DEATH
BENEFITS

D E A T H
BENEFITS

A RACHEL GOLD MYSTERY

MICHAEL A. KAHN

A DUTTON BOOK

DUTTON
Published by the Penguin Group
Penguin Books USA Inc., 375 Hudson Street,
New York, New York 10014, U.S.A.
Penguin Books Ltd, 27 Wrights Lane,
London W8 5TZ, England
Penguin Books Australia Ltd, Ringwood,
Victoria, Australia
Penguin Books Canada Ltd, 10 Alcorn Avenue,
Toronto, Ontario, Canada M4V 3B2
Penguin Books (N.Z.) Ltd, 182–190 Wairau Road,
Auckland 10, New Zealand

Penguin Books Ltd, Registered Offices:
Harmondsworth, Middlesex, England

First published by Dutton, an imprint of New American Library, a
division of Penguin Books USA Inc.
Distributed in Canada by McClelland & Stewart Inc.

First Printing, July, 1992
10 9 8 7 6 5 4 3 2 1

 REGISTERED TRADEMARK—MARCA REGISTRADA

LIBRARY OF CONGRESS CATALOGING IN PUBLICATION DATA:

Kahn, Michael A., 1952–
Death benefits: a Rachel Gold mystery/Michael A. Kahn.
   p. cm.
ISBN 0-525-93456-1
I. Title.
PS3561.A375D4 1992   91-42580
813′.54—dc20   CIP

Printed in the United States of America
Set in Plantin
Designed by Leonard Telesca

PUBLISHER'S NOTE
This is a work of fiction. Names, characters, places, and incidents
either are the products of the author's imagination or are used
fictitiously, and any resemblance to actual persons, living or
dead, events, or locales is entirely coincidental.

For my father, who always
had time to play catch,
and
For my mother, who always
had time to read me a story.

DEATH
BENEFITS

ABBOTT & WINDSOR

M E M O R A N D U M

TO: Ishmael Richardson
                Chairman

FROM: Reed St. Germain
                Acting Managing Partner
                St. Louis Office

RE: Estate of Stoddard Anderson

I learned today that the *St. Louis Business Journal* is working on a Stoddard Anderson retrospective for next week. I will do what I can to put some positive spin on the Abbott & Windsor situation down here, *i.e.*, the future looks good, plans to expand practice groups, adding new attorneys, etc.

I will continue to keep you posted on a daily basis until we meet after the funeral on Friday.

Attached below are photocopies of the press coverage last week. The paper garbled my Rock of Gibraltar quote, but you already know how unreliable newspaper reporters can be.

I look forward to our meeting, Ishmael.

1. From the *St. Louis Post-Dispatch*, June 22, Section A, page 11:

PROMINENT LOCAL ATTORNEY REPORTED MISSING; DISAPPEARED THREE DAYS AGO

Attorney Stoddard Anderson, managing partner of the St. Louis office of the law firm of Abbott & Windsor, has been missing since Tuesday, when he left his downtown law office shortly before noon to attend a lunch meeting at a private club in Clayton. He never arrived, and has not been heard from since. Anderson, 57, resides in Clayton.

Reed St. Germain, a partner in Anderson's firm, said that Anderson had been reported missing the following day. The Clayton Police Department is investigating the disappearance.

"We have no reason to suspect foul play," stated Clayton Police Lt. Donald Rimmel.

Nevertheless, Rimmel said a bulletin on the disappearance had been sent to law enforcement agencies throughout the country. The department also checked the parking lots at Lambert Int'l Airport in case Anderson's car—a blue 1990 Cadillac with license plate AW-LAW—had been left there.

St. Germain, his law partner, denied that Anderson had exhibited any unusual behavior prior to his disappearance.

"Stoddard Anderson is as steady and reliable as the Rock of Gibraltar," St. Germain stated. "This is very unusual for him. He's never done anything like this before. I'm confident that this will all turn out to be much ado about nothing."

Efforts to reach Anderson's wife for comment were unsuccessful.

St. Germain said Anderson stands about six feet tall, weighs about 190 pounds, and wears reading glasses.

2. From the *St. Louis Post-Dispatch*, June 23, Section A, page 1:

MISSING ATTORNEY FOUND
DEAD IN AIRPORT HOTEL;
PROBABLE SUICIDE

The search for Stoddard Anderson, a prominent St. Louis attorney who mysteriously disappeared en route to a business meeting four days ago, ended today with the discovery of his body in a hotel room near Lambert Int'l Airport. Anderson, 57, had been missing since June 18.

An official at the scene said that Anderson had apparently died of self-inflicted cuts on his wrists and neck. An autopsy will be performed today in St. Louis County. Officials said Anderson's body was not decomposed.

According to police sources, Anderson was last seen leaving his downtown office on Monday of this week for a lunch meeting at the St. Louis Club in Clayton. He never arrived at that meeting, and apparently had no further contact with his family or his law partners.

A hotel maid discovered Anderson's body in the bathtub today when she entered his hotel room to perform routine cleaning duties, according to Bridgeton Police Det. Mario Aloni.

Anderson was a well-known corporate attorney and the managing partner of the St. Louis office of Abbott & Windsor. Prior to joining Abbott & Windsor last year, he had been a principal in his own firm, Anderson, Raymond & St. Germain.

In the effort to find Anderson, the police had tracked bank withdrawals and credit card charges every day since Anderson disappeared, according to Lt. Aloni. Other than $800 in withdrawals from an automated teller machine on the afternoon of his disappearance, there were no transactions, Aloni said.

Anderson lived with his wife, Dorothy, at their home in Clayton. Married for 33 years, the couple had a son, now deceased, and a daughter, Rebecca, in her 30s, according to St. Germain.

Funeral arrangements have not yet been announced.

CHAPTER 1

"Call me, Ishmael," I had told him, half hoping he wouldn't. But he did—or rather, one of his secretaries did. To ask if I could meet Mr. Richardson for lunch on Monday in Cathedral Hall of the University Club. I could, and I did.

Mr. Richardson was running late, the maitre d' explained with a mournful look. I assured him that I would somehow persevere. Relieved, he led me through the enormous dining room to one of the coveted "private" tables—reserved for bank presidents, corporate CEOs, and chairmen of major law firms. The table was nestled between a pair of massive fluted columns that rose three stories to the vaulted timber ceiling of Cathedral Hall.

I ordered a glass of wine and looked around. Most of the tables were occupied. Sunlight streamed through the stained glass windows overhead, daubing muted reds and blues on the gray stone walls and white tablecloths. Although I spotted a few familiar faces, the lunch scene at Cathedral Hall still looked as if David Lynch had been in charge of production design: bankers, lawyers, and other moneychangers doing deals over charred meat in a fake Gothic cathedral.

My table was by a window overlooking Michigan Avenue. As I sipped my wine and gazed at the brown-baggers on the

6 Michael A. Kahn

grass near the Art Institute, I realized that it was at this very same table, almost three summers ago to the day, that Ishmael Richardson had retained me to investigate what he had described as an "awkward little matter" involving the identity of something named Canaan that was buried in a pet cemetery. The matter hadn't stayed little for long, and it got a whole lot more awkward before it was over. Although the firm paid my bill without complaint, there had been a definite downturn in referral business from Abbott & Windsor ever since.

Which is why I'd been delighted when my secretary told me that Ishmael Richardson was on Line 2. Summers tend to be slow for trial lawyers, largely because of overlapping vacation schedules of judges, court clerks, witnesses, and other lawyers. My next few weeks looked especially slow: A major new case I was defending had suddenly settled. So when it's July and a big case has just settled and there's a hole in your calendar and the chairman of Abbott & Windsor is on Line 2, you get off Line 1 in a hurry.

But visions of a challenging case topped with a fat fee dissolved when Ishmael told me his firm might need my services with regard to an "awkward little matter" involving an insurance policy. Although he had used the magic three words, they lost their promise when coupled with the dreaded phrase "insurance policy." Had I ever done any work for Mid-Continent Assurance Company, he asked.

I silently groaned. A "coverage" dispute.

There are trial lawyers out there—thousands—who make their living litigating the meaning of terms in insurance policies. One of the mysteries of the law is the way that basic words— words as hard and precise as cut diamonds—become warm salt-water taffy when inserted at critical points in insurance policies. Because millions of dollars can hinge on a court's explication of one of the Four Horsemen of the Insuring Clause—"sudden," "unexpected," "occurrence," and "loss"—entire law firms have been built on the legal fees paid by insurance companies, to say nothing of the cottage industry of legal publishers and law school professors that have been feasting at the insurance trough for years.

Three of the largest law firms in Chicago handle nothing but insurance coverage disputes. The sexiest man in my law school class at Harvard joined the in-house legal staff of the Chubb Group of Insurance Companies. So be it. I couldn't even force myself to read my auto policy.

"No," I had told Ishmael over the phone. "I've never represented Mid-Continent."

"Good. We may not need separate counsel on this matter, but in the event we do, it would appear that you could handle the matter without a conflict of interest."

Or any interest, I thought. "If you need me I'd be glad to help," I said, trying to force some enthusiasm into my voice.

"Call me, Ishmael."

And he had. And here I was.

"I am terribly sorry I'm late, Rachel. Please forgive me."

I looked up from my reverie, surprised. I hadn't heard his approach. "Don't be silly," I said. "I've been enjoying the view, and the wine is delicious."

It had been more than a year since I had last seen Ishmael Harrison Richardson. Although he was seventy-two years old, he looked terrific—far younger than his age. His face was deeply tanned, his white hair thick and wavy, and his eyes a pale gray. Tall and slim, immaculate as usual in a gray pin-striped suit, blue oxford cloth shirt, and red-on-navy tie, Ishmael Richardson seemed the very apotheosis of what he was: chairman of one of the nation's largest and most powerful law firms.

He had joined the firm of Abbott, Windsor, Harrison & Reynolds in 1939 after graduating *summa cum laude* from Harvard Law School. Back then, the firm had consisted of six lawyers. Now—a half-century later and two names shorter—Abbott & Windsor had more than five hundred lawyers, with branch offices in Washington, D.C., New York, Dallas, Los Angeles, Atlanta, St. Louis, Palo Alto, Taipei, Singapore, and Riyadh. It was the third oldest and second largest firm in Chicago, and, in the opinion of many, the most powerful law firm in the Midwest. Ishmael Richardson had been chairman of the firm during its remarkable growth in size, profits, and prestige over the past decade and was generally credited with much of the firm's success.

Viewed from a distance, he was an imposing, almost regal figure, made all the more so by his reputation, his press clippings (how many lawyers can boast cover stories in *Forbes* and *Vanity Fair?*), and his astounding list of clients (which included not only Fortune 500 companies and national political figures but several nation states). But to his clients, like most great corporate attorneys, Ishmael Richardson was neither imposing nor regal. He had the bedside manner of a country doctor and the ability to focus all of his considerable attention and empathy on whomever sought his counsel. During a typical day he might talk to dozens of clients on the telephone, yet each hung up satisfied that his problem was the *only* problem on Ishmael's mind. I had admired him when I was a young associate at Abbott & Windsor. During the four years since I had left the firm, my admiration had grown to include real affection.

After exchanging pleasantries and placing our orders, Ishmael turned to the purpose of the meeting. "I believe St. Louis is your home town."

I nodded.

"You may recall that Abbott & Windsor opened an office in St. Louis last summer."

"In the Boatmen's Tower on Broadway, right?"

"Correct. We have approximately fifty lawyers in the office now. We had hoped to double the size in two years."

"Had?"

"Stoddard Anderson was the managing partner of our St. Louis office." He paused to take a sip of his water. "He died last month."

"I'm sorry," I said.

He nodded. "Thank you, Rachel."

"Was it sudden?"

Ishmael leaned back. "Sudden? No. Quick? Probably. He committed suicide."

"Oh, God. How?"

"He slit his wrists and neck with a razor blade. He bled to death in a hotel bathtub."

"That's awful."

We paused as the waiter set down our salad plates and sprinkled on ground pepper with a mill the size of a Louisville Slugger.

"As you may have surmised," Ishmael said after the waiter hauled off the pepper mill, "I asked you here today to discuss an awkward little matter involving the suicide of Mr. Anderson."

I smiled. "As someone once said, this sounds like *déjà vu* all over again."

Ishmael shook his head, chuckling. "I am quite certain that this matter will seem tame in comparison to the Canaan investigation."

"Then it has to involve an insurance coverage issue," I said.

He looked at me with surprise. "How did you guess?"

"Elementary, my dear Ishmael. When we talked on the phone last week you asked if I'd ever represented Mid-Continent Assurance Company. I assume you aren't moonlighting these days as an insurance agent."

He smiled. "Your assumption is correct, Rachel. This is indeed a matter where you may be adverse to the insurance company. And," he raised his eyebrows, "possibly adverse to Abbott & Windsor, although I sincerely hope it will not come to that."

I removed a legal pad and fountain pen from my briefcase. "What kind of insurance policy?" I asked as I scribbled the insurance company's name at the top of the first page.

"Life."

I paused, and then looked up. "So my client is Mr. Anderson's widow?"

Ishmael nodded. "Dorothy Anderson. She prefers the name Dottie."

"Is the carrier denying coverage?"

"Not yet, but we anticipate a dispute over the death benefits. The insurer claims to be investigating the situation. All it has done so far is issue a reservation of rights letter in which it raises the suicide exclusion."

"Do you have the letter with you?" I asked.

"Not with me. Melvin Needlebaum should have a copy. He has conducted a preliminary investigation of the insurance issues."

I couldn't suppress a smile. "How's old Melvin doing?"

Ishmael had better luck with a straight face. "Melvin is a hardworking and brilliant young man. I am certain he will provide you with a thorough briefing on the legal issues."

"I'm sure it will be thorough." I paused to eat some of my broiled Lake Superior whitefish. "What are the issues?" I asked.

"The potential problem arises out of the somewhat unusual circumstances of the death. This was not an ordinary suicide, assuming there is ever such a thing. Stoddard Anderson was last seen alive shortly before noon on June eighteenth, when he left the St. Louis offices of Abbott & Windsor. According to his secretary, he had a luncheon meeting at the St. Louis Club." Ishmael paused. "Anderson never arrived at the club. He disappeared. Four days later, he was found dead in a hotel bathtub near the St. Louis airport. The coroner ruled it a suicide."

"How long had he been dead?" I asked.

"Not for more than a day. The medical examiner placed the time of death at twelve to twenty-four hours before the body was discovered."

"Where was he between the time he disappeared and the time he died?"

"No one knows, Rachel. He checked into the hotel on the day he disappeared. It is my understanding that the police have not yet determined whether he remained in the room during the entire three days before his death."

"Did his wife . . . his widow—did he contact her before he died?"

"I don't believe so. As far as the police can determine, he contacted no one. His activities, if any, during the last few days of his life are not yet known."

"How much insurance is involved?" I asked.

"The total package is worth over two million dollars. Melvin will have the precise figures."

"How, and why, do I fit in?"

"The amount of the death benefits payable to Mrs. Anderson may depend, first, upon whether Stoddard Anderson intended to commit suicide at the time he purchased the policy and, second, upon whether he was insane at the time he killed himself."

"When did he take out the policy?"

"Four months before he died. Prior to that, his life insurance package was somewhat modest, at least for someone at Stoddard's station in life. He more than quadrupled his coverage in February of this year and added the accidental death benefits package."

"Is Abbott & Windsor handling his estate?"

Ishmael nodded.

"What's the size of the rest of the estate?" I asked.

"Far smaller than one might imagine. Stoddard Anderson sustained significant losses in the stock market crash of 1987. Those problems were compounded by his heavy investments in commercial real estate, primarily through limited partnerships. The recent slump in that market has had a materially adverse impact on the assets of the estate."

"So the widow could use the death benefits."

"Precisely."

I mulled it over. "Suicide is not an accident. If he was sane at the time he committed suicide, the insurance company wouldn't have to pay the accidental death benefits."

"Correct, or so Melvin has concluded."

"So it might be in the widow's best interest to argue that her husband was insane when he killed himself," I mused.

"If the facts would support such an argument," Ishmael added with an edge in his voice.

"But of course," I said with a smile. "I see the conflict. It would be awkward for Abbott & Windsor to make the insanity argument."

Ishmael nodded. "Our St. Louis office opened just a year ago, Rachel. The suicide of the managing partner of that office has already been a most unfortunate source of embarrassment in the St. Louis legal and business community. Were Abbott &

Windsor to discharge its professional duty to zealously represent the estate in order to maximize the insurance payment to Anderson's widow, we could find ourselves in the position of having to argue that the managing partner of our St. Louis office was insane at the time he committed suicide.''

"If the facts would support such an argument," I added.

"But of course." He forced a smile, which quickly vanished as he leaned forward, his eyes narrowing. "At the moment, Stoddard Anderson's suicide is a local embarrassment. I cannot allow my firm to be placed in the position of publicly advocating that one of its more prominent partners was insane when he died. Clients understand that personal grief—that overwhelming personal trauma—can lead to suicide. No client, however, could ever be comfortable with the thought that an insane man was handling his affairs, or, even worse, that a firm could be so imprudent as to place an insane man in the position of the managing partner of one of its branch offices. Clients pay us handsomely for our expertise and judgment. A mentally disturbed managing partner tends to suggest a lack of both. What is now merely a provincial setback would escalate into a national scandal, suitably tailored for *The American Lawyer* and our competitors. It could subject my firm to mockery and derision in the national legal community." His eyes blazed. "I will not allow that to happen."

"So it's safe to assume that Abbott & Windsor will take the position that Stoddard Anderson was perfectly sane at the time he died?"

"It is indeed. And it is also safe to assume that Abbott & Windsor will vigorously oppose any contention to the contrary."

I let it all sink in. "Why hire me?"

"You are the obvious choice for several reasons. You are from St. Louis. Presumably you are somewhat familiar with its people and institutions. You are, as I recall, a member of the Missouri bar. Thus, you could represent Mrs. Anderson before a Missouri tribunal, if that should become necessary. But those are trivial reasons, Rachel. Stoddard Anderson was a prominent and valued partner of Abbott & Windsor. His widow deserves excellent representation on this matter, and I am determined she will receive it. I know you. I trust you. And I have the utmost confidence you will provide Stoddard Anderson's widow with excellent representation.''

"I'm flattered."

He smiled. "You should be."

I mulled it over. "We could become adversaries here."

"I am well aware of that, Rachel. I included that factor in my selection of counsel. You are trustworthy and discreet. You proved that to me beyond cavil in the way you handled that unfortunate Canaan investigation. You could have turned that into a media carnival. Others might have used it as an opportunity for self-promotion. You did not. Although this matter is far different from the Canaan situation, it could nevertheless present opportunities for attorney grandstanding. You are not a grandstander, Rachel."

"What makes you think that Dottie Anderson will want me to be her lawyer on this?"

He smiled. "She has already retained you," he said, removing an envelope from his suit jacket and handing it to me.

Inside was a letter from Ishmael Richardson to Dottie Anderson, confirming that Rachel Gold was her attorney "with respect to all matters relating to or arising out of that certain life insurance policy bearing the policy number 113-456-89J and issued to Stoddard Anderson by the Mid-Continent Assurance Company of Kansas on or about February 22nd of this year, including without limitation Endorsement No. 4, entitled 'Accidental Death Benefits Rider A.' " The final paragraph of the letter assured her that Abbott & Windsor would pay "all of Ms. Gold's fees and expenses in connection with her representation herein."

At the bottom of the letter was a place for Dottie Anderson to sign her authorization. She had so signed, in blue ink, in a fat, backward-sloping script.

We parted in the lobby of the University Club after Ishmael called Melvin Needlebaum to confirm that I would meet with him later that afternoon.

I had a court date at 2:00 P.M. On my walk across the Loop to the Federal Courts Building on South Dearborn, I reevaluated my decision.

I didn't like insurance law, and I wasn't crazy about taking on a case that could make me an adversary of Abbott & Windsor, particularly where there was the risk—if it ended up in court—of lots of publicity. No sense biting the hand that pays the fees.

But taking on the case would give me a chance to spend some time in St. Louis. Although my parents were in Israel for the rest of the summer, my sister and her two children were there. In addition, as I confirmed from the Cardinals' schedule I pulled from my purse while waiting for the light to change on State and Dearborn, the Redbirds were in town for the entire first week of August. When you live more than two hundred miles from Busch Stadium, you don't pass up the chance to return to St. Louis during a midsummer home stand.

Moreover, the case did sound intriguing. Particularly the missing days at the end of Stoddard Anderson's life. Was he insane? Or just depressed? Where was he those last few days? And what was he up to?

CHAPTER 2

Until Abbott & Windsor hired its first Irish Catholic in 1964, the columns of names on the firm's letterhead looked—at least to those who still pronounced the *h* in Amherst College or thought squash rackets was a mafia-controlled produce scam—as if some printer's imp had separated all the surnames from the Christian names, tossed the whole lot into a top hat, and pulled out pairs at random. The letterhead included Hayden James, Sterling Grant, Porter Edwards, Townsend Ward, Emerson Barnes, Rexford Dean, and—centered at the top of the letterhead—the long-dead founding partners, Kendall Abbott and Evans Windsor.

Patrick Kennedy, the first Irish Catholic, joined the firm in 1964. Stanley Handelsman, a German Jew and a third-generation Yalie but a Jew nevertheless, joined the firm five years later. Four Jews, two Catholics, and eight years later, A & W hit the Title VII trifecta when it hired Louise Simpson, a blind, black female attorney. She lasted fifteen months before going in-house at Monsanto.

By the time I joined Abbott & Windsor after graduation from Harvard Law School, the firm had enough Jews for a *minyan*, enough blacks to field a competitive basketball team in the Chicago Bar Association league, and enough women attorneys to cause most of the senior partners to stop referring to their secretaries, at least in the common areas of the firm, as "my girl" (as in, "Let's schedule a meeting for next week. Have your girl call my girl").

For the student of the legal profession, there are several criteria for determining which of the thousands of law firms across the nation belong in that most exclusive of categories, the Major League Law Firms. There are the obvious disqualifying characteristics, such as a bold-type listing in the *Yellow Pages* or the presence of any workmen's compensation work or domestic relations matters. And then there are the necessary threshold requirements, such as size (generally over two hundred attorneys), percentage of graduates from the Big Seven (Harvard, Yale, Columbia, Chicago, Michigan, Stanford, and Berkeley), and profits per partner (over $400,000).

Although taxonomists can debate the subtle distinctions for hours, on one issue they all agree: You cannot be a Major League Law Firm without at least one Melvin Needlebaum. But never more than three. Abbott & Windsor's Melvin Needlebaum is actually named Melvin Needlebaum. You can look it up in *Martindale & Hubbell*.

While the Melvin Needlebaums of the legal profession travel under many aliases, they all look remarkably like Abbott & Windsor's Melvin: pale eyes swimming behind thick glasses, thinning brownish hair slicked back, a manic laugh, scuffed brown tie shoes, a fat tie anchored by a crooked tie clasp, and a Dacron short-sleeve (even in January) white shirt with the tail hanging out.

At first glance, Melvin Needlebaums remind you of the nerds from your high school Audio-Visual Club—the extra-chromosome types who ran the film projector in driver's ed. But first impressions are misleading. Melvin Needlebaums are not nerds, at least not in the ordinary sense of the term. Yes, they are workaholics. And yes, they can crank out reams of motions and briefs on short notice. And yes, they have astonishing recall of the thousands of court opinions they have read.

But what truly distinguishes the Melvin Needlebaums of the legal profession from garden-variety nerds are their astounding reserves of hostility and aggression, all of which they can focus on opposing attorneys in the lawsuits they work on.

Within the sunken chest of a Melvin Needlebaum beats the heart of a serial killer. Staring out from behind those smudged lenses are the subzero eyes of a contract hit man.

Melvin Needlebaums are entirely at home within that peculiar version of reality known as the law—where a corporation is a "person," a claim for damages is a "prayer," and a seventy-page document is a "brief." For obvious reasons, Melvin Needlebaums are not often seen outside the prestigious firms in which they work. They don't mingle with the firm's clients at social events, they seldom appear in court, they never ever interview law students visiting the firm on job interviews, and they rarely become partners.

But they survive at the Major League Law Firms, and even prosper for many years, because they are extraordinarily profitable. The typical Melvin Needlebaum works twelve hours a day, six to seven days a week—and every minute of his time is billable to a client. Multiply 2,600 hours a year by a billable rate of $200 per hour, subtract his salary and overhead, and one Melvin Needlebaum delivers more than $325,000 of pure profits to the partnership's bottom line each year. Numbers like that invariably tap into hitherto unknown reserves of tolerance among the partners. Sterling Grant, one of those partners, was once overheard in the hall reverently describing Melvin to another partner as "a cash cow."

Melvin the Cash Cow sounded more like Melvin the Mad Dog when I walked into his office to discuss his work on the Stoddard Anderson situation. He was barking into the telephone, the receiver pinned between his neck and shoulder. His desk was a cluttered jumble of yellow legal pads, computer printouts, pleadings binders, and deposition transcripts. There were documents scattered in piles throughout the office. A dead rubber plant sagged against the wall in the corner of the office, one withered yellow leaf drooping from an otherwise bare trunk.

"Patently absurd," Melvin snorted into the phone in his nasal staccato. He was rapping a pencil on the red Lexis terminal on his desk. "Anyone with the brains God gave a goose would know that was patently absurd."

I lifted a stack of pleading files off a chair and sat down to wait. There was a beep from the Lexis terminal, and I realized Melvin was running a research project on Lexis while talking on the phone. The other computer terminal on his credenza displayed a full screen of text, no doubt the court document Melvin had been typing when the telephone rang.

Melvin slammed down the receiver and leaned forward to squint at the Lexis screen, his face gradually breaking into a manic grin.

"Superb!" he said, and he spun his chair toward the word processor on his credenza. "Just a moment, Miss Gold," he barked as he typed rapidly on the keyboard. He finished typing, spun back toward his desk, typed a new search instruction into the Lexis terminal, and then looked up, his eyes blinking rapidly. "Yesssss?"

"Stoddard Anderson," I said.

"Ah, yes. The dearly departed managing partner of our St. Louis office." Melvin removed his glasses, tilted the smudged lenses up to the light, and then put them back on. He leaned back with a lopsided grin. "I have been advised that you, Miss Gold, have been anointed special insurance counsel to the widow Anderson. Your mission is to convince the insurance carrier that her husband was mad as a hatter at the time he, shall we say, cut himself shaving."

I had to smile. Melvin was definitely a trip. "That's not my mission. At least not yet. Ishmael said you've already done some work on the matter. I came here to find out what you've learned so far, and to learn why his sanity has to be an issue."

Melvin nodded his head rapidly while he rubbed his hands together. "How much do you know about the life insurance laws of Missouri?"

"Absolutely nothing."

"Then we shall begin with the most common misconception." There was a beep from his Lexis terminal. Melvin leaned forward and squinted at the terminal screen. "Another Posner opinion! Lord have mercy." He started typing a new search instruction.

"What's the most common misconception?" I asked.

"Ah, yes." Melvin pressed the TRANSMIT key and leaned

back in his chair. "Most people erroneously believe that death by suicide is *not* covered by life insurance. Wrong. Indeed, in many states, including Missouri, the legislature has enacted a statute that forbids any attempt to deny life insurance benefits on the ground that the decedent committed suicide. Unless," Melvin leaned forward and rhythmically jabbed his index finger at me for emphasis, "unless the insured intended to commit suicide at the time he purchased the policy. If so, Miss Gold, the bastards don't have to pay."

"Is there any evidence that Stoddard Anderson intended to kill himself back when he bought the policy?" I asked.

"Nothing other than the relative proximity of his death to the date he quadrupled his life insurance."

"Four months?" I said dubiously.

There was a beep from the Lexis terminal. Melvin glared at the screen in outrage. "Two hundred and eleven cases! What kind of computer search is that? Oh, well," he said with a snort, "millions for defense, not a penny for tribute." He punched the PRINT FULL key on the keyboard. Down in the firm's library one of the Lexis printers would shudder on and start printing 211 court opinions, most of them already available in the library's enormous collection of hardbound federal and state court reporters. Melvin's print full command would keep the printer busy for hours, while print requests from other attorneys backed up like planes at O'Hare on a Friday afternoon.

I had had enough. As Melvin started typing a new search request, I stood up and lifted the lightweight Lexis terminal off his desk.

"What is the meaning of this, Miss Gold?" he demanded, rising out of his seat so that he could continue typing.

"I've got better things to do with my life than watch you play around with this damn computer. Either turn it off now, or I'm going to throw it through the window."

Melvin put up his palms and giggled. "Okay. Okayokay-okay." He reached for the power switch, paused, bit his lip, and then turned off the terminal as I lowered it back onto his desk. "Great stuff, Miss Gold. Great stuff. Some first-rate cases." He sat down.

"So," I said, "there may be a factual dispute as to Stoddard Anderson's intentions at the time he purchased the additional insurance. What about the insanity issue?"

Melvin stared at me, his eyes blinking rapidly behind the smudged lenses. He said nothing.

"Melvin?"

"Ah, yes," he said, shaking his head. "Mr. Anderson had an accidental death endorsement on the life insurance policy. This is most often known as the so-called double indemnity rider—"

"Like the James Cain novel," I said with a smile.

"Cain?"

"*Double Indemnity.*"

"Judge James Cain? Of the Maryland Court of Special Appeals?" He leaned forward to turn on the Lexis computer. "Good God, has he issued an appellate opinion on this matter?"

"No. And don't you turn that terminal back on. You were describing the double indemnity rider."

"Ah, yes. Actually, this particular policy had a triple indemnity rider. It provides that Stoddard Anderson's death benefits increase to thrice the face amount of the policy in the event that he meets an untimely demise as a result of an accident."

"And a suicide isn't an accident," I added.

"Unless he was *insane* at the time he killed himself," Melvin replied.

"And if he was?"

"If he was insane at the time he committed suicide, then his death would be deemed an accident under Missouri law, and the carrier would have to pay an additional one-point-four million dollars in death benefits."

"How insane is insane under Missouri law?"

"Excellent question. Let's see, hmmm." Melvin craned his head back toward the ceiling. "Wait, wait." His left hand shot up in the air, his fingers clenching and unclenching, his eyes squeezed shut. "Ah, yes. The case of Varley versus the General American Life Insurance Company. It's a 1984 decision by the Missouri Court of Appeals. Eastern District, I believe. Volume 664 of the South Western Reporter, second series." Melvin low-

ered his head and opened his eyes, leveling a triumphant stare
at me.

"Go on," I said. Having witnessed Melvin's astral-
projection routine dozens of times as a junior associate at Abbott
& Windsor, I was no longer amazed by it.

"The facts of that case are straightforward," Melvin said.
"On August 7, 1977, one James G. Varley, Jr., committed suicide. Mr. Varley's insurance company paid the life insurance
benefits but refused to pay the additional accidental death benefits, contending that the taking of one's life while sane does
not qualify as an accident under Missouri law. The issue at trial,
therefore, was the late Mr. Varley's sanity at the time of his
death."

"And was he?"

"Not according to the jury."

"What was the evidence?"

"On the night before he died, he told his two longtime
friends"— Melvin squeezed shut his eyes, recalling the exact
text— "and I quote, 'I can't go on. I can't function. I'm in
pain. Something in my brain snapped. I'm going to kill myself.'
Unquote." Melvin gave me a manic grin. "To put it mildly,
this was an individual who needed to get his carburetor ad-
justed."

"And?"

Melvin shook his head. "Insufficient evidence of insanity.
It's not enough that the decedent's behavior was unusual or
peculiar. Under Missouri law, the test requires proof that the
decedent's behavior, when viewed by objective standards, makes
the conclusion of insanity obvious. In the case of Stoddard Anderson, you will need to find witnesses who will testify to conduct during the last days of his life that displays psychotic
behavior. If you can do that, Miss Gold, you will have the insurance carrier by the short hairs. If not, however, you and your
client will be S.O.L."

I mulled it over. "Did you know Stoddard Anderson?"

"I never met the man. He became managing partner of the
St. Louis office after A & W acquired Anderson, Raymond &
St. Germain, which was his prior law firm."

"What kind of firm was it?"

"It was principally a tax and securities boutique, consisting of three partners and eight associates. Anderson was a securities lawyer. Allegedly quite good. And supposedly well-connected within the business and social elite of St. Louis. He was heavily involved in an absolutely bizarre native ritual known as the Veiled Prophet Ball. It's the most extraordinarily weird—"

"I know all about it," I said with a smile.

Melvin's eyes widened in surprise. "Really, Miss Gold? Are you an aficionada of urban anthropology?"

I shook my head. "I'm one of the natives."

"Ah. I see."

"Ishmael said the insurance company issued a reservation of rights letter."

"It did indeed. The letter is in the file."

"Have you talked to the claims adjuster yet?"

"I have deprived myself of that rare pleasure, Miss Gold." He turned and rummaged through the files piled on his credenza. "Here," he said, spinning back to me. "This is the entire file, which I now bequeath, assign, devise, and transfer to you, Miss Gold."

I took the file from him.

"The claims adjuster is one Cyril Burt," he said, "out of Mid-Continent's St. Louis office. The reservation of rights letter is in the correspondence section."

I found it.

Melvin leaned over to point. "The marginalia on that letter is mine, including the exclamation marks and the expletives."

The letter was three pages long, and the right margins on all three pages were decorated with the usual low-key observations one comes to expect from Melvin: at least five "Bullshit!s," several "No!!!s," and a few other similarly insightful comments, such as "Fool!" and "Give me a break!!"

"Those are merely my reactions upon reading Mr. Burt's feeble-minded attempt at interpreting the insurance policy. I have not confronted him. When I learned that you would be taking over the file, I thought it best to allow you to handle that confrontation."

"What else do you have on Stoddard?"

"The only other information I've obtained on him is in the press clippings file maintained by A & W's public relations flack in St. Louis. Let's see . . ." He shuffled through the papers on his desk and pulled a manila folder out from beneath a pile of deposition transcripts. "Here we are," he said as he scanned the photocopied news clippings inside the folder. "These are for you." He handed me the folder, which was stained with two coffee mug circles. "I had an extra copy made. Ah, yes, and I also have some computer printouts. Part of my legal research. The printouts are not directly on point, but you might as well have them. After all, Mr. Richardson instructed me to turn everything over to you. Everything but the proverbial kitchen sink."

He frowned, and his eyes took on a faraway look. "Kitchen sink," he repeated softly. "But of course!" He reached for the power button on the Lexis terminal but paused, his hands hovering over the keyboard. He looked at me. "May I, Miss Gold? I believe we were about to commence the ceremonial conclusion of our meeting. You don't mind if we truncate the farewells, do you?"

"Certainly not, Melvin."

Relieved, he switched on the terminal and started typing rapidly. "This is an excellent idea, just excellent."

"For this case?" I asked.

"Oh, no." He pressed the TRANSMIT key and lifted his hands off the keyboard, fingers twitching manically. "It's for Bottles and Cans. We have a related insurance issue in Bottles and Cans."

Abbott & Windsor represented two defendants in *In re Bottles & Cans*, the largest and oldest antitrust case in American history. The case kept sixteen A & W attorneys and more than a dozen paralegals busy full time. I had worked on the case when I was an A & W associate.

"Where are those computer printouts?" I asked. "I'll take them and get out of your hair."

"Right," he said, reluctantly pulling his eyes away from the screen. He found the printouts on his desk and handed them to me just as the Lexis terminal beeped. The beep snapped his head back to the screen, like a hooked widemouth bass.

He was squinting at the screen, his jaw thrust forward, as I left his office.

"Lord have mercy!" he shouted in dismay, slamming his fist on the top of his desk. "Another Posner opinion!"

CHAPTER 3

My office is in an older building on West Washington Avenue. I bought an afternoon edition of the *Trib* from the newsstand in the lobby and checked the West Coast scores on the elevator ride to my floor. The Cards had dropped another one to the Padres.

I glanced at my watch as I got off the elevator. 5:40 P.M. Rush hour on the el trains would be ending in another twenty minutes. That gave me enough time to check my messages, finish my dictation, and walk to the subway station at Washington. By six o'clock I ought to be able to get a seat on the northbound train. I could read Stoddard Anderson's news clippings on the ride home.

I stopped at my office door and—as I had been doing every day for the past several weeks—read the legend on the pebble-glass front and smiled. The main part had been there since I moved in four years ago:

THE LAW OFFICES
OF RACHEL GOLD
Attorney at Law

But four weeks ago the sign painters had returned to add the following legend beneath:

Benjamin Goldberg,
Of Counsel

Benny Goldberg had joined Abbott & Windsor one year before
I did. He left two years after me. I left A & W to go into practice
on my own. Benny left to become an associate professor of law
at DePaul Law School.

Because of the squeeze on faculty office space, at the end
of the school term in June the law school asked the three
most junior faculty members to find alternate office space
downtown. The office next to mine had been vacant for almost a year, ever since Mendel Klayman—the elderly Jewish
C.P.A. who kept trying to fix me up with his three-hundred-
pound divorced son Sidney ("This is a good boy, Rachel")—
had retired and moved to Arizona with his wife *and* his
three-hundred-pound divorced son Sidney. With the office
vacant, it was a perfect arrangement: The law school would
not only pick up Benny's rent but pay for the cost of knocking
out a wall to connect Benny's office with the reception area
to mine.

But what really made it perfect was having Benny nearby again. He was fat and he was crude. But he was also
my best friend, and I loved him like the brother I never
had.

I walked into the tiny reception area of my office and was
surprised to see Mary still there. She usually left before five-
thirty. Mary seemed a little flustered to see me.

"Everything okay?" I asked as I leaned against the wall
and eased off my shoes.

"Sure," she said. "Great. Everything's great."

"How come you're still here?" I asked, looking down as I
wiggled my toes.

"Oh, just catching up on my filing."

"Where's Benny?" I asked, nodding toward his darkened
office.

Mary smiled, regaining her composure. "You know him.
He said he had a hot date with one of his students."

I rolled my eyes. "We better increase the saltpeter in his coffee. Any messages?"

Mary raised her eyebrows. "A couple. I put them in your office."

I looked at her funny, and she averted her eyes. Mary normally put my telephone messages on the message spike at her desk.

"You sure you're okay?"

She blushed as she nodded.

Puzzled, I walked to my office door, turned the knob, and stepped in.

"SURPRISE!"

My office was filled with people in party hats. Benny stood behind my desk, beaming. He led the roomful of friends in a rousing rendition of "Happy Birthday," with Mary joining in from behind. The birthday cake was round and decorated to look like Busch Stadium. Written in white script on the green icing in the outfield was the message "Happy 32nd Birthday, Rachel."

I had completely forgotten that today was my birthday. As I leaned over to blow out the candles, I could feel my eyes watering. There were hugs and kisses and several gag gifts (including five pairs of edible panties from Benny, who explained to the grossed-out crowd that it seemed like a practical gift for both of us since I could use the underwear and he was always looking for a late-afternoon snack). After the cake and ice cream, the pizza and beer arrived.

The last friends left around nine that night. After Benny, Mary, and I finished cleaning up, Benny offered to drive Mary and me home. Mary said she was meeting her boyfriend at the Esquire Theater for the ten o'clock show. We dropped her off at the corner of Oak Street, and then Benny pulled onto Lake Shore Drive.

As we headed north on the Drive, I leaned over and kissed him on the cheek. "Thanks," I said. "That was the best birthday ever."

Benny shrugged. "Sure. My pleasure."

We drove in silence on the Drive.

"I can't believe I'm thirty-two," I said glumly as I stared out the window toward Lake Michigan.

"Hey, I'm thirty-three," he said as he pulled the car to a stop at the red light at the Hollywood exit at the end of Lake Shore Drive. "So what?"

I shrugged. "Do you ever want to get married?"

"Are you kidding me? Does the wild Pope shit in the woods? Married? How 'bout tonight? We could fly to Vegas."

"Not to me, you bozo. I mean in principle."

"I've never been in a principal," he said slipping into his Groucho Marx voice. "But I once had a great night with a gym teacher."

Benny turned right onto Sheridan after banging on the horn and bellowing some rather specific and impossible anatomical suggestions at the sluggish driver ahead of us.

"Benny, I'm serious."

"So am I. She was so impressed she gave me one of those President's Council on Physical Fitness Awards."

Despite myself, I had to smile. "You?"

Benny covered his heart and winced. "Real sensitive, Rachel. Never underestimate the erotic talents of a full-figured man."

"Oh?" I was laughing.

"O ye of little faith," he said with a sigh. "They laughed at Thomas Edison, too. Well, join me on my waterbed tonight, Miss Too Busy To Be A Homecoming Queen, Miss Smarty Pants Communist, and you'll discover just exactly why I've earned the rank of Tongue Ninja."

North of the Loyola campus, just beyond the 400 Theater, Benny turned onto my street and stopped in front of my apartment building. He left the engine idling.

"Give me a raincheck, Benny-san."

"Promises, promises. Rachel, someday you'll receive my generous offers with the enthusiasm they deserve."

"And someday you'll receive the electroshock therapy you so richly deserve. Listen, Dr. Demento, thank you for that wonderful birthday party." I gave him a kiss on the cheek. "See you tomorrow."

"Hey, Rachel," Benny said as I closed the car door.

I leaned against the open passenger window. "What?"

"You never told me about your meeting. What did Ishmael want?"

"Me. He retained me to represent the widow of the managing partner of A & W's St. Louis office. Her husband committed suicide last month. They think she might get the runaround from the insurance company. The firm would handle it themselves except they may have a conflict of interest."

"What's the conflict?"

I gave him the short version.

"Four days, huh?" Benny said. "The guy's missing for four days? No one knows what he was doing?"

I shrugged. "Not yet."

"That's weird. You going down to St. Louis tomorrow?"

"Probably. I have to first call a bunch of people in St. Louis. Set up some appointments. I might drive down after work."

"So I'll see you at the office tomorrow."

"Yep. Good night, Benny."

"Good night, Rachel."

I watched Benny drive off in his 1970 Chevy Nova. Attached to the rear window was Benny's version of the yellow, diamond-shaped BABY ON BOARD sign. It read ENDOMORPH ON BOARD. He had designed it himself, and used it shamelessly to get preferred parking at concerts and sporting events. "Sir," he would tell the parking attendant, "I'd be grateful for a spot near an exit. I'm an endomorph." And then he would solemnly point to the ENDOMORPH ON BOARD sign.

I watched until Benny's car turned the corner, and then I walked into the foyer of my apartment building. Ozzie must have heard my key in the mailbox, because he bounded down the stairs as I stuffed the mail into my briefcase. He was waiting for me, tail wagging furiously, on the other side of the door that separated the building foyer from the hallway and stairs leading to the apartments.

Ozzie is my golden retriever. He spends the weekdays with my downstairs neighbors/landlords, John and Linda Burns, and their two children, Katie and Ben. Linda stays home with the kids, and Ozzie keeps them company during the day. It's a nice arrangement for all of us, especially Ozzie, who loves all the attention. Tonight I had called Linda from my office to let her know I'd be late. She had fed Ozzie, taken him for a walk, and left him sitting outside my apartment door.

"Hey, Oz!" I said, rubbing him behind his ear as we walked up the two flights of stairs to my apartment on the top floor of the three-flat. As I put my key in the deadbolt lock, Ozzie jumped up, placed his front paws on my shoulders and licked me on the cheek.

Ozzie squeezed past me as the door opened, and I followed him into my apartment, kicking off my shoes in the entrance-way and dropping my briefcase and purse onto the couch in the living room. I went into the bedroom, undressed, slipped on my purple and gold boxing robe, and padded barefoot back into the living room. I clicked on the light and reached over to turn on the stereo. My favorite Marvin Gaye cassette was in the tape player, and I settled back in the couch to the opening notes of "Mercy, Mercy Me."

The mail included bills, the usual junk mail solicitations, this week's issue of *Sports Illustrated*, this month's issue of *Gourmet*, and what had to be a birthday card from my sister, Ann. It was. Signed by Ann, her husband-the-orthodontist Richie, and my niece and nephew. I smiled at the thought that I would be seeing them soon.

"I'm going to have to leave you for a couple days, Ozzie," I said as I rewound the telephone answering machine and pressed the play button.

I smiled as I listened to my parents, all the way from Israel, singing an atonal and totally wonderful rendition of "Happy Birthday."

"We love you, Rachel," my mother said at the end of the song. "Your father is fine, and my elbow is better. Well, it still hurts a little. You know who I saw at the King David yesterday? Harriet Eichler. Bob Eichler's mother."

I groaned as I listened, knowing what was coming.

"She said her Bobby hasn't stopped talking about you since

he saw you at the Kimmelman wedding in June. I told Harriet you were dying to see him again.''

"Mother!''

"Now don't get upset, Rachel. He's a doctor, and a nice Jewish boy. It wouldn't kill you to see him at Rosh Hashonah. I told Harriet to tell her son to drop by after services.''

"Can you believe this?'' I said to Ozzie, who nuzzled his head against my stomach.

"We love you, Rachel. We'll come visit to Chicago when we get back. Here, Seymour, say happy birthday to your daughter. Quick, this is costing a fortune.''

But the tape ran out before my father was able to say anything.

My departure for St. Louis was delayed by several hours, first at the office by a seemingly endless string of telephone calls and minor client crises, and then at home by a flat tire. Actually two flats, including the spare—a going-away present I remembered *after* I had removed the left front tire and reached into the trunk for the spare.

I had hoped to beat the rush hour traffic out of Chicago; instead, the rush hour traffic beat me . . . by several hours. I called my sister Ann just before I left my apartment at eight o'clock; I told her not to wait up.

Thirty miles south of Springfield I pulled off I-55 for some gasoline and to stretch my legs. It was almost midnight, and I still had more than an hour of driving ahead of me.

After paying for my gas, I bought a Diet Coke from the vending machine and walked the perimeter of the station, out where the huge moths zipped and dived around the overhead lights, like manic electrons in one of those elementary school movies on the atom. Standing at the edge of the asphalt, I popped the tab on the can and took a sip. The gas station was just off an overpass. Three trucks rumbled by, heading south. I watched the red tail lights fade into the distance.

A gas station off an interstate highway, especially at night, seems to exist in limbo between the beginning and end of journeys. Stand near the pumps at any one of them and wait for the memories to seep through. As I stood there, I remembered driving home to St. Louis from law school, twenty hours straight, drinking black coffee and smoking cigarettes to stay awake. I remembered driving to Florida with three girlfriends in college over spring break. I remembered driving to Champaign, Illinois, back in high school for a Grateful Dead concert. And most of all I remembered curling up in the back seat with my sister Ann, both of us in elementary school, as my father tried to refold the road map in the front seat, somewhere in Kansas on the drive back from a vacation in Estes Park, Colorado.

The house was dark and quiet when I arrived at 1:30 A.M. I snuck upstairs to the guest bedroom, where the sheets were turned down and a fresh towel was folded on the pillow. On top of the pillow was a crayon drawing of a baseball Cardinal by my nephew, Cory; underneath the ballplayer he had written: "Hi, Aunt Rachel. Love, Cory." I carefully placed the drawing on the nightstand.

I took the Stoddard Anderson news clippings file to bed. My day would start early, and I still didn't have a real sense of the dead attorney who had been married to my newest client.

Even a cursory browse through the clippings showed that Melvin Needlebaum was right. Anderson had been well connected, locally and nationally. His national connections within the Republican Party were evidenced by a front-page article in the *St. Louis Post-Dispatch* from last December. The article described a visit to St. Louis by President George Bush. The visit included a dinner for local GOP bigwigs hosted by Stoddard Anderson at the St. Louis Country Club.

Abbott & Windsor's arrival in St. Louis last summer merited a front-page story in the *St. Louis Business Journal* beneath the following headline:

MAJOR CHICAGO LAW FIRM INVADES ST LOUIS;
STODDARD ANDERSON TO HEAD ABBOTT & WINDSOR
BRANCH

The article mentioned Anderson three times in the first four paragraphs. He was a "legal powerhouse" with "annual billings

reputed to be in the seven figures" whose "counsel was valued
in the boardrooms of St. Louis corporations, the backrooms of
City Hall, and the dining room of the Governor's mansion."

Next in the pile of clippings was a stapled collection of
Jerry Berger columns. Berger writes a society and gossip column for the *Post-Dispatch*. Over the past year alone, he had
mentioned Anderson a half-dozen times—spotted at Cardwell's
Restaurant "huddled in conversation with Apex Oil topper
Tony Novelly," at Busch's Grove "hosting a pouring with the
glitterati" for a retiring in-house attorney ("mouthpiece," in
Bergerese) at Emerson Electric, in the "Monsanto skybox
cheering on the Redbirds and sipping the host's brew with
Mayor Vince and Parks Commish **Barney Miniver**," spotted
on "the 18th green at Norwood Hills C.C." with "General Dy-
namics top veep **Mitchell Shales** and real estate sage **Larry
Lammert**," and playing tennis at "the Lah-de-due hacienda of
Northwestern Hospital topper **Eugene Reese** and a gaggle of
medicos."

Another stapled set of news clippings opened with a surprising pair of op-ed pieces that had appeared in the *St. Louis
Sun*. Surprising, that is, considering the source. Most corporate
lawyers don't disclose any controversial political or moral views
they may hold. Stoddard Anderson, however, had apparently
been a veritable exhibitionist on the subject. The first op-ed
column was an exhortation for support of the latest anti-abortion
statute pending before the Missouri legislature. The second
column was a lengthy diatribe against a recent court decision
prohibiting the expulsion of a homosexual from the Navy band.

The latter op-ed piece stirred up precisely the sort of con-
troversy that the *Sun* fed on during its brief existence. Two days
after the article appeared, a gay rights organization staged a
demonstration in front of Anderson's home in Clayton. The
Sun was there to cover the event, and reported that Anderson
had confronted the demonstrators on his front lawn, denounc-
ing them as "Un-American deviants."

I was repulsed by Anderson's actions and beliefs. But I
knew I had come to St. Louis neither to praise nor to bury him.
My job was far more mundane and lawyerly: to determine

whether his widow could obtain an additional $1.4 million dollars in death benefits from a life insurance company.

Regardless of her dead husband's beliefs, Dottie Anderson already had my sympathies, and not only because of her recent widowhood. In reviewing Stoddard Anderson's medical history with Abbott & Windsor's health plan administrator earlier in the day in Chicago, I had learned about their two children. There was a son, Paul, born with Down's syndrome, who had died four years ago at the age of twenty-nine. And then there was a daughter, Rebecca, now thirty-one—almost my age. Rebecca had suffered severe brain damage as a result of an acute case of rheumatic fever when she was three. She had been institutionalized since she was five years old. Whenever I tried to conjure an image of Dottie Anderson—something I try to do before I meet my clients in person—all I could feel was the shattering pain she must have endured when she surrendered her little daughter to the white-coated authorities.

The next two clippings, dated June 22 and 23 of this summer, broke the story of Anderson's disappearance and then told the story of the discovery of his body in a hotel room bathtub, dead of "self-inflicted cuts on his wrists and neck." According to the second article, Anderson had apparently withdrawn eight hundred dollars on the afternoon of his death. The police officer in charge of the suicide investigation was a Bridgeton cop named Mario Aloni. I circled his name.

The last clipping in the file was a Jerry Berger column that included a color photograph of Stoddard Anderson and—according to Berger—"his ever-loving wife, **Dottie**," on their thirty-second wedding anniversary, which they celebrated at the Faust's in the Adams Mark Hotel with a long list of bold-typeface friends. I studied the photograph. Stoddard was a large man with a broad, beefy face, lots of white teeth, and a receding hairline. He looked healthy, well fed, and prosperous. Dottie looked like his mother—somewhat frumpy in a flower-print shirtwaist dress and bouffant hairdo. In the picture, he was beaming confidently, she was smiling shyly. They were standing side by side, not actually touching. I stared at my new client for a long time, and then I turned out the light.

CHAPTER 4

Clients assume that law firms have simple hierarchies: partners above, associates below. Associates grimly shake their heads at such naiveté. Yes, it is partners above and associates below. But as a guide for survival, that truism is no more helpful than observing that the jungle is divided into plants and animals. Of course it is. But if you find yourself in the jungle and hope to survive, you sure better learn to tell the difference between a lemur and a lion.

Like other carnivores, all partners are not created equal. That's the first law of survival for associates at large law firms. Every major law firm in America has the same partnership trinity: the finders, the minders, and the grinders. The finders (aka the rainmakers) bring in the big clients and big fees. The minders are the specialists who handle the clients' problems and supervise the grinders. The grinders (aka the junior partners) are the high-level grunts. And down there below the grinders are the great unwashed of the law firm pyramid: the associates. Among the younger partners at Abbott & Windsor, the associates are known as the grinning buttheads.

As any grinning butthead understands, spotting the finders is just the first step toward partnership. Scattered among the thirty to forty finders at Abbott & Windsor are the ten or so who really count. Identifying those ten megapartners is thus the next step. The few titles that do exist are not reliable signposts; nor is seniority a meaningful guide. The sixty-year-old tax partner may report to—indeed, grovel before—someone twenty years his junior, while the forty-year-old litigator may earn twice as much as the silver-haired chairman of his department. For the truly ambitious associate, the key is to somehow induce a megapartner to serve as your Chinaman during the perilous seven-year climb up the pyramid toward partnership.

While the finder/minder/grinder nomenclature has spread throughout the nation's law firms, the term for the megapartners differs from firm to firm. At Reynolds & Price, they are known as the Gorillas (as in, "500-pound gorillas") while at Ross, Charles & Peters they are the 500-pounders. The megapartners at Emerson, Rinaldi & Brown are "the Great Whites" (a double entendre, no doubt) while every megapartner at Drury & Anderson is a T-Rex (as in Tyrannosaurus). At Rimmel & Abrams, the offices of the eight megapartners are along the east side of the fifty-fifth floor, which is thus known as Embassy Row.

At Abbott & Windsor, the megapartners are known as BSDs. The acronym has been in use so long that—like SCUBA, AWOL, and RSVP—many use it in conversation, and use it correctly, without knowing what the three initials stand for. This ignorance has produced one marvelous irony: Amanda Berger, a former U.S. District Judge and now the megapartner who heads A & W's bankruptcy and reorganization practice, is one of the ten Big Swinging Dicks.

Stoddard Anderson, although located more than two hundred miles from the main offices of Abbott & Windsor, had been a BSD. Reed St. Germain, the acting managing partner of the St. Louis branch, was not. That was clear from his office alone. His secretary had placed me there a few minutes ago, explaining that Mr. St. Germain's breakfast meeting had run late.

"He just called me from his car phone, Miss Gold," she explained. "He's on Highway 40 and should be here soon."

Sipping a cup of black coffee, I looked around his office. Based on the visible evidence, Reed St. Germain was, at best, an MSD striving for BSD status. He had the mandatory framed photograph of himself standing next to George Bush, and another one of him standing next to Missouri Senator John Danforth. Both, however, were posed shots—obvious photo opportunities. If a true BSD were to display a photograph of himself with the President, the two would be casually attired and casually posed—out on the golf course, for example, or on lounge chairs by a pool.

St. Germain's office also had the mandatory framed photograph of the wife and two kids, posed stiffly against a painted scenic view. And the mandatory framed law school diploma. He was a graduate of the Washington University School of Law, where—according to yet another framed certificate—he had been articles editor of the *Law Quarterly*. Based on the date of his law school diploma, Reed St. Germain was in his mid-forties.

And finally, centered on the wall above the couch, the *piece de resistance:* his admission certificate to the bar of the United States Supreme Court, framed in gold—guaranteed to impress unsophisticated clients and other credulous visitors to the office of the acting managing partner of Abbott & Windsor's St. Louis office. Only the rarest of clients will know that *any* attorney out of law school for at least three years who sends the completed application form to the Clerk of the U.S. Supreme Court along with a check for one hundred dollars payable to "Marshal, U.S. Supreme Court," will receive, by return mail, his own certificate of admission. Throughout the nation there are thousands of Supreme Court certificates of admission, expensively framed, in the offices of lawyers who, like Reed St. Germain, have appeared before the Supreme Court, if at all, only once, in Bermuda shorts, on a tour of the building with their wives and kids.

I was standing by the window, gazing down at the Old Courthouse, when he arrived.

"Ahhh, you must be Rachel Gold."

I turned and smiled, extending my hand. "And you must be Reed St. Germain."

He was darker and shorter than I had imagined when I talked to him on the telephone yesterday. We stood at eye level.

He had dark eyes and long dark eyelashes. With his strong nose and chin, he looked more like a Lebanese war chieftain than a St. Louis trusts and estates lawyer. His black, curly hair was cut short and flecked with gray.

"It's so nice to meet you, Rachel," he said in a deep, smooth voice. He was a two-handed shaker, holding with the right while covering with the left. "I've heard wonderful things about you. We're just delighted that you were able to come down here."

"I'm glad you could arrange this visit on such short notice," I said.

"It was my pleasure. And most important, Rachel," he said, and then paused, tilting his head as his expression became serious, "we're here to cooperate in your inquiry into this tragic event." He reminded me of one of those disc jockeys on an adult lite-rock radio station.

St. Germain made the usual polite inquiries about my trip, which I answered in kind as I studied him, trying to bring the picture into focus. He was wearing a Brooks Brothers three-button gray suit, a crisp white shirt with extra starch, and engraved gold cuff links. His suspenders, tie, and breastpocket handkerchief were all in matching yellow with red dots. His cordovan Weejuns were polished to a high buff.

Although his outfit, modulated voice, and expensive haircut said *Wall Street Journal* and *Town and Country,* his gnawed fingernails suggested otherwise.

As we continued to talk, I saw him glance at my outfit. I had come prepared for first impressions—as any prudent woman lawyer would. I had on my "boardroom" outfit: a traditional navy suit with jade pinstripes. Under the jacket I was wearing a white cotton blouse with pleated front and a scalloped standup collar.

As St. Germain continued to chat, I noticed that he seemed to work my name into the beginning or end of every other sentence. Maybe it's something they teach at the Acting Managing Partner Seminar.

"Could I see Stoddard Anderson's office?" I asked, trying to move the conversation toward the purpose of my visit.

Reed St. Germain gave me a puzzled look. "His office?"

"I'd like to get a feel for where he worked."

"Well, that may be difficult, Rachel. You see, *this* was Stoddard's office. I moved in a few weeks ago."

"Where are his things?"

"The police took temporary custody of the contents of his office. They returned most of the stuff about a week ago. We had it packed in boxes and moved to one of our storage facilities. We had planned on keeping them in storage until Dottie—his widow, your client—is ready to take them."

As he talked I noticed he had a slight nervous tic that caused him to move his head down and to the right, as if he had a minor crick in his neck.

"Is his secretary still here?"

"Oh, yes. Nancy is still with us."

"I'll need to talk to her."

"Certainly," he said, standing up. "In fact, let me give you a brief tour of our offices. I'll introduce you to Nancy on the way, and I can show you the office we have for you to work in while you're here."

The firm occupied one entire floor of the Boatmen's Tower. The tour confirmed that St. Louis law offices have two things in common with their Chicago counterparts. First, both are great repositories of impressive picture frames, the cost of which apparently used up most of the art budget. Second, the design architects for both seem to have been heavily influenced by Daedalus's blueprints for the Minotaur's labyrinth. The confusing layout was exacerbated by my (non)sense of direction and inability to read maps. (Why is North always at the top when you so rarely are heading in that direction?) I stared wistfully as we passed key landmarks—the coffee machine, the women's restroom, the soda machine—wishing I had a skein of thread to unwind as I followed St. Germain through the maze.

Our tour ended at a small office six doors down the hall from Reed St. Germain's corner office. He flicked on the light and beckoned me in. I got a waft of Polo cologne as I passed him into the office.

"This can be your office while you're down here, Rachel," he said magnanimously. "You're welcome to use it for as long as you need."

"Thanks, Reed."

"Quite frankly, Rachel, I shouldn't think this investigation will take much time to wrap up. I can assure you that Stoddard Anderson was as sane as the day is long."

"Perhaps you're right."

"I know I'm right." There was an edge to his voice, which he quickly recovered. "Rachel, my job here is to make sure you have what you feel you need. I mean that. If there is anything you want, anything at all, why you just let me know."

"Good," I said, deciding it was time to play my trump card. "Ishmael Richardson assured me that you would fully cooperate in every way."

"I certainly shall."

"Here." I handed him a yellow legal pad. "I'll need a few things to get started."

He uncapped his Mont Blanc fountain pen. "Shoot."

"I'll need all of Anderson's time sheets for the past twelve months. I'll also need his correspondence files for that period. I want to see all travel expense reports filed for the six months before his death, and all phone messages for the three months before his death." St. Germain was scribbling madly. "Finally, I want to see the contents of his office— the stuff you sent to storage." I waited until he caught up. "And while your people are gathering those materials, I'd like to talk to his secretary. Okay?" I concluded with a smile.

"Fine," he said, his nervous tic acting up. "I'll send Nancy in, and then I'll start in on your list."

As he turned to go I said, "So where was he those last four days?"

Reed looked back, his eyes narrowing. "In that hotel room, I suppose."

"Doing what?"

He shrugged, putting on his world-weary mask. "Whatever it is that sad men do before they kill themselves."

"What was he sad about?"

The mask dropped away. "I have no idea," he said curtly. "I'll send in Nancy."

CHAPTER 5

"Mr. Anderson was a perfect gentleman to work for," Nancy Winslow explained. "He certainly wasn't a lecher, like you know who," she said with a jerk of her head toward the doorway, where Reed St. Germain had stood just moments ago. He had poked his head in to tell me that it would take several hours to gather all of the documents I had requested because most of Stoddard Anderson's files had been sent to storage. The documents would be there by late afternoon along with the boxed contents of his office.

"Is St. Germain hassling you?"

Nancy pushed back her long red hair. "Nothing I can't handle."

"You don't have to put up with it."

"Oh, I know that."

"You have rights."

She winked. "The girls and I feel safe when you're around."

"I don't get it."

"That big lawsuit you won in Chicago."

"Oh." Last winter I had obtained a $250,000 jury award for my client in a sexual harassment lawsuit against a senior partner in a prominent Chicago law firm. My client had been his secretary. The story of the trial was featured in a *National Law Journal* special report on sexual harassment litigation.

"All the girls read about that case," Nancy said.

"Let's hope the men did, too," I said.

She laughed. "We made sure they did. Most of us gave our bosses a copy of the article."

"Including St. Germain?"

She snorted in disgust. "He's got a wife and two kids. Almost three. She's about eight months pregnant. He's been cheating on her for years. He had an affair with one of the secretaries from his old firm. And when that ended, he started sleeping with one of the paralegals here. Until Mr. Anderson found out."

"What happened?"

She raised her eyebrows. "I know he called Reed into his office and closed the door. They were in there for about an hour. When Reed came out he looked like he'd seen a ghost. As far as I could tell, he kept his hands off the girls for a while after that. But that was six months ago." She shook her head in disgust.

"You're not one of his biggest fans."

"He moved into Mr. Anderson's office the day after the funeral. Couldn't wait to get in there, Rachel. He was horning in before anyone even knew that Mr. Anderson was dead."

"What do you mean?"

"On the second day after Mr. Anderson disappeared, I found Reed in that office going through Mr. Anderson's papers. He told me—ordered me—to bring in Mr. Anderson's calendar."

"Why?"

"He said he had to make sure that Mr. Anderson didn't have any important meetings scheduled. For the next week or so, all mail addressed to Mr. Anderson had to go to Reed. Same reason. 'A law firm is like a Broadway play,' he told me. 'The show must go on.' "

"He's probably right."

She sighed. "I know. I guess that's the kind of man you

want to have in charge of things. It was the coldness that got me so upset."

"Does he still get all of Mr. Anderson's mail?"

"No. That stopped after a couple weeks."

"What happens now?"

"I forward the client correspondence to the attorneys assigned to the matters. All the rest—the personal bills, periodicals, junk mail—I've been saving it in a box near my desk. I guess I should be shipping it out to Mrs. Anderson pretty soon."

"Tell me about Stoddard Anderson," I asked. "What was he like to work for?"

"Oh, it was very exciting sometimes. He knew a lot of really important people. You wouldn't believe some of the names on my Rolodex. I used to place calls to senators, to the governor, the mayor, you name it. I bet there've been ten times at least that I picked up the phone and the girl on the other end said, 'This is the White House calling for Mr. Anderson.' Can you believe it?" She placed her hand on her chest. "Let me tell you, first time that happened this was one South County girl you could have knocked over with a feather."

I smiled, studying her. Age seems to enhance the beauty of some women in their forties, as if experience or wisdom somehow adds that last clarifying touch. Not so for Nancy Winslow. Her two most striking features—thick red hair and dark green eyes—remained strong, but twenty extra pounds and the steady pull of gravity had blurred what must have once been cover-of-*Vogue* beauty.

"What kind of things did you do for him?" I asked her.

"The usual. Took dictation, kept track of his schedules, set up appointments, set up meetings. That kind of stuff. I screened all of his incoming calls, placed all of his outgoing calls. Of course, there was always his filing to keep up with." She shook her head in wonder. "Let me tell you, that man used to get mail by the truckload."

She didn't recall anything unusual about his business travel during the last several months. He had made several trips to Chicago for meetings at the main office of Abbott & Windsor. As for other trips, she promised to get me his travel logs.

"What was he like?" I asked. "Was he cheerful, friendly, aloof?"

Nancy pressed her index finger against her chin as she thought it over. "I liked him okay," she finally said. "He was kind of formal with me. Proper. Like, I always called him Mr. Anderson. He was different in real life than he was on the phone."

"What do you mean?"

"He was always upbeat on the phone, real charming—like a game show host. But when he hung up, that personality would vanish, just like that." She snapped her fingers. "He wouldn't get mean or anything. He'd just get real businesslike, real serious. He was—well, he was a boss."

"How about the last week?" I asked. "Did you notice anything different?"

"He seemed—well, sort of moody," she said.

"How so?"

"Sort of out of it. Ordinarily, he'd be on the phone almost eight hours straight. Some days that phone never stopped ringing. He'd get fifty calls a day. But those last couple days he had me hold *all* of his calls. All of them."

"What was he doing?"

"I don't know. Sometimes he had the door closed. When it was closed he was sometimes on the phone. I could tell because his line lit up on my phone. That was odd, too. He usually didn't place his own calls."

"And when he wasn't on the phone?"

"I don't know. When the door was open, he'd either be sitting at his desk doodling or staring out the window."

"Did you ask him if anything was wrong?"

She shrugged. "Mr. Anderson didn't have personal conversations with me."

"Anything else odd that last week?"

She mulled it over. "Now that you mention it, yeah. Little things. He had this strict rule that if a lawyer was out of the office, he had to tell his secretary exactly where he was going and where he could be reached at all times. But a couple times that last week Mr. Anderson just up and walked out of the office without telling anyone where he was going. That was odd. You know what else? He didn't do his time sheets for the last three days."

"That was unusual for him?"

"Oh, yes. Definitely. That's another rule at Abbott & Windsor. Attorneys have to hand in their time sheets every day, no exceptions. If you're more than two days late, you get fined twenty dollars a day. Mr. Anderson really enforced that rule. Since he was managing partner, he made sure he did his own daily. But that last week, well, he didn't do any. None. I asked him one of those days if he had his time sheets for me, 'cause it just really wasn't like him."

"What did he say?"

She shrugged. "He mumbled something about how he'd get around to it."

"He'd never done that before?"

"No. I take that back. Once. About five months ago, there was about a one-week gap in his time sheets. I asked him about it back then. He told me to bill the whole week to vacation. Which was odd, since he was in the office some of those days."

"How about the day he disappeared. What was he like that morning?"

She shook her head sadly. "He was in his office with the door closed when I arrived that morning. He made at least one phone call, 'cause I remember his phone light lit up around ten o'clock."

"Just one call?"

"I think so. At least I didn't notice any others. Of course, I was holding all his incoming calls. He didn't take any of them. Anyway, around eleven-fifteen I knocked on the door and opened it to remind him of his lunch date at the St. Louis Club. He was standing at the window, just staring out at the Old Courthouse. I had to say his name three times before he turned around. 'Mr. Anderson—Mr. Anderson—MR. ANDERSON.' I told him about his lunch appointment but he just kind of stared at me, or through me. So I repeated it to make sure he heard."

"What did he do?" I asked.

"Just turned back to the window. He was leaning his head against the window when I closed the door. I felt real bad for him. I figured he must have heard some bad news or something. He really seemed kind of—well, stunned."

"What happened next?"

"He walked out of his office about twenty minutes later. I was sitting at my terminal when he walked past. He was gone for maybe five minutes before I realized he'd left without his suit jacket on. I went into his office and found it still hanging on the hook in back of his door. Well, that was a problem."

"Why?"

"His lunch meeting was at the St. Louis Club. You have to wear a jacket out there or they won't let you in. So I got the firm's messenger and gave him the jacket and told him to race like the devil out to Clayton to give it to Mr. Anderson. Then I called the club to tell them that Mr. Anderson had forgotten his jacket but that we were sending it out by messenger. I first started to worry when our messenger reached the club before Mr. Anderson. But then I thought that maybe he remembered about his jacket on his way to the club and had turned back to the office to get it. I stayed by my phone through lunch, waiting to hear from my boss." She sighed. "I never heard from him. Ever." She shook her head, her eyes watering. "God, it seems so stupid."

"What does?"

"That damn jacket. I'm telling you, I was in a panic. I was worried sick about that stupid jacket. He obviously couldn't have cared less about it."

I waited as she pulled a Kleenex out of the box on my desk and blew her nose.

"Did you handle his bank accounts?" I asked. Many older partners have their secretaries handle routine deposits and withdrawals. Some have their secretaries write checks and pay all their personal bills, from credit cards to home mortgage payments.

"Mrs. Anderson handled their personal bills. I kept track

of his bank statements, deposited his draw checks, and moved money from one account to another when he told me to. I didn't write any checks."

She recalled that he had cashed in several large certificates of deposit back in January and February because of some capital calls on two of his real estate limited partnerships, but told me that Reed St. Germain would be a better source of information about Stoddard Anderson's financial conditions. "He's handling Mr. Anderson's estate," she said. "He had me turn over all the bank statements, checkbooks, and other stuff."

"During the last couple weeks of his life," I said, reaching for my legal pad, "was he working on anything unusual?"

She frowned in thought and then shook her head. She recalled no new clients or unusual matters.

"Do any clients stand out in your memory?"

"Three."

"Who?"

"They're all regular clients of the firm. And they stand out because of the people involved. Especially the Missing Link." She gave a shiver of disgust.

"The Missing Link?"

"Salvatore Donalli. President of Donalli Construction Company."

"He's the Missing Link?"

"Yes. The most disgusting man I've ever met. I always felt like washing my phone whenever I got a call from him. Do you know what he once did? He made his secretary give him a blow job, and then, while that poor girl was down on her knees with his thing in her mouth, he called Mr. Anderson and told him."

"You're kidding."

She shook her head. "I was in Mr. Anderson's office once taking dictation when Donalli called. Mr. Anderson put him on the speaker phone but forgot to tell him I was in the room. 'What's up, Sal?' Mr. Anderson asked him. 'My cock,' he says. 'In Lurleen's mouth. She gives the best head in town.' And then that disgusting man made Lurleen say hello to Mr. Anderson. Well, by then Mr. Anderson had him off the speaker box."

"Was he upset?"

"Upset? Mr. Anderson was furious, what with me being in the room and hearing it. He really let that horrible man have it."

I had jotted down: Salvatore Donalli—Donalli Construction Co.—Missing Link. "And you say Mr. Anderson was in contact with this man before he died."

She nodded. "Oh, yes. A lot."

I groaned. "It sounds like I may need to meet the Missing Link."

"Then put on an extra pair of pantyhose before you go over there."

"And keep my mouth closed."

"Or get your teeth sharpened."

We both laughed.

"Who were the other two clients?"

"Albert Weidemeir. He's okay."

"Tell me about him."

"He works for the Sewer District. Mr. Anderson represents—represented—the Metropolitan Sewer District. Albert is some sort of accountant over there. He works in the controller's office. He's real quiet. Kind of dull. Your basic civil servant model, if you know what I mean. In the whole time I've known him, he's only told me one off-color joke."

"What was it?"

"He called for Mr. Anderson last Halloween. I remember because I told him I wouldn't put the call through until he told me a dirty joke. You know, trick or treat. Well, he hemmed and hawed for a while, and then finally he asks if I know what the Sewer District's motto is."

"What's the answer?"

Nancy smiled. "Your shit is our bread and butter."

"Cute . . . I guess."

"From Albert Weidemeir? My God, I almost fell over in hysterics. It's the funniest thing that man ever said to me."

"Tell me more about him."

"Albert's real straight, real serious. But nice. Every once in a while he'll ask about my boys when he calls."

"You mean the two redheads in the picture by your PC?" I asked.

"Right." She gave me a look of surprise. "You're observant."

"Part of the job," I said with a shrug.

I had noticed a photograph of two adolescent boys, both with red hair, pinned to the wall of Nancy's secretarial station. I had also noticed that she wasn't wearing a wedding ring. I knew the type. Over the years I've represented one or two Nancy Winslows in divorce proceedings, and several others in court battles with their ex-husbands over missed alimony and child-support payments. Somehow these women manage to raise their children on their own, feed them and clothe them and nourish them on meager salaries, with no help—financial, emotional, or otherwise—from the creeps who had long since abandoned them. The Nancy Winslows of this world have their own wing in the Rachel Gold hall of fame.

"So I can reach this Albert Weidemeir at the Sewer District?" I asked, jotting it down.

"Right. The main office. I'll get you his phone number."

"Thanks. Who's the third client?"

"Remy Panzer. He owns the Panzer Gallery."

"What's that?"

"A weird art gallery in the Central West End."

"Weird?"

"I've never actually been there, but it has to be. Anything Remy Panzer owns has to be weird."

"What's the story with Remy?"

"Well, for starters he's what you might call a little light in the loafers."

"Huh?"

"You know, sugar in his gas tank."

"Gay?"

"Definitely. Although I really don't mind that part. Panzer's just plain weird. Dresses weird, talks weird, walks weird. He gives me the willies."

I added Remy Panzer to my list. "This sounds like a fun

group: the Missing Link, a boring civil servant, and a cast member from the Addams Family.''

I asked her about Stoddard Anderson's mail, especially whether he received anything unusual toward the end. She didn't recall anything out of the ordinary.

I checked my watch. It was later than I thought. I was supposed to meet with Dottie Anderson, his widow, in fifteen minutes out in Clayton. I asked Nancy if she could drop off the box of correspondence in my office before she went home, along with his appointment calendar. "Also," I added, "could you have Reed St. Germain add to his list of documents the latest summary of the financial condition of Stoddard Anderson's estate.''

"Sure thing," she said as we both stood up. "You know, for what's it's worth, Rachel, Mr. Anderson really did seem out of it those last couple days. He'd always kept a pretty tight grip on himself, but I could tell he was struggling with something. Whatever it was, it was really driving him crazy.''

CHAPTER

The Anderson home is on a quiet street in the City of Clayton, which is an affluent older suburb of St. Louis. As I got out of my car, I felt as if I had been whisked back to a Golden Books neighborhood from the 1950s. The massive trees along the street formed a green canopy of shade overhead. Sunlight filtered through gaps in the leaves—dozens of slanted yellow columns. A child's bicycle was on its side on the sidewalk across the street. I could hear the distant growl of a lawn mower and the closer ring of an ice cream truck, perhaps a block over. A dog barked. A little girl pedaled down a driveway on her tricycle and then turned and pedaled back out of sight. Four houses down, on the lawn near the sidewalk, was a child's table with a handmade LEMONADE FOR SALE sign taped to the front. The proprietor was nowhere in sight. Perhaps he was taking a nap.

There was a dreamlike feel to the scene. I half expected to see the Pevely milk truck from my childhood come around the corner, trailing a pack of chasing kids—the boys wearing cowboy hats, me with my wild curls and torn Keds—shouting at the milkman for chunks of ice. Closing my eyes, I conjured up one of those big chunks of ice—sharp edges, cold to the tongue, harder than a diamond.

The Anderson house fit right in. It was a red brick house,

circa 1900, with black shutters, a gray slate roof, three chim-
neys, and two dormers. There were several window air-
conditioning units, and all were humming away. A huge oak
tree stood in the center of the lawn, casting shade over the entire
house.

The doorbell set off chimes inside. A few moments later
my newest client opened the door.

"You must be Rachel," she said with a friendly smile.
"Please come in, dear."

Like her neighborhood and her house, Dottie Anderson
looked as if she had been beamed down from the Golden Books
childhood. Specifically, she looked like the neighborhood
grandmother—the one who gave out homemade brownies on
Halloween and was always setting out a plate of warm sugar
cookies for the kids on the block who came to visit her. She was
even wearing an apron.

"These cookies are delicious," I said as she poured me a
cup of tea.

"Thank you, dear. Would you care for a lemon slice with
your tea?"

"No, thanks."

We talked generally for a while. I explained my assignment
and the scope of my investigation. She listened quietly, nodding
occasionally.

Dottie Anderson did not seem the woman most likely to
celebrate a thirty-second wedding anniversary with Stoddard
Anderson. At best, she was the one discarded after twenty-five
years for the "trophy wife." She was overweight, plain, and
shy. Her faded shirtwaist dress with a pleated bodice made her
look older than she was. The smudge of flour on her nose
seemed the final touch.

"We were high school sweethearts," she said in answer to
my question. "We were married after Stoddard graduated from
college. I taught kindergarten at the Flynn Park School while
Stoddard went to law school at St. Louis University. I haven't
worked since my son was born." She looked down at her hands
in her lap. "I've been an active volunteer, though. In fact, I
have a Red Cross committee meeting tonight, and tomorrow is

my day at the gift shop at Barnes Hospital. I do that every week.''

She gave me a tour of the house. The upstairs seemed like a series of museum period rooms. The bedrooms of her dead son and institutionalized daughter looked the way they must have looked on the day each had departed.

"This was Stoddard's bedroom," she said as she opened the door.

My head involuntarily turned toward her bedroom, which was at the other end of the upstairs hallway. She caught the look, and I saw a brief glimmer of pain, or shame, in her face.

"Would you mind if I looked around Mr. Anderson's room?" I asked. "It shouldn't take long."

"Take your time, dear. I'll be downstairs in the kitchen."

I spent fifteen minutes searching his bedroom. If it contained a clue to his mental state, I missed it. The room was bereft of personality, and seemed more like a room in a residence hotel. The only reading materials were several *Fortune* and *Forbes* magazines on his nightstand and a pile of old *Wall Street Journal*s on the corner of his desk. The only personal papers were neat stacks of old bills and magazine subscription notices in the center of his desk. The faded English hunting prints that were framed on the wall seemed as anonymous as the rest of the room.

"What were his work habits the last week or so?" I asked Dottie. We were seated at the small table in the kitchen.

"He worked late most of those nights. But that was hardly unusual." She shook her head sadly. "Stoddard worked late most nights."

"Did he have any drinking or drug problems?"

"No. He liked a glass of wine with his meal. And he often made himself a highball before dinner. When he came home before dinner, that is. I'm afraid that an attorney's wife gets used to cooking for one. As for a drug problem, I would be shocked if he did. He wrote articles about the need for longer jail terms for drug offenders. He was chairman of the 'Say No To Drugs' campaign in St. Louis under President Reagan. I met Mrs. Reagan, you know. We had tea together at Old War-son Country Club.''

"Did you see him the night before he disappeared?''

"We had dinner here. I made my pot roast.'' She tilted her head to the side, remembering. "He seemed moody. And dis-tracted. I remember I was in the middle of telling him about something that happened at the hospital gift shop when he just . . . got up and . . . and just walked out of the room. He wasn't angry, or any such thing as that. He just wasn't even aware I was talking.''

"Did you see him again?''

She closed her eyes and shook her head. "By the time I cleaned the dishes he was in his bedroom and the door was closed. He left for work the next morning while I was in my bath. I never saw him again.''

"Did he contact you before he died?''

She looked down. "No.''

"Were you afraid he'd been kidnapped?''

After a moment of silence, she looked up, her eyes moist. "I was frightened, but not that Stoddard had been kidnapped. I'm . . . I'm so ashamed of myself, Rachel. I was afraid that he . . . that he had left me for another woman. Every time that telephone rang after he disappeared, I was afraid it would be Stoddard, calling from one of those horrible places like Reno or Tijuana—calling to tell me he wanted a divorce.'' Her lips quiv-ered.

I said nothing.

"I'm so ashamed of myself for thinking those thoughts,'' she continued, her hands tightening around the teacup. "There I was, worrying only about myself. All that time I had no idea he was in such pain.''

I reached across the table and placed my hand over hers. We sat there quietly. The only sound was the humming of the air conditioner in the dining room.

"What made you think he might want a divorce?'' I asked gently.

"Oh, nothing in particular.''

"How about in general?"

"I don't know. A woman just . . ." She stopped, head down.

I waited.

"We . . . we hadn't made . . . had relations in years," Dottie said, eyes downcast. "Although it had never been an important part of our marriage, it stopped completely about ten years ago."

"What happened?" I asked softly.

"Stoddard had problems with . . . with his functions."

"He became impotent?"

She nodded. "I thought it was my fault. I know I'm not a beautiful woman, Rachel. I tried to overcome that. I went on a diet. I bought some . . . some daring undergarments." A tear rolled slowly down her cheek. "It didn't help. I encouraged Stoddard to seek medical help. I cut out an article on male problems from *Readers' Digest*. I left it on his nightstand. That just made him angrier. He told me it was just a phase and that it would pass." She sighed, her shoulders sagging. "It never passed. He moved out of our bedroom into his own room down the hall."

She looked at me. "My husband and I never slept together again after that, Rachel. I don't mean just not having relations together. I mean not even sleeping together. Back when we were young, when we were newlyweds, we used to cuddle together, sometimes for hours." Her eyes had a faraway look. "We were poor as church mice back then, but we had each other. The happiest memories of my life were those winter nights back when Stoddard was in law school. After I finished my lesson plan for the next day and Stoddard finished his homework, we'd just cuddle on the couch together while the wind howled outside." Her smile seemed to hover there for a moment and then it faded. She glanced at me and then looked down. "Those are old memories. Stoddard and I stopped cuddling many years ago."

I gently probed for other observations of her husband, but it became clear they had been strangers for years, leading separate lives under the same roof. She didn't know about the added life insurance he had purchased four months before his death. She didn't know what he had been working on during the last weeks of his life. She knew where he went when he traveled, because his secretary would send her his trip itinerary, but she didn't know why he went where he went. She assumed they were all business trips.

Although she paid the bills, she knew nothing else about their financial affairs. Whenever the balance in her checking account got low, she would call her husband's secretary, Nancy, and tell her she needed more money in the checking account. Nancy would ask her how much she needed, and then handle the transfer of the money. Dottie literally had no idea where the money came from. All she knew was that she paid the bills and Stoddard handled all the investment decisions, because "he was a man and knew about those things."

"Did he leave a note?" I asked.

"He did," Dottie said. She stood up. "I'll get it for you."

She left the room and came back a few moments later with a thick manila envelope, out of which she extracted a folded sheet of paper. "This is a photocopy," she said as she handed the note to me. "The police have the original."

"What else is in the envelope?"

"These are the papers that the police found in the motel room. Most of them were in his briefcase, they said. You're welcome to take them with you, Rachel. Perhaps they can help your investigation."

I unfolded the suicide note and read it:

> The Quest has come to an end. The Executor is safe underground. I have become my own Executor. Dottie, this is a dying man's last request:
> Forgive me.
>
> Stoddard Anderson

"What does it mean?" I finally asked.

"I don't know."

I stared at the note, reading it again. "It doesn't make any sense." I started to copy the words down on my legal pad.

Dottie reached across the table and grasped my arm. "Please find out what it means," she said fiercely. "Find out what my husband was trying to tell me."

I put my hand over hers and looked into her eyes. Surely she had once chased her own milk truck. She had once been a young bride. And now? She had buried her only son and placed her only daughter in an institution. She had waited alone as an empty marriage ended with a suicide note she didn't understand from a stranger she had once loved.

"Take the note with you," she told me. "I don't want it until I know what it means. Find out what it means, Rachel. Please help me understand his death."

"I'll try," I promised her. "I'll try to find out what your husband meant."

As I walked to my car I peered into the manila envelope. There was a fresh yellow legal pad, the front section of the *Wall Street Journal* from the day he disappeared, a pocket calendar, a calculator, a monthly statement of his account from the St. Louis Club (which was in an envelope postmarked two days before he disappeared), and a marked-up photocopy of an article from *Business Lawyer* on sale-leaseback transactions in the aviation industry.

As I unlocked my car door, I heard a truck in the distance shift gears. It made me think again of that milk truck. I turned toward the Anderson home. Had the milkman ever handed little Dottie one of those big chunks of ice? At first, as you cradled it in your hands, the ice would seem as clear as glass. But then you would notice that your hands were distorted by the ice. Studying the ice as you tilted it this way and that, you could sometimes spot outlines of ice chunks within ice chunks within ice chunks, each invisible unless sunlight hit a surface just right.

CHAPTER 7

When I returned to Abbott & Windsor, there were several boxes of Stoddard Anderson documents in my office: his time sheets, his phone messages, his correspondence files, his travel logs, and the contents of his office. Reviewing all of the documents would take several hours.

I checked my watch. It was almost five o'clock. I called my sister Ann to tell her I wouldn't be home until late. With a sigh, I lifted the first box, lugged it over to the desk, and opened the lid.

If my friends from law school and my friends in practice are any indication, a fairly high percentage of lawyers in America were encouraged as children to become lawyers because they were "great with people" or "had the gift of gab." It is one of the many ironies of the practice. Contrary to popular belief, the legal profession is a lonely occupation. Even a trial lawyer's typical day can often resemble that of a cloistered monk. You spend hours, even days, alone in a room reviewing documents or alone in a law library researching legal issues or alone at your desk drafting court papers. And when you do have that rare opportunity to engage in an extended conversation with a living, breathing human being, more often than not he is under oath, his lawyer is at his side, and a court reporter is taking it all down.

I finished the last of the boxes of documents three hours later. I had learned several intriguing things about Stoddard Anderson, although whether any of them was important was not at all clear. Settling back in my chair and stretching first my arms and then my legs, I looked over my notes, which covered six pages of my legal pad.

Item # 1. The first gap in Stoddard Anderson's time sheets occurred two weeks before he took out the extra insurance, which was four months before his suicide. That juxtaposition could be purely coincidental. Or it could mean that during the missing days something happened that made Anderson either believe his life was in danger or decide to kill himself.

Item # 2. He took six trips during the last three months. Three overnight trips to Chicago, one to New York (two weeks before he died), one to Argentina (eight weeks before he died), and one to New Mexico (nine weeks before he died). He stayed at Hyatt Hotels each time, and all of the expenses he submitted appeared routine: restaurants, bars, dry cleaners, cab fares, tolls, parking, rental cars.

Item # 3. His time sheets did not reflect Dottie Anderson's description of his work habits and long hours. He rarely recorded more than eight hours of work a day on his time sheets. There were several possible explanations, most of them innocent. Perhaps Stoddard Anderson failed to keep track of his hours during the day, or consistently underestimated those hours. Every major law firm in America has a few workhorses who lose hundreds of hours of billable time a year by simply forgetting to write them down on their time sheets. Another possibility was that Anderson didn't record his nonbillable activities; as managing partner, he would have had a heavy load of administrative tasks on top of his billable client work. This explanation seemed less likely, however: His time sheets did include many entries for firm administration, client development, and other nonbillable matters. Then there were, of course, less innocent explanations for the long hours away from home that were not reflected on his time sheets, the most obvious of which would be charged to the nonbillable category "other woman."

Item # 4. Neither his correspondence files nor his telephone message slips contained any apparent clues other than to confirm his secretary's recollection of the three main clients he was involved with during the last few weeks of his life: There were numerous messages from, and an occasional business letter to, Albert Weidemeir (of the Metropolitan St. Louis Sewer District), Remy Panzer (of the Panzer Gallery), and M. Salvatore Donalli (of Donalli Construction Company). The letters were entirely unremarkable examples of typical attorney-client correspondence.

Item # 5. The estate of Stoddard Anderson was much smaller than one might ordinarily assume. Ishmael Richardson's comments about his stock market losses and the decline in the value of his real estate investments, along with Nancy Winslow's observations, were borne out in the financial statements. Excluding the home in Clayton and the proceeds of the life insurance policy, the remaining estate was less than three hundred thousand dollars. He had by no means died a pauper, but it was clear that his widow needed the insurance benefits.

Item # 6. His personal appointment calendar included meetings with all three main clients during the last two weeks, along with a speaking engagement before the women's auxiliary of a local hospital, a doctor's appointment six days before he disappeared, a couple of board meetings, a golf date, and numerous luncheon engagements. Conspicuously absent from the calendar were many evening meetings.

Item # 7. The box of his personal correspondence consisted almost entirely of bills, solicitations, legal publications, and newsletters and similar correspondence from literally dozens of professional organizations, charitable institutions, trade associations, and the like. Nancy Winslow was right: The task of keeping track of Stoddard Anderson's correspondence was enough to keep a secretary busy almost full time.

There were, however, two items of possible interest in his correspondence. One was a bill from the postal service for rental of a post office box downtown. I jotted down the P.O. box number and added a note to check that out. The other item was the monthly statement from the St. Louis Club that had been among the papers the police found in his briefcase. The only significant entry for that final month was a $145.78 charge for dinner on June 8, which was ten days before he disappeared. The size of the bill suggested that Anderson had not dined alone that night.

I checked his appointment calendar. There was no entry for June 8. Maybe a spur-of-the-moment dinner with someone, I said to myself.

Then I remembered his pocket calendar—the one the police had found among his papers at the motel. I pulled it out of the manila envelope Dottie Anderson had given me and flipped to the date of the dinner. He had printed the word "ParaLex" in the evening portion of that day. That was all. Maybe a new client?

I mulled that over for a moment and reached for the telephone book. I found the number for the St. Louis Club. A man named Philip answered and identified himself as the maitre d' of the main dining room. I told him briefly who I was and asked him to check his reservation book to see if he could tell who Stoddard Anderson had had dinner with on the night of June 8. A few moments later Philip apologetically told me that all that the reservation book showed was that Mr. Anderson had dined with another person that night in the Marquette Room, which was one of the club's small private dining rooms. Claude was the maitre d' on duty the night of June 8, Philip told me, but tonight was his night off. He would be back at the club tomorrow at noon, and Philip promised that Claude would call me then. I thanked him and gave him the office number.

I pulled my legal pad over and jotted down "ParaLex??" I stared at the word. Then I circled it. There. A clue, I said to myself. Just like I really knew what I was doing.

I pushed the legal pad away and looked at the two appointment calendars—the big desk one and the small pocket one. They seemed like a good source of people to contact. As I was getting up to make a photocopy of several pages from the calendars, my phone rang. It was Benny Goldberg, calling from Chicago.

"So, what do you have so far?" he asked.

I went through everything I had found in the documents. Maybe Benny would see a pattern where I could not.

"Sounds like ole Stoddard was shtupping some babe," Benny said.

"You think?"

"Sure. Just 'cause his labanzas go into vapor lock around his old lady don't mean they don't function around someone else."

"Labanzas?" I said after a pause, a smile on my lips. "Where did you get that one, Mr. Esperanto?"

"Portuguese, I think."

"I thought you said fishteras was the Portuguese term."

"Fishteras, labanzas, whatever. I'm telling you, the guy was shtupping some babe. What's his secretary look like?"

"She's pretty. But I don't think so."

"She's a likely suspect, Rachel. They usually are. Ask around the office. It might be her. Or one of the paralegals. Yeah, probably a paralegal."

"Maybe. I'll keep my eyes peeled. Hey, have you ever heard of a company called ParaLex?"

"ParaLex? ParaLex . . . nah. Listen, kiddo, you need some help down there? I could always come down. It's slow around the office, and there's a terrific barbecue joint down there. It's called Roscoe—Roscoe something or other."

"Oh?"

Benny was a barbecue fanatic. For years he had kept track of his favorites on a set of index cards that he continually updated, filling the backs and sides with arcane annotations. This summer he had transferred the entire file to a data bank in the personal computer in his office.

There was a pause as Benny was no doubt typing a Roscoe search request for his computer. "Ah, here we go," he said. "Roscoe McCrary's Hickory Bar-B-Que House. On 2719 Parnell. They serve hickory-smoked pig snouts."

"Snouts? As in piggies' noses?"

"Snouts, as in one of the best things you can put in your mouth without the consent of another adult."

"No wonder we're supposed to keep kosher."

"Believe me, Rachel, if Moses had tasted one of Roscoe McCrary's hickory-smoked pig snouts up on Mount Sinai, there'd be a special exemption in the laws of kashrut for certain parts of certain cloven-hoof mammals. God, my mouth is watering. What do you say, Rachel? I could be there tomorrow."

"I'm okay so far, Benny. I'll check in with you tomorrow. I promise."

"You sure?"

"I'm sure."

"Okay. But if I hear word of some tall, foxy white chick doing a pig snout carry-out at McCrary's, I'm going to be crushed."

"Trust me, Benny. I'll call you tomorrow."

"Rachel Gold?"

I was up at the Xerox machine copying pages from Stoddard Anderson's appointment calendars. I turned and stared at the guy who had said my name. He looked about my age, and vaguely familiar.

"Rachel Gold, right?"

I nodded.

"Sandy Feldman. We were in high school together."

I shook his hand. "Sure. Of course. I didn't recognize you with the beard. How are you?"

"Great. I heard you were coming down to do something on Anderson's estate. I haven't seen you since high school, Rachel. You look terrific."

"I didn't know you worked here."

"I came over from Thompson & Mitchell last fall."

Sandy Feldman and I had been in the same homeroom together at University City High School. Back then he had been a shy, slide-rule type who wore black pants pulled high above the waist, as if his hips were fused to his rib cage. Other than an occasional hello in the morning, I doubt if we spoke ten words to each other throughout high school. The last time I saw him, which was probably graduation day, he had fierce-looking pimples on his cheeks and a clump of dark frizzy hair hanging over his eyes. The pimples were gone, and so was most of the hair on top, replaced by a dark beard. As I followed him back to his office, I marveled at how much better he looked. He had grown a few inches since high school, filled out some, and obviously retained the services of a tailor with a better sense of the whereabouts of his waist. He looked like a neatly coiffed Allen Ginsberg.

"You have to remember," Sandy said after we were seated in his small office, "we're one of the colonies down here."

"I don't follow."

"Abbott & Windsor started in Chicago back in the eighteen hundreds. Chicago is still the motherland. This is the hinterlands. We didn't come of age singing the Abbott & Windsor fight song. Down here we didn't start off as summer clerks playing tennis at the big firm outing on the North Shore." He shrugged. "This is an office filled with opportunists. Speaking of which, have you met our new fearless leader?"

"You mean Reed St. Germain?"

He nodded. "There's a piece of work. You should see the way he sucks around the BSDs from Chicago. Practically straps on the knee pads. Especially when Ishmael Richardson comes down to inspect the troops."

"Where did St. Germain come from?"

"He started at his dad's firm, Harris & St. Germain. He joined Anderson's old firm two years before the merger with A & W. Hard to figure him out. Guy meditates almost every day after lunch, flies off to Nepal every other year, a strict vegetarian. And do you know what the end product of all that inner harmony bullshit is? He cheats on his wife, keeps a secret bachelor's pad in the Central West End, and usually takes some girlfriend with him on his business trips. He can be a real prick with everyone, except for Mrs. St. Germain."

"Oh?"

"Apparently, she's a real ballbuster. I hear he's a real wimp around her. She tries to keep him on a short leash."

"Not too successfully, I gather."

"I guess not. I don't know how he hides all those extracurricular expenses from her. She'd kill him if she found out. Maybe that tension makes him mean. I'm telling you, I've seen that guy in a negotiation. When he senses a weakness, he's like a shark scenting blood.''

"Be glad he doesn't eat red meat.''

"You're right. He'd probably grab an Uzi and head for the nearest highway overpass.''

"So you don't like him, eh?'' I said with a smile.

Sandy shrugged. "He's a fellow member of the bar. If I wanted to work with saints, I'd have become a social worker. His clients love him.''

"Your wife looks familiar,'' I said, gesturing at the photograph of his wife and two children on his credenza.

"Rhonda Jaffe. She was a year behind us.''

"Oh, sure,'' I said. I didn't remember her.

"She's lost some weight since that picture. She really ballooned up with the second pregnancy.''

"What's your area?'' I asked.

"Corporate tax.'' He gave me a sheepish smile. "Planet of the nebbishes.'' He shrugged. "Once a nerd, always a nerd. It's the curse of high school.''

"Don't say that, Sandy. I can't get over how good you look.''

"Me? Look at you.''

"Please.''

"I gotta tell you, Rachel, I had a terrible crush on you back in high school. When you used to walk into homeroom in your cheerleader outfit with that micro-miniskirt I would practically swoon.''

"Don't start,'' I said, embarrassed.

"You should have been homecoming queen,'' he said. "I voted for you.''

"Oh, for goodness sake, Sandy.''

He waved his hand in dismissal. "It was all those Jewish boys voting for that blond bomber.'' He shook his head in wonderment. "High school. It's amazing the way it stays with you, isn't it? So tell me, are you married?''

"No. Not yet.''

"You're kidding.''

"No," I said, deciding to change the subject. "Is your middle initial 'A'?"

He sat back with a puzzled look. "Yes," he finally answered.

I had recalled several "Office Conference w/SAF" entries on Anderson's time sheets from last January and February. "How much did you work with Stoddard Anderson?" I asked him.

"Not much. I did a few things for him over the last six months or so."

"On what?"

Sandy tugged on his beard in thought. "Mostly run-of-the-mill tax stuff. You know, structuring a merger or acquisition to take advantage of some tax angle."

"How about last January and February? Did you have any unusual projects from him?"

"January and February," he mused. "Well, I had one weird assignment from him sometime last winter. Maybe it was then."

"What was it?"

"Anderson had me do a big research memo on importing art objects."

"Anything specific?"

"Yeah. I had to look at Mexico's law on—what's it called—on cultural patrimony."

"Which is what?"

"The kind of artifacts that all those nineteenth-century British dudes hauled back to England from Egypt and Greece and places like that. Mummies, ancient Greek statues, that kind of stuff."

"What was the issue Anderson wanted you to look at?"

"It was a good one. That Mexican law prohibits the export from Mexico of anything that could be considered part of its cultural patrimony. If someone breaks that law, other countries, including the U.S., have agreed, by law or treaty, to help Mexico retrieve the property. Problem is, the Mexican law isn't all that old. I think it got enacted back in the 1960s."

"Why's that a problem?"

Sandy leaned forward, warming to the story. "The issue Stoddard asked me to check out was whether that law would apply to an art object that had been taken out of Mexico a long, long time ago, like back a couple hundred years, but which had somehow briefly returned to native soil."

"I'm not following you."

"Say some guy back in 1885 visits Mexico, finds some sort of a pre-Columbian artifact—an Aztec pot. Maybe buys it off an Indian. He brings it home to New York with him. Then, a hundred years later, someone brings that same pot back into Mexico, maybe to get it appraised. Assume that if that pot had *never* left Mexico in the first place it would be considered part of the cultural patrimony of the country. In other words, if it had always been in Mexico, it would be illegal to take it out of Mexico."

"So the issue is whether the law applies to something that returns to Mexico?"

"Exactly," he said. "As long as it stays in the United States, it's legal. But if you bring it back to Mexico, even for just an hour, and then go back home, can the Mexican government legally ask U.S. Customs to seize it and return it?"

"Can they?"

Sandy shrugged. "The Mexicans think they can. So do their courts. It's not entirely clear what Customs would do if asked."

"What kind of artifact did Anderson have in mind?"

"I have no idea."

"Really?"

"Really. He never told me."

"Who was the client?"

"I don't know that either. He handled the whole thing in a strange way. Anderson told me to bill my time to the office rather than to a client. When I was done with the project, he told me I had to give him all of my drafts. I wasn't even allowed to keep my notes after I finished the project."

"Why not?"

"He didn't say."

"What did he do with it?"

"I don't know. He never talked to me about the project after it was over."

I thought it over. "Do you have a copy of the memo you gave him?"

"No, he told me not to keep any copies." But then Sandy smiled. "Ah, but there has to be a copy. I did it on word processing. It'll be in the word processing department's computer. C'mon," he said as he stood up. "We can have them print out a copy."

But we couldn't. As the head computer operator on the night crew told us after she had completed her search through the computer files and back-up disks, there was no record of Sandy Feldman's memorandum. Stoddard Anderson, or someone else, must have issued instructions to delete all copies of the memorandum from the computer records.

Sandy followed me back to my office, where I was gathering my notes and papers and stuffing them in a large trial bag. It was close to nine o'clock. He still had several hours of work on an SEC filing. I was done for the day.

"Have you ever heard of ParaLex?" I asked him as I flicked off the light in my office.

He frowned. "No. Why?"

"I saw it in Stoddard Anderson's calendar. I thought it might be a client."

"We can check on your way out. Follow me."

Lugging the trial bag, I followed him down and around several corridors to a small room with a bank of facsimile machines. He reached under the counter and pulled out a bound client and matter list. It was several hundred pages long and arranged alphabetically. I found the right page and ran my finger down the column of client names:

Paradigm Incorporated

Paraform Manufacturing Corporation

Paragon Investment Research Co.

Paramount Pictures, Inc.

Paraquest Limited Partnership, Ltd.

"Is this a current list?" I asked.

"Give or take a couple weeks," Sandy said. "You can have them run the name through the computer tomorrow if you think it might be a brand-new client."

"Maybe I will."

"Hey, let me show you something on your way out," Sandy said. "You're going to get a kick out of it."

I followed him down the hall to the darkened employee lunchroom. He flipped on the lights and walked over to the support staff's bulletin board.

"You're famous down here," he said, pointing to a photocopy of the article from the *National Law Journal* on the sexual harassment jury trial I had won, the same article Nancy Winslow had mentioned earlier. Someone had circled my name in red ink and written in the margin: *She will be here next week!!*

"It's a great article, Rachel."

I shrugged. "The reporter got a little carried away. I wasn't crazy about the cowboy metaphors."

"Really? I loved that part. That Stanford Blaine sounds like he deserved it. Did he really act like he was a cowboy?"

"He had some cowboy stuff in his office," I said. Stanford Blaine had been the defendant in the lawsuit. At the time he had been chairman of a mid-sized Chicago law firm. He was now "of counsel" at a smaller firm. "He was born in Wyoming," I added.

"But he prepped at Choate and earned his law degree from NYU. Some cowboy." He squinted at the text on the bulletin board. "Here's my favorite part: 'But it was on the morning of the third day of cross-examination that the Marshall Dillon facade began to crumble,' " he read. " 'Firing questions like bullets, Rachel Gold stalked Stanford Blaine across the sagebrush, methodically cutting off every avenue of escape. That afternoon she lured him into a testimonial box canyon, and then backed him into a corner no larger than the witness stand. Finally, at twenty minutes to four, with a rapt judge and crowded courtroom looking on like witnesses to a hanging, she moved in for the kill.' " He paused, shaking his head in admiration. "Oh, yeah, the next part I love."

"Enough," I said as he was about to start reading aloud again.

He turned to me with a grin. It was as if we were back in homeroom again. "I love it," he said. "Did you really make him turn to the jury and admit that he lied?"

I nodded, unsmiling.

"Great stuff."

"It generated a lot of hate mail."

"Really?"

"A lot of male attorneys—*anonymous* male attorneys—didn't think it was so great."

"Well, they're pathetic. I wouldn't worry about them."

I nodded again, unsmiling.

I thought about that hate mail as I rode the elevator down to the lobby. The letter writers called me everything from "a castrating cunt" to a "miserable dyke." One Neanderthal sent me a rubber dildo wrapped with barbed wire; the note told me to "shove this up your twat, bitch."

What upset me most was that the hate mail authors succeeded. I was devastated by their horrible letters, by the curses they hurled at me from their anonymous rat holes. I couldn't sleep at night, I dreaded venturing out of my office during the day. When I rode an elevator in the courthouse or sat in a courtroom, I scanned each male face, trying to make eye contact, trying to determine whether I was staring at one of my correspondents. If a strange lawyer smiled at me, I stiffened. It took months before it passed, before I was able to be around unfamiliar male attorneys without flinching.

And the irony was that it had all stemmed from representing a woman I didn't particularly like or trust in a lawsuit against a man I didn't particularly dislike or distrust. Brandy Holmen was the former secretary of Stanford Blaine, the senior partner whose reputation she ruined—I ruined, we ruined—through the trial. In her occasional unguarded moments around me during the trial, I saw her use on other men the seductive, manipulative charm that she must have used on her boss over the years, that must have led him to believe she was sexually available. Now

I'm sure that up there in the rarefied atmosphere of the Pure Sisterhood, Brandy Holmen's secretarial fan dance is just further proof of her status as victim of a male culture. But down in that courtroom after the jury returned its verdict—after Brandy let out a war whoop and jumped into her new boy-friend's arms while Stanford Blaine buried his head in his hands—things didn't seem quite that black and white.

I ran into Stanford Blaine earlier this summer in the cafeteria line at the Chicago Bar Association. The jury verdict had just been affirmed on appeal. He shook my hand, no hostility apparent. Blaine is a trial lawyer. He understands. Better than I do.

CHAPTER

As I drove my car out of the parking garage and onto Highway 40 heading west, I realized that I hadn't eaten since breakfast. No wonder I was so hungry. I decided to have dinner at one of my favorite high school hangouts: the Steak 'N Shake on Olive Boulevard in University City.

Back in high school I used to go there after football games on Saturday nights with my boyfriend, who was the quarterback. On Friday nights I'd go there with my girlfriends, with our hairbrushes and Juicy Fruit gum and packs of Marlboros. There would be dozens of parked cars on the lot, each filled with high school kids, while an endless parade of cars cruised through, checking out the scene. Horns would honk, there'd be shouts from one car to another, and above all the sounds of rock music blaring from car radios. The delicious smells of french fries and catsup would drift into your car windows as you turned off the ignition. Carhops weaved between the cruising cars to deliver food on trays that hooked onto the car windows.

But times had changed at Steak 'N Shake. There was no curb service, and the drive-through lane at the McDonald's across the street had more cars in it than the entire parking lot at Steak 'N Shake. Fortunately, not everything had changed, as I discovered when the waitress placed my favorite Steak 'N

Shake meal on the table in front of me: a double cheeseburger with thousand island dressing, extra pickles, regular fries, and a chocolate malt. I must have eaten that combination more than a hundred times during high school, and it tasted just as delicious as it had back then.

"Rachel?"

During the time it took to chew and swallow a bite of cheeseburger I was able to put a name with the face.

"Timmy O'Donohue," I said.

"Been a long time, Rachel."

"It sure has. I didn't know you were a cop."

"Yeah," he said with a shrug. "I been on the U. City force going on ten years now."

The waitress came over with a white carry-out bag. "Here's your fries and Coke, Tim."

He thanked her and paid the bill. He turned back to me, a hesitant look on his face.

"You on break?" I asked.

He nodded. "Yeah."

"Don't be such a snob," I said. "Sit down."

"Sure," he said with a sheepish grin. "Don't mind if I do."

We spent a fun ten minutes reminiscing about high school days and sharing the latest intelligence on our classmates. He had married Sherry McGuire, whom I remembered from my Spanish class. They had four kids, two still in diapers.

I tilted my malt and sipped the last part through the straw until it made that gurgling noise.

"So you're not married?" he asked.

"Not yet," I said, glancing at my watch.

He checked his own watch. "Well, my break's almost over."

We both stood up. Timmy walked with me out of the restaurant.

"Maybe you can help me, Timmy," I said as we walked toward our cars. "I have to talk to some people over the next day or so. Maybe you've heard of them."

"Who are they?"

"Salvatore Donalli. He's the head of his own construction company."

"Sure. He's got a crew doing some work on the River Des Peres over by Hemen Park. Donalli's a hothead. He got into a shoving match with some sewer district inspector about a month ago."

"Over what?"

"Some sort of dispute over cement. Something about the specs. No one filed charges."

"How about Albert Weidemeir? He works for the sewer district."

"Don't know him. Of course, that River Des Peres project, the one Donalli Construction is working on, that's a sewer district project. I don't know any Albert Weidemeir."

We had reached my car. "How about a guy named Remy Panzer?" I asked.

Timmy raised his eyebrows. "He the guy with the art gallery in the Central West End?"

I nodded.

"I've heard some of the guys in vice talk about him. It's all hearsay. He's supposed to be one of the chickenhawks who sometimes cruise the Loop. I don't think we've ever busted him."

"He likes young boys?"

"So I hear. He likes them around thirteen. A real sicko, if that's the guy I'm thinking of. Watch out for him."

"Do you know anyone on the Bridgeton police force?"

"I know a few of those guys."

"How about a detective named Mario Aloni. I'm meeting him first thing tomorrow."

"Mouse? Sure, I know him."

"They call him Mouse?"

"Yeah. Mouse Aloni. He's a good man. Tell Mouse I said hi."

"I will. Thanks, Timmy. Give my best to Sherry."

"Sure. It's real good to see you, Rachel. See you around."

As I got in my car Timmy called out my name.

"What?"

He had his car door open, his hand on the hood. "You have any problems, things get a little dicey, you give me a call, you hear?"

"Thanks, Timmy."

By the time I pulled into my sister's driveway it was almost eleven o'clock. The house was dark except for the den on the first floor, where I could hear the sounds of a television show.

I stopped at the doorway to the den. Ann's husband-the-orthodontist Richie was seated on the couch, staring slack-jawed at a Cubs-Dodgers game on the big-screen television. An empty bag of Doritos and two cans of Diet Coke were on the coffee table.

"Hi, Richie," I said.

Richie snapped out of his TV daze. He was startled at first, but then flashed me one of those 50,000-watt orthodontist smiles—all those even white-capped teeth.

"Hey, Rachel. Good to see you, babe. Looking super."

Richie started toward me. I stuck out my hand. He looked down at it.

Five years ago, just after Richie and Ann had moved into their brand-new English Tudor in Ladue, they threw a big New Year's Eve party. I was in St. Louis for the holidays and went to their party. Around one in the morning I had walked into the kitchen for a refill. Richie sneaked up as I reached into their Sub Zero for a beer. He grabbed me by the hips as I straightened, pressing his crotch against my rear. I was so startled I thought he was joking. But then he turned me around and backed me up against the built-in Amana microwave oven. "God, you have magnificent incisors," he groaned as he tried to stab his thick tongue into my mouth. I had to conk him on the head three times with the beer can, splattering foam on the hardwood floor, before he loosened his grip enough for me to shove him away.

That was five years ago. We had reached an awkward truce since then, although I tried to avoid situations where we were alone together.

"Good to see you, Richie," I said, shaking hands. "Ann asleep?"

"Sure is. You know her. Early to bed, early to rise." He smiled and shrugged.

Studying him, I suddenly realized that Richie was sliding into middle age. He'd put on enough weight to have a double chin and paunch. His black hair was thinning, and he had started combing it over the top to cover the balding area. Camouflage hair. Before long he would have to eliminate rides in convertibles. (Why do bald men go the camouflage route? And what happens when they turn in their sleep so that their heads rest on the same side as their parts? Do those eight-inch hanks of camouflage hair gradually slide off the bald spots and unfurl on the pillows?)

Although I had never been crazy about him, Richie was on his best behavior tonight, playing his own version of Robert Young on *Father Knows Best*. He took me up to the guest bedroom, showed me the fresh towels Ann had left on the bed, brought in his travel alarm clock, and gave me a note from Ann.

"Oh, yeah," he said, pausing at the door. "You got a phone call from a guy named St. Something-or-other."

"St. Germain?"

"Yeah, that's it. He said to be sure to call him when you got in."

Richie ran downstairs and came back up with the message slip and the portable phone. I dialed the number after he left. Reed St. Germain answered on the second ring.

"Rachel, I just wanted to make sure you've been getting the cooperation and help you need from our people."

"Everyone's been great, Reed."

"Terrific. I'm pleased. Tell me, Rachel, how is the investigation going?"

"I'm making progress, but it's still kind of early."

"Sure. I can understand that. Any questions I can help answer?"

"Not really. I just have to work my way down the list of people. Oh, there is one thing. Do you know whether Mr. Anderson had a new client named ParaLex?"

There was a pause. "A client named ParaLex? No. Why, Rachel?"

"Just curious."

"How did that come up?"

"Just a name jotted down in his calendar. A dinner meeting, I think. I thought maybe it was a new client. If so, it might be someone I could talk to about Mr. Anderson's mental condition."

"I don't think it's a client, Rachel, but you might want to check our list of new clients tomorrow to be sure. Sorry I can't help you there. Anything else?"

"No."

"You be sure to call me if there is, Rachel. And you be sure to tell me if you need any help whatsoever. Understand?"

"Sure. Thanks."

As I hung up I thought to myself that if St. Germain had used my name one more time in that conversation I would have screamed. Maybe clients responded to his programmed sincerity, but I sure didn't. He reminded me of the boys from my sixth-grade dance class: the ones who looked like little Fred Astaires from across the room. When you were up close, holding their sweaty hands, staring over their heads, you could hear them counting to four over and over again.

Before turning off the light, I read Ann's note, written in her familiar, childish scrawl:

> Hi Rachie!
>   I know you're probably real, real busy tomorrow, but like Mom always says, a girl has to eat! My girlfriends are just dying to meet you. I told them to meet us for lunch at Briarcliff. We'll all be there at noon. Hope you can join us.
>
>   Love ya,
>   Ann

I groaned at the thought of lunch at Briarcliff, but Ann wanted me to be there and I would be. Firstborns are saps for those requests.

CHAPTER

I could have understood Stretch, since he was as tall as a professional basketball player. He was skinny, too, so they could have called him Slim. And he was bald, which could have earned him one of those antonym nicknames, like Curly, or Fuzzy.

But Mouse? You certainly couldn't tell from looking at him. There just wasn't anything mousey about Bridgeton Police Detective Mario Aloni. He was perched behind his metal desk, his shoulders hunched forward, as he peered at the notes from the Stoddard Anderson file. He had a long, solemn face with a hooked beak of a nose. His large eyes were dark brown—deep set beneath large projecting eyebrows. If anything, Mario Aloni looked like a predator—the kind that swooped down and carried off mice in its claws.

It was 8:40 A.M. I had been in Mouse Aloni's cubicle at the Bridgeton Police Department on Natural Bridge Road for about twenty minutes. Although he had been reluctant to talk to me at first, he became less guarded after I showed him the letter from Ishmael, countersigned by Dottie Anderson, confirming that I was her lawyer on this matter.

I had asked him a question and he was slowly leafing through the Stoddard Anderson file for the answer. He stopped to study a document. "Anderson checked into the hotel under an assumed name," he said.

"What was the name?" I asked, taking a sip of coffee from the Styrofoam cup.

"Unusual one. Giovanni Careri, Esquire," he read from his notes.

"Who's that?"

Aloni looked up and shook his head. "No idea, ma'am."

"Did Anderson use a credit card when he checked in?"

"No, ma'am. Paid cash in advance. For a week."

"Did he ever leave the hotel room?"

Aloni tugged at the skin covering his prominent Adam's apple. "He left the hotel, or at least his room, for some part of the next two days. The hotel maid cleaned his room both days around noon. According to her, he wasn't in the room either day."

"How about the third day?"

"Door chained shut from inside. One of those Do Not Disturb signs hanging from the doorknob. Maid didn't go in. We don't know whether he was inside the room the whole day."

"Room service?" I asked.

Aloni shook his head. "Didn't use room service. No telephone calls from his room, either. Outgoing or incoming."

"Ever?"

"Ever."

"And the fourth day?"

"Mr. Anderson was dead by the morning of the fourth day. He died somewhere between midnight and about three A.M., according to the M.E."

"M.E.—Medical Examiner?"

"Yes, ma'am." He glanced down at the notes. "On the fourth day the room was no longer chained from the inside, and the Do Not Disturb sign was gone. Maid started to go in his room around noon. Heard the shower, so she left. Came back an hour later. Went in, heard the shower, left. Same thing an hour later. Finally, at three o'clock, when she heard the shower still going, she got worried and called for the manager. They went in together. They found the body in the bathtub."

"With the shower on?"

"Yes, ma'am. He died in the rain."

"He cut his wrists with a razor?"

Aloni nodded solemnly. "Slashed his neck on both sides, then slit his wrists. From the stain lines in the tub, it appears he filled it with water, got in, turned on the shower, pulled the plug, and then started cutting."

The image made me shiver. "Was he—just sitting there when they found him?"

"Sort of slumped down. Body probably slid lower as the blood drained." Aloni leafed through the file. "Had a crime scene technician in there before we moved the body. That's S.O.P. on suicides. He took photographs of the body." He looked at me. "I have one here, ma'am."

I shook my head. "No, thanks." I once prosecuted a wrongful death claim on behalf of the widow of a man killed in a motel fire. Although the case settled quickly, the charred corpse continued to appear in my nightmares for almost a year.

"Were you able to find any evidence of what he'd been doing in the room for those three days?"

"Not much, Miss Gold. His last supper was a Big Mac, large fries, and a medium Coke. We found the McDonald's bags and containers in the bedroom. Coroner found the contents in his stomach."

"Any indication of where he went when he left the room?"

"Just general observations, ma'am. From his clothing and his car. We never sent any of it through the lab, seeing as how it wasn't much of an issue, him having committed suicide and all."

"What kind of observations?"

"His clothes and shoes were kind of muddy. There were traces of what looked like concrete on his shoes and on the floor mat of his car."

"Which tells you what?"

Aloni shrugged. "Tells me some, not much. Tells me that sometime between the time he disappeared and the time he killed himself, he was probably walking around near a construction site. That'd explain the concrete, and probably the mud as well. Since it hadn't rained for a couple weeks before he disappeared, the mud part's a little curious. Which is why I say a construction site. Then again, he could have been walking down near a river or some other body of water, but then where'd the concrete come from? Like I say, the mud and concrete tell me some, but not much.''

"Why didn't you have the lab run some tests?''

Aloni sighed. "This is a busy department, Miss Gold. We got limited resources, limited manpower. Look at it from our point of view. A suicide is the easiest homicide to solve. You always catch the killer right there at the scene of the crime. And that means it's a file you can close. We've got hundreds of files we still can't close. Mud in an open file gets sent to the lab. Mud in a closed file—well, it'd be nice if we had the time. We don't.''

"I understand,'' I said with a sympathetic smile. "I've got a few open files with mud in them. Where did you find the suicide note?''

"On the bed.''

"Not in the bathroom?''

"No, ma'am. It was right in the center of the bed.''

"Hmmm.''

"You seem surprised.''

"More confused than surprised, I guess. Did you find any rough drafts?''

"We did, ma'am. Several, in fact. Found three in the waste can. Some were torn into several pieces. Took me a while to piece 'em together.'' He reached into the folder and pulled out three sealed plastic bags. "These are them.'' He handed the bags to me.

I skimmed each draft. Anderson had tightened the language from draft to draft, a good lawyer to the end. In one draft he spoke of the Executor "having crossed the River Styx.'' In another draft he wrote that he was "the only Executor above ground.''

"It looks like his handwriting,'' I said as I compared the photocopy of the final version—the one Dottie gave me—with the earlier drafts. The handwriting seemed to match the handwriting in his appointment book and time sheets.

"Our expert agrees," Aloni said.

"What's his suicide note mean?"

Aloni shrugged. "Doesn't make any sense to us. So far."

"How 'bout these drafts? River Styx?"

Aloni shrugged and gave me a palms-up gesture.

I reminded myself of the original purpose of my trip to St. Louis. "The suicide note sounds a little crazy," I said, hopefully.

"That's because we don't have all the facts, Miss Gold. These things tend to make sense once you learn all the facts."

"When will that be?"

"Can't say."

"Are you still working on the case?"

Aloni shook his head. "No, ma'am. Like I say . . ."

I finished the thought: "Closed file."

"Yes, ma'am."

I stared at my photocopy of the suicide note. "You say you didn't find this in the bathroom?"

"Found it in the bedroom."

"Was there any evidence that he'd taken an overdose of sleeping pills or some other medicine before he slit his wrists?"

"No."

"Was he on drugs or alcohol?"

"Drugs, no. Alcohol, yes. He consumed two fifths of Scotch during his stay. Maybe more. We found two empty bottles in his room. Autopsy report showed a blood alcohol content of almost point two. No evidence of drug use—not in the room and not in the blood."

"Would you have the autopsy report?"

"Sure do." He leafed through the folder until he found it. He glanced at it and shook his head. "There just wasn't much blood to send to toxicology. The M.E. said the bathwater must have been warm. Shower was, too. Blood just kept draining out. Even after his heart stopped."

He handed me the report and then came around behind my

chair to look at it over my shoulder. He pointed to the toxicology results. "They were able to get enough blood to test for
alcohol," he said. "The deceased was pretty well intoxicated
when he died. Tests don't show the presence of any drugs. No
barbiturates, no amphetamines, no controlled substances of any
type. Not that it really matters. Cause of death was obvious,"
he said, pointing to the outline of the human body at the bottom
of the report. Someone had drawn slash marks on each wrist
and on both sides of the neck. "We found the razor blade in
the tub."

"Fingerprints?" I asked.

"The ones on the razor blade were too smudged to identify.
The decedent's were all over the hotel room. Including several
on the bathtub. Found other fingerprints as well, but that's
pretty much what you'd expect to find in a hotel room."

"Have you identified any of the other prints?"

"No, ma'am. Why did you keep asking where we found
the suicide note?"

"He was a lawyer, Detective. When a lawyer does several
drafts of a short note, you start to assume that every word that
made it into the final draft was significant."

He nodded. "Go on."

"The last sentence in the note talks about a dying man's
last request. 'Dottie,' " I read, " 'this is a dying man's last
request.' " I shrugged. "Maybe I'm being too much of a lawyer
myself."

"I'm not following you, Miss Gold."

"If he hadn't taken an overdose of sleeping pills, and if he
hadn't already slit his wrists, then he wasn't actually a dying
man when he wrote the suicide note. Right?" It had sounded
more significant before I had explained it aloud.

Aloni raised his eyebrows as he considered the point. "I
guess so," he finally said, without much enthusiasm.

"Never mind," I said, feeling like a real amateur. Rachel
the Junior G-Man, with her plastic badge and pretend wrist-
watch radio.

"Now here's something odd," he said as he reached into
his file. "Looks like the decedent even tried a note to the med-

ical examiner.'' He pulled out another sealed plastic bag. ''Took me a while to put this one back together. It was torn up into more than twenty pieces.'' He handed me the sealed bag. ''It's some sort of riddle,'' he continued. ''I showed it to the M.E. He can't make heads or tails out of it.''

I stared at the note. Like the others, it was written on the hotel's stationery:

Equation for M.E.
C = MSD/AW
RS = ROTF

''Could I have a copy of this?'' I said. ''Along with copies of those draft suicide notes?''

''Yes, ma'am. We've got extra photocopies of each one.''

I skimmed my notes to see whether I had covered all of the topics on my list. I hadn't. ''I understand you took temporary custody of the contents of his office,'' I said. ''When you returned his things to the law firm, did you keep anything here?''

Aloni shifted uncomfortably. ''We inventoried every item. Then we returned everything, except for . . . uh, certain contraceptive devices.''

''What kind?''

''Condoms.'' He glanced at his notes. ''Trojan brand. Lubricated. Reservoir tips. There was an opened twelve-pack in his desk drawer. Ten remaining.''

''You kept them?''

''We had them tagged and filed. The deceased certainly wasn't going to have any further use for them.'' Aloni paused. ''I had the opportunity of meeting Mrs. Anderson in the course of my investigation. Seemed like a fine woman to me. Woman of her years wouldn't have much need for birth control. Change of life and all.'' Aloni shrugged. ''I made a judgment call, Miss Gold. I assumed that the decedent's personal effects would eventually be turned over to Mrs. Anderson. The only thing those contraceptive devices would do for her is cause pain. So I didn't return them. It seemed the right thing to do at the time.''

''It was, Detective.''

He nodded gravely. "Ma'am."

"Any other property or personal effects that the police haven't returned?"

"None from the office. We did find a set of keys. They were on the nightstand of the decedent's hotel room. We were able to identify most of the keys. As I recall, there were two to his house, one for his garage door opener, two to his car, two to Mrs. Anderson's car, and one to the law firm." He reached into the file and pulled out a sealed plastic bag that contained a single key. "The only key we couldn't match up is this little one. Looks like it might be a key to a piece of luggage. Or maybe to a storage locker."

"Could I have a copy of that key?"

Aloni pursed his lips as he weighed the request. "Well, I suppose that'd be okay. I can go have one made for you down in the lab before you leave."

When he returned with my copy of the unidentified key from Stoddard Anderson's key chain, I wrote down the phone numbers of Abbott & Windsor and Ann's house on the back of one of my business cards and gave it to him. He promised to call if he heard anything.

"One thing I still can't figure," I said as I stood to leave.

"What's that?"

"The nickname?"

"Huh?"

"Mouse. Where'd it come from?"

His solemn face broke into an embarrassed smile. "Oh, that. Cheese," he said.

"Explain."

He shrugged. "Been on the force eighteen years. Bring my lunch every day. Every day it's cheddar cheese on white. So the boys call me Mouse."

"Cheese every day, huh?"

"I guess it's not too good on the cholesterol."

"I don't know about that," I said with a smile. "I've never heard of a mouse with a bypass."

He smiled back. "Well, I never heard of one that lived too long, either."

CHAPTER 10

From the police station I drove downtown to Abbott & Windsor. It was a typical summer morning in St. Louis—the temperature was ninety-two and rising, the humidity was holding steady at ninety-five percent. With first impressions behind me, I had dressed for the tropics: a sage-colored twill jacket with roll-up sleeves, a peach silk T-shirt, a lightweight natural-colored twill skirt, and sandals.

Once I reached the office, I put in calls to the Missing Link, Remy Panzer, and Albert Weidemeir.

The Missing Link was out on a job site, his secretary Lurleen told me. During the brief conversation, I couldn't help but recall Nancy Winslow's description of the additional duty included in the job description of the Missing Link's secretary. Lurleen told me he would be back that afternoon and she'd make sure he returned the call.

Next I tried Remy Panzer. He wasn't in either. The bored and increasingly petulant male voice that answered the phone at the Panzer Gallery informed me that Mr. Panzer was at a client's home on the grounds of the Old Warson Country Club doing a private showing of selections from art work currently featured by the gallery. Acting as if I had just asked him to drive to Chicago and paint my apartment for free, he sullenly took down my name, phone number, and a short message for

Panzer: "Called re Stoddard Anderson and work he was doing for you at time of death."

The operator at the Metropolitan Sewer District told me that Albert Weidemeir was on vacation and would not be back at work until Monday. I gave her my name and Abbott & Windsor's telephone number and told her that it was important that I speak to Mr. Weidemeir as soon as he returned to work. I called Albert Weidemeir's home telephone number on the chance that he might have stayed home for his vacation. No one answered.

As I hung up and reached for my notes the phone rang.

"Miss Gold, this is Claude at the St. Louis Club." He had a French accent—*Zees ees Claude.* "I understand you have inquiries regarding Mr. Anderson's dinner on June eighth."

"You were on duty that night, Claude?"

"Yes, ma'am."

"I understand that Mr. Anderson had dinner in one of the private dining rooms."

"This is correct."

"Do you recall who he had dinner with?"

"Yes, ma'am. Mr. Anderson dined with Mr. St. Germain."

"Reed St. Germain?"

"This is correct."

"Hmm." I was surprised.

"Pardon?"

"Did anyone else join them?"

"I do not believe so."

"Do you remember how long they were together?"

"I am most sorry that I do not. All that I can recall is that Mr. Anderson arrived first."

I tried to jog his memory with a few other questions, but he couldn't remember anything else.

"If you think of anything else about that night, Claude, please call me."

"I certainly shall, Miss Gold. There is one matter that perhaps you can be of assistance."

"What's that?"

"Mr. Anderson—or perhaps it was Mr. St. Germain—one of the gentlemen left some business papers in the room. We found them later that evening. Unfortunately, I left on holiday the following day and did not return until after Mr. Anderson was dead. It has been most awkward for us to continue to be holding these papers."

"What kind of papers?"

"They appear to be statements of account. I am most anxious to have them returned. I thought that perhaps I could send them to your attention, Miss Gold, if it would not be too much trouble."

"No problem. Send them. I'll make sure they get to the right person."

"Oh, this is excellent, Miss Gold. I shall send our runner downtown with the papers after lunch. We are most appreciative of your assistance, Miss Gold."

I walked down the hall for a fresh cup of coffee. On the way back I asked Nancy to be on the lookout for a messenger delivery from the St. Louis Club after lunch. I paused at my door for a moment, and then continued down the hall to the large corner office. Reed St. Germain was on the telephone. He waved me in when he saw me in the doorway.

"So, Rachel," he said cheerfully as he hung up the phone, "are you getting all those loose ends tied up?"

"I'm making progress."

"Think you'll finish up today?"

I smiled and shook my head. "No way. But I hope to by early next week."

"Really? That long?"

"I still have a lot of people to talk to."

"Well, I'm here to help. Don't forget that, Rachel. Anything you need now?"

"Actually, yes. Tell me about your last supper with Stoddard."

He gave me a puzzled look. "My last supper?"

"June eighth. At the St. Louis Club. According to the maitre d', you and Stoddard had dinner together that night in one of the private dining rooms."

"June eighth," he repeated as he flipped through his pocket calendar. "June eighth. Well, well. You're absolutely right, Rachel. It looks like I did have dinner with Stoddard that night."

"What did you talk about?"

He leaned back in his chair and looked toward the ceiling. "June eighth," he ruminated. "Nothing stands out, Rachel. We probably talked about the sorts of things we usually talked about at those dinners. Mostly firm administration matters. We were both on the management committee. It was hard for us to schedule meetings together during the day. Dinner was the only quiet time for us. As for what we talked about, it could have been anything from our associate hiring needs for next year to switching paper vendors. Nothing stands out."

"How often did you two have dinners like that?"

Reed leveled his stare at me, holding it for a moment before giving me what I think was supposed to pass for a good-natured power wink. "Rachel, partners of this firm aren't privy to all of the matters that come before the management committee. Partners of this firm don't receive notice that members of the management committee are meeting. While I certainly want to help facilitate your investigation, don't you think we're getting a little far afield? After all, this isn't a deposition."

I told myself that he was probably right. And anyway, no sense crossing the managing partner this early in the investigation. I forced a sheepish smile. "You're right. It must be the litigator in me. Tell me one thing about that dinner: How did Stoddard seem that night?"

St. Germain tilted his head and squinted his eyes in thought. "Frankly, I don't recall anything about that meeting. I suppose that means he must have seemed like his usual self that night."

St. Germain's telephone started ringing. He glanced at it and then back to me.

"Go ahead," I said as I stood up.

"You sure you don't have any other questions, Rachel?"

"If I think of any I'll come back and ask."

"Great. You do that." And with that he lifted the receiver. "This is Reed," he announced as I left his office.

* * *

When I returned to my office, I sat quietly for a few minutes replaying my conversation with Reed St. Germain. Finally, I glanced down at my notes. The next person on my list was Cyril Burt, the insurance claims adjuster.

As I dialed his number, I put on my game face. When he answered I was ready for the ritual known as mau-mauing the claims adjuster. I told him that I represented the sole beneficiary on Stoddard Anderson's life insurance policy, that I was in town to investigate various matters surrounding Mr. Anderson's death, and that I wanted to schedule an appointment with him for sometime early next week to discuss the death benefits payable to Mrs. Anderson.

"Perhaps next Tuesday afternoon, Miss Gold?"

Today was Thursday. By Tuesday I ought to have a fairly good feel for the circumstances leading to Stoddard Anderson's death. "That should be fine," I told him. "How does two o'clock sound?"

"Two o'clock it is."

Time for the mau-mau. "I'd like one thing understood at the outset, Mr. Burt. I'm down here for two purposes: to gather facts and to see if you're interested in resolving the coverage dispute. My expectation is that I will arrive at our meeting with facts *and* with a reasonable settlement proposal. I am assuming that you will arrive at that meeting with facts *and* with settlement authority. If you won't have settlement authority by then, then send your boss, or whoever it is in your company who can cut a check. Okay?"

"Miss Gold, my hope is that we can use that meeting to open a dialogue."

"If my client wanted dialogue, she would've hired a scriptwriter. She hired a trial lawyer. I don't want to open a dialogue, Mr. Burt. I want your company to open its checkbook."

"Let's not burden our first meeting with unrealistic expectations, Miss Gold."

"I don't have unrealistic expectations about our *first* meeting, Mr. Burt, because it's also going to be our *only* meeting.

Either we settle the claim then, or you and your company can start working on your dialogue for the jury. Okay?"

There was a pause, and then, "Okay."

"I'll see you on Tuesday."

After I hung up, I said to myself, "Bitch." Cyril Burt had no doubt uttered an even nastier noun on his end.

I spent the next half-hour interviewing some of the junior associates about Stoddard Anderson. The only thing of interest I learned was that Anderson did not regularly stay late at the office. Benny might be right about his labanzas. Or fishteras.

I sat down again with Nancy Winslow. As Anderson's secretary, she might have witnessed evidence of an extramarital affair—the sorts of things that a secretary might be privy to, such as frequent phone calls from an unidentified woman, changes in Anderson's dress style or cologne, bills from florists.

Nancy shook her head. "Nope. If he had a thing for some mystery lady, he did a good job hiding it from me."

She appeared to be telling the truth.

It didn't have to be a serious affair, though. He could have been a Don Juan type—lots of short-term affairs, even one-night stands.

"How about someone here at the firm?" I asked. "Any flings?"

Her eyes narrowed. "You mean Portia?"

"I don't necessarily mean anyone."

"Who told you it was Portia?"

"Porsche? Like the car?"

"No. P-O-R-T-I-A."

"Like the play?"

"What play?"

"Never mind. No one told me about her, Nancy. Who is she?"

"A paralegal in the trusts and estates department." Nancy snorted in disgust and leaned forward, lowering her voice. "A real prick teaser, too. All the younger guys have the hots for her. She flirts with them, but that's all she does with them. She's after bigger game than that. Believe me, she's a very ambitious little girl."

"Portia S. McKenzie?" I asked, finding her full name on the list of paralegals in the firm's telephone directory.

"That's her."

"You don't like her."

"I don't like the type. And neither do you. Wait till you meet her."

"Do you think she was having an affair with Anderson?"

"God, I hope not. She flirted with him, but then that girl would shake her tits in front of anything in pants. Most of the guys here fall for it. You should see them. They hang around her office like dogs in heat." She shook her head. "Men. I'm telling you, they're so transparent. Anyway, I never saw Mr. Anderson react to any of her come-ons."

"Did she do any work for him?"

"Some. The kind of things paralegals in trusts and estates do for lawyers."

"Stoddard Anderson wasn't in that department," I said.

"Mr. Anderson had plenty of clients who came to him for estate planning. During the first client meeting on a new will or trust he'd have one of the trusts and estates lawyers sit in. Usually, it was Reed St. Germain. Mr. St. Germain was chairman of the trusts and estates department before Mr. Anderson died. Anyway, if it was really a complicated estate plan, they'd have Portia sit in, too. She'd take notes and help the client fill out the forms. After the first client meeting, Mr. Anderson would gradually get the client used to the idea of dealing with Mr. St. Germain, or whoever Mr. St. Germain assigned to the matter. But in the early stages, Mr. Anderson would sometimes give assignments directly to Portia."

"Was she in his office frequently?"

Nancy thought it over. "Not that much."

"Nothing suspicious?"

"Nope."

"Switch subjects. Did Mr. Anderson ever mention something called ParaLex to you?"

"ParaLex? Doesn't ring a bell. Why?"

"I'm not sure. How could I find out if it's a new client of the firm?"

"That's easy enough," she said as she swiveled in her chair to face her computer terminal. She typed in a command and hit the TRANSMIT key. After a moment, a prompt message appeared on the monitor screen. Nancy looked up at me. "ParaLex?"

"Right. One word, capital 'L.'"

"If it's a client, it'll show up here," she said as she pushed the TRANSMIT key.

I peered over her shoulder at the monitor, which flashed *Searching* several times before announcing *No client with the name ParaLex has been located.*

"I guess not," Nancy said.

"Probably just a wild-goose chase anyway. Speaking of which, was your boss named the executor on many wills?"

Nancy frowned in thought. "Believe it or not," she finally said, "I have no idea."

"Would Portia know?"

"She ought to. And so would Mr. St. Germain. And so would Linda Salem. She's the other paralegal in that department."

"Maybe I'll talk to Portia," I said, more to myself than to Nancy.

But it turned out Portia McKenzie had already left the office for lunch. So had Reed St. Germain. And so had Linda Salem.

I had my own lunch date with my sister Ann and her friends. I told Nancy, who was acting as my secretary while I was in St. Louis, that I would be at Briarcliff Country Club for lunch if anyone should call.

During the few minutes before I had to leave for Briarcliff, I tracked down Sandy Feldman.

"I don't think so, Rachel," he said in response to my question.

"Not even rumors?"

"No. Believe me, if Stoddard Anderson was sleeping with his secretary, he did an excellent job of hiding it."

"How 'bout Portia?"

Sandy raised his eyebrows. "So you've met our heart-throb?"

"I understand she makes more than your heart throb," I said, and Sandy blushed. His reaction reminded me again of the corrupting influence of sharing office space with Benny Goldberg.

"No," I said, "I haven't met her. How about Anderson and Portia?"

"Don't know." He mulled it over. "Managing partner of the firm, one of the movers and shakers of St. Louis. He'd be the perfect target for her. I never saw her leave with him, but that doesn't mean they didn't. If someone like Stoddard Anderson was going to have an affair, especially an affair with someone in this office, he'd be so damn discreet no one would ever know." He leaned back in his chair. "Portia and Stoddard. Well, she seems to like managing partners."

"Reed St. Germain, huh?"

"Off and on. But that was going on back when Stoddard was alive, too. I heard that Anderson called St. Germain on the carpet for sleeping with someone in the office. Maybe it was Portia."

I don't like private clubs. I don't like the concept. I don't like the execution. I just plain don't like anything about them.

Briarcliff Country Club, however, is the very worst sort: an exclusive Jewish country club, where my people—victims of exclusion since the time of Abraham—can exclude their own people. Briarcliff strives for a white-bread Judaism. There are no Tevyes at Briarcliff, and corned beef is available only on St. Patrick's Day. Over the years it has become a Jewish version of nineteenth-century Liberia, with the natives dressing in the White Man's clothes and mimicking the White Man's rituals. And just like the Uncle Toms of nineteenth-century Liberia, the good burghers of Briarcliff have their doppelgangers lurking out there in the bush: the Eastern European arrivistes at Golden Bough (aka Goldenberg) Country Club, land of the diamond pinky rings, white belts, and platinum Eldorados.

At Briarcliff you can sip Bloody Marys on the front lawn of the main clubhouse while little Jewish girls in Easter bonnets and white pinafore dresses search for painted eggs and you can try to forget what Easter brought upon your ancestors in Europe. You can promenade with your family through the Great Hall, a kitsch homage to King Arthur, and as you pass beneath the rows of heavy flags emblazoned with English heraldry you can almost—almost—forget that your family coat of arms is, at best, a gefilte fish rampant on a field of chopped liver.

Ann and I could never have become members of Briarcliff on our own. In the Briarcliff scheme of things, the Golds were descendants of mongrel yids from Eastern Europe. Ann was a Briarcliff member solely because of Richie, and Richie—like many of his generation—was a member solely because his parents were.

As I turned into the blacktop parking area at Briarcliff, I was struck by the number of large American cars, but then I realized this was the lunch crowd, consisting primarily of women. The men of Briarcliff all drive German cars in a macabre homage to the nation that had spawned their ancestors and then tried to exterminate them. The women of Briarcliff, however, were moving into larger and ever larger American cars. My sister was typical. If you lined up the cars she had owned over the past ten years in chronological order, the result would resemble one of those food chains in the ocean. Ten years ago she had traded up from her sporty little Porsche to the mandatory maroon Volvo station wagon. A few years later she traded up in size again to a seven-seater Dodge minivan, and from there up to a nine-seater Ford Country Squire. And now, as I scanned the parking lot, the trucks of choice seemed to be conversion vans and Chevy Suburbans. (Ann had a Suburban.) If the trend held firm, in about five years the women of Briarcliff would be doing carpool behind the wheel of a Greyhound bus, the diesel engine roaring and the air brakes hissing.

Having expected the worst, I was pleasantly surprised by my lunch with Ann and her friends. Her friends clearly liked my sister a great deal, which pleased me. Several asked if I had really gone to Harvard Law School. One or two asked about a couple of the bigger lawsuits I had handled. Ann had obviously bragged to them about her big sister. I was surprised, embarrassed, and touched.

But as the lunch wore on, I came to feel as if I had stumbled into a parallel universe. These were women my age, none with jobs and all with children, who seemed to spend their days shopping in malls, going out to lunch, having their nails and hair done, issuing orders to their housekeepers. There was a ten-minute discussion of the subtle differences in the versions of a new style of blouse on display at Neiman-Marcus, Famous-Barr, Dillards, Saks, Lord & Taylor, The Limited, Teddi's, and Ann Taylor. I doubt whether a group of graduate students in a doctoral seminar on Wallace Stevens could have employed a critical vocabulary as subtle and precise as the designer jargon of my sister and her friends.

As I tried to find a way into the Great Blouse Debate— feeling like I did back on the playground in fourth grade at the start of my turn in Double Dutch, trying to time my jump in between the rotating jump ropes—my mind began to drift. We really did exist in different worlds, these Briarcliff women and I. And who was I to say that mine was the better world? Since when did we single professional career women become anointed recipients of divine grace—at least by anyone other than ourselves? It was too easy to get smug around women with sculpted fingernails. It was too easy to assume you were on the inside looking out. As I looked around the table I asked myself how I could be so sure I wasn't on the outside looking in—out there beyond the campfire circle, watching the others sing the songs and roast the marshmallows.

A waitress interrupted my reverie, touching me on the shoulder to tell me I had a phone call. I followed her to the telephone. It was Nancy Winslow at Abbott & Windsor.

"What's up?"

"Remy Panzer just called," she said. "He said he would like to meet with you at his gallery today after lunch. He told me he really wants to talk to you. I thought I'd call and save you the drive all the way back downtown."

"Thanks, Nancy. Could you call him back and tell him I'll be there in thirty minutes?"

"Sure thing."

CHAPTER 11

They were a remarkable couple. She had huge round breasts and thick jutting nipples. He had an enormous erection that arched out of his groin and rested against his chest. She was missing a hand. He was missing a testicle. Both were grinning.

They were fat, they were black, and they were short. Very short. Maybe ten inches tall. According to the placard inside the display case, they came from South Africa and were each approximately eight hundred years old. You could buy them both for $9,000.

They weren't the most expensive pieces of art in the Panzer Gallery. As I drifted around the gallery, I saw a pre-Columbian Aztec pot for thirteen thousand. At two hundred fifty dollars, a Navaho wall hanging was the cheapest thing there.

I had been greeted at the Panzer Gallery by Hans, who apparently was Remy Panzer's assistant. Hans was maybe twenty. He had hollow cheeks, dull blue eyes, and long blond hair that needed a vigorous shampoo and a comb. He was in a foul mood, but that could have been caused by his black leather pants, which cut high into his crotch and butt. The pants were tight. Although he may not have been circumspect, he clearly was circumcised.

Hans told me to wait in the gallery while he went in back to announce my arrival. He reappeared ten minutes later, clearing his throat to get my attention. "Mr. Panzer is ready for you," he said sullenly, turning to point. "His office is in back."

Remy Panzer's office had the look and feel of a study in an English country home—lots of dark mahogany, leaded glass windows, floor-to-ceiling built-in bookcases behind a captain's desk, a burgundy Persian rug, wing-back armchairs upholstered in leather, three crystal decanters and a matching set of brandy snifters on a small Queen Anne table, an antique globe against one wall corner, and a fireplace in the other.

Behind the desk, an art book open in his hand, stood Remy Panzer. He was smoking a long brown cigarette.

"Have a seat, Rachel," he said, dispensing with introductions. His voice was a full octave lower than I had expected. "Can Hans bring you some mint tea?"

Hans was still at the door. I turned back to Panzer. "I'm fine, thanks."

Panzer made a dismissive gesture toward the door. "That will be all, Hans. Close the door on your way out."

Remy Panzer took a deep drag on his brown cigarette. Tilting back his head, he blew a thin stream of smoke toward the ceiling, ending with a pair of smoke rings, each a perfect circle.

With his bushy eyebrows brushed up and out from his forehead, his close-cropped hair, and his pointy ears, Remy Panzer reminded me of a well-groomed schnauzer. He had a neatly trimmed gray goatee and a long, sinewy neck. Like a schnauzer, he was compact and looked taut. As he turned to reshelve the book, I glanced down, half expecting to see the outline of a stiff stub of a tail protruding from the back of his pants.

He was wearing a burgundy turtleneck and burgundy slacks, the same shade as the Persian rug. A pair of black horn-rim glasses with tinted lenses hung from a strap around his neck. He took another deep drag on his brown cigarette as he turned to me.

The eyes were not schnauzer eyes. The lower lids were puffed with age and dark with fatigue. Crow's nests of deep wrinkles fanned out from the corner of each eye to his hairline. The eyes themselves seemed almost inanimate—the irises a dull blue, the whites tinged gray, as if carved from old bones.

I didn't like him.

"I'd like to hire you," he said.

"For what?"

"To complete what Stoddard Anderson began."

"Which was what?"

He took a seat behind the desk. Leaning back, he blew another stream of tobacco smoke out of his mouth, ending this time with a single smoke ring that hovered above us for a moment, vibrating, and then disappeared. He shifted his stare from the vanished smoke ring to me.

"Stoddard Anderson's death came at a most infelicitous time."

"Is there a felicitous time to slit your wrists?"

"Oh, I'm sure there is. For each of us. Perhaps that time had arrived for Stoddard. Unfortunately, his death has delayed consummation of a most important matter he was handling on my behalf." He tapped the ash off his brown cigarette into a silver ashtray. His fingernails were manicured and buffed to a high gloss. "He was my attorney on the project. I will still require the services of an attorney. You are the obvious choice."

"Why?"

"You have impeccable academic credentials. And that, I should add, is not an insignificant concession from a Yale man." His facial muscles wrenched his mouth into something that was supposed to resemble a smile. It didn't. His eyes remained inert. "You have an excellent professional reputation as well. If my assumption is correct, you are presently representing the Widow Anderson in connection with some matter relating to her late husband's estate. Since I quite doubt that Stoddard's wife would have—could have—independently selected counsel, much less a young, female, solo practitioner from Chicago, I must also assume that Abbott & Windsor played a material role in your retention by the Widow Anderson."

"And if they did?"

"I view it as further affirmation of your qualifications. It confirms my decision to retain you as my attorney."

"What do you need an attorney for? What was Stoddard Anderson doing for you?"

Remy Panzer studied me. "You are representing the Widow Anderson, correct?"

"Yes."

"And that representation is in connection with some aspect of her late husband's affairs, correct?"

"It has some connection with her husband's estate. That's all I can tell you."

"But of course. The hallowed attorney-client privilege." He steepled his hands together in front of his face, fingertips touching, and bowed his head in mock deference. "Excellent, Rachel. Precisely the response I deserve. And require. For you see, the matter for which I need your services requires the highest level of confidentiality."

"If Stoddard Anderson was handling it for you, why not use someone from his firm to finish it?"

"I should very much doubt that anyone else at Abbott & Windsor knows anything about the project. Moreover, I should very much doubt that a typical Abbott & Windsor corporate attorney would have the qualities or the spunk required for my task. You, on the other hand, are not a typical corporate attorney. And you certainly have the requisite spunk."

"You assume a lot."

"On the contrary, I assume nothing. As you corporate lawyers would say, I have done my due diligence on the subject of one Rachel Gold in advance of this meeting."

Panzer stood and moved behind the desk chair. Opening a platinum cigarette case resting on the edge of the leather desk pad, he removed a brown cigarette. Lifting the case, he tilted it toward me.

I shook my head. "I quit."

"Good for you," he said, lighting his cigarette with a gold Dunhill lighter. He sat down behind the desk. "Will you serve as my attorney?"

"That depends."

"Depends on what?"

"On what you want me to do. On whether representing you would conflict with my representation of Mrs. Anderson."

"I want you to finish what Stoddard Anderson started." He paused, his eyebrows arching. "I can assure you that your compensation will be quite generous. I negotiated a flat fee with Stoddard: a quarter of a million dollars, payable upon completion of the task. Based on my understanding of Stoddard's efforts on the project, he had completed most of the work before he died. Indeed, he may have completed it all. If so, your only task would be to retrieve it for me. Nevertheless, I am willing to pay you one hundred thousand dollars for what in all likelihood is, at most, a few days' work. Indeed, Rachel, you may have earned that fee already."

Leaning forward, he exhaled tobacco smoke through his nostrils. The twin streams of smoke wheeled and churned as they hit the surface of his desk. "As for a conflict with the Widow Anderson"—he shrugged—"you can split the money with her in any way you see fit."

"That's a lot of money."

He gave a dismissive wave of his hand. "Baseball players earn ten times as much for playing a child's game."

"Baseball isn't a crime."

"And what makes you think this project is?"

"Too much money."

He shrugged. "Is fifty million dollars too much for a Van Gogh? Is fifty thousand too much for a bottle of wine? Value is relative, Rachel. No price is too high if the market will bear it." He leaned back in his chair.

"But the bottle of wine that sells for fifty thousand dollars is unique," I said.

"And so are you, Rachel. You have access to Stoddard Anderson's files and records. I do not. That makes you unique."

"It's still a lot of money."

He waved his hand dismissively. "Obviously, one doesn't earn a fast hundred thousand in fees without being willing to move out of the sunlight into . . . shall we say . . . the penumbra. But that's exactly where the truly exceptional lawyers thrive, Rachel. Indeed, that's where all truly exceptional people thrive. Artists, explorers, scientists." He paused. "And collectors. The great ones find their niche out there."

"Not if it means they could lose their law license."

"Come, come, Rachel. You're hardly June Lockhart, and I am surely not little Timmy. If you need assurance, don't underestimate the significance of Stoddard Anderson's involvement. Do you actually believe that a politically ambitious attorney—a conservative Republican, of all things, Mr. Straight Arrow himself—would participate in a criminal scheme?"

He had a point. "I'll have to make my own decision," I said. "But I won't be able to unless you tell me the facts."

"Fair enough." He leaned back in his chair and blew a stream of smoke toward the ceiling. "I shall begin at the beginning." He was staring at the ceiling and stroking his goatee with his thumb and index finger. "It is a most remarkable story, and it opens with a lawyer." He shifted his gaze to me. "If you succeed, it shall end with one as well. Are you familiar with the Spanish conquistador, Hernán Cortés?"

"Generally," I said.

Panzer nodded. "You may be interested to know that Hernán Cortés was a fellow member of the bar. He had been a Spanish attorney—a bored Spanish attorney—before he decided to get into the conquistador racket. He was motivated, if one can use that bit of psychobabble, by a powerful lust for gold."

"Sounds like some attorneys I know," I said.

"He also had a rapacious appetite for women."

"Yep."

Panzer tried to smile. It was closer this time.

"Quetzalcoatl was an Aztec god," he said. "A white god, in fact. According to the sacred texts, Quetzalcoatl was supposed to return from the East and arrive at Tenochtitlán in the year 1519."

"Arrive where?"

"The capital of the Aztec empire was Tenochtitlán. Mexico City sits today atop the ruins of Tenochtitlán."

Unbeknownst to Cortés, Panzer continued, he was about

to become the beneficiary of a remarkable coincidence. For his ship landed on the eastern shores of the Aztec empire in 1519. As he and his men began their march west toward Tenochtitlán, word spread quickly. A large white man had arrived from the East, people said. His godlike qualities seemed confirmed by the size of his sexual organs.

"For you see," Panzer said, his eyebrows arching, "Cortés wore a prodigious codpiece. The Indians had never seen one before."

By the time Cortés reached Tenochtitlán, Panzer explained, the entire Aztec nation was in an uproar of anticipation. "The Emperor Montezuma personally greeted Cortés at the gates of the city and presented him with a staggering array of gifts, including two circular calendars, each as large as a cartwheel, one of gold and one of silver."

Panzer stood and ran a finger along a row of books in the bookcase. "Cortés was a guest at the emperor's palace for almost a year," he said as he removed an old, battered volume. He turned to me. "During his stay he viewed treasures of unimaginable value." He opened the book and leafed through the pages. "He sent five lengthy letters to Charles the Fifth of Spain. Those letters have been reprinted in countless history books and translated into more than a dozen languages. But this," he said, turning the book around and sliding it across the table to me, "appears, as far as I can determine, in only two books, including this one. It is a biography of Cortés by the nineteenth-century Spanish historian Wilfredo Sola. This"—he pointed to the page—"is in the original Spanish of Cortés's time. The actual document is in the Spanish national archives—and long ignored, I might add."

The pages of the book were yellowed with age. I scanned the Spanish text on the page. It looked like a detailed list. I turned the page. The list continued. I turned the page again. More of the list. "What is it?" I asked.

"An inventory."

"Of what?"

"The lost treasures of the Aztecs."

"Who wrote it?"

"Cortés. Or more likely, one of his scriveners."

"For what purpose?"

"For the information of the Spanish king. Cortés attached the document to his second letter to Charles the Fifth. It is a partial inventory of the vast Aztec treasures he had viewed."

"You said it's been ignored by historians?"

Panzer nodded. "The text of the Cortés letter itself describes many of the most remarkable treasures, including the famous six-foot gold serpent that was literally encrusted with gems from snout to tail. As a result, this inventory has never received the attention it deserves."

"These are *lost* treasures?"

Panzer nodded. "Cortés returned to Tenochtitlán in 1521. The Aztecs were no longer friendly. Cortés eventually took the city by siege. The siege lasted seventy-five days and left a quarter of a million Aztecs dead from wounds or disease. On August 13, 1521, the capital fell. But when Cortés entered the city, he discovered that all of the treasures were gone. Vanished."

"Where were they?"

"Cortés never found out. He first tried ordinary cross-examination, but his interrogations produced no leads. So he used a branding iron to emphasize his questions. He eventually branded the faces of thousands of men, women, and children. But that brutality yielded little more than a handful of treasures that had been dumped into a nearby lake. Cortés eventually leveled the city and built Mexico City in its place, but he never recovered the bulk of the vast treasures of the Aztecs."

Panzer stood and walked behind the desk chair.

"What happened to the treasures?" I asked, caught up in the story almost against my will.

"Most are lost forever." Scholars, Panzer explained, believe that the Aztecs sneaked the treasures out of the city at night during the siege. They buried some in the jungle, hid some at the bottom of lakes, hid others in caves. The locations of the secret hiding places may have been passed down from generation to generation. But memories faded, family lines died out. He gestured toward the Spanish inventory in the book. "Very little of what is on this list has ever been found."

"But some have?"

"Oh, yes."

The mystery of Sandy Feldman's research project was revealed in a flash. "And Stoddard Anderson was helping you bring one of those Aztec treasures into this country, right?"

Panzer nodded. "You are a quick study, Rachel."

"Is it on this list?" I asked, nodding toward the inventory.

"It certainly is. Indeed, among the courtiers of Charles the Fifth, the object in question was clearly the *pièce de résistance.*" He pronounced the phrase with a thick French accent. "It was the most eagerly awaited of all the treasures of Montezuma." He pulled the book toward him and scanned the list, turning the page. "Here," he said as he turned the book to me and pointed.

"El Verdugo de Motecuzoma Xocoyatzin," I read slowly, sounding out each word.

Panzer nodded. "Literally, 'the Executioner of Montezuma the Younger.' "

"The Younger?"

"His grandfather was the first Montezuma."

I looked down at the list. There was a clump of text after the words *El Verdugo de Motecuzoma Xocoyatzin.* "What's this say?" I asked, pointing.

"That is the infamous description of El Verdugo. It was in the original inventory sent to the King by Cortés. Let me translate it for you." He took the book. " 'Blade handle,' " he translated. " 'Solid gold, with channel for insertion of itzli blade—' "

"What's that?"

"The itzli blade is a sharp knife the Aztec craftsmen made from volcanic stone. It was as hard as steel and honed sharp as a razor." He returned to the text. " 'With channel for insertion of itzli blade—sprinkled with emeralds and pearls—in shape of erect organ of generation—said to be cast from Montezuma—used in Tezcatlipoca rituals.' " He looked up. "Some of the words are archaic, but that's a close translation."

"This El Verdugo thing, it's a blade handle?"

"Exactly."

"In the shape of . . . Montezuma's penis?" I asked, my face reddening. It seemed kind of ridiculous.

"Correction: in the shape of his erection. Indeed, purportedly cast from his erection. Think of it, Rachel. In their religion, he was a god. El Verdugo was the symbol of the power and the glory of the Aztec empire. It is a truly magnificent specimen. Whether cast directly from Montezuma's genitals or from the sculptor's imagination, it is a most extraordinary link with one of the greatest empires the world has ever seen. The ultimate phallic symbol."

I shook my head in amazement. Wait until Benny heard. "You said this thing was used in a ritual?" I asked.

"The Tezcatlipoca rituals," Panzer responded.

"Which are what?"

He stood and turned to his bookshelves. "Tezcatlipoca was an Aztec god. I have a lithograph of the Aztec sacrificial rituals." He pulled another book off the shelf. "Human sacrifices played a central role in the Aztec religion," he said as he paged through the book. "By the time of Cortés, there were close to fifty thousand sacrifices a year. Most were awful, primal death orgies. Cortés himself wrote that the temple walls were splashed and encrusted with dried blood, and that the stench was horrendous. But not so at the Tezcatlipoca pyramid, which was located on the grounds of the royal palace. Ah, here we go."

He turned the volume toward me. It was a series of lithographs of a ritual Aztec sacrifice. I stared at the pictures as Panzer continued the tale.

According to eyewitness reports by one of Cortéz's men, Panzer explained, the victim at Tezcatlipoca was always a magnificently handsome young man, clothed only in a gold and green gown. In a solemn procession, he was led up to the top of the pyramid, where he was received by five priests. They removed the victim's gown and turned him naked toward the crowd below. The priests wore sable robes covered with hieroglyphics. Their hair was long and matted, like dreadlocks.

The sacrificial stone was a huge block of jasper with a slightly arched upper surface. The five waiting priests placed the naked victim in the middle of the stone and held him down by his head, arms, and legs. The convex surface of the sacrificial stone thrust the victim's chest upward.

As the five priests recited the ritual chants, their long hair swaying over the victim, a sixth priest emerged from the temple. He wore a robe made of scarlet feathers, with a hood that shrouded his features. When the chanting reached its climax, the sixth priest raised his itzli dagger toward the sun, and, with an expert downward thrust, he sliced open the chest of the victim. In a quick motion, he shoved his other hand into the opening and tore out the heart; the victim's body heaved and shuddered in its death spasms, blood spraying from the open chest. As the spectators roared in ecstasy, the red-shrouded priest held the still-pulsing organ to the sun for a long moment, and then cast it on the ground, where it rolled and bounced down the stairs of the pyramid.

"Later that evening," Panzer added with a cold smile, "the corpse would be served at a banquet hosted by Montezuma himself."

"He ate human flesh?"

"Oh, yes. According to Cortés's men, the Emperor Montezuma was particularly fond of one delicacy his chefs prepared: a stew made with the fingers of the little boys who were occasionally sacrificed to another deity."

I sank back in my chair, nauseated, as Panzer continued the tale.

Although the red-shrouded executioner at the Tezcatlipoca sacrifices was generally the highest ranking priest, Cortés himself was an eyewitness on at least three occasions when Montezuma emerged as the sixth priest. The Aztec emperor's tall, slender carriage and long, spare face were easily identifiable, even beneath the scarlet robe and hood. He wielded his unique itzli dagger with the skill of an experienced priest—which in fact he was, having spent his youth in the priesthood.

And thus, El Verdugo, cast from Montezuma's genitals and linked by his own hand to the human sacrifices and cannibalism that so titillated and repulsed the courtiers of Charles V, became the most talked of treasure among the Spanish royalty awaiting the return of Cortés. "El Verdugo was even mentioned in the diary of one of the king's mistresses," Panzer added. "When reports of the vanished treasures crossed the Atlantic, the disappointment among the courtiers was keen."

Cortés returned to Spain two decades later. By then, El Verdugo had been forgotten. Cortés, who began his career as a lawyer, ended as a frustrated litigant before the Court of Charles V, seeking a declaration of his rights in the land he had discovered.

By this point in the story, Panzer had pulled down a book by someone named Prescott. He read an excerpt:

" 'Cortés lingered at court from week to week and month to month, beguiled by the deceitful hopes of the litigant, tasting all the bitterness of the soul which arises from hope deferred.' "

Panzer looked up from the book. "Some things never change."

The lawsuit dragged on for seven years, finally terminating in Cortés's death in 1547. As for El Verdugo, rumors of its existence remained unconfirmed until 1719.

"Yet another lawyer entered the fray," Panzer explained. "His name was Giovanni Francesco Gamelli Careri."

I sat upright. "Who?"

Panzer paused, taken aback by the tone of my voice. "Giovanni Francesco Gamelli Careri." He gave it a rich Italian pronunciation, trilling the r's. "You are familiar with his works?"

"No," I said after a moment. "Just the name." I flipped back through my legal pad to my notes from my morning meeting with Mouse Aloni. "Go on," I said to Panzer.

Careri was a Neapolitan lawyer, Panzer explained. In the early 1700s, he gave up his practice and left his home to travel around the world. The trip took him eighty months, including almost a year in Mexico.

Careri wrote of his travels in a five-volume book entitled *Giro del Mondo*. Published in 1719, it included the most detailed description of Mexico to reach the outside world. Incredulous readers of Careri's descriptions of Aztec ruins included Oliver Goldsmith and Adam Smith, Panzer said. Smith labeled Careri a fraud who had written "nothing more than a work of fiction from his study in Naples." Not until the nineteenth century would explorations of Mexico confirm the truth of Careri's account of the Aztec ruins.

"How does Careri fit in?" I asked.

"He was the first European after Cortés to actually see El Verdugo. Indeed, he was the first European to actually hold it in his hands."

Careri arrived in Mexico in 1699, Panzer explained. There he met Don Carlos de Siguenza y Gongora, a sad-eyed priest in his fifties. Gongora was the chaplain at the Hospital del Amor de Dios, an infirmary devoted to treating Indians suffering from bubas. He was also an amateur archeologist with a passionate curiosity about Mexico before the arrival of Cortés. The Indians loved Gongora, and responded to his interest in their heritage by bringing him manuscripts, paintings, and treasures that had been hidden from the Spaniards during the siege of Cortés back in 1521.

The traveling attorney cultivated Father Gongora, who took him to view Aztec ruins, translated manuscripts from the time of Montezuma, and permitted him to view the Aztec treasures he had received as gifts over the years from his grateful Indians.

Careri's accounts of his travels with Father Gongora drew derision from Goldsmith and other incredulous readers, Panzer told me. But because everything about the Aztecs seemed so unbelievably fantastic, most of the derision was aimed at the big, easy targets—such as Careri's descriptions of the Moon Pyramid of San Juan Teotihuacan and the huge statue of Tonacatechuhtli on the summit of the Sun Pyramid.

"As a result," Panzer said, "no one paid attention to Careri's description of a much smaller treasure." He had pulled volume four of the English translation of Careri's *Giro del Mondo* off the shelf. "It's here on page 197. Read it for yourself, Rachel." He leaned across the desk to hand me the open book.

The pertinent text was marked with a yellow marker pen:

Don Gongora then brought out a most remarkable piece of craftsmanship. It was gold and encrusted with jewels, and it was in the unmistakable shape of that part of the body which is between a man's legs. It rested upright, like a miniature obelisk. At the apex of the object was an opening, not round as in nature but narrow and rectangular.

Don Gongora explained that this extraordinary object, through which a blade could be inserted, had been, according to Aztec legend, cast from the generative organs of Montezuma II and was occasionally used by the last Aztec emperor of Mexico in barbarous ceremonies atop a pyramid near the palace. For that reason, Don Gongora told me, the Indians call this sculpture Montezuma's Executor.

"Remarkable, is it not?" Panzer said when I looked up from the text.

I nodded, glancing down at the text again. "Executioner or Executor?"

"Good eyes, Rachel. Only a lawyer would have spotted that on the first reading. The word 'Executor' appeared for the very first time in this English translation. Either an error in translation or in typesetting. It began as a mistake but has gradually become the rule. The error was not discovered until the 1960s, when a scholar went back to the original Italian text. By then it was too late. The most influential scholarly journals on pre-Columbian art are published in English. As a result, El Verdugo has become Montezuma's Executor."

The strange tale had me enthralled. "What happened next?"

"Father Gongora died in 1719," Panzer said, "the year the first volume of Careri's work appeared."

The Jesuits in Mexico City salvaged most of Gongora's Aztec manuscripts, paintings, and treasures, including, according to church records, a gold object described as a "bejeweled dagger handle of obscene design, used in ritual executions." However, when the Jesuit order was thrown out of Mexico a few decades later, Father Gongora's Aztec artifacts and treasures were not on the bills of lading of the items shipped across the Atlantic Ocean.

"It would appear, however, that El Verdugo had left Mexico years before the Jesuits did, for it made its next appearance in the journal of Fra Carlo Lodali of Venice."

"Who was that?"

"A wealthy and eccentric cleric," Panzer answered. "One of the most fascinating art collectors of all time. He was a pack rat, a man who spent the last two decades of his life acquiring art the way junk collectors acquire junk."

By now, Panzer had an entire file of papers in front of him, which he had removed from a locked file drawer. He leafed through them as he spoke. "Fra Carlo Lodali frequented pawn shops, he cultivated rag collectors, he wined and dined ship captains on shore leave. He viewed them all as potential sources of objects to add to his extraordinary collection. During his final years the man purchased an absolutely phenomenal quantity of objects—some of it outright junk, some priceless works of art."

Panzer removed a set of photocopied materials from the file. "Fra Lodali kept a journal of his collecting years. His journal entry for August 17, 1754, mentions the acquisition"—he paused to read the photocopied text—"of a 'gold sculpture encrusted with jewels in the shape of the male genitalia.' He doesn't identify the sculpture by name, but he meticulously records its measurements. 'Twenty-two centimeters long, ten centimeters wide.' " Panzer looked at me over the text and lowered his dark glasses. "Those measurements are as unmistakable as fingerprints."

"I flunked metrics back in seventh grade," I said with a shake of my head.

"Nine inches long, four inches wide."

I raised my eyebrows.

"Yes," Panzer said, with what looked close to a leer. "Montezuma was lavishly endowed."

"Only his sculptor knows for sure. What happened next?"

"Where were we?" He put his glasses back on and perused his papers. "Fra Carlo Lodali. He died in . . . 1761," he said, checking his notes. "His vast collection was dispersed, almost helter skelter, to friends, art collectors, and scavengers. There is no evidence of who walked off with El Verdugo."

The next record of El Verdugo was 1791. In that year, one Michael Kazimierz Oginski of Lithuania offered it for sale, along with a painting, to his cousin by marriage, who was the King of Poland.

"That sale is most renowned for the main acquisition," Panzer said, "Rembrandt's celebrated painting 'The Polish Rider.' But in addition to the Rembrandt, King Stanislaus Augustus acquired El Verdugo. The records are undisputed on that point. When Stanislaus died eight years later, the last king of Poland, the Rembrandt and the Executor passed into other hands, first together, then separated. Scholars have confirmed that they both belonged to Countess Therese Tyszkiewicz. But she is the last confirmed owner of the Executor. By the time the Rembrandt reached the hands of Count Jan Tarnowski, the Executor had disappeared."

"How do you keep all this straight?" I asked.

"How do you keep all the rules of evidence straight? How does the American historian keep all the Civil War battles straight? Because it's your job. The Executor is part of my job, Rachel. Indeed, it's my life. I've been in pursuit for more than twenty years."

I nodded. "Go on with the story."

"Edward Solly is next. Perhaps. He was an English lumber dealer based in Berlin. He amassed a large and extraordinary art collection with the same tenacity that had earned him vast sums in the lumber business. He made frequent trips to Poland. His acquaintances claimed that Mr. Solly bragged of purchasing a solid gold Aztec phallus on one such trip."

"Did he?"

"We don't know. When he went bankrupt in 1821, he was forced to sell his entire art collection to King Frederick Wilhelm the Second of Prussia. There was a fifty-seven-page bill of sale. I've seen the original in the German archives. There is no listing for El Verdugo, or for anything remotely resembling it. Of course, that hardly proves that Edward Solly *never* owned the Executor. It could simply mean that he disposed of it before his bankruptcy. Or perhaps he never sold it."

Panzer paused to put out his cigarette. "After Edward Solly," he said, "there is a century of silence. Until James Hooper. Are you familiar with the Hooper Collection?"

"No."

"It is one of the most comprehensive and important collections of primitive art in the world. In 1923, according to the as-yet-unpublished memoirs of Bjorn Olson, who served as one of his assistants during and after World War One, Hooper attempted to purchase the Executor from a Mexican art dealer named Arturo Sierra-Cordova. A South African attorney named Morgan Proost allegedly acted as the go-between. Proost's letter to Hooper is the first reference to the Executor in more than a century."

"What happened?"

"The parties agreed on a price of one thousand British pounds. Alas, Sierra-Cordova was robbed and killed before he could make delivery."

Panzer leaned back in his chair, his hands steepled beneath his chin, fingertips lightly touching. "Silence again," he said, "until after the Second World War. Enter several important collectors of pre-Columbian art, including Morton D. May of this city."

"Of the May Company?"

"The same. An avid collector."

"How does he fit in?"

"In 1964, one of May's emissaries was contacted in Chile by Mose de la Lenga. De la Lenga was an Argentine attorney. He claimed to have come into possession of Montezuma's Executor, and said he was willing to sell it for the right price."

May was one of perhaps ten such collectors contacted by de la Lenga, Panzer explained. De la Lenga's goal was to induce a bidding war among the collectors.

"You must understand," Panzer explained, "that by 1964 the Executor was an object that, to avid collectors of pre-Columbian art, had become the Aztec equivalent of the Holy Grail."

May, however, along with at least two other collectors, insisted that an art expert be permitted to examine the Executor and certify to its authenticity before they would make a bid. De la Lenga agreed, since he understood that a certification of its authenticity would guarantee a lucrative bidding war. Once the authentication procedures were set, de la Lenga smuggled the Executor into Mexico so that it could be examined by one of the pre-Columbian art experts who lived in Mexico City.

"Quite by accident," Panzer continued, "Mexico's National Museum of Anthropology learned of the existence of the Executor and, even more important, its presence on native soil."

The Museum ran into court in an effort to halt the sale of the Executor. It took a full day in court, however, before the judge issued an injunction halting the sale and ordering de la Lenga to surrender the Executor to the Museum pending resolution of the merits of the case.

Because of the court delay, by the time the authorities arrived at de la Lenga's hotel room, the element of surprise was long gone. So was the Executor. "And so was de la Lenga," Panzer said.

"Where did he go?"

"He surfaced three days later. Literally. Floating on his stomach in a small lake on the outskirts of Mexico City. His throat was slashed from ear to ear."

"No Executor?"

Panzer shook his head.

"I joined the quest a few years later, Rachel. Off and on over the years I have traveled to Poland, to South Africa, to Lithuania, and to Thailand in pursuit of leads and tips. All for naught. Until ten months ago, that is. Quite unexpectedly, the Executor came on the market again. The black market, that is. Down in Argentina. Acquiring it, however, was only the first hurdle."

"It's against the law to bring it into America," I said.

"That is a most controversial legal question upon which reasonable minds can differ. For you see, after the Mexican authorities bungled their attempt to grab the Executor from de la Lenga, they pursued court process. In 1968, they *purported* to perfect their claim to the Executor as—quote—stolen cultural property—closed quote—under a United Nations convention on cultural property."

"What effect does that have?"

"Under a treaty between Mexico and the United States,

any designated article of so-called stolen cultural property that is imported into the United States is subject to seizure by Customs and forfeiture to the government.''

"So it's against the law to bring it here.''

"Is it? Come, come, Rachel. Your mind is more subtle than that. I am not a lawyer, but even I can see that there may be at least a question of law as to whether Mexico has in fact perfected its claim to the Executor. After all, the object had left Mexico hundreds of years *before* that statute was enacted. Just because some Mexican justice of the peace issues an *ex parte* judgment hardly means that an American court will afford such a decree full faith and credit. That is precisely why I retained Stoddard Anderson. As I said, acquiring the Executor was just the first hurdle. Safely delivering it inside this country was the true challenge.''

"And Stoddard agreed to do that?'' I asked, amazed.

"He did indeed. Stoddard's assignment was to deliver the Executor into the country and, in the process, evade or defeat the efforts of the Mexican government to lay claim to it. For those services I agreed to pay him the sum of two hundred and fifty thousand dollars. Don't look so incredulous, Rachel.''

"I have a hard time believing that Stoddard Anderson would agree to do that for any amount of money. How would he even know the first thing about smuggling something into the country? And why would he be willing to do it?''

"The how part is not as incredible as it may first seem. Stoddard Anderson was not without influence within the Republican Party, which, as the political party in power, controlled the patronage appointments at the U.S. Customs Service. Stoddard also had powerful friends within corporate America. As you surely must know, many major American corporations have substantial international operations, and equally substantial influence within the governments of the countries where they do business.'' Panzer leaned back in his chair and stared at the ceiling. "As for the why, it was quite simple: Stoddard Anderson needed money. For what, I have no idea. Perhaps as seed money for the senatorial campaign his friends in the GOP kept urging him to wage. Perhaps for the purchase of a summer home on Martha's Vineyard. His political ambitions were no concern of mine, Rachel. Nor was his private life. We struck a deal. The price was right. For both of us.''

I thought it over. "So where is it?"

He shifted his gaze to me. "That, my dear woman, is the one hundred thousand dollar question. If you can answer it, the money is yours. I have reason to believe Stoddard Anderson succeeded in bringing the Executor into the country before he died. Indeed, he told me so himself. I even have reason to believe the Executor was somewhere here in St. Louis at the time of his death.''

"Then why didn't he turn it over to you?"

"The U.S. Customs officers—the law enforcement types— began snooping around about a month before Stoddard's death. We both decided it was best to wait until Customs lost interest. As recently as three days before he disappeared, Stoddard told me that he still didn't believe it was safe.''

I sat back in the chair and mulled it over.

Panzer lit another cigarette. "Really, Rachel," he said as the smoke trickled out of his mouth and nose, as if he were on fire, "even if we assume that there has been a technical violation of the law, and I most sincerely doubt it, then the guilty party is already dead. Moreover, the technical violation, if any, was in bringing the Executor into the country. I am merely asking you to retrieve it from wherever Stoddard Anderson placed it before he died. Let me worry about the consequences.''

"I have no idea where, or even if, he hid that thing."

"Ah, but you have one thing I do not. You have access. To his papers. To the people he dealt with before his death. My sources tell me you are a woman of uncommon tenacity and imagination. Use those qualities. Find the Executor, Rachel.''

As incredible as it seemed, other facts—ranging from the suicide note to the hotel register—seemed to confirm Panzer's remarkable claim. It appeared that Stoddard Anderson had actually been involved in the quest for Montezuma's Executor. At the very least, I might have to revise my views about Republicans.

"If I agree to help you," I finally said, "and that is still a giant if, the fee is the same one you negotiated with Stoddard Anderson. Two hundred and fifty thousand dollars.''

His bushy eyebrows arched. ''I should think that one could fairly call that overreaching. After all, Stoddard had completed the most challenging phase of the work before his death. You surely must concede that he earned a substantial portion of that fee.''

''I couldn't agree more. He earned it. You never paid it. You agreed to pay him a quarter of a million dollars, Remy. That money belongs to his estate. If Stoddard Anderson really brought that thing into the country, then you owe his estate the entire amount, assuming I can deliver the Executor. I will work out my own fee arrangement with his widow.''

After a long stare, Panzer nodded his head in appreciation. ''You are a good attorney, Rachel. Your argument is persuasive. We have a deal.''

''Not yet,'' I said as I stood up to leave. ''But at least we have a price.''

CHAPTER 12

"I'm dead," she explained. "I used to be living, but I've been dead for six months. You'd have to ask Portia. She used to be the dead one, but we switched."

I had to smile. The ghoulish jargon of the trusts and estates department of Abbott & Windsor had not changed since my days as an associate in the firm's Chicago office. There were two paralegals in the St. Louis office's trusts and estates department. Accordingly, one was "dead" and the other was "living." The "dead" one handled the administration of the estates of dead clients, while the "living" one organized and updated the estate plans of the living ones. (In the A & W jargon, living trusts-and-estates clients are "undeads.")

And thus, Linda Salem was the "dead" paralegal. Portia McKenzie was the "living" one.

By the time I returned to Abbott & Windsor from the Panzer Gallery, it was close to four-thirty. Although I now had a fairly good idea of the identity of the first "Executor" mentioned in Stoddard Anderson's suicide note—"The Executor is safe underground"—I still wanted to follow the executor trail I had started down before my meeting with Panzer. Perhaps it would help me identify the second "Executor" reference in the suicide note. And if not, it might lead somewhere anyway. There were too many loose ends in this investigation. I wanted to tie down any that I could.

Linda Salem—the "dead" paralegal—told me that at the time of his death, Stoddard Anderson had not been the executor of any estate then in probate. According to her search of the computerized records, Reed St. Germain was usually named executor of any of Anderson's clients who, in the A & W phrase, were "no longer undead." In addition, Reed St. Germain was serving as the executor of Stoddard Anderson's estate.

But Linda couldn't help me with the "undeads." Portia McKenzie would have the records on whether Stoddard Anderson was designated as executor in any of their wills. Unfortunately, Portia was already gone for the day. I left a short note on her desk asking her to call me in the morning.

The message light on my telephone was flashing when I got back to my office. I called the message center. There was a package up front from the St. Louis Club. There were also two phone messages from Bridgeton Police Detective Mario Aloni, two from Benny Goldberg, an ASAP message from Reed St. Germain, and a call from the secretary of Salvatore Donalli (aka the Missing Link). Donalli's secretary had left a message: Mr. Donalli could meet me tomorrow at 11:30 A.M. at his office. I called her back, received a recorded message that the offices of Donalli Construction were closed, and left a confirming message at the sound of the beep.

I dialed Mouse Aloni's number next.

"I called earlier to tell you the news about Mrs. Anderson," he said. "I suppose you've heard by now."

I clenched the telephone. "No. Tell me."

"Oh." There was a pause. "I'm afraid your client was attacked last night, Miss Gold."

"Oh, no. Is she—?"

"She's alive, ma'am. But in critical condition. Head injury."

"Oh, my God. What happened?"

"We're not exactly sure, Miss Gold. The Clayton police are handling it, but they've been keeping me apprised. A neighbor found her this afternoon. She had come over to visit Mrs. Anderson. Door was open. Mrs. Anderson was on the floor in the front hall. She was unconscious. As near as we can tell, she came home last night from a board meeting of one of her charities, probably shortly after nine-thirty. That's when her meeting ended. It was only a five-minute drive from her house. Apparently, there was an intruder in the house. Her entrance must have surprised him."

"What did he do?" I could feel my heart beating.

"He struck her on the back of the head. With a hard object. We found a fireplace poker near the body. The indentation in her skull appears to match the bore of the poker."

"And that all happened last night?"

"Yes, ma'am."

"And no one found her until when?"

"Approximately twelve-thirty this afternoon."

"Oh, that poor woman. Will she live?"

"You'll need to talk to her doctor, Miss Gold. She was rushed into surgery this afternoon. She's still unconscious."

"Which hospital?"

"St. Mary's. Intensive care unit."

"Have they caught the intruder?"

"No, ma'am."

"Any suspects?"

"No, ma'am."

"What was taken?"

"Well, the Clayton police aren't sure. You see, this wasn't a typical breaking and entering."

"How so?"

"From what the Clayton police can ascertain, the intruder took nothing from the house. Mrs. Anderson's wallet was in her purse. There was close to two hundred dollars in there, along with several credit cards. The intruder didn't take the money or the plastic. Although there's clear evidence that the intruder was upstairs, there doesn't appear to be any jewelry missing. The VCR is still there. The stereo system is still there. The televisions are still there. All the usual items are still there."

"Maybe she scared him away."

"Possible, but not likely. From the look of the house, he was searching pretty hard for something specific."

"What do you mean?"

"Mr. Anderson had his own bedroom. Separate, I mean, from Mrs. Anderson's. Her room was lightly searched, but his bedroom was . . . well, it was pretty thoroughly ransacked, Miss Gold. I saw it myself. The mattress and box spring were slit open with a knife. Several floorboards were removed with a pry bar. Pictures were slashed. The place was a mess. It looked to me like the intruder was searching for something very specific. Probably something that belonged to Mr. Anderson."

On my way out I stopped at the reception desk to pick up the package from the St. Louis Club.

"Rachel?"

I turned to see Reed St. Germain approaching. He looked somber. "You've heard?"

I nodded.

"Are you going out there?" he asked solemnly.

"I am."

"I'm going to a meeting out in Chesterfield. Otherwise I'd join you. I'll walk you to the parking garage. Here," he said as the elevator doors slid open.

He put his hand on my waist to usher me into the elevator. I was keenly aware of the way his hand seemed to slide down to my hip before he moved it away.

"I spoke to the treating physician," he said as we started our descent.

"What does he say?"

He shook his head gravely. "I'm afraid Dottie has suffered a severe subdural hematoma. She hasn't regained consciousness yet."

"Will she?"

"He says they may not know that for another forty-eight hours."

"That poor woman," I said quietly, fighting to control my emotions in front of him.

Reed sensed that I was shaken up by what had happened

to Dottie. He insisted on walking me all the way to my car. He asked me nothing about my investigation. Instead, he asked gentle questions about where I had grown up in St. Louis, what high school I had gone to, whether my parents were still alive. I was surprised—even touched—by his consideration.

I thanked him as I got into my car.

Highway 40 was clogged with rush hour traffic when I left downtown for the hospital. The westbound traffic slowed to a crawl as I passed the Arena on the left. Up ahead near Skinker, the highway doglegged to the south and tilted up into the path of the late-afternoon sun, which hovered directly above the highway—a giant, shimmering ball of fire, as if a nuclear bomb had just been detonated over Clayton.

Sitting in traffic was therapeutic. With my radio turned to KSHE, the Beatles' "Back in the U.S.S.R." blaring, I tried to distract myself from what had happened to Dottie Anderson.

Traffic had come to a complete halt. I reached for the hand-delivered envelope from the St. Louis Club that I had tossed onto the passenger front seat. Inside were three quarterly statements of account—one for something called the Abramson Trust, one for the Estate of Laurence M. O'Conner, and one for the Estate of Brock Allard Fontaine. Each was a photocopy and each showed on its face that it had been prepared by Abbott & Windsor.

The formats of the three documents were similar—each was essentially an itemized list of payments made during the prior quarter. There were payments to appraisers, payments to investment advisors, payments for court transcripts, payments for photocopies, payments for postage, payments for legal fees. And on each statement of account there was a payment to ParaLex Support Systems, Inc. On the quarterly statement for the Abramson Trust, the entry appeared as follows:

April 9— ParaLex Support Systems, Inc. $175.00
               (for trust administrative services)

On the quarterly statement for the Estate of Laurence M.
O'Conner, the entry appeared as follows:

April 18— ParaLex Support Systems, Inc. $185.00
      (for estate administrative services)

On the quarterly statement for the Estate of Brock Allard
Fontaine, the entry appeared as follows:

April 11— ParaLex Support Systems, Inc. $190.00
      (for estate administrative services)

Someone—Anderson? St. Germain?—had circled each of the
ParaLex entries in red ink.

As I stared at the ParaLex entries, I sorted through my own
contacts within the main office of Abbott & Windsor. I could
probably get the answers from people in Chicago without involving anyone in the St. Louis office. I could run this down
without any more jousting with Reed St. Germain.

As traffic started to move forward, my thoughts moved back to
Dottie Anderson.

Had the intruder been looking for Montezuma's Executor?
Or for evidence of its whereabouts? If so, who was he? Or she?
Panzer had started our meeting this afternoon by offering me
$100,000 to bring him the Executor, and ended by agreeing to
pay $250,000. No matter what he said about famous paintings
and rare wine, it was still a lot of money. Was it possible that
Panzer had first tried to locate the Executor on his own? Could
he have decided to hire me only after the intruder found nothing
in Anderson's house? After all, the house was searched last
night; Panzer didn't call me until this morning.

But then again, I had called Panzer first. Yesterday. He
had merely returned my call. Still, the presentation he gave
today was far more than a mere returned phone call.

Panzer was not necessarily the only one. Could there be

someone else on the trail of the Executor? Who else knew about it? Panzer had mentioned that the Executor had come onto the black market about ten months ago down in South America. If that was true, Panzer surely wasn't the only one who knew about it, or the only one interested in acquiring it. If there were others, things could get worse. As near as I could recall from Panzer's story, every time the Executor had come on the market during this century, someone had died. If there were others out there right now in pursuit, then what had happened to Dottie Anderson might not merit even a footnote in the history of the Executor.

Or was the burglary totally unrelated to the Executor? I reminded myself that there was such a thing as coincidence. I also reminded myself that coincidence showed up more often in mystery novels than in real life.

CHAPTER
13

Weaving my hand through the tubes and monitor wires, I pressed a cool washcloth against Dottie's forehead. The resident had been checking the monitors and making notes when I had arrived. He said her chances of survival were fifty-fifty.

I leaned close to her ear. "Dottie," I whispered, "this is Rachel Gold. The doctors say you're doing super. I know you're going to make it."

I thought her eyelids flickered in response, but as I watched for a few moments they flickered again. Her arms were outside the bedcovers. I held one of her hands and looked down at her.

She was all alone now—her son dead, her daughter lost, her marriage long empty, her husband a suicide. If she survived this brutal attack, life held little promise for her remaining years. I tried to conjure up the little girl again—little Dottie in pigtails chasing the milk truck, shouting and laughing, laughing and shouting.

I wiped a tear from my cheek.

And what about the insurance money I was supposed to get for her? Although I still had people to talk to (including Anderson's doctor, I reminded myself) and evidence to locate, what I had seen so far suggested that Stoddard Anderson had been sane when he killed himself. Depressed? Probably. Distracted?

Definitely. But the standard of proof for establishing insanity required far more than that. It was an evidentiary hurdle that now seemed higher than the Gateway Arch. The best I could realistically hope for was one or two pieces of evidence that would at least *suggest* the *possibility* of significant mental instability—evidence I could use as bargaining leverage with the claims adjuster. I might never be able to prove insanity, but I might find enough evidence to shake a couple hundred thousand dollars of settlement money out of the insurance tree.

Unless. Always unless. What had caused him to take out all that insurance just four months before he died? Although the answer might be Montezuma's Executor, it was an answer that could cause insurance problems. Did he believe he was going to die back then? Perhaps. Did he plan to kill himself back then? Let's hope not, Rachel.

I gently squeezed Dottie's hand.

Nothing felt quite right about Anderson's involvement with Panzer and the Executor. There were many things one might expect to find Stoddard Anderson doing last winter: pressing the flesh at a Republican Party black-tie fundraiser, reviewing quarterly financials at a board of directors meeting, editing one of his anti-abortion or anti-gay-rights pieces, perhaps even sipping room-service champagne in a hotel room with a mistress. But not helping smuggle an Aztec treasure—a golden erection, for goodness sakes—across the border, possibly in violation of the law. It just didn't compute.

As I looked down at Dottie, I thought again of Panzer's proposal. If Anderson had really undergone the personal and professional risks of bringing that incredible object into the country, then he truly had earned his $250,000 fee. If the Executor was already in St. Louis, and if I did find it, maybe Panzer was right. What was so terrible about turning it over to him and collecting the fee? At least I would have obtained something of value for Dottie.

And what an experience to actually see that thing, to touch it, to hold it. According to Remy Panzer, no one in the United States—with the possible exception of Stoddard Anderson—had ever seen it. In fact, there had been no confirmed sightings of it for more than 150 years. You'd have to be cold on a slab not to respond to the chance to find Montezuma's Executor.

Removing the washcloth, I leaned over Dottie and kissed her on the forehead. "I'm coming back tomorrow, Dottie," I told her softly. "I expect to see you up and around by then. I have some exciting things to tell you about. We've got a real adventure ahead of us."

I called Benny Goldberg from a hospital pay phone. I told him about Dottie, and I told him vaguely about Remy Panzer's proposition.

"I'm coming down."

"Benny."

"Hey, I'm not all that busy. You can take me up that ridiculous golden arch."

"It's silver. And I'm okay down here."

"Rachel, I need a couple days' vacation. I was thinking of Monaco, but what the hell, they don't call St. Louie the Monaco of the Mississippi for nothing. We'll take your niece and nephew to a baseball game. Just like last time. I'll finally take a tour of that fucking brewery. Maybe have me a couple orders of barbecued snouts at Roscoe's. And if we run out of things to do, hell, it's August in St. Louis. We can always work up a sweat and go to the Galleria. Think your sister is willing to put me up again?"

"Probably." I was smiling. "We Gold girls have an inexplicable soft spot in our hearts for you."

"Anyway," he said, "I got a phone call this morning from the dean of the law school down there."

"Washington U?"

"Yep."

"Wow. Are they serious?" Last winter Benny had published a law review article proposing a radical new approach to resale price maintenance agreements under the federal antitrust laws. It was a brilliant piece (which I would say even if Benny hadn't thanked me, in the very first footnote, for my editorial suggestions). During the months since its publication Benny had received inquiries from several law schools around the country.

"Don't know. The dean invited me to come down for a morning of interviews with some of the professors. I thought maybe I could schedule that for Saturday or Monday."

"That's wonderful. You should definitely do it."

"I just might. So tell me again how to get to your sister's house. I can't remember."

I told him.

"I've got a meeting tomorrow afternoon," he said. "I won't hit the road until around five o'clock. So don't expect me until ten or eleven."

"Thanks, Benny."

"Hey, what are friends for?"

The prospect of Benny Goldberg's coming to St. Louis had blown away the blue fog that had descended on me with news of Dottie's assault. I was feeling good as I took the elevator down to level four of the underground parking garage. I was feeling good as I stepped out of the elevator on level four. I was still feeling good as I spotted my car and started toward it. That's because my mind was operating on tape delay. Nothing clicked until I actually reached the car.

"Oh, no," I gasped.

Someone had bashed in the back window and the window on the passenger side in front. There were thousands of pieces of shattered glass everywhere—on the ground, inside the car, on the seats, on the floor of the car.

I peered in the window on the driver's side. Last week's *New York Times Magazine* was still on the back seat, although now covered by a sprinkling of broken glass that for some reason made me think of the coarse rock salt that road crews spread during snowfalls. The documents I had received from the St. Louis Club—the three quarterly statements of account—were still on the front seat.

I walked around to the back of the car. Feeling a little woozy, I put my hand on the trunk for balance. The trunk moved, and I jumped back. I tried to breathe slowly as I stared at the trunk. Someone had pried it open, breaking the lock in the process.

I stepped forward and lifted the trunk lid, my heart racing. There had been nothing in it other than my trial bag, which had been stuffed with my notes and documents related to Stoddard Anderson. The trial bag was still there. It had been closed when I put it in the car this afternoon. It was still closed, but now all of my notes and documents were strewn throughout the trunk.

I stared at the trial bag. Someone had smashed in the car windows, broken into the trunk, rifled through the contents of my trial bag, and then . . . closed it back up? My fingers twitched as I reached into the trunk for it. From the weight alone I knew the trial bag was empty. Balancing it on the rear fender, I opened it. There was nothing inside but a single, folded sheet of white paper.

I pulled out the note and unfolded it. The three-word-message was printed in big block letters:

GO HOME BITCH

As I slowly lowered the trunk lid, I became aware of how isolated my car was. The garage had been crowded when I pulled in. I had been forced to drive down four levels before I could find a space. Rush hour had come and gone while I was inside the hospital, and now most of the spaces on level four were empty.

I looked around quickly. It was quiet and it was dark. There was no sound other than the hollow drip-drip-drip of liquid from somewhere on the other side of the garage. I got in the car, pulled the door closed, and locked it. Inserting the key into the ignition, I prayed it would start. It did.

By the time I reached the cashier on level one, I was feeling a little better. By the time the police got there (I had the cashier call them), I felt even better. And when the crossbar lifted and I finally pulled into traffic forty minutes later (after telling the police very little beyond the outlines of my relationship to Dottie Anderson), I could almost shake my head sheepishly. How come Philip Marlowe was never spooked? Or Spenser? Being a man might have something to do with it. Nah. Being a fictional character had everything to do with it.

Dinner with Ann and the family was a delicious break from the day's events. You can't imagine how good it felt to be called Aunt Rachel again. I was determined to have a wonderful evening.

After dinner, while Ann cleaned up and Richie plopped down in front of the tube to watch the ballgame, I took my niece and nephew upstairs to get them ready for bed. I had brought each a present: a new book. *Tales of Amanda Pig* for Jennifer and *Owl Moon* for Cory. I read them the books, sang them several songs, and tucked them in.

Richie was watching baseball highlights when I came downstairs. I joined Ann in the kitchen, where she was making brownies. Tomorrow was Cory's treat day at baseball practice, she explained. I greased the baking pans as we caught up on our lives and Ann filled me in on our parents. As I listened to her tell me about Mom's latest craze, I noticed something about Ann that I hadn't seen at lunch.

"Have you been lifting weights?" I asked.

"Weights?" Ann responded. "Me? Are you serious? You were the jock in the family."

"Well, it's just that you look more, uh, developed."

Ann laughed. "These?" she said, cupping her breasts. "I had my boobs done in March."

"Done?"

"You know, enlarged."

"You mean by a plastic surgeon?"

"Of course, silly. Who else would do them?"

"Why?"

"Why do you think? To make them bigger."

"Did Richie make you do that?"

"No. Although"—she let the word hang out there a moment—"I haven't heard any complaints. He loves them like this."

I absorbed the information in silence. "He shouldn't have made you do that to yourself," I finally said.

"I didn't do it for him, Rachel. I did it for me. You can't imagine how much better it makes me feel. You should see me in that black cocktail dress." She winked and made an ooh-la-la gesture with her hands.

"I thought your boobs were nice before."

"And now they're even nicer. Jesus, Rachel. Sometimes you are such a prude."

Forty-five minutes later, I closed my Jane Austen novel (*Emma*—again) and pulled up the covers. I thought back to when Ann and I were in elementary school. I had felt closer to her back then than I have ever felt to anyone. We slept in the same bed, bathed in the same bath, walked to and from school together, invented our own language, protected each other from our parents. I can close my eyes and still recall her little-girl scent or the smell of her breath in the morning. When I was eight and Ann was six we formed the T.W.A. club, our secret and extremely exclusive club (only two members). I smiled as I remembered our vow to never reveal that the initials stood for Tushy Wipers Association. Were we ever really that young? Or that close? And what had happened over the intervening years? How was it that my idea of a great concert moment was James Taylor at Ravinia singing "Sweet Baby James" while Ann's was Barry Manilow at the Dunes singing "I Write the Songs"? How was it that the junior member of the T.W.A. club now had bleached hair, silicon boobs, and sculptured fingernails?

As I reached up to click off the reading lamp there was a knock at my door. It was Ann.

"You have a call, Rachel," she said as she handed me the portable phone.

As she turned to go, I touched her shoulder. "I love you, Ann."

She smiled. "I love you, too."

I padded back to bed, sat down, and said hello into the phone.

No one answered.

"Hello?"

No answer.

"Hello?"

And then a male voice came on. "Today was a warning," he said slowly. His voice was deep, fuzzy, far away.

"Who is this?"

No answer.

"Who is this?" I repeated.

"Go home, bitch."

And then there was a click. And then there was a dial tone.

CHAPTER 14

Ann shook me awake at four-fifteen in the morning.

"Rachel, there's a man on the phone. He needs to talk to you. He says it's important."

I was immediately alert, buzzing on that jolted-awake sensation unique to the middle of the night.

As I reached for the telephone, I suddenly recalled my last phone call—the one that had left me staring into the darkness for close to an hour after it ended.

"Hello?" I said, guardedly.

"Ah, Miss Gold. It would appear that I am in need of legal counsel."

"Melvin? Is this Melvin Needlebaum?"

"It is indeed."

"What's wrong?"

"Wrong? Shall I begin with the Justice Department's totally inadequate enforcement of the Clayton Act *and* the Hart-Scott-Rodino Act in the context of airline mergers? Or should I open with the Reagan administration's ill-informed, ill-conceived, and ill-advised decision to deregulate the airline industry?"

"What are you talking about?"

"Miss Gold, I am a victim of airline piracy, a prisoner of

political pandering, a sacrificial lamb to supply-side econom-
ics.''

"Melvin, are you on drugs?"

"Don't be absurd, Miss Gold. My consciousness has not
been chemically altered, and I am certainly not high. I am in
jail. I need an attorney."

"You're in jail?"

"Precisely what I just said, Miss Gold. Is there something
wrong with this connection?"

"No. Go ahead."

"This conversation we are having constitutes my one telephone call."

"What jail?"

"I am presently incarcerated in what is known as the hold-
over facility at police headquarters."

"You mean here?"

"I do indeed."

"In St. Louis?"

"But of course. As you may know, Miss Gold, the due
process clause of the Fourteenth Amendment prohibits this
Missouri Gestapo from holding me without issuance of a proper
judicial warrant for a period longer than twenty hours. Ordinarily, I would be content to allow the full twenty hours to
expire, if for no other reason than to increase my consequential
and incidental damages at the trial of my civil rights suit against
this hillbilly junta. However, my twenty hours will not expire
until ten forty-one this evening. I am scheduled to commence a
deposition of an Anheuser-Busch VP at precisely nine A.M. in
the offices of Thompson & Mitchell in downtown St. Louis. It
is a Bottles & Cans deposition, Miss Gold, and it is imperative
that I be there on time."

"Okay, Melvin. I'll come downtown and see if I can spring
you."

"Excellent, Miss Gold. I knew I could depend upon you.
I can assure you that Abbott & Windsor will compensate you
handsomely for your emergency services."

"Let me ask you something, Melvin."

"Certainly. Fire away, Miss Gold."

"Why exactly are you in jail?"

"As I stated earlier, I am a victim of airline piracy, a prisoner of political—"

"Come on, Melvin. It's almost four-thirty in the morning. What are you charged with?"

"Disorderly conduct. Assault third degree. And some species of theft. It is nothing short of a total perversion of the system of justice, Miss Gold. Worse yet, I have been physically assaulted by a fellow prisoner."

"Sit tight. I'll be right down, Melvin. Don't talk to anyone until I get there."

"Excellent, Miss Gold. You have my gratitude. Indeed, I would be pleased to afford you the right of first refusal on both my civil rights suit against these S.S. troops and my RICO suit against the airline."

In the background I could hear someone—a police officer, I assumed—say to Melvin, "Okay, pal, time's up."

"I AM NOT YOUR PAL!" Melvin shouted in outrage.

"C'mon, pal," the officer said, his voice closer to the phone. "Time to go back upstairs."

"Can you believe this shocking misconduct?" Melvin said to me. "Officer, I must remind you that I am a member of the bar and an officer of the court. I insist upon my rights! I insist—"

There was a click, and then a dial tone.

Two and a half hours later I was seated in the small living room of the south St. Louis home of Circuit Judge Robert Schmeizing. To my right sat Jim Wortz, the chain-smoking bail bondsman who'd met me at police headquarters. When we had arrived at the judge's home, the acting bailiff (aka Mrs. Schmeizing) answered the door. She said the judge would be out in a few moments. I leaned back in the chair and tried to sort through what I had learned since Melvin's call.

I had driven downtown in the dark. The plastic taped over the rear and side windows of my car flapped violently on the highway. I reached the police headquarters near Tucker Boulevard at 5:10 A.M. I learned that court would not open until nine—almost four hours from then. The only way to get Melvin out in time for his deposition would be to contact the duty judge (the judge on call that night), see if he would hear me, and then try to convince him to issue an appearance bond. A call to a bail bondsman yielded the identity of the duty judge: the Honorable Robert Schmeizing. I called Judge Schmeizing, clearly waking him from a dead sleep. He groggily agreed to hear me in his living room at 7:00 A.M.

From what I had been able to piece together at police headquarters, Melvin Needlebaum had outdone himself this time. Although urban police officers, particularly desk sergeants, have perfected the art of stonewalling lawyers attempting to see clients in the middle of the night—the favorite tactic being the "shift change in progress," a changing of the guard which purportedly renders the entire police force incommunicado for hours—Melvin's activities over the past twenty-four hours had already become the stuff of legend down at police headquarters. There were plenty of officers eager to fill me in.

According to the police, Melvin had been in Philadelphia reviewing documents in a warehouse yesterday. He caught a flight for St. Louis last night. Engine problems forced the plane to land in Indianapolis. The next flight to St. Louis was the following morning.

At that point, a normal human being would have rescheduled or delayed the deposition. Not so with Melvin. He jawboned an airline official for fifteen minutes, and then—apparently acting in accordance with what he believed to be official authorization—leaped into a taxi outside the Indianapolis airport and instructed the cabby to take him to the Hyatt Hotel . . . in St. Louis.

The taxi pulled up to the Hyatt at Union Station at approximately 2:00 A.M. The fare was $456.60. Melvin told the driver to collect it from the airline. The driver explained that he hadn't just hauled an airline across two state lines. He told Melvin that if he thought the damn airline was responsible for the damn fare, he could go talk to the damn airline—after he paid the damn fare.

Enraged, Melvin quoted (from memory, of course) various

federal aviation regulations regarding the obligations of an airline in the event of an inability to complete a flight to the original destination. The driver was not persuaded. Extremely not
persuaded. When the police arrived, Melvin was pinned beneath the driver on the sidewalk outside the entrance to the
Hyatt.

He was neither contrite nor polite with the police officer on
the scene, who, accordingly, became the arresting officer. Back
at police headquarters, they tossed Melvin into the holding cage,
where he got to spend some quality time with several winos, a
one-armed pimp named Maurice, an elderly child molester who
claimed he was Captain Kangaroo, and a bug-eyed white man
named Earl who had fired a bullet through the erect penis of a
homosexual named Gene, who had had the extraordinary bad
luck of inserting his erection through a glory hole cut into the
only toilet stall in all of Tower Grove park that was occupied
that evening by an armed, high-strung, violently heterosexual
Vietnam veteran suffering from profound constipation.

At some point during his first hour in the cage, Melvin
jumped to his feet, raised his fist, and started chanting "Attica!
Attica! Attica!" as he paced the cage. Maurice, the one-armed
pimp, told him to shut the fuck up or he'd slap him upside the
head. Melvin ignored Maurice, who eventually did slap him
upside the head. One of the winos, while bending over to see if
Melvin was okay, vomited all over Melvin's shoes and slacks.

The constitutional guarantees can get kind of rarefied by the
time they reach the lofty environs of the Supreme Court. There
was nothing rarefied down here in Judge Schmeizing's living
room. No elegantly attired bailiff opening court with the solemn
chant of Oyez-Oyez-Oyez. His Honor wore a red plaid bathrobe
and needed a shave. He was chewing on an unlit, half-smoked
cigar. He glanced over at the bail bondsman and said, "How's
it hanging, Jimbo?" Then he fired up his cigar and studied me
through the blue haze. At 7:15 A.M., night court came to order.
Although it was a far cry from an appearance before the Su-
premes, this court was in session and ready to hear my plea—

which was a lot more than you could say for the Supreme Court
at this hour of the morning.

Judge Schmeizing heard my plea and set Melvin's appearance bond at five hundred dollars. He signed the necessary papers, stood up, scratched his behind, and shuffled down the hall
out of sight. Melvin Needlebaum had just received some due
process, compliments of the U.S. Constitution.

He had also received some white adhesive tape, compliments of
the St. Louis Police Department. During his scuffle with the
taxi driver his glasses had broken in half at the nose bridge. He
repaired them with a glob of white tape. As a result, his glasses
hung off-kilter. It was just one of several remarkable features
about the Melvin Needlebaum that emerged from police headquarters at 8:35 A.M. that morning.

His hair was mussed and his tie was askew. The breast
pocket of his suit jacket was ripped, and the torn flap hung
down. There were smudges of dirt and grime on the front of
his white shirt, which was missing two buttons in the middle
and was untucked in back so that the tail of the shirt hung
below the bottom of his suit jacket. Although the police had
returned his belt, Melvin had stuffed it into his briefcase. As a
result, his baggy pants hung low, and the back of the cuffs
curled under the heels of his shoes. From the knees on down
the pants were splattered with brown and gray splotches that
gave off the sour odor of dried vomit.

Help was not on the way. He had forgotten his suitcase in
the overhead compartment of the grounded plane in Indianapolis. No clothing store would open until after the scheduled
starting time of his deposition. Not that it mattered. Melvin was
completely oblivious to his appearance. A change of clothes was
out of the question. His only concern was for me to get him to
the deposition on time.

As we walked to my car, Melvin launched into a diatribe
about his mistreatment at the hands of the police. He gesticu-
lated madly—his arms jabbing in all directions. People stepped
out of our way as we moved down the sidewalk.

"Melvin, why not postpone the deposition for an hour?" I said as I pulled the car into traffic. "You can bathe, get some clean clothes, have some breakfast and coffee, relax, get your thoughts organized."

"Out of the question." He shook his head rapidly. "My thoughts are tightly ordered. Adrenaline is raging through my veins. Miss Gold, I can assure you that this will be an unforgettable deposition. By ten A.M. I plan to be charging through the rice paddies and taking no prisoners."

Triumphantly, he yanked open his briefcase. Pulling out a sheaf of papers and a yellow marker, he hunched forward.

At the stoplight, a bleep of a horn drew my attention to the car on my left. I turned. A cherry red Porsche. Two guys in the front seat. Big, beefy guys. Both wearing muscle shirts and both flashing toothy grins.

The driver signaled for me to roll down my window. I did. He leaned forward, flashing his white teeth. "Hey, honey, what's happening?"

"Oh, brother," I mumbled to myself.

"What are you doing with the dork?" the driver's companion said, gesturing toward Melvin, who was rapidly paging through his papers and muttering under his breath.

"Hey, babe, how 'bout dumping the dork and coming with us? We're going over to the track."

I stared at them for a long moment. What a pair of creeps. "Is your Porsche new?" I finally asked.

The driver nodded proudly. "Three weeks old, baby."

"You should try out his stickshift," his witty companion added, winking to make sure I caught the clever double entendre.

I studied the Porsche. "How much did it cost?"

The driver grinned. "Fifty-two thousand dollars."

"Fifty-two?" I said, feigning astonishment.

"You better believe it. Tell her, Joe."

"Fifty-two grand, mama," said Joe with a leer.

The light turned green. I took my foot off the brake pedal and leveled my gaze. "Wouldn't it have been a lot cheaper for you guys to have your dicks lengthened?"

As I pulled away, Melvin's head snapped up. "Did you say something, Miss Gold?"

"No, Melvin. And please, call me Rachel." Glancing in my rear view mirror, I could see that the Porsche still hadn't moved from the stoplight.

I pulled up in front of the Mercantile Tower at five minutes to nine. Melvin started to reach for the door handle, paused, and turned to me.

"I can't tell you how grateful I am, Miss—Rachel."

"You're welcome, Melvin. I'm glad I was able to help."

"I would like to demonstrate my gratitude."

"Don't worry, Melvin. It's what I do for a living. Same as you. I'll bill the firm."

"But this was above and beyond the call of duty. I insist, uh, Rachel. I would be most appreciative if you would allow me to, uh, purchase dinner for you this evening."

"Don't be silly, Melvin." I was going to say more, but I saw that he was blushing.

"Please allow me to purchase dinner for you tonight," he repeated, eyes averted.

"You mean, go out to dinner with you?"

He looked down, even redder. He nodded. "Or words to that effect," he said.

I paused. "Well, Benny Goldberg is coming down tonight," I said. "I'm not sure when he's going to get here."

"If Mr. Goldberg is here by dinnertime, I would be pleased to purchase dinner for him as well."

I weighed my options. Ann and Richie were taking the kids to a tennis social at Briarcliff that night. They had invited me, but I told them that I couldn't make it because I might have to work late. Then again, I might have opted for elective retina surgery over a tennis social at Briarcliff.

But Melvin? Of course, it wasn't as if he had asked me out on a real date. After all, if *he* had just bailed *me* out of jail, I would have wanted to do something nice for him, and I would have been hurt if he put me off.

"Sure," I said. "I'd be happy to have dinner with you."

"Excellent!" Melvin burst out. "I shall see you at the

Abbott & Windsor offices at the conclusion of today's deposition.''

"Buy yourself some clean clothes. Get something snazzy for a change.''

"Snazzy?''

"Sure. Something wild and crazy.''

"I shall, Miss Gold. Wild and crazy. I certainly shall.'' Triumphantly, he yanked open the door and hopped out of the car.

A few minutes later I pulled into the parking garage across the street from the offices of Abbott & Windsor.

As I removed my briefcase from the back seat, I heard the sound of approaching footsteps. I straightened and turned to the sound.

Moving toward me was a heavy-set man, fat enough to have to walk around his thighs.

"Rachel Gold?'' he said, his breath rasping. He was maybe fifty. Gray crewcut, lumpy nose, green-tinted aviator sunglasses, no neck.

"What?'' I said, trying to inject a little belligerence into my voice.

He had on a brown suit and thick-soled black shoes. The cuffs of his pants ended above his ankles, exposing argyle socks. Unbuttoning the suit jacket, he reached around to remove his wallet from his back pocket. His belly hung over his belt. The buttons on his white shirt strained against the pressure.

"Ferd Fingersh,'' he rasped, flipping open the black wallet to reveal a badge on one side and an ID card with photo on the other. "U.S. Customs.''

"Ferd what?'' I repeated.

"Fingersh, ma'am. Ferd Fingersh.'' A gold tie clasp kept his skinny black tie in place.

"May I?'' I asked, reaching for the wallet.

He handed it to me. I studied the ID card, I studied the badge. They both said Customs, and the ID card said Ferdinand M. Fingersh. I looked up at the real Ferd. He was chewing on a kitchen match. He looked like a sleazy private eye. I handed him back the wallet.

"Am I safe in assuming that this is not a chance encounter?"

He grunted and ran his palm over the top of his crewcut. I couldn't translate the grunt. "We'd like to talk to you, Miss Gold." He turned and gestured toward a black Lincoln Town Car down the lane. The moment he pointed the car started to creep down the lane toward us. It pulled to a stop even with us. The windows were tinted black so that you couldn't see the inside.

"Now?"

"Now would be best." He removed a cellophane-wrapped cigar from the breast pocket of his suit and twirled it between his thumb and index finger, making the wrapper crackle.

I looked over at the car. "That doesn't look like government issue."

"It isn't. We seized it in a drug raid. It's best if you ride with us in our car. We think you're being followed."

"By whom?"

"We're not sure. We need to move quickly, Miss Gold. You've been in the garage for a while. It'll be safer in our car. Windows are tinted. You can't see in from outside. Whoever's following you won't know you're with us."

"What do you want to talk to me about?"

"Stoddard Anderson and Remy Panzer."

"What about them?"

"I think we should go now, Miss Gold."

CHAPTER 15

It's a short drive up Market Street from the parking garage across from Abbott & Windsor to the massive gray building across from City Hall. The building covers an entire city block, as tall as it is wide—WPA architecture in the Franz Kafka mode.

To St. Louis lawyers, this massive block of cement is known as the federal courthouse. To the antitrust litigators of Abbott & Windsor—along with their counterparts at the scores of law firms around the nation feeding at the trough of *In re Bottles & Cans*, an antitrust leviathan that has been pending in St. Louis in front of U.S. District Judge Harold Greenman up in Courtroom M since it was filed more than thirty years ago—the building has come to be known as "Eleven Fourteen," which is its street number along Market Street. But the official name of this Depression-era edifice is the U.S. Court House and Custom House. For the first time in my career, I was here to see the Customs people.

We drove into the garage beneath the building, the one reserved for government officials. The driver dropped Ferd Fingersh and me off at a special elevator that required a key to operate it. We took the elevator up several floors, exited in an empty corridor, and followed it around to Ferd's small, cluttered office.

There were two men waiting for us. The first was a younger, tighter-wrapped version of Ferd—the same flat-top crewcut, lumpy nose, brown suit, white shirt, and kitchen match, but a lot more nervous energy. His name was Bernie DeWitt. He was burly like Fingersh, but without the beer belly. His close-cropped hair was red, his eyes were slate gray.

When Ferd introduced Bernie, the younger man clicked his tongue against the back of his mouth a couple times and said, "How ya doin' there, Rachel?"

"Don't know yet," I said. "You tell me."

Bernie pointed his index finger at me, thumb in the air, like a handgun, and he sighted down the barrel, squinting. "So far, so good, kid," he said good-naturedly.

"And this here's Mr. Rafael Salazar," Ferd said. "He's a lawyer from Santa Fe, and he's gonna sit in with us today."

Rafael Salazar towered over the rest of us when he stood up. "It's a pleasure, Rachel," he said softly, extending a hand.

I have a weakness for strong, gentle hands. His were strong and gentle.

"I have friends from law school living in Chicago," he said. "They tell me wonderful things about you."

"Oh," I said, blushing. No other words came to mind. Mental vapor lock. Just sit down, Rachel. Smile and sit down.

Rafael Salazar was at least six foot four, and—for want of a better cliché—breathtaking. His skin was bronze and his eyes were coal black. With his high cheekbones and strong nose, he looked like a Comanche warrior—but a Comanche warrior dressed by Brooks Brothers. He was wearing a khaki poplin suit that looked freshly pressed, a blue Oxford cloth button-down shirt, and a red and navy striped tie. His straight black hair was pulled back in a short pony tail that ended just below his shoulders. His smile revealed perfect white teeth. There was no gold band on the third finger of his left hand.

"Let's get started," Ferd Fingersh said. "We gotta get you back in an hour, Miss Gold. If anyone asks, you can tell 'em you went shopping at Famous-Barr, or something like that to explain this lag."

"Why don't you explain this lag?" I said. "What am I doing here?"

"Fair enough. You working for Remy Panzer?"

I paused to collect my thoughts. "If I were," I said, "I probably wouldn't tell you without first getting his consent."

"You know anything about Remy Panzer?" Ferd asked.

"I met him for the first time yesterday. He has a nice gallery."

Bernie DeWitt—the younger clone of Ferd Fingersh—snorted in disgust, his right knee bouncing. "You think that's a nice gallery. Hah! You ought to see what's going on upstairs. It's just like that damn movie about the Roman king, what's his name, Ferd?"

"Caligula."

"Yeah, that's him," Bernie said. "Like Sodom and Gomorrah up there, man. Panzer gets his rocks off with young boys. So do his clients. Panzer the pansy. He's running a whorehouse for chickenhawks and faggots up there. It's fucking disgusting, lady."

"For Christ's sake, Bernie, watch your language," Ferd said harshly. "Sorry, Miss Gold. Bernie's on target, though. We think Panzer procures young boys for his clients."

"Are you guys Customs or vice?" I said.

"Touché," Ferd said, pronouncing it "touchie." "You're right. He likes boys, that's a problem for the police. We're telling you because we think you ought to know what kind of a man you're dealing with."

"Is that all?" I asked, starting to get up.

"No, ma'am," Ferd said. "We're looking for something called Montezuma's Executor. I assume you've heard of it?"

"Maybe," I said, keeping my expression neutral.

"We think Stoddard Anderson was working for Remy Panzer, as crazy as that sounds." Ferd frowned and ran his hand over his flat-top. "Even crazier, we think Anderson helped smuggle the Executor into this country."

"And?"

"We think Anderson died before he turned the Executor over to Panzer."

"Okay."

"You want to help me out here, Miss Gold?"

"You're doing fine on your own. It's a fascinating story."

"Which you're probably hearing for at least the second time, right?"

"Where is the Executor?" I asked.

"We were hoping you could tell us," Ferd said.

I shrugged. "Sorry, I can't help you."

"Can't," Bernie DeWitt barked, "or won't?"

I stared at Bernie. He stared right back.

"Cool it, Bernie," I finally said. "Acting tough isn't going to do anything. I came down here voluntarily to answer some questions. You don't like the answers, don't ask the questions."

"Lady, you keep dodging our questions," Bernie retorted, "and we might just decide to call you before the grand jury. Make you answer under oath."

"You do that," I said to Bernie. "But make sure you give me a couple extra copies of the subpoena so I can pass them out at my press conference. For your sake, Bernie, I just hope this isn't supposed to be some hush-hush investigation."

"For Christ's sake, put a fucking muzzle on it, Bernie," Ferd said, shaking his head and muttering under his breath. "I'm sorry, Miss Gold. We appreciate you coming down here to meet with us. We really do, ma'am. Bernie's a little bit on edge these days. We all are. We've been on the trail of the Executor for almost six months now. We just don't know whether you fully appreciate that smuggling that thing into the U.S. is against the law. The fact that it's now in this country doesn't make it any less a crime. We want to remind you that you could get in a lot of trouble if you're involved."

"I'll consider myself reminded."

"Good. I'd kind of like to think we're all on the same side here." Ferd sighed as he ran his hand over his flat-top. "Frankly, Miss Gold, we also want you to understand that this could be a lot bigger than just Stoddard Anderson and Remy Panzer. It could be even more complicated than you think it is." He glanced over at Rafael Salazar, who nodded. Ferd turned back to me. "Have you ever heard of a man named Tezca?"

"Tezca," I repeated, searching my memory. "Is he the guy with the cult out west?"

"New Mexico," Ferd said.

"He's got all those jets?"

Ferd nodded. "Seven Lear jets. One for each day of the week."

"I read a magazine article about him a couple years back," I said. "Wasn't there a story about him on *60 Minutes*?" I glanced sideways at Rafael Salazar, who was seated against the wall to my right. He nodded with a friendly half-smile.

"There was," Ferd confirmed.

"I didn't see the show," I said, trying to focus on Ferd. "But I heard about it from friends."

"We got some copies of the show on videotape." He turned to Bernie. "Go check with Lucille. See if we can get Miss Gold a copy to take with her."

"No prob," Bernie said as he bounced to his feet and left.

"Is Mr. Salazar with the government?" I asked, turning toward him. He was truly gorgeous.

"Nope," Ferd said. "Ralph here represents the Mexican National Museum of Anthropology. The Museum, as I understand it, represents the government of Mexico. I got that right?"

Rafael nodded. "I'm in private practice, Rachel. A solo practitioner, like you. I have my own firm in Santa Fe. On a few occasions in the past the Mexican National Museum of Anthropology has sought my advice on international tax matters. Specifically, bequests to the Museum by citizens of the United States. They retained me here to represent their interests in securing the return of El Verdugo to its native soil."

"And you think Tezca is involved?" I asked.

Salazar deferred to Ferd.

"We do," Ferd said.

"I'm trying to remember that article on him," I said. "Didn't he used to be a CPA?"

"Yep," Ferd answered. "And he used to be Arthur Nevins. First he changed his profession, then he changed his name."

"He was a tax accountant at Price Waterhouse," Salazar explained. "In their Houston office."

Bernie DeWitt returned with a videocassette in his hand. "Here you go," he said as he handed it to me. "Take a look at it when you get back to the office."

"Thanks." I turned to Ferd. "Tell me about Tezca."

"About seven years ago, according to most versions of the story, one Arthur Nevins, C.P.A., of Houston, Texas, found religion."

"Oh, yeah," Bernie chimed in with derision, "some religion. Spelled S-E-X."

"It's your classic religious cult," Ferd continued, trying to ignore Bernie DeWitt. "Lots of losers. Plenty of Ph.D.'s. Men in their thirties and forties, women in their twenties and thirties. They all seem to dedicate their lives to him. Eventually turn their property over to him. Most of them have moved to that town they built in New Mexico. Town's called Aztlan. His cult's called the Aztlana movement. It's supposed to be based loosely on the Aztec religion."

"You can say that again," Bernie added. "Real loosely. Instead of cutting out hearts on top of that pyramid of his, he gets girls to give him head up there. That whole fucking town of ex-yuppie wimps watches him get his rocks off."

"Sex is a big thing in his cult," Ferd Fingersh said with an awkward shrug.

Rafael Salazar leaned forward. "Aztlan is the mythical lost homeland of the Aztecs." Although his voice was low—almost serene—it held everyone's attention. "Tecza bought three thousand acres out in the middle of New Mexico. He and his followers built the town of Aztlan from the ground up. It's a rather remarkable accomplishment."

"How many people live there?"

"Close to four thousand," Salazar said. "They've gradually become a political force in my state."

"All that from a C.P.A.?" I said with amused wonder.

Salazar smiled. "Tax accountants from the Big Six firms form the backbone of his organization. The earliest recruits were C.P.A.'s from the other big firms, along with a few tax attor-

neys. He met them all at tax seminars and conventions while he
was still with Price Waterhouse. Dozens of them. They run his
operations today.''

"The Internal Revenue agents are pulling out their hair,"
Ferd added. "They've been trying to build a tax fraud case
against him for years. Problem is, Tezca's got the equivalent of
Ernst & Young's tax department handling all of his business
affairs.''

"IRS can't lay a fucking glove on him," Bernie DeWitt
snorted.

"He's created an elaborate corporate structure," Salazar
explained. "Holding companies within holding companies
within holding companies. Some are located outside the United
States, principally in tax havens down in the British Virgin Islands and the Netherlands Antilles.''

"And don't let the C.P.A. part fool you," Bernie said.
"This ain't some pussy accountant. This guy's a psycho.''

"He has a short fuse," Ferd explained, "and a history of
violent outbursts that seem to go back a long way.''

"Really?" I asked.

"Hit his high school shop teacher in the back of the neck
with a ballpeen hammer," Bernie said. "Damn near killed
him.''

"He has his own security force out there," Ferd said.

"More like a goon squad," Bernie added.

Ferd nodded. "He seems to use them as enforcers and
thugs. The New Mexico police have several unsolved homicides
in the Aztlan area, including a couple cult members who had
had a falling out with Tezca. The police are convinced that all
of the deaths can be traced back to Tezca's security force.''

"To be fair," Salazar gently interjected, "there've been no
arrests and no indictments of any of his people in connection
with those deaths." He turned to me with a sheepish smile.
"That's the criminal lawyer in me talking.''

"Still," Ferd added, "he's a violent, dangerous man, with
or without his security force.''

"Tell me about the jets," I said.

"There are seven Lear jets," Salazar said. "The sun god

was the centerpiece of the ancient Aztec religion. Tezca has woven the sun into his religion, too. Every day at noon, when the sun is at its apex, all work in Aztlana comes to a halt and all of the town folk turn to the East, which is where the jet approaches from. Tezca flies one of the jets—a different one for each day—back and forth across the sky for maybe fifteen minutes or so.''

"He flies it himself?" I asked.

Salazar nodded. "He's quite a good pilot. I've seen him fly a few of those jets."

"Is the IRS still after him?" I asked.

Ferd nodded. "And the FBI. And the New Mexico state police. Everyone's trying to build a case against him. Up until Mr. Anderson killed himself, Miss Gold, we thought Customs had the inside track."

"What makes you think this Tezca is trying to get the Executor?"

"Sources within his cult," Ferd said. "Also former members, who've told us that Tezca is obsessed with the history of the Executor."

"No question," Bernie DeWitt chimed in. "The guy's got a major blue-veiner over it."

"Are your people in New Mexico keeping an eye on Tezca?" I asked, trying to ignore Bernie. Blue-veiner? I'd have to pass that one on to Benny Goldberg.

Ferd grimaced. "Well, he's disappeared."

"Tezca's disappeared?"

Ferd nodded.

"When?"

"A week before your man killed himself."

"Why? What's he up to?" I asked.

"There's a lot of speculation, but nothing solid."

"What's the speculation?"

"We think Anderson may have been about to deliver the Executor to Panzer. We'd been tailing Anderson for a couple months. We thought all along that Panzer might have been fronting for Tezca."

"Why?" I asked.

It was Salazar who responded. "Because we believe Mr. Panzer is fronting for someone. Tezca is the most likely choice."

"Why does Panzer have to be fronting for someone? Couldn't he be going after it for himself?"

"Not likely," Salazar said. "Mr. Panzer is a go-between in the art world. A fixer. Although he occasionally buys for his own account, it wouldn't be logical for him to make this acquisition for his own account."

"Why not?"

"Because of the substantial risk that Customs would seize it for my client."

"Your client's claim to the Executor is not necessarily beyond dispute," I said to Salazar. "Panzer could challenge Customs in court."

"He could," Salazar agreed. "But he'd probably lose."

"He might win."

"He might. But it would be a gamble. Panzer has money. He may even be a millionaire. But here, Rachel, the stakes are far too high. I can't imagine that Mr. Panzer is willing to play courtroom roulette with nine million dollars on the line."

I leaned back in my chair. "That's what the Executor sold for?"

"According to Mr. Fingersh," Salazar said.

I turned to Ferd.

He nodded. "Give or take a million. Believe me, Miss Gold, Panzer don't have that kind of money. He'd never be able to raise those funds from a legitimate source, like a bank. What kind of security could he pledge? Probably couldn't raise it from an illegitimate one, either. Hell, the vig on a juice loan like that has to be about eight hundred a month."

"You think it was Tezca's money?"

Ferd said, "We've been tracking the U.S. bank accounts for Tezca and his various Aztlana entities. Six months ago, back around the time we believe someone bought the Executor on the black market, Tezca and his entities made several international wire transfers totaling just over nine million dollars."

"Where'd the money go?"

"We traced it as far as an account in the Cayman Islands. We don't know where from there."

"If the stakes are too high for Panzer," I asked, "why is Tezca different?"

Bernie DeWitt snorted. "Nine million? Shit, that's flash money for Tezca. The dude's worth double that at least."

"How?" I asked.

Ferd gestured to the *60 Minutes* videocassette on my lap. "It's on there. His followers turned all their assets over to him. You're talking millions of dollars. Tezca and his C.P.A.'s formed some sort of investment fund."

"He devised a fairly sophisticated investment strategy," Salazar explained. "He used the investment fund to finance acquisitions of assets held by debtors in Chapter Eleven bankruptcy cases around the country. It was an innovative approach. Other investment bankers have followed his lead, but Tezca was first. He made a healthy return on his investments."

"So you think Remy Panzer is fronting for Tezca?"

"We do," Ferd answered. "Right around the time Tezca disappeared, at least another fifteen million was transferred offshore. We traced those funds as far as Bermuda. Our best guess is that Tezca planned to take the Executor and flee the country. That may still be his plan. For all we know, he's in St. Louis right now."

I sat back with a frown. "That doesn't make much sense."

"What doesn't?" Rafe asked.

"Why would he go through all the risk of smuggling it *into* the country if all he planned to do was take it with him when he *left* the country?"

"We doubt that that was his plan back when he bought it," Ferd said. "That was back before all the criminal investigations started heating up. Back then, his plan was probably to just stay put out there in New Mexico. Things have changed for him. I think he's figured out that sticking around in this country is getting to be hazardous to his freedom. He's starting to get the idea that it may be only a matter of time before grand juries start returning indictments."

"And when that happens," Bernie said, "he's got to figure that some hardass judge may not be too eager to set bail for a guy who owns seven Lear jets, three of which can reach Mexico on one tank of gas. Shit, if he had any sense, he'd be out of the country already."

"Why hasn't he left?" I asked.

"He's got a problem," Ferd said. "He's got nine million dollars of his money tied up in that old Montezuma's Executor."

"It's like that fucking American Express commercial," Bernie added. "He don't want to leave home without it."

"Exactly," Ferd said.

I mulled it over. "Why are you telling me all this? What if I *am* working for Panzer? How do you know I won't just go back and tell him all this?"

Ferd looked at Salazar. Salazar looked at me. "This was my idea, Rachel. I assume that Panzer tried to hire you yesterday afternoon. Based on what I have heard about you, I didn't believe you would give him a firm commitment the same day. And even if you did, I hoped we'd be able talk you out of it."

"What made you think you could talk me out of it?" I asked with a smile.

"Mr. Greenbacks," Bernie DeWitt interjected. "Ralph here's got an expense allowance that'd choke a horse."

I kept my eyes on Rafael Salazar. "You mean, pay me to cooperate?"

"No," he answered. "Never. I said I hoped we would be able to *talk* you out of working for Mr. Panzer, not bribe you out of it. El Verdugo is the rightful property of the people of Mexico. It is a tangible link with their heritage, part of their cultural patrimony. Helping my client would be the right thing to do, Rachel." Although his smile was gentle, there was intensity in his eyes. "My client is willing to compensate you for your time, the same as it would for any attorney, including me."

"Think it over, Miss Gold," Ferd added.

"I will," I said.

"As this thing develops," Ferd said, "we'd like to stay in close contact with you. Although not directly."

"Panzer the pansy knows all of us," Bernie DeWitt said.

Ferd nodded. "In his line of work, he comes in contact with the local Customs agents on a regular basis. He's a very suspicious man."

"More like nervous as a queer at a weenie roast," Bernie chimed in.

Ferd grimaced and shot Bernie a put-a-lid-on-it look. "This would not be a good time for Panzer to see you with one of us," Ferd said to me. "If you don't mind, we'd prefer that your primary contact be Ralph here."

I glanced over at Salazar.

"Okay," I said.

As I waited for the elevator, sorting through my thoughts, close but not quite ready to sign on this Customs mission, I heard my name.

It was Rafael Salazar. "Are you walking back to your office?"

I nodded.

"Could I walk with you? I need to talk to you"—he paused to glance back toward Ferd's office—"in private."

We stopped for soft drinks at the outdoor café near Kiener Plaza.

All the way down Market Street I had peppered him with questions about himself. He already knew something about me while I knew nothing about him.

As I quickly discovered, Rafael Salazar had an impressive résumé. Born in the Santa Fe *barrio*, he was a graduate of Stanford Law School, where he had been notes editor of the law review. After graduation, he fulfilled his ROTC obligations by spending four years in the Air Force, where he served as a criminal defense lawyer in the JAG corps. He learned to fly fighter jets on the weekends. After the Air Force, he joined the New York City law firm of Sullivan & Cromwell. It was a far way from home for, as he called himself, "a half-breed from Santa Fe." Too far, in fact. After three years as an associate specializing in international tax and bankruptcy, he returned to Santa Fe to set up his own practice.

The waitress returned with our drink orders, batting her eyelashes at him. He was polite to her, but nothing more. Two tables over, a pair of women in their twenties stared at him. One of them unconsciously bit her lower lip. As we had walked down Market Street, several women had turned to gawk at him. I felt like I was having a drink with a rock star. He was oblivious to it all, or at least pretended to be.

"Do you have a specialty?" I asked when Charo finally left.

He smiled. "My specialty these days is whoever happens to come through the door to my office. House closings, wills, worker's compensation claims, criminal defense, traffic tickets, domestic relations. It's a long way from Wall Street."

"Do you like it, though?"

"Oh, yes. Back at Sullivan & Cromwell I used to work on huge, complex tax and bankruptcy matters that involved so many unique issues that each one could have been the subject of a law review article." He shook his head ruefully. "A rather boring law review article, that is. Now I have living, breathing clients with real-life problems. I still handle bankruptcy matters, but they're now filed under Chapter Thirteen."

"From brain surgeon to country doc, eh?"

"Yes. Exactly. And every once in a while I still get the opportunity to perform some brain surgery. My friends at Sullivan & Cromwell still send me an occasional legal matter in New Mexico, and some of the clients I worked with back at S and C have sought my counsel with legal problems."

"Such as the Mexican Museum of Anthropology?"

"They have been a good client over the years."

"How long have you been in St. Louis?" I asked.

"For just a few days this week. I've been coming here on and off for at least four months. This is the first time I've stayed longer than a few days."

"Are you getting along with the Customs guys?"

He shrugged.

"Ferd called you Ralph," I said. "What should I call you?"

"My name is Rafael. My friends call me Rafe." He smiled. "Call me Rafe."

"I will. He's—well, unique."

"Ferd or Bernie?"

"Both. Are they any good?"

"I'm certain their abilities and skills are fine. That part doesn't disturb me. What disturbs me is their priorities. You heard them mention the FBI and the IRS. It's become a race for them, a game. Each agency wants to catch Tezca. They're all caught up in some macho interagency rivalry."

He shook his head in anger. "It reminds me of the street gangs—back in the Santa Fe *barrio* when I was a kid. I don't care about Tezca. So long as he doesn't flee with El Verdugo, I couldn't care less about him. Customs shouldn't either. They forget that they are involved here primarily as agents of the Mexican government pursuant to a treaty between the two countries. Ferd and Bernie are obsessed with Tezca. You heard Ferd back there talking about Customs being on the inside track until Stoddard Anderson died. *Inside track.* They're so eager to win that race that they've blinded themselves to the real problems."

"Such as who really owns it?"

"Exactly. You can assume that Panzer, or whoever is financing Panzer, will hire the best legal talent money can buy. It could take years to get the ownership issue resolved. Although I believe that my client has the better legal claim, who knows what will happen by the time it reaches the court of appeals? But Ferd and Bernie—they don't want to hear about that. They're like the cops who only care about making the bust and don't worry about making it stick."

"So you'll do the worrying for them. That's reason enough for your client to have you here."

He sighed. "I worry about it. I worry too much. I am afraid my professional mask keeps slipping off in this case. My mother's family came from Mexico, Rachel. From the Yucatán, in fact. It is a brutal legacy. Starting with Hernán Cortés, the Europeans—and then the Americans—pillaged and sold off the cultural patrimony of her people—of my people. El Verdugo has become a symbol for me." He paused and gave me a sardonic smile. "A phallic symbol, eh? Appropriate, perhaps. A symbol of the white man's rape of Mexico." He stared in my eyes, his own ablaze. He exhaled slowly through his nose. "I would like to help my mother's homeland reclaim El Verdugo," he said, his voice almost a whisper.

"So would I," I said, surprising myself, the words tumbling out before I realized I had made that decision.

He looked at me with gradually dawning comprehension. "Thank you, Rachel." He reached for my hand across the table. "Thank you."

It lasted a moment, and then the spell broke. He withdrew his hand, almost embarrassed.

"I get carried away sometimes," he said, checking his watch. "You need to get to your office." He reached for his wallet to pay the bill. "Please go. We will talk later."

I thanked him for the soft drink and said good-bye. The relentless St. Louis summer sun was already heating up the plaza. I weaved through the umbrella-topped tables and moved toward Broadway. I had reached the fountain across the street from the Old Courthouse when I heard my name shouted.

I turned. It was Rafe, up at the cash register paying the bill. "Can we talk some more later?" he called.

"Sure," I yelled back over the traffic noise.

"Dinner?"

I nodded happily.

"Tonight?"

I nodded again.

He smiled broadly. "I shall call you later."

I waved good-bye. When the light changed, I practically skipped across the street.

I felt positively dazzled, the same way I had felt back in my sophomore year of high school when Bobby Hirsh, the varsity quarterback—a senior, no less, with dark blue eyes, dimples to die for, and a *mezuzah* around his neck—had casually dropped by my locker on his way to class to ask me out on a date for after the game on Saturday. I had leaned against my locker, hugging my notebook against my chest, my heart pounding, as I watched him amble down the hall, averting my eyes as he turned to nod at me before ducking into his classroom.

This time, however, the dazzled feeling lasted only until I reached the elevator bank inside the Boatmen's Tower. It took me until then to remember.

Melvin Needlebaum.

I had already agreed to go out to dinner with Melvin Needlebaum.

"Oh, shit," I groaned.

I spun around and ran to the exit, pushing through the revolving door. But by the time the traffic light changed and I dashed across the street, Rafael Salazar was nowhere in sight.

"Oh, shit," I moaned as I turned back and trudged toward the building.

Things are going just great for you, Rachel. Couldn't be better. First the *National Law Journal* turns you into the hanky-panky angel of death, the infamous black widow of litigation—a surefire way to meet guys. Hey, fellas, remember me? You pat hers, I'll sue yours. And then you join the search for a gold cast of a dead Aztec's humongous erection. What could be a more normal pursuit for a single woman in her thirties? And now, at last—just when the Cherokee version of Prince Charming happens along—you get to turn him down for an evening with Melvin Needlebaum. Perfect. What girl in her right mind would want to have dinner with Paul Newman when she can dine with Don Knotts? Who would want to spend an evening with Mel Gibson when you could spend it with . . . Mel Needlebaum?

CHAPTER 16

I was in a foul mood when I stomped off the elevator into the lobby of Abbott & Windsor.

When I reached my office, my message light was flashing. There was a returned-your-call message from Portia McKenzie, the "live" paralegal in trusts and estates. I tried her line. Busy. I left a message with her secretary and banged down the receiver.

Okay, calm down, I told myself. *Tonight's not the only night. Meanwhile, you've got things to do here. Worry about Rafe later.*

I checked my watch. It was 10:50 A.M. I was supposed to meet with M. Salvatore Donalli (aka the Missing Link) in forty minutes. After that meeting I was supposed to drop my car off at a body shop on Kingshighway and pick up a loaner car for the weekend.

The upcoming meeting with the Missing Link reminded me of the life insurance matter, which certainly wasn't going to solve itself. Today was Friday. People might be leaving the city for the weekend. I checked my watch again and reached for the list.

From Stoddard Anderson's appointment calendar and telephone message slips I had compiled a list of close to forty people to contact. Nancy Winslow had typed up the list of names, along with an address and two telephone numbers (home and office) for each. I had about ten minutes to work the phones before I had to leave for the meeting.

I started with Dr. Jacob Bernstein, the physician Stoddard Anderson had seen during the last week of his life. If there was any witness out there with an opinion about Anderson's mental condition—especially an opinion that might be admissible at trial—the most likely candidate was Dr. Bernstein. With any luck, he was Stoddard Anderson's personal physician. With more luck, he was Stoddard Anderson's psychiatrist. With lots more luck, Dr. Bernstein was to straitjackets what Dr. Scholl was to corn plasters.

"Dermatology Consultants," the receptionist cheerfully answered.

"Doctor Bernstein, please."

"I'm afraid the doctor is with a patient. Is this about an appointment?"

"No, I need to talk to him about a former patient. Please have him call Rachel Gold. Tell him I'm an attorney. Tell him I represent Mrs. Stoddard Anderson." I gave her the phone number at the office and also the number at Ann's house. "Please tell him it's important we talk."

I hung up confused. A zit doctor? Stoddard Anderson was seeing a zit doctor?

I returned to the list of names. I was able to get through to three more names: (1) a "headhunter" named William Aronson, who had called Anderson about a lateral associate looking to leave a firm in Des Moines; (2) an occasional golf partner whom Anderson had called to cancel out of a match three days before he disappeared; and (3) an attorney at Gallop, Johnson & Neuman who was on the other side of a loan closing. None of them had any relevant information about Anderson.

I checked my watch. There was enough time. I dialed the Chicago office of Abbott & Windsor. When the operator answered I asked for Tyrone Henderson. He answered on the third ring.

"Hey, Ty. This is Rachel."

"What's happening, girl?"

"That's 'woman' to you."

"Shee-it. I'll call you woman, girl, when you finally come to your senses and become *my* woman."

"How'm I supposed to become *your* woman when you still haven't converted to *my* religion?"

"Hey, baby, you ain't talking to Sammy Davis, Jr."

"And you ain't talking to one of your honkie bimbos. Listen, Ty, I'm in A and W's St. Louis office and I need you to work some magic with your computer."

Tyrone and I had been buddies back at Abbott & Windsor. He had joined the firm as a messenger in the mailroom. He took night-school courses in computer programming and eventually applied for an opening on the firm's *In re Bottles & Cans* computer team. By the time I joined the firm after law school, he was the head programmer for the entire *Bottles & Cans* defense steering committee. Over the years he helped design many of Abbott & Windsor's computer systems, including the network link-up with all of the offices.

"Okay," he said. "What's up?"

"I've got three quarterly statements of account from the trusts and estates department down here."

"Deads or undeads?"

"Two deads, one trust."

"Go on."

"All three show a payment to some outfit called ParaLex. That's one word, capital *P* and capital *L*."

"Got it."

"I need to find out what's going on with this ParaLex outfit. Are these the only payments? Is it a regular vendor? How long has it been going on? Is there any pattern? That sort of thing."

"I'll do some ParaLex searches," Tyrone said. "From up here I can access the last three years in the St. Louis files."

"That ought to be enough."

"What should I do if I find anything? I can output it on one of the laser printers down there or I can fax it to you or I can mail it."

"If it's short, fax it. If it's long, can you send it to the printer my secretary down here uses?"

"No problem. What's her name?"

"Nancy Winslow. I'll tell her to look for it. Thanks, Ty."

"No problem, Rachel."

On my way out, I put in a call to Ferd Fingersh. I was hoping I could reach Rafael Salazar through Ferd, since I didn't even know where Rafael was staying in town. The Customs receptionist told me that Mr. Fingersh was out of the office. So was Mr. DeWitt. She didn't know whether Mr. Salazar was with either of them. I left my name and a message for Mr. Salazar to call me.

Lurleen had big round glasses and straight brown hair. She looked like a shy student teacher. She looked nothing like the secretary who placed Salvatore Donalli's calls on the telephone and his penis in her mouth. But then again, she probably didn't think I looked like the hanky-panky angel of death.

She brought me a cup of coffee and led me to the doorway of Salvatore Donalli's ornate office. Donalli was talking on— correction, shouting into—the telephone.

"What are you talking, twenty seventy-five, you fuck!" He followed that with an Italian curse. "You tole me twenty-five even on Monday. Don't try to yantz me, you guinea bastard."

He was short and he was dark. His skin was dark, his hair was dark, his eyes were dark. He had black hair on top, going silver on the sides, cut close and slicked straight back. Everything about him seemed compact and thick and hairy. He was wearing a white short-sleeve dress shirt, no tie, top button open, exposing a thick growth of black and gray chest hair. His arms were hairy, the backs of his hands were hairy, and the clock for his five o'clock shadow was set on Greenwich mean time.

The gold-plated telephone was cradled between his neck and shoulder. His head bobbed as he listened to someone's spiel. He reached for an enormous cigar that was resting in a marble ashtray. It was unlit and well chewed.

"Yeah?" he growled, as he jammed the cigar into his mouth. "Bullshit. . . . You heard me, Vinnie. Bullshit. Wha? . . . C'mon. You think I just got off the fucking turnip boat, Vinnie? . . . So what? . . . You think maybe I don't got no overhead neither?'' His face was flushed and he gestured with both hands. "Hey, don't talk about your Teamsters. Your Teamsters got nothing on my Teamsters, so don't start pulling that shit on me. . . . Let me tell you something, Vinnie, my goddamn Teamsters make Saddam Hussein look like Mr. Rogers, okay?''

He noticed me in the doorway and waved me in. With the cigar he pointed to a seat across from his shiny black desk, which was roughly the size of the main deck of the *U.S.S. Missouri*. He had diamond rings on both pinkies. Behind him on the wall was a portrait of the Virgin Mary hung in an elaborately carved gold frame.

He put his hand over the mouthpiece. "I'll be with ya in a minute, miss. My brother-in-law. He's selling me carpets for a building we're putting up out near Chesterfield Mall." He rolled his eyes heavenward and shrugged, his hand still over the mouthpiece.

Then his head snapped back down and he frowned in response to whatever Vinnie had just said. "Hey, Vinnie, read my fucking lips. Forget twenty seventy-five, that number don't even reside in my vocabulary. . . . Right. That's what I said. . . . Yo, Vinnie, you're talking industrial grade, this ain't no fucking Persian rug. . . . Yeah. . . . Now you're talking, you fuck. . . . Right. . . . Friday, and no excuses. . . . Yeah, I know. . . . I know, Vinnie, it's breaking my fucking heart. . . . You, too. . . . *Mangia mio gots,* Vinnie.''

Donalli replaced the receiver and shook his head. "Take my advice," he said to me as he pointed the cigar for emphasis. "Family and subcontractors don't mix. Fucking guy tries to nickel and dime me every fucking time." He leaned back in his chair and jammed the chewed cigar back in his mouth. "So you're Rachel Gold. What are you, twenty-five?''

"Over thirty.''

"Get out of here, thirty. You look like a kid. I'll tell you one thing: You don't look like no lawyer.''

"Thanks.''

"Hey, I'm not jerking your chain.''

"I'm not jerking yours, Sal.''

"Yeah?" He chuckled as he removed the cigar and studied it as he picked a piece of tobacco off his lip. "Hey, you hungry?"

I was. I hadn't eaten breakfast that morning, and I'd been up since four-fifteen. "I'm starving."

"You like Italian beef?"

"So long as there's lots of grilled onions and peppers."

Donalli's smile broadened. "Hey, you're okay." He leaned forward and punched the intercom button with a fat finger.

"Yes, Sal," said a voice over the speaker.

"Make it two, Lurleen. Extra onions and peppers. Aw, make it three, kid. Have one yourself. Unless you got some hot date tonight," he said with a chuckle, winking at me.

"Sal!" she whined over the phone.

Thirty minutes later, Lurleen brought in two huge Italian beef sandwiches, two cans of Coke, and two cannolis. By then, I had explained my involvement in the estate of Stoddard Anderson and had briefly sketched the ins and outs of the insurance issues.

Unfortunately, he wasn't much help on Stoddard Anderson. Sal had talked with him frequently during the last couple months, mostly about one or more of the five construction projects Donalli Construction had going at the time. Legal issues kept popping up on each job site.

"Especially with that River Des Peres project," he said. "Between the U. City bureaucrats and the pencilnecks from the MSD, I was probably on the fucking phone with Stod once a day."

Mention of the Metropolitan Sewer District reminded me of Albert Weidemeir. Did Donalli know him?

"Weidemeir? Don't ring no bell. I know Stod did some work for the MSD. Had some contacts. Told me a couple times he'd try to get them off my back on that River Des Peres project. But I don't recall any names."

"What about the last week or so before he died?" I asked. "Did you notice anything unusual?"

"Unusual? Like what?"

"Did Mr. Anderson's personality change? Did he seem like

a different person? Distracted? Jumpy? Depressed? Anything like that?''

Sal put the cigar back in his mouth and turned toward the window. Leaning back in his chair, he chewed on the unlit cigar, rotating it between his thumb and forefinger.

''He seemed to have trouble focusing,'' Sal finally said, still looking out the window. ''He'd kinda fade in, fade out.'' He turned to me. ''Old days, I used to shoot the shit with him, know what I mean? Not that he was a real cut-up or anything. The guy was a WASP down to the end of his . . . end of his toes. Still, he used to get a charge out of when I yantzed him. But not the last couple times we talked. I tried to. I even tried a trick that used to shake him up a little, but it didn't work.''

''What was the trick?''

''Aw,'' Donalli shrugged and waved his hand dismissively. ''Just a private thing. Not important.''

I watched him. His face reddened as he pretended to study his cigar.

''You mean that private thing between you and Lurleen?'' I said.

He winced. ''Who told you that?''

''Sal, these are the nineteen-nineties. If Lurleen gets a good lawyer, do you have any idea what it's going to cost you? Per blow job? She's going to own your company.''

''Hey, whoa. C'mon. You don't think I really had her do that, do you? For chrissakes, Rachel, she's my niece. What kind a man you think I am? Jesus Christ, you mean Stoddard Anderson thought she was—that we were—that I actually made her do it?''

I nodded my head.

''Hey, I'm no saint, but I got my limits. Lurleen, she's a good kid. My niece. I'm going to do that to her?'' He turned and gestured toward the portrait of the Virgin Mary. ''Right under you know who?'' He shook his head. ''Those fucking WASPs, a school kid could fool them. You ever meet my wife, you know I'd be crazy to try that. For chrissakes, she'd hang my balls from the chandelier." He shuddered, and then he leaned forward, pointing a pudgy finger at me. "You tell that goddamn Nancy back at the office that I never done that to Lurleen. Never. I swear on my mother's life. On the life of my six kids, you understand?"

CHAPTER

Nancy Winslow handed me a thick computer printout when I returned. "Tyrone Henderson up in Chicago printed this out for you," she said.

I took it in my office, closed the door, and settled down behind my desk. The first page showed the start of his search through the St. Louis files:

```
INQUIRY MODE:    NAME SEARCH
KEY WORD(S) :    PARALEX
OFFICE      :    STL
DATE RANGE  :    3 YEARS TO PRESENT

SEARCHING . . .

    RESULTS:     PARALEX SUPPORT SYSTEMS, INC.
                 THE NAME PARALEX APPEARS IN
                 FOLLOWING FILES:
                 1.  VENDOR FILE
                     OFFICE: STL
                 2.  TRUSTS & ESTATES PAYEE FILE
                     OFFICE: STL
```

So the first search had yielded the news that the name ParaLex appeared in the vendor file and the trusts and estates payee file of the St. Louis office of Abbott & Windsor. The following page described the next search.

```
NEW SEARCH?
YES . . .
INQUIRY MODE:      VENDOR RUN
KEY WORD(S)  :     PARALEX
OFFICE       :     STL
DATE RANGE   :     3 YEARS TO PRESENT


SEARCHING . . .
```

This was a search through the vendor files, which were the files for the companies that sent invoices to the St. Louis office of A & W. The vendor files would include everything from A & W bills (for law books, desks, paper, electricity, periodicals, typewriter ribbons, coffee filters, etc.) to client expenses that A & W paid and then charged back to the client (such as court filing fees, court reporter fees, travel expenses, licensing fees, etc.). I flipped the page to see what the computer found:

```
RESULTS:
      VENDOR:   PARALEX SUPPORT SYSTEMS, INC.
                P.O. BOX 23127
                ST. LOUIS, MO 63125
      TOTAL CHECKS:  602
      TOTAL AMOUNT:  $108,450
      FOR DETAIL, SEE TABLE BELOW
```

I was surprised. Over the last three years, A & W had cut 602 checks to ParaLex for a total amount of $108,450.00 The chart detailing those payments ran on for twenty-two pages and looked like this:

INVOICE #	CHECK #	CHECK AMOUNT	CHECK DATE	CLIENT/ MATTER
11735	39675	$175.00	4/15	23145/006
11731	39612	$175.00	4/12	34597/008
11723	39587	$200.00	4/02	18792/031

The next page of the printout described the final search:

```
NEW SEARCH?
YES . . .
INQUIRY MODE:     TRUSTS & ESTATES PAYEE FILE
KEY WORD(S) :     PARALEX
OFFICE      :     STL
DATE RANGE  :     3 YEARS TO PRESENT
SEARCHING . . .
RESULTS:
    PAYEE:   PARALEX SUPPORT SYSTEMS, INC.
             P.O. BOX 23127
             ST. LOUIS, MO 63125
    TOTAL CHECKS:   196
    TOTAL AMOUNT:   $35,220
    FOR DETAIL, SEE TABLE BELOW
```

Set out below was a chart, similar but not identical to the vendor chart. This one covered seven pages and showed all payments to ParaLex out of trust funds administered by Abbott & Windsor:

INVOICE #	CHECK AMOUNT	CHECK DATE	CLIENT/ MATTER	TYPE
11467	$185.00	4/25	24352/003	TRUST
11451	$175.00	4/22	14365/021	TRUST
11365	$195.00	4/12	19862/030	TRUST

Unlike the vendor chart, which included the Abbott & Windsor check number for each payment, this payee chart didn't have that information. Presumably, that was because each trust fund had its own checking account and thus paid its bills directly.

The two charts showed a similar pattern: hundreds of payments to ParaLex, each in the $175 to $200 range. By looking for matches in the client matter column, I was able to determine that a typical estate or trust fund was making an average of four ParaLex payments per year, spaced at regular intervals of three months, each payment in the $175 to $200 range.

The printouts showed a St. Louis address for ParaLex. I reached for the white pages and flipped to the business section. No listing for ParaLex. I picked up the phone and dialed 411. They had no listing either. That was strange.

I buzzed Nancy Winslow on the intercom line. "Hey, Nance, could you check with the Missouri and Illinois Secretaries of State to see if they have a listing for a company called ParaLex?"

"Sure."

I stared at the address for ParaLex in the computer printouts:

PARALEX SUPPORT SYSTEMS, INC.
P.O. BOX 23127
ST. LOUIS, MO 63125

I remembered the bill that Stoddard Anderson had received for rental of a post office box. I found it in the desk. Nope. Different box number, different zip code.

I sat back in my chair and frowned. This made no sense.

I leaned forward and dialed the Chicago number of Abbott & Windsor. I asked for Tyrone Henderson.

"Thanks, Ty."

"My pleasure, Rachel."

"Can I ask one more favor?"

"At your service, girl."

"You know the client/matter column on those two charts?

Can you find out who the originating partner for each of those clients is?'' Under the Abbott & Windsor system, the originating partner is the partner who brought the client into the firm.

"Hang on. Let me retrieve one of the charts.'' As I waited I could hear him humming an old Temptations song. "Okay,'' he said. "It's coming up on my screen.''

"What's it show?''

"A lot of names. There must be twenty different lawyers on the list.''

"Really? Any names more than others?''

"Well, got four, five, six, seven, eight—got a bunch here for Stoddard Anderson. Let's see. Got a bunch for Reed St. Germain. Five, six, seven—got a bunch for Prentice Ellebrecht, got some for Taylor Randall. Those four dudes have the most clients on the chart, but there's still lots of other lawyers with one or two clients on there.''

"How about the responsible partner?'' I asked. The responsible partner is the one in charge of handling the matter once it is brought into the firm.

"Hang on. Let's see.''

"I bet it's Reed St. Germain for every last one of them,'' I said.

"Damn, girl. You're right. How'd you know that?''

"He's head of the department here. Ty, you came through for me again. I owe you a dinner when I get back to Chicago.''

"It's a deal, Rachel. Take care of yourself down there.''

"Portia's in Mr. St. Germain's office,'' her secretary told me.

Reed St. Germain's door was closed. His secretary wasn't at her desk. I knocked on St. Germain's door.

"Come in,'' he said.

As I pushed open the door, the first person I saw was Reed St. Germain, seated behind his desk. Then I saw a stunning woman in a white dress. She was on the couch along the side wall, facing St. Germain, her legs crossed, lots of leg showing. She had a pen in her hand and a yellow legal pad on her lap. Presumably, Portia McKenzie.

And then I saw Remy Panzer, seated in the chair across

from St. Germain's desk. He turned toward the doorway and
our eyes met. He nodded and smiled.

"Hello, Rachel," Reed St. Germain said, adjusting his
managing partner mask. "I think you already know Mr. Panzer."

"I do."

"What can I do for you?" he asked.

"I was looking for Portia McKenzie," I said. "I didn't
realize you had a client in here as well."

"No problem. Portia's almost done, aren't you?"

She nodded stiffly, slightly miffed, perhaps at the fact that
St. Germain had overlooked her in the introductions.

"I'll send her down in a couple minutes, Rachel. Okay?"

"Fine."

Back in my office there was a message that Rafael Salazar
had returned my call. The number he left was the main number
for Customs. I called. He was out. I left my name and phone
number with the secretary.

I got through to two more people on my Stoddard Anderson telephone list—neither any help—and was dialing a third
when Portia McKenzie appeared at my doorway. I put the phone
down.

"You wanted to see me?"

"Come in," I said, gesturing toward the sole guest chair in
the little office.

Portia had shoulder-length black hair parted on the side.
She had a striking face, almost Eurasian, with a little pug nose.
Lots of make-up, but expertly applied. She was wearing a simple white silk dress that highlighted her tan and hugged her
high, round breasts. The dress was hemmed at mid-thigh, ac-
centuating dancer's legs. Her full lips were just this side of
swollen. The total effect was somewhere between *Vogue* model
and *Penthouse* Pet.

"I understand you have some questions about Stoddard,"
she asked.

"Stoddard?" In my experience, paralegals referred to senior partners, especially dead ones, by last name. "Did you call
him that when you were around him?"

Portia gave me a cool, up-yours gaze. Nancy Winslow was right. I knew the type, and I didn't like it.

"Maybe," she said. "I don't remember."

"Are you the 'live' paralegal?"

"I'm live this month, probably dead the rest of the year."

"They call the living clients undeads down here, right?"

She nodded. Her almond-shaped eyes were a chilly green.

"Was Mr. Anderson designated executor by any of the undeads?"

She unfolded a sheet of paper. "April told me you needed that information. I checked yesterday. He isn't sole executor for anyone. He's co-executor on four wills."

"Whose?"

She glanced at the sheet of paper. "His wife's. His daughter's. A man named M. Salvatore Donalli. And a man named Albert A. Weidemeir."

"That's it?"

"That's it."

"What about Remy Panzer?"

She didn't flinch. "What about him?"

"Was Mr. Anderson named executor in his will?"

"I don't believe so. I had the computer sort through the undead files for those where Stoddard was designated executor. It turned up the four names I mentioned. No one else. If Mr. Panzer had us do his will, he must have designated a different executor."

"What's Remy Panzer doing here today?"

Again the poker face. "I'm afraid I can't answer that."

"Why not?"

"One of the rules Abbott & Windsor tells its paralegals their first day is that we're never allowed to discuss attorney-client matters with *anyone* who isn't a member of the firm. Violation of the rule is grounds for termination."

"It's a good rule," I said. "If I had a gold star, I'd give you one."

"Thank you." She gave me a Miss Manners smile as she stood up. Pausing at the door, she turned to me. "I wasn't fucking Stoddard," she said.

"Ever?"

"Never."

I studied her. "Would you have told me if you had been?"

She studied me. "Probably not. Who I *don't* fuck might be your business. Who I do fuck isn't. Probably not all that different from your own rules." She turned to leave. "I'm here if you have any other questions," she called over her shoulder as she strolled away.

Five minutes later Remy Panzer was at my office doorway. He was wearing black slacks and a black turtleneck. I had assumed he would show up eventually, whenever his meeting with Reed St. Germain ended.

"Good afternoon, Rachel."

"What brings you down to the firm, Remy?"

"What keeps you away so much?"

I shrugged. "Yours is not the only matter I'm handling."

"Likewise, Rachel."

We had a Mexican stand-off, in more ways than one.

"Well, am I looking at my attorney?" he asked.

"You are not," I said. I had rehearsed variations of this conversation several times since my meeting this morning with Rafael Salazar. "I view this as more of a salvage operation than a legal matter, Remy. To the extent that your pursuit of Montezuma's Executor might someday require legal services, you are definitely *not* looking at your attorney."

"Understood. Am I looking at my salvager, then?"

"I'm still not convinced that someone hasn't committed a crime here. Nor am I sure about my own culpability. Obviously, none of us knows how this could all play out—assuming, that is, that I do find it. So, here's how it's going to have to be, Remy. You are *not* looking at your attorney and you are *not* looking at your salvager. But you are looking at someone who's going to be trying to find Montezuma's Executor. If I should find it, I understand that you have offered my client, Dorothy Anderson, two hundred and fifty thousand dollars for the object. My client has been in a coma since before you made that offer. Should I find the Executor before she recovers from that coma, then I will have to do what I think is in her best interest. A quarter of a million dollars would seem to be in her best interest. Accordingly, I do not plan to shop your offer.''

He nodded. ''That is an acceptable position. Very lawyerly. But let's cut to the chase for a moment. Are you any closer to finding the Executor?''

''Hard to say. I'm looking at records, talking to people, trying to puzzle it together. I'll keep you posted.''

''You do that. Tomorrow is Saturday. I'll be out of town tomorrow through Sunday evening. If you need to reach me, leave a message with Hans.''

After Panzer left, I went down to Reed St. Germain's office to find out why he had met with Panzer. St. Germain was out of the building, according to his secretary.

''I just met with Mr. Panzer,'' I told her. ''He said he had a meeting with Mr. St. Germain.''

''Oh he did,'' she answered. ''Mr. St. Germain already met with him.''

''Earlier this afternoon, you mean?'' I asked, acting confused.

''Right. They had a three o'clock appointment.''

''Do you know what it was about?''

She shrugged helplessly. ''I'm sorry, I really don't. Mr. Panzer called this morning. He said he needed to talk to Mr. St. Germain. Mr. St. Germain hasn't had me open a new-matter file, yet. If you'd like, I can leave Mr. St. Germain a message. He won't be back in the office today, but he usually calls in for his messages.''

''It's not important,'' I said. ''Don't even bother him with it.''

''Are you sure?''

''Positive. Don't worry about it.'' I made a mental note to check on Monday, perhaps through Sandy Feldman, to see (a) whether St. Germain did open a new file, and (b) how St. Germain and Portia described their meeting with Panzer on their time sheets.

As I started to leave I had an idea. ''That reminds me,'' I said to his secretary. ''I just had a little question about one of the trusts the firm is administering. Maybe I don't even need to bother Mr. St. Germain. Perhaps I could ask one of the paralegals. Do you know who helps him with the trusts?"

"That would be Portia."

"Would she have the files or would they be in the file room?"

"I think Portia keeps those files in her filing cabinets."

"Great. I'll see if Portia can help me out."

My phone was ringing when I got back to my office. I hoped it was Rafael Salazar. It was close to five o'clock. I had to get in touch with him before dinner.

I lifted the receiver and said hello.

"So what did the cocksucker want?" It wasn't Rafael.

"Which one are you referring to?"

"Only one. I'm using the term descriptively, not merely derogatorily."

"'Descriptively, not merely derogatorily.' Who is this, Bernie DeWitt or William F. Buckley?"

"Hey, I'm not some Joe rent-a-cop working at minimum wage and playing pocket pool, for Christ sake. I been to college, Rachel. I got a fucking B.A. in psychology. Now what did Mr. Pansy want?"

"How did you know I met with him?"

"Except for our meeting this morning, I've been trailing that slimeball for the last twenty-four hours. I watched him go in your building, I watched him come out two hours later. Even if he spent most of the time trolling the men's rooms, I assumed he at least dropped by."

"Not for long," I said. "He wanted to know if I'd made a decision."

"What'd you tell him?"

"That I sort of had. That I should try to find the Executor."

"Did you tell him you'd work for him?"

"Sort of."

"Sort of? What the fuck's 'sort of' mean?"

"That as long as it didn't turn out to be a crime, I'd try to find it for him."

"It *is* a crime, for Christ sake. That's the whole point. That's why I'm tailing him. That's why I'm calling you. I don't get it. Ralphie told us you were with us on this. He said you signed on. Did you or didn't you?"

"I did. Cool it, Bernie. You have your rules, I have mine. I had to make sure he understood I wasn't acting as his attorney. I'm willing to help you guys, but I draw the line at letting him think I'm his lawyer, letting him think that the stuff he might tell me is covered by the attorney-client privilege. That's a line I won't cross."

"Okay, Joan of Arc. I hear you. How'd he take it?"

"He seemed satisfied. He wanted to know if I was making any progress."

"And?"

"Well, not much. I told him I was working on it."

"That's it?"

"That's it. I told him I'd call him. He said he'd be out of town until Sunday night, but that if I needed to leave him a message I could leave it with Hans."

"Hans." He snorted in disgust. "Mr. Hot Buttered Buns."

"You know, Bernie, to listen to you talk on the subject one might almost suspect that you harbor some prejudice toward men with homosexual leanings."

"Don't worry. I don't like lesbos neither."

"That's certainly reassuring. Listen, do you know where Rafe is?"

"Rafe?"

"Rafael."

"Rafe, huh? No. I'm sitting here all alone in my fucking car outside Panzer's place, where it's close to a hundred in the shade. I ain't seen Ralph since lunch."

"Well, I've been trying to reach him since before noon. You know, if he's supposed to be my contact, you guys need to work out a better way for me to contact him."

"I'll tell Ferd. He's gonna relieve me at six. See if we can't get Ralph a beeper, or maybe one of them portable phones."

"That'd be good."

"Hey, speaking of relief, you got any dinner plans? I could

swing by, pick you up, take you out for something to eat, maybe a few brewskies.''

''Sorry, Bernie. I already have plans.''

''Well, maybe some other time, huh?''

''Maybe some other time.'' Like maybe the next geologic era, I thought as I hung up the phone.

My message light was on. I called the message center.

''I have two for you, Miss Gold. A Mr. Benjamin Goldberg called. He said he'll probably be at your sister's house by ten tonight. And a Mr. Salazar called. He said he'll meet you for dinner tonight at seven o'clock.''

''Oh, no.''

''There's more. He said he'd be out for the rest of the afternoon, so he'd have to meet you at the restaurant.''

''Oh, no. Did he leave a number?''

''No, he didn't. But he did leave the name of the restaurant.''

She gave me the name and I wrote it down. Then I called Customs. After twenty rings, I hung up and checked my watch. 5:17 P.M. The federal government closes down at five o'clock on Friday afternoon.

I called the Abbott & Windsor receptionist out front.

''Is Portia McKenzie still here?'' I asked. ''I just tried her line,'' I lied, ''and she didn't answer.''

''No, Portia's gone for the day.''

I thanked her and hung up. I checked the office map, figured out where Portia's office was, and set off to find it. I brought along the printout of ParaLex checks listed on the trusts and estates payee chart.

As I expected, Portia McKenzie had a small interior office. As with most law firms, partners at Abbott & Windsor get two windows, associates get one, and paralegals get walls. The metal filing cabinet took up most of the side wall of her office. According to the labels on the file drawers, the bottom two rows contained the trust files.

I tried to pull one of the drawers open. Locked.

I opened the top drawer of her desk. There were a couple small keys in the pencil tray. Poking my head out of her door,

I looked both ways down the hall. No one coming. I ducked back in and started trying keys. The third one fit.

I pulled open the drawer and started comparing the client numbers on the file jackets with the client numbers on my printout. I located three files, removed them, closed the file cabinet, and left her office.

Back in my office, I found the checkbooks in each of the files. I flipped through the stubs for the dates and check numbers for ParaLex payments. Portia, God bless her, maintained very neat files. I found each ParaLex invoice and each canceled check to ParaLex. All of the checks had been endorsed by way of a stamp (PARALEX SUPPORT SYSTEMS, INC.—FOR DEPOSIT ONLY) and deposited into Account No. 113456792 at the First State Bank of Creve Coeur. I went to the photocopy machine and made copies of the invoices and the fronts and backs of the canceled checks.

Then I returned the invoices, canceled checks, and checkbooks to the files and carried the files back to Portia's office. I put them back in the file cabinet, locked the cabinet, and returned the key to her desk drawer.

As I walked back down the hall to my office, my pulse gradually returned to normal. I mulled over my next step. Tomorrow was Saturday. The First State Bank of Creve Coeur would likely be open until noon. One phone call before noon ought to be enough.

When I returned to my office, I called the hospital to see how Dottie Anderson was doing. I had already been there today, after my meeting with Sal Donalli. Her condition was stable, and her physician was—in DocTalk—"guardedly optimistic." The hospital switchboard patched me through to a nurse in the intensive care unit. She told me that Dottie's vital signs were strong, but that there was no indication yet that she was coming out of the coma. I thanked her and hung up.

I turned to the office window behind my desk. I had a fine view of the Mississippi River and the Arch, which at that very moment framed a tow and the two barges it was pushing upriver. As I watched the tow and its barges pass under the Eads

Bridge and out of sight to the north, I softly recited the Jewish healing prayer for Dottie: *"Boruch ataw adonai rofay haholeem."*

"Wellll?!"

I turned toward the door. It was Melvin Needlebaum.

"Good God," I mumbled, gaping.

Melvin looked down at his outfit and winced. "It would appear," he said in his nasal staccato, "that the rule of *caveat emptor* applies *a fortiorari* in the context of the telephonic acquisition of clothing. I fear the sales clerk misunderstood my preferences."

"You bought that outfit over the telephone?"

"I did, indeed. I ordered it during a break in the deposition."

"Melvin," I said, fighting the urge to burst into laughter, "you look like you're about to audition for the lead in 'Son of Superfly.' "

He looked puzzled. "Do you really think so, Miss Gold? I discern no resemblance to an insect. To the contrary, these clothes look to me rather like the style more commonly associated with the casual attire of an urban Afro-American."

The color theme was purple, from the shoes on up. The purple slacks had gold glitter material blended into the polyester fabric, which made them sparkle. They were cut full at the thigh and tapered tight at the ankle. They were beltless, high-waisted, and had a crease that looked sharp enough to slice cheese. The shirt was a white silky material with a purple pattern that, upon closer inspection, turned out to be a repeating design of tiny cans of King Cobra malt liquor. The shirt collar had the wingspan of a California condor.

"Who did you order this from?"

"A clothier doing business as Famous May's."

"How did you get end up there?"

"I dialed information. I informed the operator that I believed there was a division of the May Company located in St. Louis. He asked if I meant Famous. Famous what? I asked. He told me he had more than fifteen listings for what must be some local restaurant franchise operation."

"What was this place called?"

"Famous, uh, Famous Saloon? No. Ah yes, the Famous Bar. That's it."

"It's Famous-Barr, Melvin. B-A-R-R. That's a department store owned by the May Company."

"Ahhh. That certainly clarifies matters. For you see, I insisted that the clothier would likely have the name May in it. He did have a listing for Famous May's. In north St. Louis, I believe."

"Oh, Melvin," I said, shaking my head.

"I must say, Miss Gold, they were quite responsive. I advised the clerk that I needed to acquire a casual outfit on an expedited basis for a dinner engagement this evening. I gave her my clothing and shoe sizes and credit card number over the phone, and instructed her to select a matching outfit appropriate for a man of my age. This is what she selected. Although not my taste in clothing, I must say that everything fits quite well. So," he said, rubbing his hands together, his shoulders hunched forward, "are you getting hungry, Miss Gold?"

I nodded weakly.

"Will Mr. Goldberg be joining us?"

"No, but another person will. I've been trying to reschedule my dinner with him, but I haven't been able to reach him. He left a message with the name of the restaurant where I'm—we're supposed to meet him. I have the address, but I'm not exactly sure where it is."

"That should pose no problem, Miss Gold. I have a map of the city in my briefcase. I am quite certain I can navigate us to our destination. Shall we?"

I forced myself to stand. Numbly, I followed Melvin to the elevator. All he needed was a huge gold pendant and a gold felt top hat. I couldn't believe I was going out to dinner with this man. Worse yet, I couldn't believe I was bringing him with me to have dinner with Rafe Salazar.

"Rafael is going to be surprised to see you," I said as we stepped into the elevator.

"Rafael, eh?"

I nodded.

"I'm surprised he didn't tell you to meet him in the sewer

for Domino's pizza." He gave me one of his lopsided, demented grins.

"What?"

"The turtles, Miss Gold. The Teenage Mutant Ninja Turtles."

"Huh?"

"One of them is named Rafael. They reside in sewers. They consume pizza in large quantities. It was a joke, Miss Gold." To prove it, he gave two barks of laughter.

As the elevator began its plunge to ground level, I muttered a silent prayer for courage.

CHAPTER 18

"Aha, here's another one!" he said, squinting at his map of St. Louis. "How do you pronounce it?"

"Melvin, can't we just drive?"

"C'mon, Miss Gold. One more time."

He held up the map and jabbed at it with his mechanical pencil. I glanced over quickly, long enough to see where he was pointing, and turned back to the traffic. This time he had selected a street: Courtois Avenue.

"Okay," I said, wearily. "Coat-a-way."

"Hah! Incredible." He let out one of his demented snorts. "Half the streets and landmarks of St. Louis have French names, and the natives mispronounce them all."

We were driving to a restaurant called Chaco Charlie's, which was where we were to meet Rafe Salazar. The restaurant was located in south St. Louis, somewhere near Kingshighway. Melvin had found it on his map while we were still in the parking garage, announcing that the restaurant was about three blocks south of "Grahv-wah."

"Three blocks south of what?" I had replied as I pulled out of the parking garage and turned south on Broadway.

"Grahv-wah."

"Let me see that map."

He pointed to the street on the map. Gravois.

"Not Grahv-wah, Melvin. Gra-voyz," I said, pronouncing the second syllable to rhyme with noise.

"But the word is French, Miss Gold."

"Not when it's in south St. Louis."

His Gravois discovery set him off on a manic search through the map of St. Louis for every street, park, and suburb with a French name so that he could hear me give it the St. Louis pronunciation. Bellefontaine Road is Bell-Fountain Road, Debaliviere Boulevard is De-bolliver, and the town of Creve Coeur rhymes with Leave Door.

Although Melvin's French pronunciation riff was a typically bizarre diversion for him, it did at least get my mind off our imminent arrival at the restaurant, where I was sure Rafe Salazar was already waiting. Waiting for me, that is. And soon to learn he was also going to be dining with a man dressed to audition for *The Gong Show*.

"Here's another one, Miss Gold," he barked, poking at the map. "The river we shall soon be traversing on our way to this eating establishment."

He was referring to the River Des Peres.

"Allow me, Miss Gold." He made a big show of clearing his throat. "The River Dez Perez."

I smiled and shook my head. "Wrong. We call it the River Des Peres," I said, pronouncing Des Peres "dah pear."

"But—but that's the correct pronunciation," he protested.

"Of course it is. It's our sewer."

"Sewer?"

"The River Des Peres, aka the River da Stink. Back in the old days, the river channel used to carry raw sewage. Now I think there's a sewer line buried directly under the river. All the city's raw sewage flows through it to the treatment plants. The river channel carries storm water."

He studied the map. "This is most perplexing. According to this map, the entire river vanishes north of Forest Park."

Forest Park is the St. Louis version of New York's Central Park or San Francisco's Golden Gate Park—a huge municipal park with woods, ball fields, golf course, playgrounds, picnic areas, tennis courts, jogging paths, a zoo, museums, and midnight muggers.

"The river goes underground just north of Forest Park," I explained. "Into a tunnel, I guess. I think it surfaces somewhere south of the park."

Melvin searched the map and then grunted in satisfaction. "You are correct, Miss Gold. Quite fascinating." He folded the map and leaned back in the passenger seat, his arms crossed over his chest. "Query: Who were these fathers?"

"What fathers?"

"The River Des Peres, Miss Gold. Des Peres."

"Yes?"

"It's French for 'the fathers.' My question is thus: Whose fathers?"

"I have no idea."

"It does make one speculate, does it not? If the fathers were the founding fathers of your city, Miss Gold, shall we say the St. Louis version of Romulus and Remus, then I should think one might fairly contend that the christening of a sewage line in their honor is, at the very least, passing strange. If, however, these fathers were Roman Catholic fathers—i.e., members of the clergy ranking below a bishop and above a deacon—one hopes that the river's appellation does not reflect anti-Papist sentiments."

I looked over at Melvin with a puzzled frown. "What?"

"The point being, Miss Gold, that the River Des Peres is apparently nothing more than an estuary of excreta, a torrent of turds, as it were. I was simply stating that if 'the fathers' after whom this stream of sewage has been named were Catholic priests, one would hope that the name references specific priests—in particular, the clerics who discovered it—rather than the generic category priest."

"What in the world are you jabbering about?" I asked, having trouble concentrating on both Melvin's ramblings and the street traffic.

"By way of analogy, Miss Gold, I should think that you, as a Jewess, might take offense if you found yourself in a city whose main sewage line was known as the River of the Rabbis and, upon further inquiry, discovered that it was named not in honor of two talmud-toting trailblazer rebbes but instead as an anti-Semitic smear against your people.''

I slowed the car to a stop and turned to Melvin. ''Jewess?'' I said.

His eyes were blinking rapidly behind the smudged lenses. ''A woman of the Jewish persuasion. I prefer it to the harsher-sounding, albeit gender-neutral, 'Jew.' ''

I stared at him, thinking, Why me, Lord? And why to-night? In his purple zoot suit, with a manic grin on his face, Melvin seemed a character right out of a lost chapter of *Alice in Wonderland*.

''Listen, Melvin, you said your deposition is over at noon. Tomorrow afternoon you can go over to the Missouri Historical Society. Ask them how the River Des Peres got its name. Okay? That's for tomorrow. For tonight, though, you and I are going to eat with a friend of mine. We're going to be at that restaurant in five minutes. That means you have five minutes to think of something—*anything*—besides that damn sewer line to talk about at dinner. When I pull up to the restaurant, Melvin, I'm going to ask you if you've thought of something else. If you haven't, you're going to stay in this car until you do. Okay?''

He nodded his head rapidly.

Chaco, it turned out, was the name of a canyon in New Mexico. Chaco Canyon was not far from the home of Charlie Sierra-Ruiz, who was the owner and head chef of Chaco Charlie's New Mexico Restaurant.

All things considered, it could have been far worse. Rafe was already seated in the booth when we arrived. He saw me approach from across the room, Melvin in tow, and stood to greet us.

''Hello, Rachel,'' he said, covering my hand with his. He had a warm smile of welcome—not a trace of surprise or irrita-tion over the unexpected presence of another male.

He turned to Melvin, extending his hand. ''I'm Rafe Sa-lazar.''

I had a confused flood of explanation ready to spill out, but Melvin, bless his soul, took care of it all—and with a touch of class I would have assumed was beyond him:

"Mr. Salazar, I am Melvin Needlebaum, a former associate of Miss Gold at her prior law firm, to wit, the Chicago offices of Abbott & Windsor. Miss Gold was good enough to obtain my release from jail early this morning after I had been unjustly incarcerated for the crimes and misdemeanors of the airline industry. In addition to ensuring that she is properly remunerated by my law firm for her fine representation, I insisted upon purchasing her dinner this evening as an additional show of personal gratitude. When she advised me of a potential scheduling conflict involving yourself, I insisted that you be allowed to join us as well, with the express proviso that I also be permitted to purchase your meal—including, of course, any beverages that you may elect to consume during the meal."

I could have kissed Melvin.

"Thank you," Rafe said, "that's very kind." He snuck me a good-natured wink as Melvin, oblivious, settled into the booth with a harumph.

We received the royal treatment from Charlie: a booth in a darkened corner, red candlelight, guitar music gently piped in. It was a truly romantic setting: Rafe on one side of the table, the candle flame sparkling in his dark eyes, and Melvin and me on the other.

Rafe had ordered the entire meal in advance. A brief exchange in Spanish with Charlie Sierra-Ruiz took care of expanding the portions from two to three.

Dinner was superb. We began with a bowl of posole (a hominy soup) and Indian fry bread dipped in honey—neither of which I had ever even heard of before. After that came blue corn tortillas stuffed with a spicy and spectacular New Mexico sausage, chicken sopapillas with a hot green sauce, and a thick, dark, spicy stew Rafe said was called carne adovade. All washed down with icy cold bottles of Dos Equis. Charlie served us himself, waiting with hound-dog eyes as we sampled each new course, beaming and clapping his hands together when we told him it was delicious.

Melvin lived up to his promise of finding a topic of conversation other than the River Des Peres. Armed with the knowledge that Rafe had once been in the tax department of Sullivan & Cromwell, Melvin launched into a monologue—which eventually became a quasi-dialogue—over Section 168 (f) (8) of the Internal Revenue Code, an unusual and short-lived provision added by the Economic Recovery Tax Act of 1981 (which Melvin—like most tax lawyers—calls ERTA). This ERTA provision created something called a Safe Harbor Lease, which apparently enabled owners of certain business property to sell the tax benefits in that property while still owning the property itself, or something like that—one of those bizarre Internal Revenue Service versions of reality where actions get severed from consequences, where Taxpayer A eats the chocolate sundae but Taxpayer B gets all the calories.

Nevertheless, and incredibly enough, the two of them had something in common. Rafe, it turned out, had worked on a deal where Pan Am bought an L-1011 and sold the tax benefits (i.e., depreciation and investment tax credits) to a hotel chain. At least I think that's what Pan Am did.

Their conversation provided a total contrast in styles. Rafe would listen politely, nod occasionally, and add a comment during a rare break when Melvin surfaced for air. Melvin, by contrast, grew increasingly strident as the conversation moved forward. His hands punched the air in emphasis of points of tax law. Flecks of food and salvos of saliva exploded from his mouth as he delivered a rapid-fire diatribe against the Internal Revenue Service. His speech got louder and louder and faster and faster. You could have filmed the conversation between the two of them and used it for one of those this-is-your brain/this-is-your-brain-on-drugs commercials.

And then, like a sudden summer squall, it was over. Just like that.

In midsentence Melvin abruptly checked his watch and stood up. "Good grief. You will have to excuse me. I have a deposition that reconvenes tomorrow morning at precisely eight A.M., and I must prepare for it. Moreover, as Miss Gold can attest, I have not been to sleep for thirty-six hours. Please continue without me. I will handle payment of all meal charges up at the cashier, along with an appropriate gratuity."

"Wait a minute," I said half-heartedly, experiencing a rush of pure ambivalence. "You don't have a car."

"Not to worry, Miss Gold. I am quite confident that the proprietor of this fine establishment can arrange for my transportation via a taxicab." He raised his hand as I started to protest. "Please, Miss Gold. You forget that I am down here on an expense account. This is a Bottles and Cans deposition. The clients will certainly not object to a cab fare. Mr. Salazar, I thank you for joining us, and I thank you for a most stimulating discussion of the laws of federal taxation. Now, if you will both excuse me, I shall take my leave."

And with that, he was gone.

I took a deep breath and exhaled slowly. "Well, now you've met Melvin Needlebaum."

Rafe smiled and shook his head. "We had one just like him at Sullivan & Cromwell."

"So does every big firm," I said. "You were awfully nice to him."

"I assumed he was a friend of yours. That meant he was entitled to my respect."

"You hardly know me," I said.

"I know enough about you to know that Melvin Needlebaum was entitled to my respect."

A few minutes later Charlie arrived with dessert: fried ice cream. A New Mexico treat, Rafe told me. It was wonderful. Charlie assured us that Melvin had left safely in a cab a few minutes ago. We both ordered espresso.

When Charlie left the table, Rafe leaned back and studied me. "Tell me about yourself, Rachel," he said.

"What's to tell?" I felt light-headed, perhaps from all the beers.

"Tell me about the real Rachel Gold."

"You're looking at her. I fired my body double. I do all my own stunts."

He smiled. "Most of the lawyers I know wish they had chosen another career."

"Do you wish you'd picked another career?" I asked.

"Do you?"

I shook my head. "No."

"Never?"

"Not really. As corny as it sounds, I think it's an honor to be allowed to do what we do—representing people in courts of law, advocating the rights of our clients. Being a lawyer has always seemed a worthwhile job to me."

There was an amused smile on his lips. "Fair enough, Rachel Gold. You love your job. But a job is hardly a life."

"True."

"Do you like to read?"

"I love to read."

"Who's your favorite author?"

"Jane Austen. I love her."

"Jane Austen," he mused. His dark eyes sparkled with delight. "Do you ever dream of writing a novel?"

"Me? No. I don't have the talent."

"But how do you know? How do you know there isn't a novel somewhere inside you?"

"I think that's just gas."

"I couldn't be more serious, Rachel."

"Nor could I." I sat back in the booth. "There are already too many lawyers writing too many novels. When it comes to fiction, lawyers should stick to their time sheets."

"Okay," he said, putting his hands up in mock surrender. "Not a novelist then. How about a trapeze artist?"

I laughed. "Novelists are just like trapeze artists—they're performers. But don't forget: All performers need spectators. I'm a spectator."

"A mere spectator? That's far too passive for someone like you."

"Oh, but there's nothing passive about it. At least not if you put your heart into it. I'm a fan of movies and baseball and novels. I certainly can't write like Jane Austen or play shortstop like Ozzie Smith, but I can sure enjoy watching them in action. I can read *Pride and Prejudice* the way you can ride a rollercoaster, the way you can eat a bucket of steamed clams, with the juice on your chin and the melted butter on your fingers.''

I paused as Charlie delivered our espresso.

"You make reading sound like making love," Rafe said, his dark eyes twinkling.

Blushing, I took a sip of coffee. "I get carried away."

"I understand what you're saying." He paused. "We animate what we see, we see only what we animate."

I looked up in wonder. "Yes. That's—that's exactly what I mean."

"Ralph Waldo Emerson," he said.

And he quotes Emerson, I marveled.

"Tell me about movies," he said.

"Moments, mostly. I collect scenes."

"Tell me one."

I leaned back in the booth with a smile. "Katharine Hepburn, in *The African Queen.*"

"Which scene?"

"Near the end, when she and Charlie Allnut are prisoners on that German ship, with that fat German admiral interrogating them."

"Oh, yes."

"Her hair's mussed, her dress is torn, and—oh—she's so beautiful in that scene, Rafe. So beautiful. That horrible German asks how she and Charlie got there and she tells him, 'We came down the Yulanga river.' 'That's impossible,' he sputters. She pauses one beat, gives him her proud look, and says, 'Nevah . . . theless.' Oh, it's so perfect."

He was nodding. "I remember," he said softly as he reached across the table and placed his hand over mine. It was a strong hand, and it completely covered mine. I stared at the veins bulging under the brown skin, at the small scab across one knuckle, at the callous on his thumb. So different from the soft, pink hands of most lawyers.

We sat there in silence. Finally, I lifted my espresso cup with the other hand and took a sip.

"And what about you?" I asked. "Is there an artist in there?"

He smiled and shook his head. "Not much of a spectator, either."

"What are you when you're not a lawyer?"

"A redneck bachelor."

"With a pick-up truck?" I asked with a smile.

He nodded. "And a gun rack."

My smile faded. "Really?"

"It gets even worse. I play poker. I fish. I fly planes. And I hunt."

"Oh."

"Sometimes all four together."

I said nothing.

He calmly studied me. "I don't kill Bambi. I don't kill Thumper. For the most part, I eat what I kill. When I was at Sullivan & Cromwell, I lived on the Upper West Side. My liberal friends told me they were disgusted by my hunting." He shook his head in wonder. "I would sit at the dinner table and watch them ooh and ah over their veal or venison. All a matter of perspective, I suppose. They had someone offstage—some anonymous blue-collar worker in an Iowa slaughterhouse—do their killing for them. Somehow that made it okay for them."

"I've never been hunting," I finally said.

"Not counting the meat section of the grocery store, of course." He gave me a good-natured wink.

"I suppose you're right. I've just never understood the sport of it."

"Words can't make you understand it. At least my words. You should try it once. You'd be a good hunter."

"I couldn't pull the trigger."

"You might surprise yourself, Rachel."

"I wouldn't want that kind of surprise. I got all the hunting I needed back in high school from Ernest Hemingway."

"But you can't be just a spectator in life."

"But I'm not. I'm a lawyer, too. And a friend, and an aunt, and a sister, and a daughter."

"Have you been a wife?"

"No," I said as I looked down at my hands. "And never a mother, either. At least not yet. Although"—I smiled—"I already have most of the books. I'm a sucker for children's books. It seems like every time I go into a bookstore to buy a book for my niece or nephew, I end up with one or two for me. Well, not for me, but for my kids. Oh, listen to me.'' I blushed, my ears burning. "For my kids?" I repeated, embarrassed, still looking down.

"I remember one book from my childhood."

I looked up, still red.

He smiled. "It was already old and dog-eared when we got it. My mother used to read it to me when I was in elementary school. My father was dead by then. It was just her and me. She read it to me every night until it finally fell apart."

"What was it called?"

"Horton Hatches an Egg."

"Oh, yes," I murmured, flashing back to my own mother, seated on the edge of my bed, as she read bedtime stories to Ann and me. "I meant what I said, and I said what I meant . . ."

He finished it: "An elephant's faithful one hundred percent."

We smiled at the shared memory.

And so it went. It was such a wonderful evening. I almost never talk to anyone about myself. But that night I seemed to talk about little else. Rafe Salazar was so different from the men I usually meet—the ones whose idea of conversation is a recitation of their "accomplishments" or a soliloquy on life's broken promises or a session of brandname-dropping (as in, how many ways can you work the phrases "my Saab" and "my Aspen condo" into the conversation). Rafe, by contrast, seemed to radiate calm strength and inner contentment. And not to be ignored—impossible to be ignored—he was absolutely gorgeous, at least if you like your men tall and dark and handsome. And he could quote Ralph Waldo Emerson from memory. Tall and dark and handsome and able to quote Ralph Waldo Emerson. I would have pinched myself but for the fear that I might have woken up.

We took a stroll through the quiet surrounding neighborhood after dinner. It was a cloudless night and the moon was full. We had been talking and talking and talking, but now we were quiet, walking side by side.

And then I remembered Benny Goldberg. I checked my watch. It was almost ten o'clock. Benny was probably at my sister's house already.

"I have to go," I said reluctantly.

He stopped and gazed down at me. "So soon?"

"I'm sorry, Rafe. This has really been some night. First, I show up for dinner with Melvin Needlebaum. And now I just realized I have to meet this guy from Chicago who's coming down to St. Louis tonight. He's been worried about the stuff I'm doing, which I told him is really silly, but when he heard about Stoddard Anderson's widow getting attacked, he insisted on coming down. He's a friend. Well, he's really my best friend." Arghh. Come on, Rachel. "Not, you know, my boy-friend or anything like that." Cut to commercial. Go to the video. "It's just that I'm the reason he's coming down—"

Rafe mercifully interrupted. "I understand. You don't need to explain yourself to me. Let me walk you to your car."

By the time we reached my car, I was feeling awkward again. Like a first date back in high school.

"Maybe we could have dinner again," I said.

"I would like that, Rachel."

"Let's see. Tomorrow night I'm taking my niece and nephew to the Cardinals game. I bought baseball tickets for them and for Benny Goldberg—that's his name, the guy coming down—he had me get him a ticket too."

"Sunday would be fine, Rachel. And feel free to ask Benny, too."

"Benny's kind of unusual," I said, wondering why I was apologizing for him in advance. "Benny and I, we're like brother and sister," I stammered, looking up. "We've been through a lot together."

Rafe leaned over and kissed me softly on the lips. "He must be very special," he said, slipping his right arm gently around my lower back for support.

"Yes," I sighed, kissing him back. "He . . . is."

Rafe pulled me against him as the kiss shifted from tender to urgent.

When we separated, my knees were actually wobbly. "Well," I gasped, my eyes wide.

With a hint of a smile on his lips, he watched me fumble for my car keys. I rolled down the window when I got in the car.

He leaned down to the open window and brushed his lips gently across mine. "Call me," he whispered.

"Okay," I whispered back, inhaling his musky scent.

I was still in a daze when I pulled into my sister's driveway. An unmarried urban professional woman in her thirties is like a barmaid in a Navy port of call—we've seen or heard it all. We're hard to impress. But when Rafe kissed me, I had felt like Lois Lane in Superman's arms. He could make the president of NOW swoon.

My reverie ended when I reached the den. Benny Goldberg and my brother-in-law Richie were seated on the couch in front of the television, a huge bowl of popcorn between them and several empty cans of Budweiser on the coffee table. They were watching the baseball game on cable. Benny leaned forward to grab a handful of popcorn, and as he did his shirt back pulled up from the waist of his jeans, exposing the top half of his large, hairy butt.

I arrived just in time to see one of the Cardinals picked off second base.

"Hah!" Benny shouted. "What a schmuck!" He turned and saw me in the doorway. "Hey, Rachel, you sure you want to go see these dogs tomorrow night? This ain't no major-league ballclub, kiddo. These are nine assholes in search of a colon."

"And nice to see you, too," I said to Benny.

And welcome back to reality, I said to myself.

CHAPTER 19

"It's just not enough money," Benny said.

"I know," I said glumly. "It's been bothering me all day."

We were still in the den. Richie had gone upstairs about thirty minutes ago, after Ann brought down fresh sheets and a pillow for the pull-out couch, which would be Benny's bed for the weekend.

"Was he having financial problems?" Benny asked.

"He was."

"Bad?"

"Bad enough," I said. "He certainly could have used the money. Even so, a quarter of a million dollars doesn't seem near enough for that kind of risk."

"What do you think that guy was making?"

"Managing partner of Abbott & Windsor's St. Louis office," I mused.

"A BSD?"

I nodded. "Definitely."

"Half a mil?"

"At least that much," I said.

"You're probably right about him. I just can't see a guy making that kind of bread agreeing to smuggle that golden schlong into the country for two-fifty. Two-point-five million—maybe. But two hundred and fifty—no way, Jose."

"He probably didn't think he'd get caught."

Benny shook his head. "Still not enough. At some point he'd have to weigh the risks. Jesus, look at the risks. If he gets caught, he loses his license, he's out of the firm, his career's in flames, he might even get to spend some time in the cross-bar motel."

"Panzer could have agreed to pay him a lot more than two-fifty," I said. "Anderson would have had a good sense of the true value of Montezuma's Executor. Two-fifty would have seemed small in comparison to that. Anderson worked on big deals with investment bankers—he's seen the way those vultures calculate their fee as a percent of the deal."

"Maybe," Benny said, leaning back. "Maybe the guy's willing to take the risk for that kind of money. But I don't know, Rachel. Don't forget, the guy was a fucking corporate lawyer. Talk about weenies."

"Maybe he just wanted to finally *do* something," I said, "instead of just writing it up. Corporate lawyers never get to *do* the deals, they just write up the papers that describe the deals. Maybe he wanted to get in on the action."

"Look, Rachel, to the extent Anderson got his rocks off 'doing deals,' he got plenty of that action as the managing partner. He got to 'do' the office lease, 'do' the firm's line of credit with the bank, 'do' the office supplies deal. For a corporate lawyer, that's like an all-you-can-eat weekend at the Mustang Ranch."

I paused and shook my head. "I just had a truly chilling realization."

"What?"

"I think that I've lost the capacity to be shocked by you."

"Now that," he said with a grin, "sounds like a direct challenge."

"God forbid. I surrender. Let's get back to Anderson. So you don't like my theory. Okay, if he didn't want the thrill of finally doing a deal, why did he do it?"

"Hey, who do I look like? The Incredible Karnak? I have

no fucking idea what made that guy tick. Now what about this ParaLex thing? Where does that fit in?''

I shook my head. "I don't know if it even does."

"What is it?"

"I don't know. It has a post office box. It has a bank account. And over the past three years it's been paid more than a hundred thousand dollars by the St. Louis office of Abbott & Windsor and close to forty thousand dollars by trusts administered by A & W. All in payment of invoices, each for two hundred dollars or less. Hundreds of invoices, apparently issued on a quarterly basis. And all for 'services rendered.' ParaLex sent invoices to Stoddard Anderson's clients. It sent invoices to Reed St. Germain's clients. It sent invoices to dozens of other A & W attorneys' clients."

"And this ParaLex outfit doesn't even have a listed telephone number?"

"Nope. And according to Nancy Winslow, the State of Missouri has no record of its existence. Same with Illinois."

Benny leaned back and crossed his arms. "That dog won't hunt."

I nodded. "I know. And someone else discovered that, too."

"Anderson?"

"Or St. Germain. They had a private dinner meeting ten days before Anderson disappeared."

"How do you know they talked about ParaLex?"

"An educated guess," I said. "I checked Anderson's pocket calendar. He had penciled in the word ParaLex on the night he met with St. Germain at the St. Louis Club. One of them left some papers there that night. They were three quarterly statements of account for A & W trusts and estates clients. Someone had circled the ParaLex payment on each statement."

"What does St. Germain say about the meeting?"

"He doesn't recall anything specific. He said that he used to have dinner meetings with Anderson. They would talk about management committee matters."

"What's he say about ParaLex?"

"When I first saw the name, I thought maybe Anderson

was having dinner that night with a client or maybe a prospective client named ParaLex. That was before I knew that Anderson had dinner that night with St. Germain. So when I asked St. Germain, all I asked was whether ParaLex was a new client.''

"And?"

"He said he didn't think so."

"Have you gone back to him since?"

"Not about ParaLex. I want to first pin down the facts. St. Germain's a slippery guy. I want to have as clear a picture as possible before I go back to him."

Benny rubbed his chin. "Hundred and forty grand over three years. What's that? Forty-seven grand a year?"

"Roughly."

"That's chickenshit. What do you think the annual revenues of the St. Louis office are?"

"Fifty lawyers in the office," I said. "At least fifteen million in revenues."

"Forty-seven grand." Benny mulled it over. "So you think Anderson caught him?"

"Maybe he caught Anderson," I said.

"Or maybe they were in it together."

"Or none of the above," I said. "But I just don't see the connection to Montezuma's Executor."

Benny shook his head. "You figure it out. Me, I'm like Rick in *Casablanca*. I came here for the waters. Speaking of which, you want a beer?"

"Maybe some apple juice. I had a lot of Mexican beer at dinner."

"Where do you have all those drafts of the suicide note?"

"In my briefcase. I'll get 'em and meet you in the kitchen."

"So how's your brother-in-law like the view in silicon valley?"

"What?" I asked, clinking a couple ice cubes into my glass of apple juice.

We were in the kitchen. Benny was at the table studying photocopies of the suicide note and the drafts that Mouse Aloni's people had found in the hotel room. I yawned as I closed the freezer door. It was close to midnight and I was feeling the lack of sleep. I'd been up for almost twenty hours.

"Your sister's new balcony."

"Oh. I haven't asked. Knowing him, I'm sure he loves it."

"Did you talk to Ann about it?"

"Yes."

"Why'd she do it?"

"Benny, it's none of your business."

He looked up, his nose scrunched. "Benny," he mimed, "it's none of your bees wax." He took a gulp of beer. "How much you think those knockers cost her?"

"I have no idea, Benny."

"I bet all her friends are getting theirs done, too." He leaned back and shook his head. "God, think of the money. I was a visionary, Rachel. A fucking prophet. Admit it. It was the best new franchise idea of the 'eighties. I could have put one in every city in America. By now I'd be on a first name basis with Robin Leach."

"Not with a franchise name like 'Breasts 'R Us.' "

"That's where you were always wrong, Rachel. It's a user-friendly name. Look at the stats. Most of the women getting boob jobs are mothers in their late thirties, early forties. Baby boomers. Growing kids and shrinking tits. They're looking in the mirror after the shower, maybe feeling a little depressed. Then they hear a radio commercial for 'Breasts 'R Us'—with a catchy little jingle. The name makes them smile. All those good memories come rushing back."

"Just think, Benny, you could have been the Ray Kroc of boobs."

"More like Burger King," he said. "Home of the Whoppers."

"I still think you would have had trouble staffing up the franchises with that name."

"That was always the easy part, Rachel. Plastic surgeons? Shit, those guys have no more shame than those baboons at the Lincoln Park Zoo that jerk off in their cage while everyone watches. Plastic surgeons are made to order for franchising. You think a self-respecting physician is going to do a liposuction? I mean, can you picture Marcus Welby or Dr. Kildare standing there holding something that looks like one of those Hoover vacuum cleaner accessories—one of those crevice tools—standing there sucking globs of fat out of some old lady's butt? Plastic surgeons? 'Breasts 'R Us' would have been a step up for most of those jackals.''

He leaned forward to study one of the drafts of the suicide note, instantly shifting gears. "The River Styx, eh?''

"The actual suicide note said it was 'safe underground.' Maybe he buried the Executor.''

"Now this is the strangest one," Benny said, studying the version that had taken Mouse Aloni so long to puzzle back together:

> Equation for M.E.
> C = MSD/AW
> RS = ROTF

"Why's he want to leave a message in code for the medical examiner?'' Benny mused.

I shrugged. "Got me.''

"You think it wasn't a suicide? You think he's trying to tell us that? You think that's why your mystery caller is trying to scare you away?''

"The police are convinced it was a suicide," I said. "And if it wasn't, why'd he tear up that note?''

"Maybe he decided he didn't want them to figure it out," Benny said. "Why else tear it to shreds?''

I was seated across the table from Benny, reading the message upside down. Maybe it was the upside down view that did it. Maybe it was finally being able to talk it out with someone. Whatever the reason, the meaning of "M.E." suddenly clicked.

"My God, I've got it, Benny. M.E. doesn't mean medical examiner. I bet it stands for Montezuma's Executor.''

"You think?''

"Sure. That's not an equation for the medical examiner. It's an equation for Montezuma's Executor. I bet it's a clue for how to find it!''

" 'C equals M-S-D slash A-W,' " Benny read. "C? What's C stand for?"

"Don't know." My heart was racing. "But I do know at least two MSDs. The Metropolitan Sewer District and the Missing Link."

"What the fuck is the Missing Link?"

"M. Salvatore Donalli."

"Who's that?"

"Client of Stoddard Anderson."

"How's he connected to this?"

"I don't know."

"You think the A and W is Abbott & Windsor?"

"Maybe. Or maybe Albert Weidemeir." I rummaged through my briefcase for my notes.

"Albert who?"

"Weidemeir. He works for the MSD." I kissed Benny on the forehead. "You're a genius."

"Not so fast. Who's RS? And ROTF?"

"RS could be Reed St. Germain."

"Think so?"

I shrugged. "It could be. He's not easy to figure out. I walked into his office this afternoon and guess who was in there with him? Remy Panzer."

"No shit. What was he doing in there?"

"I don't know. I walked in on a meeting. Three of them. St. Germain, Remy Panzer, and a hot little paralegal named Portia McKenzie."

"How hot?"

"Forget about her. From what I hear, she only goes for BSDs."

"Still, one can't be too careful these days, especially in light of what they did to your car. It may be prudent for me to frisk Miss McKenzie. Perhaps a body cavity search is in order."

"In your dreams, Goldberg. Actually, I tried to get her to tell me what the meeting was about, but she wouldn't."

"Did you ask St. Germain?"

"He was gone when I tried to find him."

"What department is that paralegal in?"

"Trusts and estates."

Benny pondered the issues as he took a sip of beer. "Who's the executor of Stoddard Anderson's estate?"

"Reed St. Germain."

Benny drained the beer can. "Curious." He looked down at the "Equation for M.E." sheet. "Who's ROTF?"

"Don't know."

Benny leaned back in the chair and crossed his arms over his chest. "Weird. Anderson carefully writes out this equation, and then he tears it up."

"Assume it's a clue to where he hid Montezuma's Executor. Maybe he decided that the clue was too easy. Maybe he was afraid that the wrong person would figure it out."

"Who's the wrong person?" Benny asked.

"I don't know. But I'm going to ask Sal Donalli tomorrow morning. I had this feeling he was holding out on me today when I asked him about Stoddard Anderson's last days."

"You think the Missing Link has the missing link?"

"It's worth a try."

CHAPTER

"Do you know Stoddard's widow?"

Sal Donalli took off his cap and ran his fingers through his hair. "I think I met her once."

"She's had a hard life, Sal."

"I guess so, losing her husband."

"It's a lot worse than that. Her only daughter is in an institution. Her only son had Down's syndrome. He's been dead for years. On top of all that, she's in a coma in intensive care. She's been there since she was attacked in her own home last week."

Sal winced. "Jesus Christ, that's awful."

I let him think about it.

It was Saturday morning. Benny had left early for his interviews at Washington University School of Law. We had agreed to meet at my office around noon.

Benny had been upset when he heard I was going to visit Donalli without him, but I explained that it was going to be tough enough getting Sal Donalli to open up to me alone; he'd never talk around someone new, especially someone with no affiliation to Stoddard Anderson's widow.

I had tracked Sal down at a construction site in South County, where he had been going over change orders with one of the foremen, who left shortly after I arrived. It was just the two of us now, standing out by the freshly poured foundation.

"If she recovers," I said to Donalli, "she'll still have a tough life ahead of her. Stoddard lost a lot of money in the stock market and in his real estate investments. He didn't leave her much. That piece of art is worth a lot of money, Sal. Stoddard took a big risk to get it. He wanted her to have it. It belongs to her, Sal. It's going to help her have a comfortable old age. Think if it was your wife."

Donalli shoved the cigar in his mouth and turned away. He walked around the perimeter of the concrete foundation, scratching the back of his head. I followed him. He stopped by a bulldozer and turned to me.

"How big you say this piece of art is?"

"About this big," I said, showing him with my hands.

He studied my hands and removed the cigar from his mouth. After a long pause, he took a deep breath and exhaled. "This conversation never took place," he said, pointing his cigar at me, "and I'll deny it on a stack of bibles. You understand?"

I nodded. "Of course."

"I didn't want to get involved in the first place. I did it only 'cause Stoddard done me some favors over the years."

"Tell me what you did."

"I hid a box for him."

"What kind of box."

"Steel. Like one of your safe deposit boxes at the bank, except this one had its own lock."

"When?"

"About a month before he died. Stoddard called me at home on a Sunday. Asked me to meet him at my office that night. I did. He showed up with that box. He told me he needed to hide it for a while. He knew I had one of them big safes in my office, and that we had round-the-clock security guards. Said he couldn't tell me what was in the box. Wanted my promise that I'd keep it secret, that I wouldn't open it."

"You mean it's in your office?" I asked in amazement.

"Was. Not anymore."

"What happened?"

"I had it in there for about a month. Practically forgot it was even there. Then one afternoon, out of the blue, Stod calls to tell me he wants it back. Sure, I say, come on by. He says to me he don't want anyone to see him there, could he pick it up that night? After dark. Somewhere away from the office, where no one would see us. Sure, I say. So I meet him at a job site that night around nine o'clock. I had the box in the trunk."

"When was this?"

Sal studied the foundation walls. "Wednesday, June nineteenth," he finally said.

"That was the day after he disappeared."

Sal nodded. "Didn't know it at the time. Found out later. Should have known something was up, though."

"Why?"

Sal turned to me. "Guy looked like shit. You gotta understand, Rachel, Stoddard Anderson don't never look like shit. Guy like that looks sharp even when he's taking a dump, you know what I mean. But that night, he looked worse than a bum. His clothes looked like he'd been sleeping in 'em, he smelled of booze, his hair was all messed up, hadn't shaved. The poor guy was going nuts."

"How so?"

"When I got out of the car without the box he went crazy. 'Where is it, where is it?' he yells. I tried to calm him down, but all he wanted was the box. So I opened the trunk and gave it to him. He thanked me like crazy, tears running down his face, begged me to promise to never tell anyone, which I did. And I kept that promise until today. I never told no one until you, Rachel."

"What happened after that?"

Sal shrugged. "He left. Got in his car, revved the engine, and laid a patch getting out of there." Donalli shook his head. "I gotta tell you, Rachel, his brain wasn't hitting on all cylinders that night."

"Where did he go?"

"No idea. That was the last time I seen him. Two days later I open the paper over breakfast and about coughed up my poached egg when I seen that article on him disappearing. I almost called the police, but I remembered my promise to him. And anyway, what could I tell the cops? I hadn't seen him since that night. I didn't know where he'd gone. So I kept mum.''

"You never heard from him again?''

"Nothing. Last time I saw him was that night. I don't know what was in that box, and I don't know what he did with it.''

As I got out of the car, I decided to do it by telephone instead of in person. I thought the odds might be better that way, especially on a Saturday morning. So I placed the call to the First State Bank of Creve Coeur from the pay phone in the parking lot of the First State Bank of Creve Coeur. The receptionist connected me to someone named Doris in account inquiries.

"Doris, this is Annie Goodman at Kendell Exports," I said, trying to sound just a tad breathless. "I'm Mr. Kendell's secretary. Mr. Kendell Senior, that is. I'm calling to check on a wire transfer.''

"Incoming or outgoing?" Doris asked.

"Incoming. Mr. Kendell told me to make *sure* that First National wired eleven thousand dollars into one of your accounts yesterday afternoon. He wants to confirm that it got there.''

"What's that account number?''

I gave her the ParaLex account number I had copied off the back of the canceled checks I'd found in Portia McKenzie's files. Doris told me to hold while she checked on the computer.

"I'm sorry, Miss Goodman," she said after a minute. "There was no wire transfer into that account yesterday.''

"None? That can't be. Are you positive?''

"I'm sorry, Miss Goodman. Nothing yesterday.''

"Wait a minute, wait a minute. Oh, maybe I have the wrong account number. I'm supposed to have the number for the ParaLex account.''

"You have the right account number. That's the ParaLex account.''

"Oh, no," I said, sounding more frantic. "Could you check

the other ParaLex accounts? Maybe the money got sent to one of the other ParaLex accounts.''

"I'm showing only one account for ParaLex, Miss Goodman.''

"Oh, no. Oh, no. What do I do?''

"I don't know. I wish I could help.''

"My boss is out of town. I don't know how to reach him. He thinks the people at ParaLex already have the money. My heavens, the ParaLex people must think they have the money, too. Have they called to confirm the transfer?''

"I don't believe so, Miss Goodman.''

"I've already tried their office number. No one answers. I've got to get in touch with them. Today. Who should I call?''

"I don't know, Miss Goodman. Who do you normally deal with at ParaLex?''

"That's the problem,'' I moaned. "I've never talked to them before. Do you know who their president is?''

"I don't,'' she said.

"Well, who has signing authority on the account?''

There was a pause. *C'mon, Doris,* I silently begged, my fingers crossed.

"I'm sorry, Miss Goodman. We're not supposed to give that information out over the phone.''

"Oh, please, Doris. I have to let them know. My boss will absolutely kill me if I don't.''

Another pause. "I don't know,'' came the reply, but this time with less conviction.

"I won't tell anyone, Doris. I promise. All I want to do is call them and tell them the money will be in their account first thing Monday morning. I just have to reach them before Mr. Kendell does. You have no idea what a terrible temper that man has. Please, Doris.''

Another minute of groveling did it. Doris took a deep breath, paused, and then told me the name of the person with signing authority on the ParaLex account.

I absorbed the information in silence. "Are there any other names on the account?''

"No. No one else.''

"No one added in the last month or so?"

"No one."

"Thank you, Doris."

I hung up the phone and stared at the passing traffic on Olive Boulevard, weighing my options. After a few minutes, I removed my long distance credit card and dialed a familiar Chicago number.

Reed St. Germain had on his Saturday-at-the-office outfit—an all Land's End set featuring a white crewneck sweater over a green Oxford cloth button-down shirt, khaki pleated twills, tan ragg socks, and tan bucks. He was seated against the edge of his desk, posed, arms loosely crossed over his chest, sleeves of his sweater and shirt pushed back toward the elbows.

"Isn't this somewhat far afield from the focus of your investigation?" he said, ignoring the pending question.

"I don't know," I answered. "Remy Panzer is one of the last people Stoddard Anderson spent time with before he disappeared. I interviewed Panzer on Thursday. He never mentioned anyone at the firm other than Stoddard Anderson. I was surprised to see him in your office on Friday. To the extent your meeting with him related to Stoddard Anderson, I don't think it is 'far afield.' "

"Now Rachel," he said, his face softening into Smile No. 7 from *The Managing Partners Handbook* (Legal Press, 1988), "there's nothing sinister going on here. Remy Panzer happens to be a client of the firm. As with any client, he has a legitimate expectation that the legal affairs he entrusts to us are protected from disclosure by the attorney-client privilege. I can assure you that our legal services for Mr. Panzer have no relation to the insurance matter you are investigating. How *is* that going, Rachel? Any idea when you'll be wrapping it up?"

"I have a meeting with the claims guy from the insurance company on Tuesday morning. It all depends whether I can get all my ducks in order by then. Look, Reed, I don't need to know the details of your work for Panzer. But I do need to know whether Panzer's matter touches on *anything* having to do with Stoddard Anderson.''

"Really, Rachel. As we both know, you've been retained *solely* on the insurance matter. I've seen the retention letter. If and when Mrs. Anderson elects to expand the scope of your services, we can discuss this again. Until then, you are going to have to take my word for it: What we are doing for Remy Panzer has no bearing on what you have been retained to do for Mrs. Anderson.''

"You better be right, Reed.''

He chuckled, Smile No. 7 ("We're in this together") replaced by Smile No. 4 ("Don't fuck with me, honey"). "I *better* be right? Come now, Rachel, we are hardly adversaries.''

"That's my assumption, too. But you have to understand: I have a client to represent. I don't know you well enough to take your word for it—at least not when it might affect my client. As far as I'm concerned, the only one whose word counts here is Ishmael Richardson's. He's the one who retained me. You can surely tell him what you're doing for Panzer without breaching the attorney-client privilege. If Ishmael tells me to take *his* word for it, then I will.''

I gave him back a Smile No. 4. His right eye twitched.

"I have to talk to Ishmael tomorrow afternoon, Reed. He wants to hear a report on the status of my Stoddard Anderson investigation. I think he wants to hear from you, too. In fact, he asked if you'd be available. I told him I assumed you would be. I'm supposed to call him at three o'clock. I told him I'd make the call from the office. That way, if we miss connections he'll know where to contact me. And you, I guess. Here's what I'll do. I'll step out of the room during the call and you can tell him what you're doing for Remy Panzer. Then you can call me back in. We'll let him make the decision. If Ishmael tells me it's none of my business, I'll drop it. Okay?''

I said it all with a pleasant smile on my face—my we're-in-this-together smile.

By the time I finished, Reed St. Germain looked like he

was about to pop a few rivets. Breathing deeply through his flared nostrils, he stared at me. "I'll be here at three tomorrow," he finally said.

So much for future referral business from Reed St. Germain, I said to myself as I walked out of his office.

CHAPTER

The phone was answered on the third ring.

"Yo."

"Hi. This is Rachel Gold. Is Nancy Winslow there?"

"Just a sec. Mom! . . . Mom!! . . . For you. . . . Don't know. Some gal."

A moment of silence.

"Hello?"

"Nancy, it's Rachel Gold. Sorry to call you on a Saturday."

"No problem. I was just cleaning the garage. What's up?"

"I've been trying to get in touch with a Dr. Bernstein. Mr. Anderson saw him about a week before he disappeared, according to his appointment calendar. I called Bernstein's office yesterday and left my name with his receptionist. He never returned my call. I called again this morning. I got his answering service. They told me they'd give him my message, but I still haven't heard from him."

"Dr. Bernstein?"

"He's a dermatologist."

"Okay."

"Ring any bells?"

"Name sounds familiar. I probably made the appointment for Mr. Anderson."

"Did he tell you why he was going to see a dermatologist?"

"I doubt it, Rachel. If he did, I sure don't remember."

"Any ideas?"

"A skin doctor. Hmmm."

"Acne? Eczema?"

"I don't think so."

"You notice any sort of rash?"

"All I can think of is maybe dandruff? Don't dermatologists treat dandruff?"

"I think so," I said. "Did he have bad dandruff?"

"I never noticed it much before. But over the last month or so, I guess it must have flared up—if that's what dandruff does."

"How do you mean?"

"You could really notice it when he wore a dark suit. It'd be all over the shoulders. I'm sure it bothered him. He was real fussy about appearances. He never said anything to me about it, but I'd see him brushing it off his jacket when he left the office."

"Anything else besides dandruff?"

"Not that I noticed, Rachel."

"And Mr. Anderson never talked to you about his visit to Dr. Bernstein?"

"Not that I recall."

"Dandruff?" Benny repeated. "You got to be shitting me."

"Not necessarily dandruff," I said. "It could have been something else. Dandruff is what his secretary guessed."

It was 12:30 P.M. Benny had just arrived at the office after a morning of interviews with faculty members and the dean of the law school.

"From a gold Aztec dildo to a case of dandruff," Benny said, pacing the office. "Talk about going from the sublime to the ridiculous."

"Which is the sublime?"

He stopped and grinned. "Good point." He sat down in

the chair across from the desk and propped his feet on the edge of the desktop. "Any luck finding that guy at the sewer district?"

"Still no answer at his home. He's due back at work on Monday. I'm hoping he'll be home by tonight or tomorrow."

"So what's your guess now? Does MSD stand for that Donalli guy or for the Metropolitan Sewer District?"

"Probably the sewer district," I said. "Donalli had no idea where Anderson went after he left with the steel box. I don't know why Anderson would have used Donalli's initials if Sal didn't know where it was."

"Maybe Anderson wrote that note the first night in the hotel. Before he saw Donalli. Maybe that's why he decided to tear the note up. Because it was no longer an accurate clue."

"Or maybe he wrote it after the second night, and MSD stands for the sewer district."

"All I know is I am starved," Benny said, standing up. "I got me a powerful hunger for some hickory-smoked pig snouts. How's that sound?"

"Absolutely disgusting."

"Ribs?"

"Better."

"Shall we?"

I looked over at the list of names I still hadn't contacted. I looked at the *60 Minutes* videocassette I still hadn't viewed. I looked up at Benny and gave a weary sigh.

Benny gave me an elaborate bow. "Of course, my darling. I would be delighted to bring you back some ribs. Perhaps madam would like some cole slaw and fried sweet potatoes as well?"

"My hero. Benny, you are really going to make a wonderful husband for one of those blond, leggy shiksas of yours."

He put his hand over his heart. "I'm saving myself for you."

"Which reminds me, Benny. Speaking of blond, leggy shiksas, what's the story with you and Gwendolyn the runway model? The one with stilts for legs."

"The story?"

"Is it getting serious?"

He blushed, caught off guard. "Depends on what you mean by serious," he said, trying to sound offhand.

"You know what I mean. Are you guys doing it?"

"Jesus Christ, Rachel."

Behind him, Melvin Needlebaum suddenly appeared in the doorway.

"Aha!" Melvin barked. "The receptionist was not hallucinating. It is indeed you, Benjamin."

Benny turned and grinned. "Mel, baby, how's the main vein?"

Melvin giggled. "Uhh, up tight," he recited, "and, uhh, out of sight."

It was the opening riff to their old routine, back from the days when we were all young associates at Abbott & Windsor. Benny and Melvin had shared an office their freshman year at A & W. For the first six months or so, Benny detested Melvin, whom he called "the Geek."

But then something magic happened. Benny returned to the office one night after having downed several beers with a few college buddies passing through Chicago. Melvin was still there—Melvin was always still there. For the first time, Benny and Melvin actually had a conversation, the substance of which Benny never disclosed. And then, wonder of wonders, Benny invited Melvin back to his apartment, where Melvin smoked his first—and only—joint and listened to all of Benny's Firesign Theater albums. Benny had listened to those albums hundreds of times—enough to have memorized most of the comedy routines, a feat Melvin matched after just one play of each record. From that night on, Melvin was no longer "the Geek." Instead, Benny called him "my science fair project." He and Melvin worked up a bizarre routine—a grab bag of rock lyrics, Firesign Theater routines, and other stuff—that lasted fifteen minutes. They sprang it on the rest of us in the firm cafeteria the next morning, and it became an instant associates' classic.

"My liege," Benny said to Melvin, "what has happened to your nose?"

"I, uhh, just returned from Rome."

"What-what?"

"What-what-what-what?"

"Excellent, Mel, excellent." Benny looked at me and winked. "This fucking guy is totally insane. This guy is beyond New Wave. M.C. Eraserhead." He turned to Melvin. "Are you sure you didn't do a lot of acid back in college?"

"Hydrochloric or sulfuric?" Melvin answered, punctuating it with a machine-gun burst of laughter.

"Hey, Mel, I heard you took Rachel out to dinner last night."

"Indeed I did. An excellent meal. We also dined with a tall Hispanic attorney by the name of Salazar. Mr. Salazar and I engaged in a most stimulating discussion of the sale of tax benefits under ERTA's Safe Harbor Lease provision."

"You talked about the sale of tax benefits, eh?" Benny turned to me. "My condolences, Rachel."

"You're very kind," I said.

"Say Mel, you want to put on the old feed bag?"

"What?"

"Satisfy the inner man? Stuff your face?"

"What?"

"Eat lunch, you douche bag."

"I regret that I must decline your offer, Benjamin. Earlier today I arranged in advance for delivery of a sandwich, a dill pickle, and a large iced tea to the southeast conference room at precisely one P.M." He checked his watch. "I am due back at my deposition in fifteen minutes." He nodded at me. "Good day, Miss Gold. Good day, Benjamin."

And with that, he was gone.

Benny stroked his chin. "You notice, you never see him and Joe Montana in the same room at the same time. Makes you wonder, doesn't it?"

"Now that you mention it, I've never seen you and Roseanne Barr in the same room, either."

"Very astute, Miss Gold. You think I sing off-key by accident?"

"Speaking of keys, that reminds me. Can you do me a favor when you go get lunch?" I sorted through my purse and removed a small, folded-up envelope. "Here," I said, handing it to Benny. "There's a key in there."

"To what?"

"I don't know, but I have a hunch. It's the only key on Stoddard Anderson's key chain that the police couldn't match to a lock. Anderson apparently rented a post office box downtown. I saw this month's bill." I leafed through my notes on the yellow legal pad. "It arrived after the police inventoried his stuff. They don't know about it. Ah, here's the number."

On a separate piece of paper I copied down the post office box number and address and handed it to Benny. "See if he got any mail since he died," I said.

"Aye, aye."

After Benny left, I reached for the *60 Minutes* videocassette on Tezca and the Aztlana religious cult. I still hadn't seen it. If Tezca was behind the quest for Montezuma's Executor, as Ferd Fingersh and the Customs people suspected, there might be something worthwhile on the videotape.

I walked down the hall in search of a television and a VCR.

CHAPTER 22

Even in black silhouette, with the background darkened as well to protect her identity, you could see her lips quiver.

"Then," she said, her voice quavering, "he opened his robe. I could hear all those people down below. They were standing all around the pyramid and they were chanting, 'Tezca, Tezca, Tezca.' Over and over and over. And then that horrible woman told me—ordered me—to take his . . . to put his penis in my mouth."

"And did you?" asked the offscreen voice.

She was motionless, rigid. And then, slowly, she nodded her head twice, stopping with her head pointed down, her shoulders slumped.

"Was that the first time they made you do that? Up on the pyramid?"

She shook her head.

"How many times?" asked the offscreen voice.

She didn't say anything, but you could see her shoulders beginning to shake. "Ten times," she finally gasped, collapsing in tears.

The scene shifted to Ed Bradley, facing the camera, no jacket, top two buttons of his khaki shirt unbuttoned, squinting into the New Mexico sun. Visible in the background was the great pyramid of Aztlana—a four-sided pyramid, built in steep, receding blocks. There was a broad stone stairway leading from the base to the apex of the pyramid. At the top of the stairs was a large ceremonial courtyard paved with elaborate patterns of aquamarine and scarlet tiles. Beyond the courtyard was Tezca's ritual chamber, which had white adobe walls and a multicolored slate roof.

The ceremonial courtyard was where, once a month—the scene illuminated by the full moon, his chanting followers ringing the base of the pyramid—the former Arthur A. Nevins, one-time C.P.A. with Price Waterhouse, ejaculated onto the face and neck of one of his sacrificial maidens.

"It is a town of stark contrasts," Ed Bradley said into the camera. "Named after the mythical homeland of the ancient Aztecs, it has become the real homeland of four thousand modern Americans, most of them drop-outs from the world of investment banking, law, and accounting—a town where J.D. means John Deere and C.P.A. stands for three of the town's crops, corn, potatoes, and apricots. But set against this pastoral background are tales of a complex web of offshore investments, tales of torture and beatings and homicide, tales of sexual slavery, tales of women forced to perform sodomy atop the pyramid on the man known simply as Tezca."

The camera panned slowly along the base of the four-sided pyramid, where hundreds of smiling men, women, and little children were milling around, many shading their eyes as they look heavenward.

"It is noon in Aztlan, town of contrasts, and Tezca's followers are gathered around the pyramid to greet their leader."

The camera panned heavenward, slowly sweeping the cloudless blue sky, freezing on the sun, which seemed on fire. You could hear the sounds of mothers talking to young children, people laughing, someone selling lemonade—sounds you might hear along Main Street before the Fourth of July parade.

"Like the ancient Aztec sun god, Tezca appears from the sky. Unlike the ancient Aztec sun god, Tezca arrives in a Lear jet."

The distant roar of an approaching jet. Buzzing among the

crowd. Mothers pointing to the sky. A dark dot emerging from among the mountains. A black jet, high above the desert floor. And then it tilts, and then it goes into a screeching dive toward the pyramid. Pulling up at the last minute, the jet spins, slowly corkscrewing, as it climbs toward the sun and disappears. The crowd cheers.

The story shifted to several scenes of pastoral life in Aztlana, intercut with sound bites from angry or frightened New Mexico citizens and national commentators on the town's growing power. The speakers included a UCLA professor of religion on the distortion of Aztec religious customs, a psychiatrist from Manhattan on why former Wall Street investment bankers are so attracted to a religious movement that attaches evangelical significance to the moment of orgasm, a Connecticut D.A. seeking to indict Tezca on charges of taking money under false pretenses, a teary mother and father of a cult member ("He was such a good boy"), a C.P.A. who had worked with Tezca back at Price Waterhouse ("Arthur was just your basic quiet, conservative type"), a New Mexico highway trooper with photographs of three corpses (all dissident former members of the cult) that he believed were executed on direct orders from Tezca.

Then the story cut to a black-and-white portrait photograph from a high school yearbook circa 1968. The subject of the photograph had longish brown hair, bangs almost to his eyes, muttonchop sideburns, thick horn-rim glasses slightly askew, bad teeth. He looked like a slide-rule nerd. The black print under the photograph identified him as Arthur A. Nevins. The list of activities beneath his name read:

> Esperanto Club 3, 4; Model United Nations 3, Audio-Visual Club 4.

His quote was:

> "Quiet conceals great movement beneath."

The Ed Bradley voice-over summarized his high school years in Cleveland and then his years at Ohio State, as the high school shot dissolved into his college yearbook photograph: hair now shoulder length, glasses now wire-rim but still askew, face now adorned with a chin-strap beard, white T-shirt with a red silk-screened clenched fist. Then his years at Price Waterhouse's Houston office, the college yearbook photograph dissolving into his accounting firm glossy: hair shorter now and neatly trimmed, wire-rims replaced by the old horn-rims (but now perfectly level), face clean-shaven but a little pudgy, crisp white shirt, repp tie, dark three-button suit.

The voice-over moved through his years at Price Water-house, the murky origins of his religion, the recruiting of accountants and lawyers at tax seminars and conferences around the nation, his following gradually growing, until the founding of the town of Aztlana.

And then the black-and-white glossy from the Price Water-house days slowly dissolved into a live color shot of Tezca, staring into the camera. The softness was gone, the flab burned off, the flesh pared down. A narrow, bony face. Hollow cheeks, lines around the mouth, thin lips.

From the neck up, Tezca looked like a battle-hardened marine: close-cropped hair, veins at the temples, sinewy neck, sun-darkened skin, no glasses. From the neck down he was all cult leader: He wore a long, multicolored caftan decorated with orange serpents, a red sash at the waist, and thick leather sandals.

He sat motionless as he listened to Ed Bradley's questions. He paused before each response, his nostrils flaring. His voice was low, almost without affect, the words precise. He didn't rise to the bait of Bradley's allegations of sexual misconduct and financial irregularities. But when Bradley raised the state troopers' investigation into the violent deaths of the three former members of the cult, Tezca shook his head in disgust and announced, "This interview is over."

The report ended with a close-up freeze frame of his glowering eyes.

I popped out the videocassette and returned to my office. No leads to Montezuma's Executor, but a fascinating, almost chilling, glimpse of the man who might be out there in pursuit of the Executor, who might have had a hand in the attack on

Dottie Anderson. According to Ferd Fingersh, Tezca went into hiding just around the time Remy Panzer thought that Anderson had smuggled the Executor into the country.

Putting the videocassette in the top drawer of the desk, I reached for the list of names I had put together from Anderson's calendars, correspondence, and message slips. I still had about ten names left to contact.

The few who were in that day couldn't recall anything helpful other than that Stoddard Anderson had seemed somewhat distracted some of the time. So do I. So do you. Clues don't come easy.

I was studying the photocopies of Anderson's appointment calendar when Benny returned. I looked up at the crinkling sound of the two grocery bags full of barbecue goodies. The hickory smoke followed him into the room.

"If you've got snouts in there," I said, "you'd better eat your lunch down in the confer—" The look on his face stopped me.

"What is it?" I asked.

"I visited your man's post office box."

"The key fit?"

He nodded, setting down the big brown bags. "I think we may have stumbled on an alternative explanation for why it had been so long since Stoddard Anderson had his knob polished at home." He peered into one of the bags.

"Did you find love letters?"

Benny glanced over with a rueful smile. "Hardly." He reached into the bag and pulled out two glossy magazines. "Check these out," he said as he tossed them onto the desk. "Not exactly *U.S. News and World Report*."

The one on top was entitled *Naughty Boys*. The cover had a gray-haired man kneeling behind a naked boy of maybe twelve years of age; the man had his tongue pressed into the crack of the boy's buttocks. I leafed through the magazine. Its clinical explicitness made *Hustler* look like *Better Homes & Gardens*—except there wasn't one female in the entire magazine. Page after page of preteen boys and older men—masturbating each other; engaging in anal intercourse; urinating on one another;

performing fellatio; ejaculating onto stomachs, backs, and faces; arranged in various S & M poses; wearing masks; wielding whips; preening in leather. Dizzy, I closed the magazine, and found myself staring at a color ad for a gay phone sex outfit called Wet Daydreams. The ad featured a blond stud "named" Sean who was holding a telephone and wearing nothing but thigh-high leather boots and a pair of tiny white briefs stretched tight over an ominous bulge. Sean took Mastercard and Visa. I took a deep breath.

"It could have been put in his P.O. box by mistake," I said.

Benny shook his head. "It came in this." He pulled a brown wrapper out of the grocery bag and handed it to me. "See that?"

The mailing label had Anderson's post office box number on it.

I put the wrapper down and reached for the other publication, which turned out to be a catalog from some mail order house called The New Greek Isles. Anderson's post office box number was on this mailing label, too.

"Oh, God," I mumbled as I opened to page one, which featured rows of dildos and leather restraining devices. There were pages of ads for hardcore gay kiddie porn videotapes, ads for sets of hardcore kiddie porn photographs, sexual devices, varieties of lubricants, a rainbow of condoms. Much of the ad copy was clearly geared toward pederasts and chickenhawks. There was even a page of kinky outfits for boys, including crotchless lederhosen.

I pushed both publications away from me and turned toward the window. Benny unpacked our lunch behind me.

Each piece of evidence clicked into place, one after another. His sexual "impotence" with his wife. The opened twelve-pack of condoms the police found in his desk drawer. The unaccounted-for activities after work. The absence of any rumors about sexual affairs.

The public Stoddard Anderson—family man, conservative Republican, member of Civic Progress, St. Louis establishment, gay basher—was a facade, carefully constructed around a private life of pick-up sex with preteen boys.

"That son of a bitch," I muttered.

"Anderson?" Benny said, gnawing on a barbecued rib.

"No. Remy Panzer."

CHAPTER

"Come, come, Rachel."

"You were blackmailing him, weren't you?" The anger made my ears ring.

"Blackmail?" Remy Panzer repeated, swiveling his chair so that he was facing me. Slowly, calmly, he placed his arms flat on his desk. "Such a vulgar word." He gave me a frigid stare. "It conjures such crude images."

"Crude images?" I said, outraged. "From what I hear, you're the expert in crude images." I paced over to the antique globe in the corner of his office. "You supplied him with boys, didn't you?"

His eyes were cold, dead.

"Of course you did," I said. "Stoddard Anderson wasn't the type to cruise the streets and parks for boys."

"I detect disdain in your voice."

"Disgust is more like it."

"Such a disappointment, Rachel. It suggests such a conventional—such a provincial set of values in what I had hoped was neither a conventional nor a provincial woman. Look to history. Take the grand view. What puritan America outlaws, Plato celebrated."

"Come on, Remy. The gay part doesn't bother me."

"You're needlessly overwrought, Rachel. Try to understand, not all of us are breeders."

"Stoddard Anderson pretended he was until the end. He had to. And you used that. Like a noose around his neck."

"Stoddard wore a mask. A mask of convention for a conventional world. I was honored to know the real Stoddard Anderson."

"You were *honored* to know him? Honored to know someone who got his jollies screwing eleven-year-old boys in the butt? Don't B.S. me, Remy. Of the many words you could use to describe your relationship with Stoddard, honor wasn't one of them. What was the evidence you used to blackmail him? Photos? Videotapes?"

He averted his eyes momentarily when I said "videotape." Just a fraction of a second, and then he forced himself to meet my stare. "Come, come, Rachel. This isn't an episode of *Police Woman.*"

"No wonder he agreed to help you get the Executor. If he didn't do your bidding, you could destroy him. Ruin his career, ruin his future." I paused to catch my breath. "I just knew it had to be something besides the money."

He gave a world-weary sigh. "Money? It hardly matters now, does it?"

I said nothing. Benny was out in the gallery, waiting for me.

"Rachel, let us assume, arguendo, this overheated hypothesis of yours. Let us assume I blackmailed him. I forced him to do my bidding. Okay? Let's assume it all. Nevertheless, how in the world could a dead Stoddard Anderson further my goals? Indeed, how could a dead Stoddard Anderson do anything other than threaten to completely vitiate my quest? And just at my moment of triumph. How, Rachel? Explain that."

I paused. "I can't," I admitted.

"Nor can I. Now listen to me. Somewhere in St. Louis, even as we speak, is the most remarkable treasure of the Aztec empire. It's there. I know it. You know it. Stoddard Anderson is dead. I can't change that. You can't change that. He's dead.

Forever. We're still alive. But not forever. You can't simply walk away from this, Rachel. This is history. You've become one of the links reaching back in time to the Emperor Montezuma himself.''

He paused to remove a cigarette from his gold case. He tapped it on the case to pack the tobacco and then he lit it. Leaning back in his chair, he blew a stream of smoke toward the chandelier overhead. As the smoke dissipated, he turned to me.

"You don't like me, Rachel.''

"That's irrelevant,'' I answered.

"Precisely my point. Like a doctor and his patients, a lawyer does not select clients based on whether the lawyer happens to like them. Liking a client, admiring a client—completely irrelevant.'' He leaned forward, pointing the cigarette at me. "I'm just another client, Rachel,'' he said slowly, forcefully. Then he leaned back. "Actually,'' he mused, "not just another client. I happen to be a client willing to pay your client a handsome fee for the return of what belongs to me. I bought it, Rachel. It's mine. You may not like me. But surely that is not a disqualification under your professional code. Correct?''

I quelled my disgust with thoughts of Ferd Fingersh leading Remy Panzer away in handcuffs, shoving him into the back of a blue government sedan. I obviously couldn't bring down Remy Panzer alone. If there ever had been a videotape of Stoddard Anderson, it was long gone. Panzer was no fool. The police would never find evidence of blackmail, and even if they did, so what? Any decent criminal lawyer could throw enough reasonable doubt onto the blackmail scenario to get an acquittal. And meanwhile, the resulting hoopla could seriously sidetrack, or even fatally undermine, the Mexican government's quest for Montezuma's Executor. I thought of Rafe Salazar. *Play along, Rachel, play along. Stoddard Anderson's dead. You're not going to bring him back to life. Getting mad won't help. Get even.*

I softened my look and tried an abashed shrug. "Correct,'' I said, trying to sound submissive.

"Good.'' He smiled. "If the money is insufficient . . .'' He let it linger out there.

I shook my head. "A deal is a deal," I said. "The money's fine."

"Then find it, Rachel. Bring it to me. It's more than just a quarter of a million dollars. It's your moment in history. It's the adventure of a lifetime."

Ten minutes later, on the way to the car, I turned to Benny. "So help me God, whatever else happens, I want to make sure we nail that creep."

From Panzer's gallery we drove west. I had four box-seat tickets to the Cardinals' game against the Mets that night. Benny and I got back to my sister's house with enough time for me to change into the red clothing that all true Cardinal fans must wear to the stadium. For me, that meant an oversized red cotton mock turtleneck with the sleeves pushed up, matching red cotton canvas espadrilles, and a pair of baggy khaki shorts with double front pleats. My niece and nephew were literally jumping with excitement about the game. On my way out the door I had time to skim the telephone message my sister had taken from Melvin Needlebaum:

> Melvin Needlebum (sp?) called from airport. On his way back to Chicago. Said he found answer to question. The fathers were Jesuit priests. Father Gabriel Marest and Father Francois Pinet. Built Indian mission around 1700 at mouth of river. Indians part of Cahokia empire. Largest Indian empire since pre-Columbus (sp?) Aztecs.

"What fathers?" Benny asked when he read the message.

"It's a long story," I said as I ushered my niece and nephew into the car.

At quarter after twelve that night, after the baseball game (Cards won), after the postgame Ted Drewes' custard concretes for the four of us, after tucking the kids in bed, after saying goodnight to my sister and Richie—after all that, as we sat in the kitchen, Benny had a thought.

"I have a thought," he said. He was staring at the draft suicide note, the one headlined "Equation for M.E." "The RS doesn't have to be Reed St. Germain. The real suicide note says it's safe underground. Another draft mentioned the River Styx. Maybe the RS is the River Styx. Maybe Anderson hid it near some underground river. It says RS equals ROTF. You know any underground river or cave with those initials?''

"The only river I know of that runs underground is the River Des Peres.''

"RDP. Nope.''

"Caves?'' I mused. "Meramec Caverns. Onondaga Cave. There are supposed to be hundreds of little caves in south St. Louis. The Mississippi carved them out of the limestone. I guess it could be in any of them. I sure can't think of one that starts with an R.''

"If it's a cave,'' Benny mused, "then RS doesn't stand for River Styx. He'd have used some other code name.''

"You're probably right. Unless there was a river in the cave.''

"River on . . .'' Benny tried, letting it hang there. "River over . . . river of . . . River onto . . .''

"Melvin!'' I said. "God bless him. It *is* the River Des Peres. Remember that crazy message from Melvin? The names of the fathers. Well, last night he told me Des Peres is French for 'of the fathers.' River Des Peres means River of the Fathers. He had called to give me the names of the two fathers.''

"God damn, that's it. RS equals ROTF. So the River Styx is the River Des Peres.''

"And the C,'' I nearly shouted, "the C has to be Charon, ferryman of the River Styx.''

"C equals MSD slash AW,'' Benny read. "You think the AW is that guy on vacation. The one with the Metropolitan Sewer District.''

"Due back in the office on Monday. I hope he's back from vacation tomorrow. He's got to be our man. I've got to talk to him.''

"Maybe he's home now.''

I checked my watch. "Now?''

"You tried him before the ballgame, back around dinner.

What was that? Six hours ago? Maybe he's home now. Call him now, we might catch him off guard."

Five minutes later I was dialing Albert Weidemeir's telephone number. Benny was in the den by the extension, waiting for my signal that the call was going through.

"Okay," I shouted softly. I heard Benny lift his receiver. "You ready?"

"Yeah, yeah," he said.

"You've got to do the talking if his wife answers. I don't want her to think I'm some girlfriend."

"Don't worry, Rachel." There was the clicking noise on the line that signaled the phone was about to start ringing on the other end. "They don't call me Cool Hand Luke for nothing."

"I've never heard *anyone* call you Cool Hand Luke." It started to ring. "Okay," I whispered.

A woman answered on the fourth ring. "Hello?" She sounded flustered.

"Howdy, Miz Weidemeir," Benny said in a deep, friendly voice. "This here's Jenner Block down at the Sewer District. We got ourselves a little problem up at the Backwash Station. One of them Kirkland Ellis screws went out on us, ma'am. I just wanted to ask your husband a couple questions about it, seeing it's in his territory, so to speak. Be much obliged, ma'am."

"Certainly, Mr. Block. Let me put him on." I could hear her in the background waking him up.

"Jenner Block?" I whispered to Benny. "Backwash Station? Kirkland Ellis screws?"

"Yes'm," Benny said, still in the role. "You have one of your Kirkland Ellis screws lock up on you and might as well bend over and kiss your sorry ass good-bye."

There was a fumbling with the phone on the other end, and muffled voices.

"Hello?" said a male voice.

"Mr. Weidemeir," I said, my voice level but insistent, "just listen to me and nod your head every once in a while so that your wife won't get nervous. My name is Rachel Gold. I'm investigating Stoddard Anderson's death. You had an important meeting with him that the police don't know about. Yet. I'd like to keep it that way, Mr. Weidemeir. Now, why don't you say something like—like, 'Yep, you'll need to clear the pipeline.' It'll make your wife think you're talking to someone from the Sewer District. Go ahead.''

He cleared his throat. "Uh, yeah, you'll, uh, need to clear, uh, clear the, uh, pipeline.''

"Good,'' I said. Sir Laurence Olivier he wasn't. Nervous, though, he was, and that was just fine for my purposes.

"Mr. Weidemeir,'' I continued, "I'd especially like to make sure we can help you avoid legal problems with some of the activities that Mr. Anderson was involved in during the last weeks of his life. Some of those activities may have violated the law, Mr. Weidemeir. Now I don't presently believe that you did anything wrong.''

"I didn't,'' he blurted out before catching himself. "Uh, right,'' he stammered, "uh, you'll need to, uh, clear the pipeline.''

"As I say, I don't have any reason to think you did anything wrong, but the police might not see it that way. Neither might the FBI.''

"The FBI?''

"Exactly. Which is why you need to meet with me. Tomorrow. Understand?''

"Yes.''

"How does noon sound?''

"Okay.''

"Somewhere public. How about the Dinosaur Park behind the Science Center in Forest Park. By the triceratops. At noon?''

"Okay.''

"Very good. Now, why don't you end this call like I'm from the Sewer District. For your wife.''

There was a pause. He cleared his throat. "Okay. Uh, well, right, uh, just remember that, uh, you'll need to, uh, clear out the, uh, pipeline. So long.''

Click. Followed by Benny's click.

A moment later Benny walked into the kitchen.

"Well?" I asked.

He grinned. "I think our buddy Albert Weidemeir may be dunking his pajama bottoms in the toilet about now."

"I wanted to make sure he'd be nervous."

"I think you made sure of that. That boy just had himself a fiber optics enema compliments of Southwestern Bell."

CHAPTER 24

I was leaning against the left front leg of the triceratops with my arms crossed over my chest. I stared up at the tyrannosaurus that towered overhead. Its open mouth revealed a menacing set of teeth—dozens and dozens of long white daggers. Kids had thrown five, six, seven tennis balls into its mouth. The yellow balls rested against the bottom row of teeth like a mouthful of lemon drops.

I was in Dinosaur Park, a small hollow in the southeast part of Forest Park that was screened from view by a circle of trees. Dinosaur Park is just below and behind the Science Center, which is perched on a hill overlooking Highway 40. It has two permanent residents: a triceratops and a tyrannosaurus rex, both full scale. They face each other in classic battle pose—the gray triceratops with its horn tilted up toward the exposed brown belly of the tyrannosaurus, which is turning for the attack, its tiny forelegs clutched, its huge tail about to swing around, its head frozen in a silent roar.

At the moment, Dinosaur Park had one visitor. Me. I was alone, wearing a cinnamon polo shirt, long pleated twill shorts, aviator sunglasses, and a stone-colored canvas islander hat. I didn't have a .357 magnum in my purse, but I did have good running shoes on my feet and Benny Goldberg standing watch up at the Science Center.

I didn't hear him approach.

"Are you Miss Gold?"

I turned.

He was pure-bred civil servant, right down to the small details: wire-rim glasses; a brown, pencil-width mustache; four Bic pens in the plastic pocket protector of his white, short-sleeve Dacron shirt. He was bald on top, with close-trimmed sidewalls, the hair a mixture of brown and gray, no sideburns. His stomach bulged below the high waistline of his brown Sansabelt slacks. He was wearing gray Hush Puppies.

"Albert Weidemeir?"

He glanced around, nervously scratching the back of his neck, and then he nodded.

"Are you alone?" I asked.

He glanced around again and nodded. "Are you?" He had a nasal voice.

"No."

He started.

"I have a colleague nearby," I explained. "He's here to make sure we aren't being followed. We don't want to be followed."

He nodded.

"I represent Mrs. Anderson," I said. "Did you know her?"

He began with a shake of his head but ended with a nod. "I met her once. No, twice."

"The property belongs to Mrs. Anderson, Albert."

He shoved the fingertips of both hands into the waistband of his brown pants. "I don't know where it is."

"I can help you, Albert. I don't want you to get hurt. Your best bet is to tell me what you know."

I waited.

He avoided eye contact, glancing down.

"Don't you see?" I continued. "You tell me all about it, and then it's my problem, not yours. If the FBI knocks at your door, you just tell them to talk to me."

"The FBI?" he whined, sliding his hands further down the front of his pants.

236 Michael A. Kahn

"At least the FBI," I told him. "Probably the police. U.S. Customs, too. Maybe others. There are lots of law enforcement agencies involved. Everyone is looking for it. You're about to hit the big time, Albert."

His face was flushed. He pulled one of his hands out of his pants and tugged at his thin mustache.

I studied him, watching as the scope of his predicament sunk in. "Tell me about it," I said softly.

After a long moment, he sighed. "I should have just said no."

I uttered a silent thanks heavenward. "No to what, Albert?" I asked gently.

"To Stoddard. When he called. I should have just said no."

"When did he call?"

Albert had the date and time of the call committed to memory. The date and time meant that Anderson had contacted Albert the morning after he picked up the lockbox from Sal Donalli, which meant that Anderson met Albert the morning of the day after he disappeared.

"Stoddard caught me off-guard. I mean, he sounded—well, desperate on the telephone. In fact, that is precisely what he said he was. He actually said he was desperate. He said that to me over the telephone. That just was not like him at all. I had never heard him talk like that."

"What did he want?"

"He wanted me to meet him. He said it was an emergency. He said he needed my help. But then he said that I had to swear that I would keep it a secret. I was so—so startled that I told him I would. He made me swear. I did. I swore that I would keep it a secret." He jammed his fingers back into the front of his pants. "Of course, I had no idea at the time of what he was . . . that he was going to, you know . . . do that thing."

"What thing?"

Albert shuddered. "Kill himself."

"What happened after Stoddard called you that morning?"

"He told me to meet him. At a deserted warehouse on the south side. That morning. He gave me directions."

"Did you go?"

Albert nodded.

"He met you there?"

Another nod.

"Tell me about the meeting."

"He was very . . . agitated, Miss Gold. He had not shaved. His clothes were wrinkled. His breath smelled of alcohol. I distinctly remember that. Mind you, this was ten in the morning."

"Did he have anything with him?"

He shook his head. "He said it was in the trunk."

"What was?"

"Whatever it was he wanted me to help him hide," Albert said, his tone now peevish, almost shrill. "He never told me what it was. Never."

"What did he tell you, Albert?" I asked, trying to keep my voice soothing.

"He . . . he did tell me it was very valuable. And . . . and from the way he talked about it . . . it—that thing—did not sound like it was a large object."

"What did he say that made you think it wasn't large?"

Albert Weidemeir looked down as he talked, staring at his shoes. He took a couple slow, deep breaths. "I don't recall specifics, Miss Gold. I just got the feeling that whatever it was, it was something small—something a person could carry."

"Okay."

"Stoddard said that it was imperative that he hide that thing in a safe place. He said it would have to remain hidden for a lengthy period of time. Perhaps years. Somewhere safe and secure. He asked me if I knew of a good place to hide it in the sewer system."

"And you suggested the River Des Peres?"

Albert's head snapped up and he stared at me, slack-jawed. "He told you?"

"Sort of. What part of the River Des Peres?"

"You have to understand, Miss Gold, this was all against my better judgment. All of it. I am hardly the type of man to get involved in this sort of thing." He was jittery, his arms jumping at odd angles as he spoke. "If I had any inkling that there were criminal overtones—well, I can assure you." He took a deep breath and held it for a moment, shaking his head. "I work in the accounting department at the Sewer District," he whined, as if that were explanation enough.

"What part of the River Des Peres?" I repeated.

"Section D," he answered, head down.

"What's that?"

"Section D is the double-arch section that runs under Forest Park."

"Is that where he hid it?"

Albert shrugged and shook his head at the same time, palms up. "I don't know."

"Why not?"

"Section D wasn't my only suggestion. I told him about several other locations in the sewer system."

"Such as what?"

"I told him about two brick feeder lines that might be better for hiding something in."

"What made them better?"

"You could chisel out a few bricks instead of having to cut out a hole in cement. He listened to what I said, but in the end he hid it himself. He didn't want me to know where it was hidden. He told me he didn't want anyone to know besides himself. That way no one could be threatened. Or compromised. At least that is what he told me. But now look what's happened to me. He's barely dead a month and I am practically on the FBI's most-wanted list. I should never have gotten involved with this. Never. Neverneverever."

"So you don't know where it is?"

He shook his head. "I surely do not. You must tell that to the police. And the FBI. Please make them understand, Miss Gold. I don't know where he hid that darn thing, and I never ever ever want to know. I am an accountant, for heaven's sake."

"He hid it himself?"

"Yes. Yes. Yes. That is what I am trying to make you understand."

"How did he know where to go?"

Albert made a helpless, distressed gesture with his hands.

"He asked me for blueprints. For several parts of the sewer system. He also asked me for some tools and supplies to help him hide it. He was quite despondent, Miss Gold. I was afraid he was going to have a nervous breakdown. He had always been a good lawyer and friend." Albert shrugged helplessly. "I agreed to help him."

"You were a good friend to him, Albert. You did the right thing."

"That's what I thought. He was a very important lawyer, Miss Gold. A very important man here in St. Louis. He knew the president of the United States. And yet, when he was in trouble, he turned to me. I—I was—honored." He reddened. "Stoddard waited there at the warehouse for me. I went back to the headquarters, got the tools and supplies, and then I drove back there."

"What did you bring him besides the blueprints?"

"I brought him a hammer, a chisel, a shovel. I brought him a small bag of concrete. I brought the bucket to mix the concrete in. I brought him a big flashlight, too."

A dad and three small boys came charging into Dinosaur Park. The boys ran around to the back of the triceratops and started climbing up its tail.

I gestured to Albert, and he followed me through the trees and down toward the pond.

"What happened after you gave him all that stuff?" I asked.

"He left. First he thanked me, and then he left."

"That's it?"

He nodded.

We had reached the edge of the pond.

"Did you talk to him again?"

Albert didn't answer. He watched as a pair of swans glided past.

"Did you talk to him again?"

He glanced over at me. "How can I be sure you are really who you say you are? How do I know you are really her lawyer?"

"Here," I said, reaching into my purse for the photocopy

of my retention letter. It was getting dog-eared from being shown to people.

He read it once, and then he read it again. He handed it back to me.

"He called me the next day," Albert said. "After dinner. I could not believe it. I mean, he had told me the day before that he would never ask me to do anything else for him. He had promised." Albert shook his head in outrage. "Well, I finally agreed to meet him back at that warehouse."

"And?"

"He looked terrible. Haggard. His shirt torn. His pants smeared with dirt or mud. He still had not shaved. I should have known then."

"What happened at the meeting?"

"It did not last long. He gave me a large envelope. It was sealed with tape. He told me that the plan had changed slightly."

"What plan?"

"I have no idea," he whimpered. "I never knew of any plan. You must tell that to the FBI, Miss Gold."

"What was in the envelope?"

"I have no idea. None whatsoever."

"What happened at this second meeting, Albert?"

"He made me promise to put that envelope in my safe deposit box. He gave me very specific instructions. He told me I should wait for exactly one year. Then I should call his law firm to find out who is representing his wife. Then I should contact that lawyer and give him the envelope. When I give him the envelope, I am supposed to tell him that it describes an extraordinarily valuable asset of the estate. Except, when Stoddard told me that, I thought he said 'state.' An extraordinarily valuable asset of the state. I—I didn't know he was talking about his own estate. I didn't know he—he was going to commit suicide."

"What else happened?"

"That was it. He gave me the envelope. He gave me the instructions. He made me recite them. Then he made me swear that I would follow them. And then he left."

"Did you hear from him again?"

"No. Never. The next thing I heard, he was missing. And then, well, then he was dead."

"Did you do what he told you to do?"

Albert nodded. "The very next morning. I went directly from home to my bank. I put the envelope in my safe deposit box."

"Is it still there?" I asked, trying to keep my voice calm.

"Yes."

I felt like doing one of those crazy touchdown dances football players do in the end zone. But I remained motionless, forcing myself to consider the best approach to landing this fish. Ironically, Albert Weidemeir also happened to be the best witness of Stoddard Anderson's mental state just prior to his suicide. And he was clearly spooked by the thought of having to deal with the FBI.

"I must tell you, Miss Gold, I was quite anxious about that envelope, even before Stoddard was dead. But then, after his suicide, well . . ." He paused to shake his head. "Even though I feel a certain obligation toward his wishes, I am most uncomfortable about having continuing custody and control over that envelope."

I waited a few beats and then said, "I'd like to help you, Albert."

He glanced at me. "You would?" He sounded hopeful.

"I can shield you from the criminal authorities. I'm willing to do that. But I'm going to need something from you in return."

"Money?"

"No. Mrs. Anderson is my client. She'll pay my fees. What I need from you is a written statement of your observations of Stoddard Anderson's mental condition during the last time you saw him. The way he looked, the way he acted, even the way he smelled. I need it for the life insurance matter. The matter described in the letter I showed you. I can promise you that I will show that statement to no one but the insurance company. Okay?"

"I suppose I could do that for you."

"And," I continued, watching closely for his reaction, "I won't tell anyone that you gave me the envelope."

He gave a sigh of relief. "Then you *will* take it?"

In my mind, I leaned back, punched my fist into the sky, and shouted a YES!! that reverberated across the city. With my body, though, I pretended to carefully weigh his request.

"I will," I finally said. "Since I represent his widow, Albert, you'll always know that you kept your promise to him. You were a good friend to the end."

"This is excellent. I must tell you, Miss Gold, you cannot imagine how relieved I will be to finally get that dreadful envelope out of my safe deposit box."

We made arrangements to meet outside his bank at twelve-thirty the following afternoon. I really wanted to do it first thing in the morning, but Albert couldn't get to the bank any earlier than lunchtime because of the Monday morning staff meetings he had to attend on his first day back at the office after his vacation.

As we were parting, I asked, "One more thing, Albert. This Section D—the tunnel under Forest Park. You say Mr. Anderson seemed more interested in that than the other places you told him about?"

"Yes, but that doesn't mean he hid it in Section D. As I told you, I do not know where he hid it. I cannot impress upon you enough—"

"How did Stoddard know how to get into Section D?"

Albert looked down at his feet. "I told him how. The river comes out of those tunnels over at Macklind and Manchester. The mouths of the tunnels are wide open. No fences or gates or anything like that. Anyone can walk in. I told him about that entrance."

"How long are the tunnels?"

"From Macklind through Forest Park, I would say about three miles."

As Albert Weidemeir walked briskly away toward the parking lot, his arms pumping and his hips rolling, Benny casually passed by him as he walked toward me, tipping his Yankees cap at him. It only made Albert speed up his pace.

"Nu?" Benny asked me.

I gave him a thumbs-up. "Albert's our man. And he's going to cooperate."

"No shit. Good old Albert. Tell me about it. And do it in the shade, for Christ's sake. Look at me. I'm shvitzing like a hog. Summer in this goddamn town is like living in a fucking steam bath."

We walked back to the Science Center, where I finished filling Benny in while he chugged a large Sprite, refilled the cup with water, and chugged that as well.

"Way to go, Albert," Benny said when I finished. "Tell him I want to have his children. For lunch. I'm starved."

When we got back out to the parking lot, I told Benny I had to go downtown for the meeting with Reed St. Germain.

"I still don't see why you have to be the one," Benny said.

"I'm the emcee," I said. "I set it all up."

"Well, you know I'm going to have to be there."

"You can't be."

"Hey, I *can* be. You won't even know I'm there. I'll stay out of your way. Give me a research project, stick me in the library. Christ, it's air-conditioned down there. I've got to get some place in this fucking city where the heat index is under a hundred. The climate control center of my brain has already gone to DEFCON-Two."

Eventually, I relented. "I just don't want a circus down there," I told him. "Here's the car keys. Wait for me by the car. I want to call both of them one more time."

CHAPTER

Reed St. Germain appeared at the doorway of my small office at ten minutes to three, briefcase in hand. I looked up from my legal pad, as if I had been engrossed in my investigation notes.

"Come in, Reed."

"Let's make the call from my office," he said. "It's more comfortable."

"We're not making the call. Ishmael is. I gave him my direct dial number. I think we better wait for the call here. Have a seat. And close the door."

He did both, which put him at an immediate disadvantage. Some wit once said that big-firm lawyers are like wolves: They travel in packs. They share another trait as well: Big-firm lawyers—at least the male ones—are highly territorial, and view their offices as their lairs. Reed St. Germain was now in my den.

He slid around in his chair, trying to find a comfortable position. Fortunately, these were Abbott & Windsor guest chairs, selected by an all-male committee of lawyers. As a result, there is no comfortable position in those chairs. That's the whole point. In addition, the chairs sit a couple inches lower than standard ones, which means that the visitor is always just a tad below the lawyer behind the desk. The people in charge of a law firm's interior design play the same role as the grounds crew at the ballpark—in dozens of little ways they can tip the odds slightly in favor of the home team.

"Are you sure he even remembers about this call?" Reed said.

"Why do you say that?"

"He's out of town."

"How do you know that?"

"I called earlier today. First his office, then his home. His wife said he was out of town until tomorrow."

"Why did you call?"

"Uh, management issues. Certainly of no concern to you. Speaking of which, what's the story with this investigation?" Having faltered for a fraction of a second, he was now attempting to take charge, but from the wrong side of the desk. "When do you plan to wrap it up so we can get back to business around here?"

"Soon."

"Define soon."

"Come on, Reed," I said with irritation. "I already told you that I'm meeting with the claims adjuster on Tuesday. My goal is to have everything wrapped up by then."

"Well, that's good to hear. What have you decided to tell him?"

I smiled. "Now it's my turn, Reed. I don't think that's any concern of yours. I represent Mrs. Anderson, not the firm."

He gave a snort of disgust, trying to sound gruff. "Last time I looked, we were paying your fees."

"Reed, if you have a problem with my interpretation of my ethical obligations to Mrs. Anderson, I suggest you raise that with Ishmael. He's the one who retained me."

"I just might," he snapped, his face coloring. He checked his watch. "He should have called by now—if he's going to, that is."

"He told me he would. I'm certain he will."

"Don't be so sure. He's getting older, more forgetful. He's not the man he once was."

Involuntarily, I glanced down at the button for the intercom line between my desk and Nancy's. The light was still on.

"While we're waiting," I said calmly, "maybe I can tie up some loose ends. Help speed things up. Can I ask you a few questions?"

He crossed his arms and leaned back in his chair. "Go ahead."

"Were you the one who did that to my car?"

The question seemed to land with palpable force, pushing him further back so that he momentarily lost his balance before righting his chair. "Your car? I won't even dignify that question with a response."

"Did you call me later that night?"

"Did I what?" he sputtered.

"You heard the question."

"Good God, lady, get serious."

"I am serious."

"And I am indignant. You can rest assured that Ishmael will hear about this."

"Tell him. But first answer my question."

"This is ludicrous."

"What is ludicrous?"

"Even the suggestion that someone in my position would stoop to making that kind of call."

I paused, nodding slightly. "What kind of call?"

He had realized his mistake. I could see it in his eyes as he tried to replay the last minute of our conversation in his head. "The kind of call you described," he finally said, trying to sound belligerent.

"I didn't describe the call. I didn't say anything about it. I just asked if you were the one who called me later that night."

"Word games," he sneered. "This isn't cross-examination, lady."

"It took me a while to figure it out," I said, leaning back in my seat. "For a long time I really did think someone was trying to scare me off the Anderson investigation. I kept looking for a motive and couldn't find one. But that was before I pieced together the ParaLex scheme."

If I needed any further confirmation, I got it from the way his eyes jumped when I mentioned the word ParaLex. I waited for him to say something, but he was waiting for me. I opened my desk and pulled out the ParaLex payment charts that Tyrone Henderson had printed out for me—the ones that listed each payment to ParaLex over the last three years. I slid them across the table.

I watched as he leafed through page after page of the lists of checks to ParaLex.

"Did you get this from our accounting department?" he finally asked.

I shook my head. "I got it from Chicago."

"Who?" His voice was just a little hoarse now.

"Someone."

"Ishmael?"

"Of course not."

He tossed the printout on my desk. "You think ParaLex has something to do with Stoddard Anderson?"

"I think ParaLex has something to do with you."

"Obviously it does. You don't need to be a rocket scientist to figure that out. And we certainly don't hide ParaLex from our clients. As you can see from these lists, we use ParaLex for administrative assistance in connection with many of our trusts and estates. As the head of that department, I suppose that makes me involved with any of our vendors, including appraisers, investment advisors, and other purveyors of services, such as ParaLex. But that doesn't make me any more *involved* with them than one of my litigation partners is *involved* with a court reporting service. Indeed, I should think these ParaLex bills pale in comparison to the fees we've paid to certain court reporting services over the years. Do you have any idea what those depositions in Bottles and Cans have cost over the years? Over a million dollars." He lifted the printouts. "According to these, the ParaLex payments average under fifty thousand dollars a year." He shook his head and he tossed the printouts onto the desk. "Compared to other vendors, that's peanuts."

"Yes, but there's one difference."

"What's that?"

"Those other vendors actually exist."

That earned a facial twitch. "I'm not following you," he said, trying to look confused.

"The court reporter exists. The property appraiser exists. The copy service exists. ParaLex doesn't."

He forced a laugh. "Ridiculous. Of course it exists."

I reached under my desk and lifted the St. Louis Telephone Directory. I heaved it onto the desk, where it landed with a heavy thud. "Call them," I said.

He studied the telephone book, his arms again crossed over his chest. He raised his eyes to meet my gaze. We stared at one another. "You're on a wild-goose hunt, lady. Believe me, you're in over your head."

"One of us sure is, Reed."

I opened my desk drawer and pulled out a photocopy of the front and back side of one of the canceled checks to ParaLex. I slid it across the desktop. "That," I said, "is a check in payment of a ParaLex invoice. Look at the back. It's been deposited into the ParaLex account at the First State Bank of Creve Coeur."

He looked up, his eyes cold. "Where did you get that check?"

"That's not important."

"Did that little prick-teaser give it to you?"

"Portia? She doesn't even know I have it. Is she in on this, too?"

"That check is client property. I could have you up on charges before the disciplinary commission. You've invaded a client's privacy. You've trespassed client property."

"Oh, come on, Reed. Trespassed client property? You've *stolen* client property. I've talked to the bank, Reed. I figured out what's going on. That ParaLex bank account is your account. You own it. All these checks—all the money—they all go to you. ParaLex doesn't exist except as a name on an invoice, a name on a post office box, and a name on a bank account. You're ParaLex."

He seemed to be fighting for control of himself. "You're wrong. You don't understand."

"Stoddard Anderson found out about ParaLex, didn't he? That's why he had that meeting with you at the St. Louis Club."

"Goddamn you," he said, his eyes flaring. "No one knew. No one. No one. Not even Anderson."

"Then why did he meet with you about ParaLex?"

"He never figured it out," he said with contempt, his fists clenched. "All Stoddard wanted to know was why we were paying ParaLex to perform services that we might be able to have our paralegals perform. He wanted to know if we could phase out ParaLex, phase in our paralegals, and bill their time at a profit. I told him we could. I told him I'd start transferring those functions to our paralegals. All Stoddard Anderson wanted to do was increase the profit ratios in the trusts and estates department. He was satisfied with my explanation. He had no idea. None. No one did."

He looked down, shaking his head. Suddenly, he slammed his fist on the desktop. "Goddamn you!" he shouted as he jumped to his feet and unzipped his briefcase. "I stopped ParaLex right after that meeting with Stoddard. It's done. It's over. No one ever figured it out. If you think I'm going to let you destroy me . . ." He started around the desk and pulled what looked like a short, wide crowbar out of his briefcase. "If you think I'm going to let you tell Ishmael about ParaLex . . ."

As I stood up, backing against the window, my office door burst open. In stepped Detective Mario Aloni, holding a gun in both hands.

"Sit down, sir," he told St. Germain, pointing the gun at his head. "Drop that bar on the carpet. Now."

Stunned, St. Germain staggered back to his chair. He looked down in confusion at the iron bar grasped in his right hand.

"Oh, Reed."

St. Germain looked up at the sound of the familiar baritone. Standing in the doorway was Ishmael Richardson, shaking his head sadly. "A petty thief and a petty thug. I am so disappointed."

Coming from the chairman of Abbott & Windsor, that last sentence was the equivalent of a judge imposing capital punishment. St. Germain winced, his head hanging down. He dropped the bar on the carpet. Aloni reached over and snatched it up.

Ishmael turned to Aloni and me. "Rachel, Detective—I would like to have a few moments alone with Mr. St. Germain. I would appreciate it if one of you would turn off that intercom device at the secretary station. Reed and I have some matters to discuss in confidence."

We left after Aloni made St. Germain assume the position against the desk so that he could pat him down. On the way out, Aloni took the briefcase and the iron bar.

An hour later, Ishmael joined us in the conference room. He looked fatigued.

"Detective," he said glumly, "I have attempted to achieve some justice today. I have done so because I realize that my firm must take full responsibility—morally if not legally—for Mr. St. Germain's malfeasance. Beginning on Monday, this law firm will implement all necessary measures to ensure that by the end of the week every client of this firm that has ever paid money to ParaLex will be reimbursed in full, plus interest accrued at prime rate. I will be more than happy to provide you with evidence of that."

Ishmael gave a weary sigh before continuing. "I have also attempted to mete out appropriate punishment. Mr. St. Germain is in the process of clearing out his personal belongings. He has resigned from this firm. I have urged him to withdraw from the practice of law and turn in his license. He has promised to consider my recommendation. I intend to make him accept it, and I have reason to believe he will. Although the firm will repay the clients, Mr. St. Germain will, in turn, make full restitution to the firm. As of last Friday, his capital account with the firm stood at roughly ninety-five thousand dollars. He has signed papers relinquishing his claim to that account. He has also signed a promissory note for the balance, to be paid in full over the next eighteen months. Detective, I can show you those documents as well."

Ishmael took a deep breath and exhaled slowly. He looked at me with melancholy eyes, and then turned to Aloni. "I realize that you are here today in an unofficial capacity, Detective. I am telling you what has transpired between Mr. St. Germain and myself because of what Rachel has told me about you. She has good instincts about people, Detective. She believes that you are a man of compassion. Your presence here today on your day off is eloquent testimony of that compassion. I give you my word that my law firm will take all necessary steps to fully compensate any client whose funds were used to pay phony ParaLex invoices. I give you my word that Mr. St. Germain is leaving this firm today and, I believe, the practice of law shortly thereafter. He has been punished, Detective. The punishment is severe. I have questioned him closely about the attack on Stoddard Anderson's widow. I am convinced to a moral certainty that he had nothing to do with it. If you reach the same conclusion . . ." Ishmael let the thought complete itself.

"We still have the act of vandalism on Rachel's car," Aloni said. He rubbed his chin. "That's a serious offense, although it is outside my jurisdiction."

Ishmael nodded gravely. "Rachel and I spoke over the telephone at length on the subject this morning. Under my questioning, Mr. St. Germain confirmed her suspicions. He did it all—the car windows, the trunk of her car, the threatening phone call. He acted in the misguided belief that he could scare her off." Ishmael looked at me with a weary smile. "He is hardly the first attorney to underestimate Rachel Gold. However, I have the sense that Rachel may be willing to walk away from that incident without pressing charges."

Aloni looked at me.

I nodded. "I don't want to have anything further to do with him."

"I intend to talk to the man," Aloni said. "Alone."

"Certainly," Ishmael said. "But when you're finished asking questions, Detective, don't forget about the people who don't have to become his victims." Ishmael leaned forward, the fatigue gone. "This law firm suffered a grievous blow earlier this summer with the loss of Stoddard Anderson. The departure of Reed St. Germain will add yet another layer of instability. So long as I can keep the true reason for his departure a secret, I believe his loss will not be a mortal blow to this firm. I believe we can hold this office together, maintain the client base. Detective, this office employs close to one hundred and fifty people—secretaries, messengers, word processors, and the like, as well as attorneys. These people are all innocent, as are the spouses and children who depend on them. Yet these are the very people who will suffer if this office cannot recover from this . . . this entanglement. Please consider the innocents when you decide whether anything further must be done here.''

Aloni promised to keep that in mind. He said he would call Ishmael that night after he finished questioning St. Germain.

Ishmael remained seated after Aloni left. His shoulders were slumped as he stared at the far edge of the conference table. His speech about all the people who depended on the firm reminded me of the weight of his responsibilities and the pain he felt over what he viewed as St. Germain's betrayal. I remained silent until he concluded his meditations with a sigh.

"Why?" I asked. "Reed St. Germain must be earning close to three hundred thousand dollars a year. This ParaLex scheme added less than fifty thousand dollars a year to his income. Why even do it? Surely he didn't need the money.''

Ishmael shook his head sadly. "But he did. Reed St. Germain achieved through marriage what he may never have been able to attain on his own, namely, admission to St. Louis high society and, through his wife's family's business, a handsome book of business. The price has been a marriage to an abusive and domineering woman. He appears to be quite intimidated by her—as well he should, since his social and professional status depend upon the continuation of that marriage. To that add the fact that she controls all of his personal finances. He literally hands her his draw checks twice a month. She deposits the money, handles the checkbook, pays the bills. She can account for every penny of their income. And apparently she does.''

"Okay.''

"That is the crux of Reed's predicament: His wife controls the finances, and she is a suspicious woman. For you see, Reed St. Germain has one very expensive compulsion: fornication. He quite literally appears to be addicted to extramarital sexual relations. To feed that habit, he needs, among other things, an apartment in the city and a sufficient supply of money to entertain and buy presents for his various paramours."

"And so he invented ParaLex," I said.

Ishmael nodded. "He kept the individual ParaLex invoices small enough so that the clients would not ask questions. Indeed, the heirs of a multimillion-dollar estate or the beneficiaries of a multimillion-dollar trust fund would hardly notice a quarterly payment of two hundred dollars or less. ParaLex served as a ready source of cash that his wife could never detect."

"Until now."

Ishmael nodded gravely. "I am afraid that the punishment I imposed upon him this afternoon will pale in comparison to what awaits him at home. I understand that the wrath of Janet St. Germain is wondrous to behold."

He sat up and forced a smile. "Enough of this thoroughly disheartening topic. Let us turn to something upbeat, such as suicide. Tell me about your investigation of Stoddard Anderson."

I filled him in generally—very generally. I told him of my upcoming meeting with the claims adjuster and I told him that in all likelihood I would try to settle the accidental death issue. He seemed satisfied. Of course, I left out a few minor details— such as everything having to do with Montezuma's Executor, including my meeting with Customs tonight and my rendezvous tomorrow with Albert Weidemeir to receive the contents of his safe deposit box. Why make it worse by telling him that the former managing partner of the St. Louis office—the one whose suicide had already caused a damaging scandal in the legal community—had probably also violated U.S. and international law by arranging to smuggle into the country a pre-Columbian golden blade handle in the shape of Montezuma's phallus.

I promised to call Ishmael after I met with the claims adjuster.

As I got up to go collect Benny and head off, Ishmael said, "I almost forgot."

"What?"

"I did ask Reed about his meeting with that Mr. Panzer."

"And?"

"Routine estate planning. Stoddard had handled Panzer's estate planning. Panzer came in to meet his new trusts and estates attorney and to ask some questions about the advantages of a living will."

CHAPTER 26

"You put his nuts in a vise and you turn the screws. You want Tezca, you first gotta squeeze the faggot." Bernie DeWitt reached for another slice of pizza and leaned back against the headboard. He looked smug, as if he had said something profound. For all I knew about nuts and vises and the like, maybe he had.

Ferd Fingersh nodded slowly and looked over at me. "He's right. We arrest Panzer in the act of paying you for the Executor. We make sure it's a clean arrest. Then we lean on him. He might just cooperate. If he does, he could lead us to Tezca, using the Executor as bait. When Tezca surfaces—boom."

Bernie nodded, chomping on the pizza. "Tezca surfaces and it's 'Assume the position, motherfucker.'"

Fingersh shrugged. "He gets to spend some time down at Marion. Mr. Salazar returns to his client a hero. Not a bad day's work."

It was Sunday night. We were in Cottage 14 of a motel along Watson Road in south St. Louis that rented these tiny cottages by the week, by the night, or by the hour. We had ours until 2:00 A.M. There were five of us: Ferd Fingersh and Bernie DeWitt of Customs, Rafe Salazar, Benny, and me. Bernie had just returned with four large pepperoni and mushroom pizzas and a case of cold beer.

I had finally gotten in touch with Ferd Fingersh around five o'clock. He located the other two, and we all met at the motel at 8:00 P.M. I told them that I thought I might know where the Executor was by sometime tomorrow afternoon, although I didn't tell them how I was going to find out. I kept my promise to Albert Weidemeir.

"I don't like the plan," Benny said as he twisted the cap off a longneck bottle of Budweiser beer. "Why should Rachel take that kind of risk? What makes you think this Remy Panzer is just going to pay her the money? What if he has no intention of giving her the money? What if he plans to hurt her? Or kill her, for Christ's sake?"

"Don't worry about that faggot," Bernie DeWitt said, pointing at Benny with his beer bottle.

"Rachel will be perfectly safe," Ferd Fingersh interjected. "You have my word on that. If we couldn't guarantee her safety, we wouldn't even consider it."

"How can you be so sure?" Benny asked.

"It's not difficult when it's done right," Fingersh explained. "We know how to do it right. Once Rachel figures out where Anderson hid the Executor, she'll call it in to us. We'll set up an exchange with Panzer for tomorrow night. We'll make sure it's in a safe place. By the time Panzer arrives that night, we'll have an army of men in position, including five or ten sharpshooters. We'll be monitoring everything with high-powered audio equipment and video cameras with telephoto lenses and night vision."

"If he's wearing a watch," Bernie said, "we'll be able to read what time it says. Better yet, we'll have half a dozen sharpshooters about to put a bullet right through the center of the dial."

I was seated on the desk against the wall. I leaned over and lifted another slice of pizza out of the box on the bed nearest me, stealing a glance at Rafe Salazar as I did. Benny was on one bed, shoes off, back against the headboard. Bernie DeWitt was in a similar position on the other bed. Ferd Fingersh was seated on the well-worn armchair.

Rafe Salazar was leaning against the wall near the bathroom, his arms crossed over his chest. Earlier, just after Benny and I arrived, Rafe had pulled me aside to ask if he could buy me a drink after the meeting. I had said yes. I glanced over at him now. He was wearing stone-washed jeans, a black T-shirt with a Telluride Film Festival logo, and brown cowboy boots. The T-shirt accentuated his strong arms and lean torso. The tight jeans accentuated his narrow hips and certain other fine qualities. He looked awfully good.

"We're going to cover some other things with you, Rachel," Fingersh said. "Such as what to do when you make contact with Panzer. We're going to tell you some of the instructions you'll have to give him. What he should wear, things like that."

"I should be Rachel's contact," Rafe said in a soft but authoritative voice.

Ferd looked over. "You?"

Rafe nodded solemnly. "Let's not forget that the only real party in interest here is my client," he said. "My reason for being here is to ensure the safe return of El Verdugo. My client is willing to cooperate with the federal government's ancillary goal. So long as your pursuit of Tezca does not jeopardize the return of El Verdugo, my client will continue to cooperate. I want to make sure we don't lose our focus." He glanced at me. "I also want to make sure we don't lose Rachel. You're using her to bait the trap. I want to make sure there's a safe way out of the trap before it slams shut."

"Hey, Ralph, we're not going to put her at risk," Bernie DeWitt said. "We ain't the fucking Mexican federales."

"I'd feel better if Rafe was my contact," I said.

Ferd put up his hand to silence Bernie. "That's great," he said, smiling at me. "We can always use the help. Bernie and I will be plenty busy tomorrow making all your security arrangements anyway."

Benny cleared his throat. "As long as we're all looking out for Rachel's interests," he said, "I think we ought to address the issue of her fee for all this." He turned to Rafe. "I understand your client is willing to compensate Rachel."

"Yes," Rafe answered.

"According to what Rachel's told me," Benny continued,

"Panzer, or whoever Panzer represents, paid millions for that golden woodie. Panzer's offered to pay Rachel a quarter of a million dollars for finding it. He claims that's the fee he promised to pay Stoddard Anderson. Rachel's planning to turn that fee over to her client, Mrs. Anderson. Now, if this thing came on the market legally, I assume your client would have been willing to pay millions, right?"

"Perhaps," Rafe answered.

"Seems to me the *least* they can do is match Panzer's offer to Rachel," Benny said as he turned to me. "Doesn't that seem fair to you? Your client could use two hundred and fifty thousand dollars, right?"

Benny's proposal caught me off guard.

Rafe answered before I could. "That's a reasonable request," he said. "I'll pass it on to my client tomorrow morning with a recommendation that they agree to it." He shifted to me, a hint of a smile on his lips. "I will try to have an answer for you by noon."

I smiled back.

"Which reminds me," Ferd said, lifting a large briefcase onto one of the beds. "We're all going to be moving around tomorrow. Bernie told me about Rachel's problems getting in touch with Rafe the other day. Can't have that happen tomorrow."

He opened the briefcase and pulled out two portable telephones—one for me and one for Rafe. He explained how to use the phones and recharge the batteries. He had us each write down the other's portable telephone number, along with emergency numbers for reaching Ferd and Bernie.

"These are open lines," Ferd said. "That means you could have other people listening in—usually by accident, but sometimes not. It's safest to assume someone's listening. So be careful what you say when you're on these phones."

Rafe and I never got to have our drink. The five of us were in the motel room until midnight. Ferd and Bernie went over everything—from what I should say to Remy Panzer to how to select the best place for Remy and me to exchange the money for the Executor. Benny asked dozens of questions about the security arrangements, each of which seemed to elicit a long answer punctuated with acronyms and names of electronic devices. By eleven-fifteen I was stifling yawns. By quarter to twelve I had dozed off once, my head slumped forward onto my chest for maybe thirty seconds before I snapped up in surprise, my eyes coming into focus on Rafe Salazar, who was watching from across the room. He smiled. I shrugged. He winked. I stretched, trying to stay alert.

As the meeting droned on, I stood up and stepped outside the motel room into the hot, humid August night. There was a full moon and the sky was cloudless. Rafe joined me moments later.

I leaned against him, staring up at the moon. "I'm glad you'll be my contact."

"So am I." He put his arm around my shoulders.

"Think they have room service?" I asked.

"Why?"

"For that drink you promised me."

"Here?" He looked down at me.

"You said the meeting's almost over." I raised my eyebrows. "We have the room until two."

He shook his head. "Not tonight, Rachel Gold. Not the night before a day like the day tomorrow may be. When we finally"—he looked at me and smiled—"have our drink together, it most definitely will not be in a seedy motel like this."

"Oh? And where will it be?" He had a delicious, musky scent.

"I know a special beach on the east coast of Africa."

"Africa?"

"Miles of pure black sand that sparkles like black diamonds. Palm trees along the beach, the jungle rising behind you like a dark green wall. You can rent one-bedroom cabanas right on the beach. They bring the drinks to you on the little veranda in front of your cabana as the sun sets. The sunsets are spectacular."

"You've been there?"

"Oh, yes. It's magnificent, Rachel."

We were silent for a moment.

"Africa's far away," I finally said.

"Most exceptional things are," he said.

"What if I can't wait till then? What if I get real thirsty?"

The door behind us opened. As we turned, Benny, Ferd, and Bernie walked out. The meeting was over.

An hour later I was in my bed, staring at the ceiling, when I heard what I first mistook for the chirp of a cricket. After the second chirp I realized the noise was from the portable telephone on the carpet by the bed. I lifted it onto my stomach and unhooked the receiver.

"Hello?" I said.

"You didn't get an answer to your last question," Rafe said.

I snuggled back against the pillow and smiled into the dark. "I can't remember the question."

"You wanted to know what happened if you couldn't wait for Africa, if you got thirsty before then."

"That's right. Well, what's the answer?"

"It's in my hotel room. I got it tonight, after we parted."

"Sounds intriguing. But remember what Ferd said: This isn't a safe line."

"I don't mind who hears."

"Then tell me the answer."

"A bottle of French champagne. Moët et Chandon. For tomorrow night. For when this is all over. To celebrate. If you think you might still be thirsty."

"That's sweet, Rafe. I'll be thirsty. I guarantee it."

"Sweet dreams, Rachel."

"Good night, Rafe."

I fell asleep with a smile.

CHAPTER 27

It was 10 A.M. Monday morning and I was still waiting to see Dr. Jacob Bernstein, the dermatologist. According to Stoddard Anderson's personal calendar, Dr. Bernstein had been the last physician Anderson saw before his death. I had come to Dr. Bernstein's office because Albert Weidemeir would not be retrieving the mystery envelope from his safe deposit box until noon. This had seemed a good time to wrap up this loose end.

I was in the reception area of Dermatology Consultants, absently leafing through a tattered issue of *People* magazine. I'd been there since eight-thirty, and my rage had been building steadily ever since. Bernstein hadn't returned my call on Friday. He hadn't returned my call on Saturday. He hadn't returned my call on Sunday. And now he'd let me cool my heels in his reception area for an hour and a half.

By the time the nurse finally opened the door to the inner sanctum and said, "Miss Gold?" the Dr. Jacob Bernstein of my imagination had become a white-coated Hermann Goering.

The real Bernstein was anything but. He was short, chubby, and bald, with a gray walrus mustache and sad brown eyes. He stood to shake my hand when the nurse showed me into his small, book-crammed office, and he profusely apologized for not returning my calls.

"I was at my nephew's bar mitzvah in Cleveland, Miss Gold. He's my younger brother's only son. I was there from Thursday until late last night. I'm very sorry I didn't call you. One of the other doctors was on call for all emergencies. I only returned calls from patients I was worried about."

It sounded plausible. "How was the bar mitzvah?" I asked.

"Beautiful. Thank you for asking." He removed a pipe from the pipe rack on his desk. "Do you mind if I smoke?"

I shook my head. "I like the smell."

"I know you've been waiting out there for a long time. There was nothing I could do. When you arrived I had a patient in every examination room—a basal carcinoma in Room A, a terrible outbreak of herpes zoster in B, and inflamed acne in C."

He paused to tamp the tobacco into the pipe bowl. After he got it lit, he looked up, his face surrounded by smoke. "How can I help you?" he asked, waving away the smoke.

"Tell me about Stoddard Anderson."

Bernstein sighed. "Such a sad ending."

"He saw you a week before he died."

Bernstein leaned back in his chair and crossed his arms over his chest.

"His appointment with you is in his personal calendar," I explained. "Doctor, I represent his widow. Here," I said as I fished the retention letter out of my briefcase.

As he read it, I explained the nature of my representation of Dottie Anderson.

"There are two issues," I said. "First, did he intend to kill himself when he took out the policy less than five months ago? And second, was he sane at the time he killed himself? As far as I can tell, you're the last physician to see him before he died. You may be the best witness as to his mental condition."

Bernstein frowned as he puffed on his pipe. "I'm a little reluctant to talk about these matters, Miss Gold. I don't mean to be difficult, but I have always tried to honor the privacy expectations of my patients. After all, Mr. Anderson was a patient of mine."

I had already anticipated this concern—indeed, I'd thought

of it yesterday as Benny and I drove down to the Abbott &
Windsor offices after my meeting with Albert Weidemeir. I'd
had Benny research the scope of the physician-patient privilege
while I had my encounter with Reed St. Germain.

I explained to Dr. Bernstein that the privilege in Missouri
belonged to the patient, not the doctor. Even if Stoddard Anderson's privilege had somehow survived his death, it could be
waived by his heirs, his representatives, or any beneficiary
under his life insurance policy.

He was still uneasy, but I persisted.

"He took out the insurance policy about four months ago,"
I said. "Was he a patient of yours back then?"

Bernstein shook his head. "I saw him only once. About a
week before his death."

"Why did he come to you?"

"Mr. Anderson had a severe case of seborrheic dermatitis."

"Which is what?"

"Dandruff."

"Did you treat it?"

"I prescribed some medication."

"Anything else?"

Bernstein puffed on his pipe, staring at me with his sad
eyes. "I drew a blood sample. I sent it to a laboratory for test-
ing."

"Why?"

"I must tell you, Miss Gold, I'm most uncomfortable dis-
cussing this matter. Mr. Anderson swore me to secrecy."

"Doctor, Mr. Anderson is dead. Nothing can hurt him
now. His widow is alive. She is the sole beneficiary of his life
insurance policy. The reason he decided to kill himself could
have a direct bearing on how much money she receives. Now,
he came to you with a bad case of dandruff. Why did you take
a blood—" I leaned back in my chair. "Is bad dandruff a symp-
tom of AIDS?"

Bernstein nodded. "Occasionally it is. A severe case of seborrheic dermatitis, especially in one who has never previously
had such a problem, can be a sign of AIDS. I explained that to

Mr. Anderson. I attempted to ask him about his personal life, but he refused to answer any of my questions. He agreed only to let me send the blood sample to the laboratory."

"And did you?"

Bernstein nodded sadly.

"When did you get the results?"

"It took a week."

"Did you call him?"

"He called me. He'd call every morning."

"You talked to him on the day he disappeared, didn't you?"

Bernstein nodded.

"Did you tell him over the telephone?"

Bernstein sighed. "I asked him to come to my office to discuss it. He refused. He wanted to hear it over the phone. 'Do I have AIDS?' he asked."

"And what did you tell him?"

Bernstein's eyes were moist. "When I told him he moaned. Like a wounded animal. I begged him to come see me. He said he needed a few days alone. He made me promise I wouldn't tell a soul." Bernstein pulled a handkerchief out of his pocket and daubed the corner of one eye. "I never dreamed he would kill himself."

It was quarter to eleven when I walked out of Dermatology Consultants. My meeting with Albert Weidemeir was still almost two hours away. I had enough time to drop by the hospital to check on Dottie Anderson and then swing by Washington University to pick up Benny from his interviews at the law school.

I had been to the hospital each day, and each day her status had been unchanged. But today the news was dramatically better. According to the doctor, Dottie had come out of her coma late last night, around two in the morning. She was asleep when I arrived, and still under medication, but her doctor was confident she would fully recover. I was ecstatic.

As I sat by her bedside while she slept, I thought about the last days in the life of her husband. Ironically, AIDS would have destroyed Remy Panzer's power over him. Up until then, Panzer could blackmail Anderson with the threat of exposing his homosexuality and pederasty. For someone of Stoddard Anderson's generation and in his position—especially someone who had publicly cast himself in the role of the archconservative Republican gay basher—exposure would be devastating. But more was at risk than simply being humiliated before his peers. Anderson had to know that disclosure of his appetite for young boys would lead, at best, to social exile and, at worst, to jail. And nothing could be worse or more dangerous than being a convicted child molester in a state penitentiary.

But when Anderson learned he had AIDS, the threat of exposure must have given way to the certainty of exposure. Far more powerful men of his generation with far more at stake—men such as Roy Cohn and Rock Hudson—had died exposed, and Anderson surely must have realized that he would as well, if he *allowed* himself to die of AIDS.

With Panzer's hold over him destroyed, Anderson would have taken steps necessary to keep Montezuma's Executor out of Panzer's grasp. He surely must have detested Panzer by then. Once he had completed the task of hiding the Executor, he killed himself. Even his manner of suicide—bleeding to death under a shower—was probably an attempt to hide his disease. He must have hoped that by the time someone discovered his body most of the blood would have drained out, leaving too little to test for AIDS.

The various drafts of the suicide note, along with Albert Weidemeir's last meeting with him (the meeting where Anderson said the plans had changed), suggested that Anderson's first plan had been to leave a message that would lead someone—the police? Dottie's attorney?—to Albert Weidemeir, who would then presumably lead them to the hiding place. That must have been the origins of the note entitled "Equation for M.E." But then Anderson may have worried that the wrong person could figure out the message, that the wrong person could lean on Albert Weidemeir, that the wrong person could find the Executor. So he changed his plan and tore up the note. Instead, he instructed Weidemeir to lay low for a full year and then turn the information over to Dottie's lawyer.

I thought again of the last line of the suicide note: "a dying man's last request." And now the mystery of the phrase "dying man" was solved. He had chosen his words carefully.

I checked my watch. It was time to go. I leaned over and kissed Dottie softly on the forehead. Next stop: Albert Weidemeir.

CHAPTER

Two hours later, Benny and I were parked in the shade in a secluded spot behind the zoo in Forest Park. Blueprints of the River Des Peres sewer system were spread on the front seat between us.

The rendezvous with Albert Weidemeir had gone smoothly. His bank let us use a private room in the safe deposit area. He read through his witness statement three times, asked a few questions about two of the phrases, and then signed it. That statement would be exhibit number one for my meeting tomorrow afternoon with the insurance claims adjuster.

After he signed his witness statement, I waited in the room while he visited his safe deposit box. A few minutes later he returned, holding the thick manila envelope away from his body as if it might bite. He dropped it on the table in front of me, pulled a pair of sunglasses out of his suit pocket as he turned, and left without a word.

Putting the envelope and the witness statement in my briefcase, I walked out of the bank and got into my car, where Benny was the getaway driver. I waited to open the envelope until we had parked in a secluded spot in Forest Park.

The envelope contained three things:

1. A two-page letter to Dottie's attorney in Anderson's handwriting. The letter consisted primarily of instructions for locating and then selling what Anderson called "an unusual but extraordinarily valuable piece of Aztec craftsmanship." The letter warned of the importance of maintaining confidentiality, hinted at possible legal problems with regard to the manner in which the object entered the U.S., and advised that it be offered for sale directly to a Mexican museum (rather than to a U.S. collector or through Customs). He signed the letter and dated it June 21, which was the day before he killed himself.
2. A small key. (According to the letter, the key was for the lockbox in which he had placed Montezuma's Executor.)
3. Blueprints and maps of the River Des Peres sewer system.

Benny and I studied the maps, trying to get our bearings. Across the top of the Section D blueprint Anderson had scrawled the following message:

> Six archways in from the end of Section D. Look inside the archway.

According to the blueprints, each of the twin tunnels of Section D was twenty-nine feet wide and, at its apex, twenty-eight feet high. One tunnel carried raw sewage and the other carried storm water. The floors of the two tunnels were slightly concave, which meant that when there wasn't storm water running through the system you could probably walk down the storm tunnel along one of the walls and not get wet. At least that's what I hoped as I glanced wistfully at my new Nike Airs.

"These tunnels are solid poured concrete," Benny said. "Unless he schlepped a jackhammer in there with him, how the hell did he chisel out enough to hide that thing?"

"You're asking me?"

"What's he mean by 'six archways in'?"

"Probably these things," I said, pointing to the bottom of the page of blueprints, which had a series of cross-sections and side profiles of the twin tunnels. The tunnels shared a common center wall that was three feet thick. According to the blueprints, there were passageways cut into the common wall at regular intervals, apparently to allow access from one tunnel to the other. The blueprints stated that there was a passageway cut into the wall every one hundred yards down the entire length of the twin tunnels.

"So the Executor is in the roof of the sixth one," Benny said. "That means it's six hundred yards down those tunnels, about a third of a mile."

I nodded. "The exchange point is obvious," I said.

"Where?"

"I'll show you. Let's go."

Ten minutes later we were cruising slowly across the bridge over the dry channel of the River Des Peres at Macklind Avenue. Macklind Avenue crosses the River Des Peres channel about four hundred feet downriver from the huge tunnel openings. I stopped my car in the middle of the short bridge over the river channel.

There were three tunnel openings—a smaller one on the right, a large one in the center, and another large one on the left. They were set in a huge cement wall. Just over the tunnel openings, etched in block letters in the wall, was the legend DES PERES DRAINAGE WORKS 1928.

"Hard to believe, huh?" Benny said as we stared upriver toward the tunnel openings.

"I know," I said. "I keep trying to conjure up the image of Stoddard Anderson walking into one of them."

"So where's the water?"

The River Des Peres channel was dry.

"I don't know."

When there was water in the River Des Peres, it would pour out of the tunnels into the open channel, which ran below street level like a huge ditch. The riverbed was concrete—

cracked in places, with big chunks missing. The embankment on either side of the riverbed was pitched at a forty-five-degree angle.

I opened the blueprints and found where we were. According to the blueprints, the smaller tunnel on the right was a feeder line that brought storm water in from the local area. The identical large tunnel openings in the center and on the left marked the end of the double-arch tunnels of Section D.

I studied the blueprints. The twin tunnels headed north, burrowing under Oakland Avenue west of St. Louis University High School, and then under Forest Park, curving west until, just under Union Boulevard at the edge of the Park, Section D connected into Section E, which extended west along the edge of Forest Park under Lindell Boulevard and beyond any concern of Benny or mine.

"You're right," Benny said. "That's the perfect spot. Right down there in front of the tunnel openings. Hell, you could hide a hundred sharpshooters in all that jungle up there."

I nodded in agreement. The tunnel openings were set in a wide cement wall, like a dam in a river. The wall rose up to street level. Above it was a dense growth of trees and bushes and other vegetation.

"Good spots along the riverbanks, too," I said.

Up at street level, lining the banks of the river on both sides were factories and warehouses, with train tracks running along the north bank—plenty of places to put Ferd Fingersh's SWAT team. The overpass we were on was another good spot.

"I guess Anderson got down over there," I said, pointing to a concrete stairway to the left of the tunnels. The stairs went down from street level to the riverbed.

At the entrance to the left tunnel was a pile of junk—a mangled shopping cart, branches, pipes, and other trash, presumably washed through the tunnels by storm water.

"So where's the damn water?" Benny asked.

"Let's go see," I said, pulling the car over to the side of the road on the south side of the bridge.

There was a white gravel pathway along the top of the riverbank that led all the way to the tunnel wall. Benny and I got out of the car and walked along the path until we were almost even with the tunnel openings down below.

"There," I said, pointing. "It looks like it goes in there."

There were huge steel grates set in the cement floors about ten yards inside the tunnel openings. From where we stood you could just make out the water in the center tunnel flowing down through the grates.

"So there's another part of the river underground?" Benny asked.

"It looks that way." I studied the blueprints. "The sewage line goes down there. The riverbed handles the storm water, I guess."

"Un-fucking real."

I turned to Benny. "What?"

"Stoddard Anderson. The guy was un-fucking real. Think about him. Running around in the sewer system of St. Louis with a bucket of cement and an ancient golden dildo. Let me tell you something, Rachel, Stoddard Anderson was one funky managing partner."

I turned at the sound of a train horn. A freight train was crossing a trestle over the river channel way off in the distance, about a half mile further downriver from the overpass we were on.

"Look," I said, pointing downriver. On the left side of the riverbank about one hundred yards away was a vehicle ramp leading down to the concrete riverbed. "Ferd could have a couple cars waiting off in the distance down there."

"It's a good spot," Benny agreed. "Let's set it up."

"For tonight?" I asked.

"Definitely. Ferd has all his troops ready to do it tonight. And I'm getting *shpielkes*. Now that we know where it is, the longer we wait the higher the risk. What if Panzer is having you tailed? Or what if he's questioning Weidemeir? And don't forget that fucking Tezca and his goon squad. Set it up for late tonight. That'll give us enough time to go in there and find that damn thing."

* * *

My first call was to Rafe Salazar. I made the call on the portable phone, the antenna sticking out of the car window.

"I found a spot for our party tonight," I said, mindful of Ferd's warning that we were talking on an open line.

Although I was vague about the nature of the party, I was very specific about the location. He said it sounded perfect, but that he would drive by with Ferd to make sure. He told me to leave the area and wait for his call.

"Do you think I can tell our friend about the party now?" I asked. "I can call him later with the location. Since he may need some time to get ready, I want to let him know as soon as possible that the party's going to be tonight."

"Good idea. Call him now. Tell him the party's tonight. Tell him you'll call him later with the location."

"What time should I tell him to come to the party?"

"Well, it's a surprise party. We want to make sure everyone else is there first. How about eleven o'clock?"

"Sounds perfect."

"I'll call you within an hour, Rachel."

Next I called Remy Panzer. For this call I used a pay phone.

"This is Rachel. I found it."

"Wonderful, wonderful. Where is it?"

"Safe. I'll deliver it tonight. At exactly eleven o'clock. I'll call you later to tell you where."

There was a pause. "Why the intrigue?" he finally said.

"You were the one who told me Customs was still snooping around. From what I can determine, there could still be serious legal problems. What if they have your gallery staked out?"

"What did you have in mind for our rendezvous?"

"I'm not sure yet. I want our exchange to be in a safe, open place. I'll call you later with the location."

"Very well. I shall, of course, have your fee with me."

"In cash."

"Certainly."

"Now here are a few more things, Remy." I took him through the various instructions Ferd Fingersh and Bernie DeWitt had covered with me—the clothing he had to wear (white or beige, nothing loose-fitting, turtleneck or T-shirt, no jacket or sweater), the type of carrying case for the money, etc. etc.

"And what about you, Rachel? How will I know you won't be planning to rip me off and keep the Executor?"

"I'll be alone. When I pick the location, I'll make sure that from where you'll be standing tonight you'll be able to see I'm alone."

"As for the clothing, Rachel, I should think the same dress code should apply for you, too."

"Agreed. I'll call you again with the location."

Rafe called an hour later. He called on the portable phone.

"Perfect," he said. "You'll need to make sure our guest doesn't get too close, though. I'd tell him to wait in the center of the riverbed, no closer than one hundred feet from the opening."

"That's what I'll tell him."

"Good." Then his voice softened. "You call me after you talk to him. Okay?"

"Sure."

"You'll be pleased to know that my client agreed to your fee."

"That's nice. I have one more request for your client."

"Tell me what it is."

"When your client finally puts that thing on display, I want there to be a little plaque on the display case that gratefully acknowledges it as the gift of my client. That poor woman deserves at least that much out of it."

"I'd be honored to convey that request, Rachel. I'm sure they will agree to it. Meanwhile, call our guest of honor and then call me back."

Remy Panzer's line was busy, and then he was out. I didn't get through to him until close to four o'clock.

I told him where the meeting spot was to be.

"Fine," he said. "Now, here are my two rules. First, you must be alone. Rest assured that I will be there well in advance of our eleven o'clock meeting. If I see or if I hear anything suspicious, I'll leave. And if I do leave, I will have nothing further to do with you. Ever. I will assume you have betrayed me, and I shall act accordingly. Second, I shall be at the meeting spot precisely at eleven. You chose the place, you chose the time. I choose to wait there no longer than five minutes. If you are not there by then, I will leave, and I shall be extraordinarily reluctant to schedule any further meeting with you. Understand?''

"Understood."

My final call was to Rafe. I told him Panzer's additional conditions.

"Those shouldn't be a problem," Rafe said. "I'll let Ferd know. We'll call you back immediately if there's a problem. If you don't hear from me, it's a go."

"Okay."

There was a pause. "How do you feel?" Rafe asked softly.

I took a deep breath and exhaled. "This is one course I forgot to take in law school."

He chuckled. "You'll be able to teach the course after tonight."

"I guess so."

"Listen to me."

"I'm listening."

"Don't take any risks tonight, Rachel. It's not worth it."

"Okay."

"I mean it."

"I know you do."

Another pause. "I'll be there," he said.

"I know that."

"I'll have that champagne on ice back in my room."

I smiled. "Good. 'Cause when this is over, I'm going to be one thirsty cowgirl."

"You're a special woman, Rachel. May God be with you tonight." And then he hung up.

I pushed the antenna down and put the phone under the car seat. Leaning back in the seat, I sighed.

"So you really like this guy, huh?" Benny asked.

"Yeah," I said.

"You don't think you're moving a little too fast?"

"Too fast?" I looked over at Benny. He was gazing out the windshield.

"What's so fast?" I asked. "I met him on Thursday. We had a soft drink together at Kiener Plaza. In broad daylight. On Friday I went to dinner with him *and* with Melvin Needlebaum. And then, to top off that romantic evening, we were together again last night along with you and those two guys from Customs."

Benny rubbed his chin. "Well, that sure sounds to me like three times in four days."

"For goodness sake, Benny. You sound like my father."

He looked over at me. "If I were your father, I'd be reminding you that Mr. Salazar wasn't Jewish."

"Jewish? Who says we're getting married? C'mon, Benny. And look who's talking about Jewish: the original shiksa maven himself."

That forced a sheepish grin from him.

Close to an hour later we were sitting on two swings in the playground behind my old elementary school, sort of killing time and sort of going over the evening ahead of us. I had the blueprints spread out on my lap. I was studying the portion of Section D that ran under Forest Park.

"I've been thinking," Benny said.

"Yes."

"Let's say Remy Panzer decides to get there early. To case the joint."

"Okay."

"Let's say he's there right now."

"Okay."

"He's looking around, trying to figure out where we're going to emerge. Right?"

"Right."

"Maybe we're going to come up that riverbed, he thinks. Maybe we're going to walk out of one of the warehouses, he says. But probably, we're going to come out of one of those tunnel openings. Right?"

"That's probably what he'll think," I said.

"So he says to himself, 'Hmmm. I see three tunnels. I wonder which one they're going to come out of?' Okay?"

"Okay."

"And let's imagine he's got a couple thugs with him to help out. 'Cause Remy Panzer isn't exactly Ward Cleaver, okay?"

I looked over at Benny. "Go on."

"He doesn't know which tunnel we're going to come out of. He doesn't have blueprints for any of the tunnels, so he doesn't exactly know where each of those tunnels is coming from, either. Okay?"

"Okay."

"The guy's no dummy, right?"

"Right."

"So maybe he says to himself, or says to his thugs, 'Let's hide somewhere around here. Because,' he says, 'whatever comes out has got to first go in.' " Benny raised his eyebrows. "You following me?"

I nodded.

"Think about it," he continued. "According to Stoddard Anderson, Montezuma's Executor is hidden in the top of one of those arched passageways. You said those archways are one hundred yards apart, right?"

"Right."

"So that means we're going to have to walk six hundred yards down that tunnel. That's going to take some time. Then we're going to have to find out where the hell he hid the damn thing, unlock the box, and carry it out. That's going to take some more time. Right?"

"Right."

"You have to meet him at eleven o'clock sharp. You know we're going to want to go in that tunnel hours before then to make sure we can find that thing and get it out of there. Right?"

"Go on."

"If Remy Panzer and his thugs are hiding out there, they're going to see us go in. They're going to see which tunnel we enter. Shit, they might just follow us in there, wait till we get that goddamn Aztec dildo, and then kill us." He shook his head

in disgust. "No wonder he agreed to meet you there. Jesus,
Rachel, we fucked up."

"It's worse than that," I said.

"Huh?"

"He told me I had to be alone. He told me if he saw me
with anyone else, he'd *never* show up. Think about that for a
moment. If he's hiding out there, he not only sees *me* go in the
tunnel—he sees *you*, too."

Benny shook his head. "We're really a pair of idiots."

"What do you mean 'we,' keemosabe?"

Benny looked at me with a puzzled frown. "What?"

"We can't enter through those tunnel openings. It's way
too risky."

"Agreed. But how are we supposed to get in?"

"Right here," I said, placing my index finger on the blueprint. "That's what I've been doing for the last fifteen minutes,
you bozo. Trying to figure out an alternate route into the tunnels."

Benny stood up and leaned over my shoulder to stare at
where I was pointing. "Where is that?"

"Near Union Boulevard. On the north part of Forest Park,
just off Lindell Boulevard."

"What is it?"

"A way to get into the underground portion of the River
Des Peres."

"No, I mean what is it? What's there?"

I looked up at Benny, who was peering over my shoulder.
"I have no idea. It says 'Surface Access to Section D.' Let's
drive over and find out what that means."

I drove east into the city along the northern edge of Forest Park,
passing the stately nineteenth-century mansions of Lindell Boulevard on my left. The light was red at Union.

"We should be almost there," Benny said, studying the
maps.

The light turned green. I turned south onto Union and
drove slowly into Forest Park. There were ponds and intercon-

nected waterways on both sides of the road, part of the canal system built for the 1904 World's Fair.

"It should be on the left," Benny said. "There!" He pointed. "That must be it."

I slowed down long enough to spot the long black cage before the driver behind me leaned on his car horn. I pulled ahead and turned left onto a road that crossed over one of the ponds.

"Keep going," Benny said. "Park it up there. We can walk back real casual, like we're just out for a late afternoon stroll."

I drove another two hundred yards down the park road and pulled over. We were north of the Muny Opera in an open part of the park. There were two elderly black men fishing in the pond nearest us. They had long bamboo poles and were both smoking pipes.

Benny and I crossed the road and walked down the footpath along the pond back toward the arched bridge. When we reached the end of that pond, just before the bridge, we turned right and walked along the edge of the larger pond toward the black cage we had spotted from the road into Forest Park.

About twenty yards from the cage I slipped my arm through Benny's and gently pulled him to a stop.

"Let's look at the pond," I said, glancing back down our path. No one was following us. "Pretend like we're out for a stroll."

"Ah, yes, such a lovely pond," Benny said as he casually looked around. The stagnant pond was covered with a greenish gray growth. "Can you imagine what would happen to you if you fell into that thing?"

"The skin fungus from hell?"

"At least," he said with a shudder.

"I don't see anyone."

"Me neither."

"Do you hear a waterfall?"

"It's that thing," Benny said, gesturing at the square concrete embankment rising out of the water near the edge of the pond. It had an opening right at water level, and a steady flow of water was passing over the concrete lip.

"It's a sluice," Benny said. "That's where the water drains out of these ponds. That way the ponds never overflow."

The black cage was just beyond the end of the pond and to the right of the concrete sluice.

"Shall we, my darling," I said, nodding toward the cage.

"Yes, my sweetness. Let us promenade."

The cage was four feet wide, five feet tall, and thirty feet long. It covered a cement stairway down into the sewers. We slowed as we passed. The stairs disappeared into the darkness. Cool air drifted up from below. The sounds of the sluice waterfall echoed from somewhere down there.

We continued maybe fifty feet beyond the cage and turned back. This time I studied the cage door as we passed.

"A padlock," I said.

"I think we'll need to pay a visit to our friendly hardware man before we descend into the sewers."

"I know just the place. We'll need some other supplies, too."

"Let me ask you something," Benny said as we approached the car.

"Shoot."

"We cut the lock and go down those stairs," he said, turning back toward the cage. "Once we get into the sewer tunnels, how long of a walk is it?"

"About three miles."

"Three miles? We gotta walk three miles through that sewer tunnel?"

"Yep."

"Shit."

"There'll be plenty of that," I said.

CHAPTER 29

Snap.

"Got it," I said, laying the metal cutters on the ground and removing the padlock.

I was crouched by the gate of the black stairway cage in Forest Park. Benny was standing in front of me, using his bulk to shield me from the view of any passerby—although at eight-thirty on a Monday night there were no passersby, and hadn't been since we arrived thirty minutes ago. We had waited in the car until it started to get dark.

"All clear?" I asked, picking up the metal cutters and the old padlock.

Benny glanced around. "Let's go."

Still in a crouch, I swung the gate open, went down a few steps, and turned to wait for Benny. He ducked around the gate and pulled it closed behind him.

"You have the other lock?" I asked, my heart pounding.

"Yeah. Yeah." He held it up for me to see.

It was a heavy-duty combination lock that I had purchased at the hardware store. Just in case someone was following us. Benny reached through the bars, hooked the new lock into place, clicked it shut, and spun the dial a couple times.

From where I stood on the steps, my eyes were just above

ground level. I peered through the bars, anxiously surveying the area.

"You see anyone?" I asked.

Benny looked around. "Naw." He turned to me. Although his face was partly shrouded by the growing darkness, I could see the smile. "We must be fucking nuts, huh?"

"Turn around and let me get the flashlights."

Benny had on a backpack. The portable phone was in there, along with some of the blueprints, extra batteries, a white turtleneck for me to put on later, and three flashlights. We had bought two regular flashlights and one of those high-powered park ranger types that has a handle. I had insisted on the extra flashlight, just as I insisted on the extra batteries and the combination lock to replace the one we destroyed—just to be safe.

I pulled the high-powered flashlight and one of the regular ones out of the backpack, dropped in the metal cutters, and closed the strap. I handed Benny the high-powered flashlight and turned to face the stairway down.

"Ready?" I asked as I clicked on my flashlight.

"Let's do it."

It was about forty steps down into the sewers. At the bottom of the stairs and to our left was the waterfall created by the run-off from the pond above. The water splattered onto the sloped cement floor about fifteen feet away from where we stood and ran down the center of the tunnel in a narrow stream that you could step across. We both shined our flashlights at the cascading water. There was nothing behind it but the back wall of the concrete sluice, which rose up to the water level of the pond overhead.

To the right of the stairs was a large tunnel that, according to the blueprint, ran at a right angle into the twin tunnels of Section D about one hundred feet further on. I pointed the flashlight down the tunnel. Sure enough, you could see where it intersected with a much larger opening.

"This way," I said, moving along a low ledge near the side wall of the tunnel.

Benny followed.

We were both wearing jeans, dark cotton turtlenecks, and work gloves. I had on my Nike Airs (new), and Benny had on his Top Siders (battered).

The tunnel emptied into a huge area that marked the beginning of Section D and the end of Section E. The waters of Section E flowed into the twenty-nine-foot horseshoe-shaped twin tunnels of Section D. Section E was to our left—upriver. It was a thirty-two-foot tube of reinforced concrete that brought the storm water and raw sewage down from the northwest part of the city. We were standing at the edge of what was, according to the architect notations on the blueprints, the largest pipe joint in the world.

"Whew," Benny said, waving his hand in front of his nose. "Help me get that phone out of there," he said, turning his back to me. "Let's double check with your federal bodyguards. Make sure everything's set."

I pulled the portable phone out of his backpack.

"You got Ferd's number?"

"Here," I said, removing a small pad of paper from my back pocket. "First page."

As Benny dialed, I looked around, flashing the beam of light this way and that.

The flood and sewage waters of Section E separated here and continued their flow downriver—to my right—into Section D. As shown on the blueprints, the two twenty-nine-foot arched tunnels had a common center wall that was several feet thick. The twin tunnels were enormous—you could easily drive a Mack truck down either one.

I shined my flashlight down the arched tunnel closest to me. Nothing but tunnel, stretching down as far as the beam of light could penetrate. Somewhere three miles down was the end of the tunnel. Two and a half miles down there, hidden somewhere in the ceiling of an arched passageway, was Montezuma's Executor.

"This piece of shit doesn't work," Benny growled, shaking the phone.

"What's wrong?"

"My call won't go through."

I looked around. "We're underground. These sewer walls must be several feet thick. Maybe you can't transmit a signal from down here. Go back to the stairs and give it a try."

"Okay," he said. He lumbered back down the smaller tunnel toward the waterfall and the stairs.

I looked around as I waited. There was a big pile of junk—logs, pipes, wire, sticks, oil cans, and other stuff—piled against the center wall at the entrance to the Section D tunnels. Floodwaters must have washed the debris downriver, and some of it got hung up against the center wall.

I flattened one of the blueprints against the wall and shined the flashlight beam on it. The Section D tunnels would gradually curve to the right as we went farther down them. I studied the blueprints, occasionally glancing at the tunnel entrances and then back to the blueprints for reference. The tunnel on the right was the storm-water tunnel. The tunnel on the left was the raw sewage tunnel. Although I couldn't see into it from where I stood, the stench alone was reason enough to do our trek through the storm-water tunnel.

"It worked," Benny hollered as he came down toward me. "You were right."

"Who'd you talk to?"

"Ferd. He said his men are all in position. He's got twenty sharpshooters out there waiting for us, along with about a half dozen air raid spotlights they're going to turn on as soon as Panzer hands you the money. Those guys are pumped."

"That's good."

I peered down the storm-water tunnel. There was a narrow stream of water running down the center. As the blueprints had indicated, the floor of the tunnel was concave, so that the middle of the floor was almost three feet lower than where the floor met the walls. I took a deep breath and exhaled. "Well, Mr. Kurtz? Shall we?"

Benny nodded. "Lead on, Marlowe. Let's exterminate the brutes."

We started off like sewer tourists. We could have been strolling through some 20,000-Leagues-under-the-Park exhibit at Disney

World—or at least that's how we acted, probably to keep our minds off what lay ahead.

Despite the tension we both felt, it was fascinating for the first mile or so. I was surprised—pleasantly surprised—by the animal life in the stream. I had expected—dreaded—rats, but we didn't see any. Instead, we spotted frogs, albino crawdads, snapping turtles, and even a pair of muskrats. Although the water was no more than four or five inches deep, there were places where the last flood had left logs or rocks or trash in the middle of the tunnel, which formed little dams. Hovering in the pools of water behind these dams were bluegill and catfish.

As we moved farther down the tunnel the original waterfall sounds faded but were replaced by new ones created by run-offs from the smaller sewer lines that fed into the main tunnels of Section D. First you would hear the waterfall sounds in the distance, muted at first, gradually louder as you approached, and then you would see it, shooting out of an opening in the arched ceiling, a spout of water splashing and splattering into the tunnel through a run-off from one of the feeder lines.

Occasionally there would be a shaft of light coming through what looked like a round vent in the ceiling. The vents were grates in the street above, the light from a street lamp. Once in a while there was a loud metallic bang, which was a truck running over a manhole cover overhead.

Because of the way the ceiling arched, there was no way to run a ladder all the way up to those manholes. However, sometimes we came across a metal ladder that went up the side of the tunnel and disappeared into a vertical tube, which presumably led to a way out of the tunnel.

We stopped at the first arched passageway we came to. It was about four feet wide and seven feet tall, and was cut into the common wall between the storm-water tunnel and the sewage tunnel. Since the common wall was almost three feet thick, there was ample room for both of us to stand in the passageway.

We stepped up into the passageway and peered across into the sewage tunnel. Benny slowly swept the beam of his high-powered flashlight back and forth along the surface of the water.

"Yechh," he spat in disgust.

His flashlight beam illuminated a broad, slow-moving brownish river of raw sewage. The river was at least two feet deep—the water line was maybe eight inches below the bottom of the passageway we were standing in. Benny shined the beam at the water passing near our feet.

"That's definitely raw sewage," I said.

Benny waved his hand in front of his nose. "Almost makes you feel sorry for sewer rats."

I shined my flashlight up at the arched ceiling of the passageway. Right in the center of the arch, where the keystone would go, was a corroded light fixture.

"I bet that's where Anderson hid it," Benny said.

I checked my watch. It was almost 9:40 P.M. We had at least another two miles ahead of us. "Let's go."

We had walked in silence for twenty minutes. I had been counting passageways since the first one. According to my calculations, the sixth passageway from the end of the tunnel was also the thirty-ninth passageway out from where we had started.

"Thirty-five," I said as we passed another one.

"How many more?"

"Four."

Benny glanced at his watch. "Ten minutes after ten."

"We're still on schedule," I said.

"Did I tell you my latest brainstorm?" Benny asked a few minutes later.

"So you've given up on Breasts 'R Us?"

"I've changed sex."

"Boobs for men?"

"Better."

"I'd sure hope so."

"Balls."

"Balls?"

"Balls."

"As in testicles?"

"Actually, as in scrota."

"As in what?"

"Scrota. The plural of scrotum."

"You've got more than one?"

"One today. Millions tomorrow. Someday I could be the Sultan of Scrota. Play your cards right, Rachel, and you could be my Sultana."

"Okay," I sighed. "Let's hear it."

"Take your average, affluent, recently divorced, sixty-year-old guy, okay?"

"Go on."

"He's squirting Grecian Formula on his hair, working out five times a week at the health club, maybe even hired his own exercise guru. Low-fat diet, lots of veggies, nice tan, new wardrobe. Cruising around in his Porsche or his red Beemer. All for one purpose, and one purpose only."

"To feel young?"

"To get laid. Specifically, to get laid by some twenty-five-year-old potential trophy wife. It's what makes the world go around."

"It already sounds ennobling. What's the gimmick?"

"I'm getting there. Got our guy in mind? Dyed hair, body whipped into shape, lots of dough, fancy car, great clothes. Everything's perfect—with one exception."

"His scrotum?" I asked incredulously, caught up in Benny's goofy scheme even as I laughed.

"Do you have any idea what happens to a man's balls when he gets old?"

"I can't say that I do."

"It's pathetic. Worse, it's an irrefutable sign of old age. That's the key, Rachel. Our sixty-year-old stud finds himself a twenty-five-year-old babe, squires her back to his newly decorated bachelor pad, pours her a glass of Dom Pérignon, pops a CD into his $50,000 sound system with speakers roughly the size of the ones the Stones used at Soldier's Field."

"What's the album?" I asked. "Frank Sinatra?"

"Nah. Our hero's too savvy for that. He'd have asked some younger guy in his office what the chicks love these days. Probably Dire Straits. Sounds like fingernails on a chalkboard to him, but he'd never let on. Anyway, at some point in the evening, he's going to have to take off his clothes. And things have

sure as hell changed in that jurisdiction since the time he was
married. These days the lights stay on. So when he takes off his
underwear, there they are, lo and behold, dangling down around
his knees.''

"His balls?'' I was giggling.

"He can practically play soccer with 'em.''

"My God, you've got to be kidding.''

"I'm serious, Rachel. His balls are a dead giveaway. It's
like they've got the words 'old fart' branded on them, one word
on each.''

"Let me get this straight: You see financial opportunities
here?''

"A fucking gold mine.''

"I'm afraid to ask.''

"A scrotum lift.''

"Oh, come on.''

"I'm serious, Rachel. A scrotum lift. Like a face lift, or a
tummy tuck. In a half-hour you can have the balls of a twenty-
year-old.''

"For heaven's sake, Benny.'' I was laughing. "That's the
most ridiculous idea I've ever heard.''

"That's where you're wrong, Rachel. Women just don't
understand. Men are already obsessed with their dicks. With
the right marketing pitch, I can make them obsessed with their
balls, too. Then all I got to do is round up a bunch of plastic
surgeons. Put together some franchises. Hire a spokesman.
Someone like Johnny Carson. Or maybe Paul Newman. I could
make a fortune.''

"Paul Newman?'' I said, laughing so hard there were tears
in my eyes.

"Sure. I bet his *cojones* are halfway down his thighs already.''

When I finally stopped laughing I said, "Have you got a
name yet?''

"Not yet. I've been toying with Highballs—''

I burst into laughter again.

"—but maybe it's a little too cute.''

"I've got your motto. 'Highballs: For a Vas Deferens.' ''

I was still laughing, staggering against Benny as we walked on, when the beam of his flashlight fell on something that stopped us cold.

We stared in silence.

"Jesus," Benny finally said. "You think that's from Stoddard?"

I stared down, and then glanced over at the passageway. "Yep," I said. "We're here."

CHAPTER

What had caught our attention was a green plastic bucket and a brown grocery bag on the floor of the tunnel near the arched passageway—the thirty-ninth passageway from where we started, and thus the sixth passageway from the end.

The bucket had a small amount of hardened concrete in it, and one of those wood paint stirrers was stuck in the concrete. On the ground next to the bucket was a chisel that was six or seven inches long and looked like it was made out of a heavy metal. I peered into the grocery bag. It was one-fifth full of what looked like a mixture of sand and gravel.

"Is this concrete?" I asked, pointing the flashlight beam at the grocery bag.

Benny leaned over to see. "Yep. It's the ready-mix stuff. You just add water. Stoddard must have brought it in with him. There's certainly plenty of water for mixing."

I stepped up into the arched passageway and shined the flashlight into the ceiling. Right in the center was a corroded light fixture. You could see traces of fresh concrete around the edges. I reached up and tugged on the light fixture. I could move it back and forth. Benny joined me.

"Let me," he said, grasping hold of the light fixture with both hands. "Back up," he said.

He gave three big pulls, and on the third one the fixture came loose in a shower of crumbling concrete and dust. As Benny brushed the junk out of his hair and off his face, I stepped in and shined the flashlight at what he had exposed.

"Bingo," I said.

Anderson had chiseled out a large area above the light fixture. Set back in the archway and anchored in concrete was a metal lockbox, turned on its side so that whatever was in it would not fall out when the door was opened.

"That's it," Benny said. "Goddamn."

I pulled the key out of the front pocket of my jeans. I stood on my tiptoes, but the lockbox was just barely out of my reach. "Give me that bucket," I said to Benny.

"Here," he said, bending down and wrapping his arms around my thighs. "I'll pick you up."

He lifted me high enough to insert the key.

"It fits!" I said in excitement as I turned the key in the lock. The door swung open and I reached inside. I pulled out something heavy wrapped in a plastic bag. "Okay," I said, and Benny lowered me with a grunt.

We sat down on the edge of the passageway, our legs resting on the floor of the tunnel. Slowly, carefully, I unrolled the black plastic bag on my lap. Inside was a canvas bag, wrapped with three lengths of duct tape. My hands were shaking as I yanked off the last piece of duct tape, reached into the bag, and pulled out Montezuma's Executor.

"My God," I breathed as Benny shone the flashlight on it. "It's incredible."

I turned it slowly in my hands. Montezuma's Executor was in the unmistakable shape of an erect penis. The gold column gleamed in the light, the emeralds and rubies sparkled. The craftsmanship was magnificent.

"Jesus Christ," Benny said. "Look at the size of that thing. That fucking Indian was hung like a horse."

I rested its base on my thigh. "Look," I said, pointing at the slit in the head. "That's where the knife blade went."

"Jesus."

I turned it over. There was a wider slit between the two

little globes at the base of the column where the knife blade was inserted. As I sat there, holding that remarkable object in my hand, thinking back to who had originally wielded it, up there on the sacrificial pyramid, and for what specific purpose, I shivered—part in awe and part in revulsion.

I checked my watch.

"What time is it?" Benny asked.

"Ten-thirty."

He shifted his weight from side to side. "Whew," he said, taking a deep breath. "Not too long now, huh?"

"Turn around," I said as I gently laid Montezuma's Executor on the floor of the tunnel. "I need to get that white turtleneck out of your backpack."

He did.

"Don't look," I said as I grasped hold of the dirty turtleneck I was wearing and pulled it off over my head. "Ferd said his men were already in position, right?" I asked Benny as I unfolded the white turtleneck and pulled it over my head.

"He said they're all set."

"Did he tell you where all those sharpshooters are?"

"Let's see," Benny said, trying to recall. "He said most of them were up on the train trestle. A few were on the edge of the ditch. A couple on the rooftops, a couple on the water tower."

"You can look," I said as I tucked the turtleneck into my jeans. I stretched my neck, trying to relax. "Twenty-five minutes to go. It'll take maybe ten minutes to walk down there, and then—wait a minute. He said most were on the train trestle?"

"Yeah. That's what he—oh, shit. Where the fuck is that train trestle?"

"Oh, no. It's at least half a mile from the tunnel opening. He told you he had a couple on the water tower, too? Benny, I don't even remember a water tower."

"It must be down there by that fucking train trestle. Jesus Christ, that pinhead's got his men in the wrong goddamn place. They're too far away." Benny slipped off his backpack and pulled out the portable phone.

"Is it safe to call him?" I asked.

"Sure," he said as he dialed the number. "Those knuckleheads are so far away Panzer won't hear it ring." He held the phone to his ear. "Oh, shit. This fucking phone won't work in here. I can't believe this."

My mind was racing. "How far back was that last ladder?"

Benny shook his head helplessly. "I don't remember. Quarter of a mile? Half a mile? Shit. Shit!"

"Go back there fast," I said. "That ladder leads up to the surface. Call Ferd from there. Tell him to move his men closer to the tunnel." I checked my watch. 10:35 P.M. "Tell him where you're calling from, too. Tell him to send some of his men down that manhole."

Benny was nodding his head. "Okay. Got it. You stay here, Rachel. Wait for me." He reached down to pick up his backpack, but then he handed it to me. "I don't need this. There's an extra flashlight in there, and some batteries, too."

"Go, Benny. Hurry."

"Okay. I'll be back. Just wait here."

I watched Benny jog down the tunnel and out of sight. I turned toward the direction of the tunnel opening, which was out of view about six hundred yards further down. I checked my watch. 10:38 P.M. Panzer told me he would wait exactly five minutes and then he'd leave. Which meant I had no more than twenty minutes to figure out what to do, and do it.

I rifled through my options. I was probably safer meeting Panzer without Montezuma's Executor than with it. He wouldn't try anything funny if I didn't have it with me. I could tell him some story, maybe have him follow me into the tunnel with his money, or see if he would wait there while I went back into the tunnel to retrieve it. By then, Benny would have gotten the feds back in position, with several coming down the tunnel from the opposite end. Ferd and his men couldn't be that far away now. Maybe a few blocks.

Panzer was no bigger than me, I thought, trying to rationalize it. Without a weapon, he shouldn't be that dangerous. If I could stall Panzer for a while, the feds would either descend on him out there or be waiting for him in here.

I thought of Rafe Salazar. When he finds out about the screw-up, he's going to be furious, I told myself. The thought of his rage gave me some comfort.

I checked my watch again. 10:43 P.M.

What if everything's screwed up? I said to myself. Don't think that way, Rachel. Benny must be up that ladder by now. He's probably moving them into position even as you stand here.

I looked down at the flashlight in my hand. The light was growing weaker. There was another flashlight in the backpack. I shined the beam on the Executor. Even in the dimmer light, the sparkling of the jewels made the Executor seem incandescent.

But what if Benny hadn't reached the ladder? What if he'd dropped the phone? What if everything was screwed up?

I studied the Executor, my mind fully revved on adrenaline now. I couldn't just leave it out there on the ground. I moved the flashlight beam slowly around. I held the beam first on the metal chisel on the ground by the bucket. I reached down and picked up the chisel. I moved the beam to the grocery bag, and then over to the backpack, and then back to the bucket.

I stared down at the flashlight, and then over at the Executor.

I checked my watch. I had exactly eight minutes before I had to start walking down the tunnel.

It might work.

CHAPTER 31

At precisely 11:05 P.M. I emerged from the tunnel and stepped out onto the concrete riverbed of the River Des Peres. One hundred feet in front of me, standing beneath the full moon, was Remy Panzer. He was alone and he was facing me. On the ground to his right was a large metal briefcase.

I walked toward him slowly, my eyes scanning back and forth. The concrete banks of the river sloped steeply up toward street level. We seemed to be alone down here. But because the riverbed was so far below street level, I had no way to tell who or what was up there. *Don't count on anyone else,* I said to myself. *Assume it's just you and him.*

I stopped ten yards from Panzer and turned off my flashlight.

"You're late," he said.

"My watch must be slow. Is that the money?"

"It is."

"Let me see."

"You let me see," he said.

"You first."

"Very well." He bent down, his eyes never leaving mine, and turned the briefcase on its side. Clicking open the clasps, he raised the top. I stepped a few feet closer. In the bright moonlight I could see the neat stacks of green bills packed into the briefcase.

"How do I know it's all there?" I asked, trying to stall for time.

"Because I say it is."

"Maybe I should count it."

He lowered the lid and locked the briefcase. Standing up, he crossed his arms over his chest. "Your turn. Where is the Executor?"

I gestured over my shoulder toward the tunnels. "Back there."

"Then go get it," he snapped. "And hurry."

"I can't."

"What do you mean, you can't?" He said the words slowly, precisely, his anger starting to show.

I shrugged. "You'll have to help me. I know where it is, Remy. But I can't get at it."

"I cannot believe my ears. We had a deal, young lady," he snarled. "I bring the money, you bring the Executor. Here is the money. Now bring me the Executor."

I was surprised by the force of his anger. "You don't understand, Remy. I know where it is. I found the Executor. I just can't get it out of where Stoddard hid it."

Panzer ran his fingers through his close-cropped hair in furious exasperation. "I cannot believe this. I cannot believe this."

"Listen to me," I said. "I know where it is. Do you understand that? I found it. It's in the tunnel. In a lockbox. In the ceiling of a passageway in the wall. It's there. I've seen the lockbox. I just can't get it open."

Panzer put his hands on his hips, fists clenched. "AND WHY NOT?"

"Two problems. First, it's just a little too high for me to reach. Second, the lockbox is anchored in cement. The only way to get the Executor out is to open the lockbox. I don't have a key. You're going to have to break the lock. When I called you this afternoon, all I had was Stoddard Anderson's map. I didn't find out about these problems until I went in there to-night to get it.''

Panzer stared at me, his jaw clenching and unclenching. And then he spun away, his back to me.

I quickly looked up both sides of the riverbank, straining to see any movement. To my immediate right was the stairway leading down from street level. Why weren't there twenty FBI agents charging down those stairs? What was taking them so long?

"Look, Remy, I'm sure we can get it if we work together. The lockbox doesn't look that strong. You could probably break the lock with a crowbar. Remy?'' He still had his back to me, shaking his head.

And then I heard the crunch of tires on loose concrete and the low-pitched rumbling of a car engine. A Pontiac Firebird with a dark-tinted windshield was slowly coming down the riverbed toward us, headlights off. It came to a halt in front of Remy Panzer, who now had his face raised toward the moon. A perfect mirror image of the moon was reflected in the tinted windshield.

Both of us stood there in silence for a moment, facing the car. The only noise was an occasional metallic *thock* from the cooling engine block.

And then both car doors opened simultaneously. A short, bearded man stepped out of the passenger side. He was wearing a baggy white dress shirt (sleeves rolled up), baggy khakis, and wire-rim glasses. A moment later, Rafe Salazar stepped out from the driver's side. He was wearing a black T-shirt and black jeans. Both of them were carrying handguns. The bearded man's handgun had a silencer screwed onto the end of the barrel.

Rafe stared at me. "Are you okay?'' he asked, his voice flat.

I smiled bravely. "Sure," I said a little uncertainly, my mind shouting, *What's wrong with this picture?* "I was kind of nervous there for a while," I added.

He nodded curtly. No smile, no warmth.

The bearded man took a step toward Panzer. "Where is it?"

Panzer gestured angrily toward me. "She says it's in the tunnel. In a lockbox. She says she couldn't reach it, and she says she doesn't have a key to open it."

"Shit," the bearded man said harshly. He turned to me, pointing the gun. "What kind of lock?"

I looked at Rafe. "What's going on?"

Rafe's eyes were cold. "Answer his question, Rachel."

"Where's everyone else?" I asked as the earth began to tilt. "Where's Ferd? Where are his men?"

Rafe's stare met mine. "Twenty miles north of here," he said. "Staking out the playground behind an abandoned elementary school, which is precisely where I told him tonight's rendezvous would take place. He and his men have been there since six o'clock."

It took a moment to grasp the extent of the miscommunication that had occurred when Benny had called Ferd from the tunnel. Ferd had assured him that he and his men were in position. Both had assumed that they were talking about the same position. Rafe read my facial expression. He gave me a sad smile and shook his head. "You're all alone, Rachel."

The bearded man stepped in close. "What kind of lock?" His voice was low and controlled. His eyes were like laser beams.

I stared at him, trying to place a name on the face. I had seen him somewhere before. "It's just an ordinary lockbox," I said, feeling dizzy.

He turned to Rafe. "Get a crowbar out of the trunk."

As Rafe went behind the car and popped the hood, Remy Panzer reached down for the briefcase. "I don't believe my services are needed anymore."

"Services?" the bearded man repeated. "Your services have been worthless, you miserable faggot."

Panzer smiled as he straightened up, his hand clenched around the briefcase. "A deal is a deal, Mr. Nevins. Moreover, I have even delivered a special bonus, at no extra charge. I've brought you a sacrificial maiden for your next little soiree up

on the pyramid. She's really quite lovely, if I say so myself."
He turned to me. "I've enjoyed doing business with you, Rachel. Although Mr. Salazar's script called for you to betray me,
I don't take it personally. Moreover, the contents of this briefcase have placed me in a forgiving mood. You played your role
to perfection, with the exception of this minor foul-up at the
end. Assuming these gentlemen will allow you to grow old, my
best wishes for continued success in your career."

He turned and walked toward the stairway leading up the
side of the riverbank to the street. He was four stairs up when
Tezca shot him.

With the silencer on the gun, all I heard was a *thwip*.

The bullet hit Panzer in the middle of his back, punching
him forward, his back arching in pain. He started to turn toward us, his face contorted in shock and pain, his free hand
reaching for the wound.

And then I heard another *thwip*.

The second bullet tore into Panzer's neck below his ear.
The impact spun him off the stairs and onto the sloped riverbank. He landed on his side, the briefcase still clutched in his
hand. He seemed to be just resting there, propped on an elbow,
staring at us, awful, motionless but for the blood pulsing and
bubbling out of his neck wound. And then he rolled onto his
back. Dark blood ran down the concrete slope in rivulets as his
body started to twitch.

The first thing to drop was the briefcase. It slid down the
incline and clattered onto the riverbed. A moment later, Panzer's body started to follow. It slid slowly down the concrete
slope, gradually turning as it slid, no longer twitching, leaving
a dark trail of blood. The body came to a rest near the briefcase
at the bottom of the riverbank, head first, eyes wide open, twin
moons reflecting in the sightless pupils.

Rafe walked over to Panzer's body. He was carrying a gun
in one hand, a crowbar and a flashlight in the other. He
crouched beside the body for a moment and then straightened
up. He looked down at the bearded man. "That was stupid,
Arthur."

Arthur Nevins aka Tezca ignored the remark and grabbed me roughly by the arm. "Panzer was right, lady. You want to live to see your grandchildren, you show us where it is. And quickly."

"Show us, Rachel," Rafe said.

"Now!" Tezca hissed in my ear.

"Okay," I said dully.

The three of us walked into the dark tunnel.

"You lied about everything," I said to Rafe.

He didn't answer, and I couldn't see his face in the darkness.

"That call last night," I said, close to tears. "Remember your call?"

He grunted.

"There wasn't any champagne, was there?" My voice was shaking. "It was all a lie, wasn't it?"

"There was no champagne," he finally said.

"What kind of monster are you?" I asked, more hurt than angry.

"Be quiet, Rachel," he said. "This has nothing to do with you."

"My God, were you the one who attacked Dottie Anderson?" I asked.

"No," Rafe answered. "Never."

"Then who did?"

Tezca twisted my arm behind my back. "Shut up, bitch," he snarled in my ear.

I was so upset I could barely concentrate. I walked as slowly as they would let me and pretended that I was unsure of where we were going. I knew that they had to keep me alive until we reached the lockbox. I also knew that they had no incentive to keep me alive afterward.

Finally, we reached the sixth passageway.

"Up there," I said wearily, taking some small pleasure in the fact that I had at least remembered to heave the bucket, the grocery bag, and the backpack into the sewer tunnel, where the currents had carried them down the river out of sight.

As Rafe shined the flashlight into the arched ceiling of the passageway, I started inching away, hoping they would become too engrossed in the lockbox to notice.

But Rafe must have sensed my movement. He spun around and shined the beam on me. I froze.

"Hold her," he ordered.

Tezca grabbed me from behind with his left arm, pulling me against him, his left hand clasped over my breasts. He pressed the gun against the right side of my neck. His breath was hot and sour.

I watched as Rafe reached up with the crowbar and poked it around under the edges of the lockbox, looking for good leverage. He found a spot and jammed the crowbar into it. Getting a better hold, he started to apply pressure, slowly pulling the crowbar down. I could see the lockbox door starting to creak and bend, slowly bowing out. Rafe yanked on the crowbar and the door gave way with a pop.

"THIS IS THE POLICE!"

The shout came from somewhere further down the tunnel.

Rafe immediately turned off his flashlight. We were in total darkness. Tezca grabbed me even tighter around the chest.

"Release the girl," the voice shouted, "and throw down your guns!"

I recognized the voice. I prayed that Rafe wouldn't.

"Dammit," Tezca hissed.

"Quiet," Rafe commanded in a low voice. Then he hollered, "WHAT?"

"Release her!" Benny shouted. "Throw down your guns!"

"Give me your gun," Rafe said to Tezca in a low voice.

"No way, man."

"You want to walk out of here?" Rafe asked calmly. "Then give me that gun. I know what I'm doing."

"I don't know, man."

"Don't be a fool," Rafe told him. "Give me the gun and hold Rachel."

Tezca tightened his grip on me. "Okay," he said, handing Rafe the gun.

Rafe clicked on his flashlight. "Here!" he shouted as he

heaved the gun in the direction of the voice. He used the flashlight as a spotlight, following the arc of the gun with the beam of light. The gun landed thirty feet in front of us. It bounced along the concrete and slid into the shallow stream of water. Rafe held the beam of light on the gun in the water.

I realized what was happening too late.

"Go back!" I screamed as Rafe shifted the beam of light up and found the moving target seventy-five yards away. "It's a trap!" I shouted just before Rafe fired the gun.

There was a howl of pain as the body twisted and fell.

"Oh my God," I moaned. "Benny! Benny!"

Tezca turned me around. "Shut up," he hissed into my ear as he hooked an arm around my neck and increased the pressure.

Rafe shined the flashlight in my face. "Be quiet, Rachel. We're almost done."

Tears of anger and frustration blurred my vision. "You bastard!" I croaked, unable to shout because of the pressure on my neck.

"Hold her," Rafe said to Tezca as he turned back to the lockbox and stepped into the archway.

The door to the lockbox was hanging open. Rafe reached up and removed the black plastic bag. Still standing in the archway, he carefully unrolled the plastic and pulled out the canvas sack, which I had rewrapped with the duct tape. He gripped the canvas sack in his left hand, judging its heft.

He turned to Tezca, the hint of a smile on his lips. "At last," he said quietly, stepping down from the archway. He turned to set the canvas sack on the floor of the passageway and pick up his gun.

From somewhere far off I could barely hear the sounds of police sirens.

"Let's kill this cunt," Tezca growled, "and get out of here. We're running out of time."

Rafe stepped closer, until we were just an arm's length apart. He had the gun in his right hand, the flashlight in his left.

I stared into his eyes—terrified but determined not to show it.

"You lost," I said, trying to sound confident.

He looked puzzled as he started to raise his gun. Tezca released his hold on me and stepped to the side.

"Lost?" he repeated, holding the gun at waist level.

The sirens seemed to be getting louder, but they were still so far away.

"Come on, man," Tezca said. "Let's go."

"No, Rachel," Rafe said to me. "I won."

He started to raise the gun and in one fluid motion shifted toward Tezca and shot him squarely in the chest. The roar of the gunpowder was deafening.

Tezca staggered backward, weaving toward the left, splashing through the narrow river in the middle of the tunnel, blood bubbling out of his chest, his mouth moving but no sound coming out. Rafe followed, the gun in one hand and the flashlight in the other. He shot him in the chest again as Tezca stumbled back against the wall. Tezca slid slowly down into a sitting position, leaving a black smear of blood along the wall. Rafe stood over him, gun ready, flashlight trained on his victim. Tezca tilted his head up with a look of total bafflement. Spotlighted in the beam of the flashlight, a rivulet of blood trickled down into his beard from the corner of his open mouth. He frowned, and then his head dropped onto his chest. I watched in horror as the body listed slowly, slowly to the right, and then tipped over, the head thonking against the cement.

My ears were ringing from the gun shots. Stunned, I turned to Rafe.

He lowered the gun and turned to pick up the canvas sack. Turning back, he stared at me for a moment. "Go help your friend," he said.

He turned away and started to run, the gun in one hand and the tape-wrapped canvas sack in the other. Far off in the distance, you could just detect the light at the end of the tunnel. The tunnel curved slightly to the right up ahead. I watched until he disappeared, and then I turned.

"Benny!" I shouted as I ran into the darkness.

EPILOGUE

The preliminary injunction hearing was supposed to last through the following week, but it ended suddenly on Thursday afternoon when, during a short recess between witnesses, the other side doubled their settlement offer and my client said yes. We signed the settlement papers and the stipulation of dismissal the following day, which meant I could enjoy the weekend.

And a glorious weekend it promised to be. Although it was early October, the sky was blue, the temperature was seventy-three, and the water was calm as Benny and I walked across Loyola Park toward the lake. Ozzie had already reached the sandy beach and had turned to wait for us, his tail wagging exuberantly.

"Did you bring his Frisbee?" Benny asked as we approached the beach.

"Of course," I said as I reached into the beach bag and pulled out the red Frisbee.

Ozzie started barking as soon as he saw it. I handed the Frisbee to Benny, who sailed it over the water. Ozzie leaped joyfully into the lake and started paddling after the Frisbee. Benny jogged across the sand toward the water line.

The mailman had arrived as we were leaving for the beach, and I had stuffed the mail into my beach bag. I could read my mail while Benny and Ozzie played Frisbee. Walking halfway down the pier, I picked a nice spot, kicked off my shoes, and sat down with my legs dangling over the side. Watching Benny run along the beach, I was pleased to see that his limp was completely gone. If he could run on it, his ankle must have completely healed. I leaned back and closed my eyes. The sun felt good on my face.

Benny's healed ankle brought back memories of the strange and violent resolution of my Stoddard Anderson investigation. Fortunately, Benny hadn't been hit by the bullet Rafe fired at him. But he had badly sprained his ankle when he slipped trying to dodge the bullet. Adding the proverbial insult to injury, he had hobbled over to one of the arched passageways and had just scrambled into it when Rafe shot Tezca. The sounds of the gun shot reverberating down the tunnel so startled Benny that he fell off the passageway into the river of raw sewage—head first.

Salazar escaped in a new Lear jet registered in Tezca's name. By the time Customs got to the airport, Salazar was thirty minutes from Mexican air space. Although the Mexican government was able to scramble two jet fighters in pursuit, Salazar shook them somewhere over the Yucatán and disappeared.

Under court orders, the FBI seized records from Salazar's office and safety deposit box and subpoenaed several individuals from the inner circle of Tezca's religious organization. Rafe Salazar was revealed as the power behind the throne, handling many of the legal and financial affairs of Tezca's operations, including the secret bank accounts in the Cayman Islands and the Netherlands Antilles. Indeed, Rafe had been a signator on each of those accounts. Based on what the FBI and the State Department were able to learn, most of the money in those accounts had been removed within days of Salazar's disappearance over the Yucatán.

Ironically, Rafe Salazar had in fact represented the Mexican National Museum of Anthropology, although they had obviously had no idea that he was representing Tezca as well. Even more surprising, he had in fact communicated to them Benny's request that they pay me $250,000—a fact I learned when Dottie

Anderson and I flew to Mexico for the ceremonial placement of Montezuma's Executor on display at the museum. It was a beautiful ceremony. The Executor looks magnificent in the elevated display case, which is bathed in spotlights. Although *Life* ran a stunning color photograph of the Executor last month, my favorite shot remains the Polaroid I keep in the top drawer of my desk. Bernie DeWitt snapped it moments after Ferd Fingersh found the Executor. In the picture, Ferd is standing in the middle of the sewage tunnel, not too far from the archway where I had carefully dropped the Executor into the sewage river before walking out to my final rendezvous with Remy Panzer. Ferd is wearing hip waders, and the sewage is up to his knees. He is holding the Executor in both hands and has a triumphant grin on his face.

Anyway, if you're ever in Mexico, you should definitely go see it. And when you do, be sure to read the bronze plaque on the display case. At the unveiling ceremony, the plaque stated that "The People of Mexico gratefully acknowledge the gift of Dorothy Anderson of St. Louis, Missouri." But Dottie insisted that they change it, and they did. The plaque now gratefully acknowledges "the gift of Mr. and Mrs. Stoddard Anderson of St. Louis, Missouri"—an acknowledgment that enabled Abbott & Windsor's public relations firm to place an extremely favorable and mostly fabricated story about the late Stoddard Anderson in the *St. Louis Business Review* and the *National Lawyer*.

After the ceremony and the cocktail reception, the head of the museum's *asuntos juridicos* (legal affairs department) handed me an envelope containing a check made out to me for $250,000. I promptly signed it over to Dottie, which started an argument between us that we eventually settled on the airplane flight back with Dottie's forcing me to agree to take half of it. After all, Dottie kept telling me, you earned it *and* you convinced that insurance company to pay me all that money.

(By the time I finally met with the insurance adjuster, I had, in addition to the statement from Albert Weidemeir, signed witness statements from Sal Donalli, Nancy Winslow, and Dr. Bernstein regarding Anderson's mental and physical condition at the time of his suicide. The insurance company agreed to pay

the full amount of the life insurance portion of the policy—
$750,000—and we agreed to settle the accidental death benefits
portion for $450,000 plus a $200,000 donation to an AIDS foundation. The donation was Dottie's idea. All told, Dottie received $1.2 million in insurance payments.)

I sat up and shaded my eyes in time to see the red Frisbee
land in the water about fifty feet from the shore. There were a
half dozen kids hanging around Benny and watching Ozzie pad-
dle out to fetch the Frisbee. No one was watching me.

I reached into my beach bag and pulled out the thick envelope with the Nicaraguan postmark. It had arrived in the
morning mail. The moment I saw it, I had known who it was
from. I didn't tell Benny. I just casually stuffed it into my beach
bag along with the rest of the mail.

As I held it now, I could see my hand shaking. The pain
and the betrayal had overwhelmed me during the days after the
tunnel. I had forced myself to exorcise him from my memories.
He had ceased to exist in my mind. Until that morning's mail.
With a mixture of excitement and dread, I tore open the envelope. Inside was a handwritten letter and an airplane ticket. I
unfolded the letter on my lap:

> Dear Rachel:
>
> I was flying over Texas when I finally opened the
> canvas bag. You can imagine my reaction when I
> discovered that I had risked my life and forever banished
> myself from my country in order to smuggle out a
> flashlight filled with a chisel in concrete. But time heals
> all wounds and, I suppose, wounds all heels. You were a
> formidable adversary, Rachel, and you won.
>
> Four days ago I viewed El Verdugo in its new home.
> It is magnificent—even more so than I had imagined.
> Although you may find this difficult to believe, I have
> come to understand that El Verdugo is where it belongs.
>
> I hope your friend did not suffer serious injury. I
> aimed wide, trying only to scare him. He showed great
> courage.
>
> Why am I telling you this? I can't hope to receive

your absolution. Perhaps I can receive your understanding. When Arthur Nevins and I formulated our plan, we were partners and there was no Rachel Gold. You changed everything, including me.

We never had our celebration, Rachel. Should you ever want to, just send a message with the date to the post office box at the bottom of this letter. I'll bring the champagne. As I told you, the black sand beaches are marvelous and the sunsets are spectacular. I promise separate cabanas and no strings attached.

Rafe

The roundtrip airplane ticket was to a city on the coast of Africa.

As I reread the letter for the third time, Ozzie came padding down the pier to where I sat and shook himself off all over me. I quickly stuffed the letter and airplane ticket into the envelope and back into my beach bag as Benny approached.

"C'mon, Rachel. Read your mail later. Ozzie and I are starving. Let's go put on the feedbag."

"Okay," I said, standing up and hoisting the strap of the beach bag over my shoulder. I gave him a brave smile. "So tell me about this hot date last night," I said as we stepped off the pier onto the sand.

"A big letdown."

"Oh?" I said, only half listening.

"You ever met some guy who just—pow! you go nuts for him, it doesn't matter how crazy it might seem, you just know he's for you? But then you spend some time with him, and you realize that what seemed so awesome wasn't really—Rachel?"

I had stopped by a trash can. Reaching into my beach bag, I removed the thick envelope and stared at it.

"What's up?" he asked.

I tore the envelope in half and jammed it into the trash can.

"What was that?" Benny asked. "One of those goddamn solicitations?"

"Sort of," I said as I turned toward him, reluctantly raising my eyes.

"Hey, are you okay?"

"Sure."

"What's wrong, Rachel? You're—your eyes are—"

"Hold me, Benny."

"There, it's going to be okay. Ssh."

I squeezed my eyes shut as I burrowed against him.

"It's okay, Rachel." He gently patted my back. "Everything's going to be okay. Hey, guess what's playing up at Northwestern tonight? One of our favorites. We can have dinner at Dave's Italian Kitchen and then head on over to see it. Wanna guess? I'll give you a hint." He cleared his throat. "We came down the Yulanga River."

I smiled against his shoulder. God bless him.

"Well?"

I sniffed and lifted my head. "That's impossible," I said with a German accent.

Benny tenderly wiped a tear from my cheek. "Nevahtheless," he said.